# Sleeping Dogs

*Also by Mark O'Sullivan*

*For Young Adults:*
MELODY FOR NORA
WASHBASIN STREET BLUES
MORE THAN A MATCH
WHITE LIES
ANGELS WITHOUT WINGS
SILENT STONES
MY DAD IS TEN YEARS OLD


*Literary Fiction:*
ENRIGHT


*Crime Fiction:*
CROCODILE TEARS

# Sleeping Dogs

## Mark O'Sullivan

TRANSWORLD IRELAND

TRANSWORLD IRELAND
an imprint of The Random House Group Limited
20 Vauxhall Bridge Road, London SW1V 2SA
www.transworldbooks.co.uk

Transworld Ireland is part of the Penguin Random House group of companies
whose addreses can be found at global.penguinrandomhouse.com

Penguin
Random House
UK

First published in 2014 by Transworld Ireland,
a division of Transworld Publishers
Transworld Ireland paperback edition published 2015

A CIP catalogue record for this book
is available from the British Library.

ISBN 9781848271623

Typeset in 11/13¾pt Minion by Kestrel Data, Exeter, Devon.
Printed and bound by CPI Group (UK) Ltd, Croydon, CR0 4YY.

MIX
Paper from
responsible sources
FSC® C016897

1 3 5 7 9 10 8 6 4 2

For Joan, Jane and Ruth

*Sunday 1 May*

Sunday 3 May

# 1

Hers was the last face some people ever saw. Some never got to see her, never knew how hard she'd worked to save their lives, strained every sinew to drag them back from whatever abyss they'd fallen or been hurled into. For the lucky ones, hers was the face that welcomed them back to the world of the living.

Eveleen Morgan walked slowly along the passage of the Intensive Care Unit. Five beds to her right, five to her left, each one overlooked by a phalanx of small screens. Time moved glacier-like now in the eternal dusk of the ICU ward. In the early hours it had positively raced. Two new admissions, and Eveleen, as senior ward nurse, had been going flat out all night. She wondered how long this spell of calm would last. How long before the families, in the first shock of catastrophe, came running? For her, proximity to death was easier to handle than proximity to grief.

In ICU there were no favourites, no judgements made on a patient's character, no moral conclusions drawn from the circumstances of their admission. A gangland casualty, a hit-and-run victim – both were equal in this ward. That was the theory. And yet, through the night, it was the hit-and-run boy she'd kept the closest watch on.

David Goode wasn't a boy really, she thought, but not yet a man. Eighteen, nineteen at most. His face unmarked, almost angelic, his neck broken, his spine snapped. He'd been wearing a helmet when he was knocked from the motorbike somewhere above Kilmacud, south of the city. It hadn't saved him. When they'd brought him in from A&E a few hours earlier, his eyes had briefly opened. At first, he seemed not to register anything of his surroundings nor did he speak. Then, as she helped a younger nurse to put the neck restraint in place, he looked directly at Eveleen with that knowing sadness of the dying, an expression she'd become too familiar with. Thirty years of experience told Eveleen that David would soon never open his eyes again.

In the bed opposite was Harry Larkin. His stomach mountainous in this prone position, his breath came loudly and wheezily through the oxygen mask. He'd been discovered in his car on the western outskirts of the city in Lucan. He had taken three bullets. One in the right shoulder, one in the neck and one in the head. They'd removed two; the third was lodged in his brain. All night the big man had been a handful. Angry grunts and groans emerged from him as he'd tried to lift himself from the bed before falling back after gaining a mere few inches, clasping his bruised neck in pain. His temperature fluctuated wildly, his blood pressure too.

An air of trepidation prevailed around the nurses who attended to him. They'd seen the Guards stationed in the lobby of the hospital. Eveleen was less apprehensive having seen it all before in Derry, Boston, Riyadh. Harry Larkin, for all his distress, seemed aware of this, attempting to speak only when she was in view. His words had been indecipherable at first and then made no sense. It was too early to tell whether the man was suffering from a temporary dementia or was permanently brain-damaged.

Liam Neeson was in the hospital, he'd told her, making a film with Kevin Costner. Sally Field had a role too, on the run with her daughter from *a bunch of fucking Arabs*. Eveleen promised to find out what she could about the film, but suspected he'd have forgotten about it next time he woke. Meanwhile, she waited for a decision from the consultant on whether Harry should be put into an induced coma to ease the swelling in his brain. For now, a stillness had come over his great bulk.

Eveleen checked his chart again, the current measurements on the screens above him. She wondered idly what her new life in Dubai would be like. Not, she hoped, a repeat of her brief stay in Kuwait in 1990 – there less than a week when the First Gulf War started and she'd had to high-tail it and leave half her belongings behind. People thought she was mad, of course, venturing off again at fifty, but she had no attachments to speak of. A brother and some nieces she saw little of. And the man who a year before, after a paralysing stroke, had gone back to his wife and kids.

Harry Larkin groaned again and the vice-grips of a bony hand caught Eveleen's wrist. The thin arm, its flesh loosened with age, still retained great force. Pain never panicked her. Not the pain of others nor her own. She ran her free hand soothingly along the hairy arm. From beneath the oxygen mask, he murmured.

'What is it, Harry?' Her voice barely stirred the hush of the ward.

She raised the man's mask a fraction and listened. His face wizened, elderly, his voice came muted and slow and thick with smoker's phlegm.

'Is Leo here?' he asked.

'Liam?' Eveleen said, mishearing the name. 'Ah, Liam Neeson? No, Harry. No sign of him yet.'

Her attention divided itself between the sweat-streaming face and the screens above. Heart rate reaching three figures and rising. His agitation on the upswing, the big man tightened his hold.

'Not Liam. Leo. I have to talk to Leo.'

'Who's Leo, Harry?' she asked, wondering if he meant Leo DiCaprio.

'Leo . . .' He struggled for breath. The oxygen escaping from the raised mask evaporated on his heated face, made a cascade of his sweat. 'Leo Woods. Get him for me.'

'Leo Woods?'

'Yeah,' Harry gasped, his blood pressure shooting down. Fast. 'He's a Guard. A detective. He's . . .'

Eveleen released herself and paged the senior registrar while increasing the flow from the infusion pump. She could tell by Harry's eyes that he was beginning to spin away into an oblivion and was fighting it with all his strength.

'Tell him to find . . . find Whitney,' he muttered through gritted teeth. 'She's been . . . taken.'

'No problem, Harry. I'll do that. I'll tell—'

The big man's head slumped sideways. Above him, the screen displays outdid one another in the intensity of their alarms. Soon, Harry Larkin's bed had been curtained off and a team of six doctors and nurses did their utmost to banish death from the ICU ward. For a little while, at least.

The sliding doors of the hospital entrance weren't ordinarily in operation at six-thirty in the morning. This was no ordinary morning. The Guards were everywhere. Two of them down at the carpark. A few more in a squad car at the ambulance bay out back. Another pair at the front entrance.

All of them had been in place for two hours now, shivering in the frosty fog that cloaked the hospital. They were in no mood for pleasantries. Only the petite black-haired woman defied them.

She appeared, small and wraith-like, out of the fog. Her blue raincoat flowed out behind her as she ran as though held by ghostly retainers. The taps of her high-heeled shoes punched out an insistent staccato. Beneath the coat she wore a short gold dress. The flesh exposed by its low cut was at one with the deathly pallor of her face. The older of the uniformed Guards stood in her path while the younger one stuttered an uncompleted sentence.

'Are you . . . are you here to see . . . to visit Harry Lar—?'

The woman had all the qualities of beauty in her face but was, at this moment, not beautiful, the symmetry of her features compromised by panic. Instinctively, the younger Guard stepped back and the doors slid open. Before he and his companion could close ranks, the woman had ghosted through the gap between them.

'That can't be this Larkin guy's wife, can it?' the young Guard said as they watched her sprint along the hospital corridor. 'I mean the guy's seventy if he's a day, right?'

His colleague shrugged. 'Maybe he's got a daughter.'

A spectacularly tall and thin middle-aged man, his prematurely greying hair stiff with fright, approached the entrance, a lanky, dreadlocked teenage girl at his side. He wore an astonished look and a suit that seemed to belong to a smaller man, long hands and bony wrists hanging uselessly by his side. The pair hesitated, seeming unable to move any further, unwilling to descend into the terrors this hospital contained for them.

*

Nurse Eveleen Morgan sat in the ICU ward station updating the PC files and the paperwork that made mere numbers of the long, arduous night they'd just been through. Four more days, she thought, and she'd be gone from here and soon forgotten. Such was life. She'd been forgotten before and done her own fair share of forgetting. But Harry Larkin's deluded ramblings wouldn't stay forgotten. The consultant had finally decided to put Harry under. The anaesthetist would be here before lunch, but meanwhile a vague sense of urgency bothered Eveleen.

Dementia was far from uncommon among post-operative patients or among the brain-injured. Neither was it uncommon that their delusions centred around the world of film and TV where people got most of their stories these days. Delusions were, after all, merely stories that dulled the pain of reality. She should know, Eveleen reflected wryly, she'd deluded herself often enough. Most delusions made no sense at all. Some did. Some held at least a grain of truth amid the chaff of improbabilities. She wondered if Harry's delusions fitted in this last category.

Most of what he'd said, Eveleen had figured out by now. Liam Neeson had starred in the film *Taken* in which his daughter is kidnapped by an Arab sheikh. In *The Bodyguard*, she seemed to remember, Kevin Costner protected Whitney Houston from some similarly dire fate. When Eveleen had Googled Sally Field, she came across a movie called *Not Without My Daughter* in her filmography. A woman whose Iranian husband was trying to grab their child. Another bad Arab movie, Eveleen thought.

As for Leo Woods, was he perhaps a character from some Irish film or TV series, or some real-life detective Harry had crossed swords with?

She rang the front desk, asked to speak with one of the

Guards posted out front. As Eveleen listened to the echo of her breathing down the phone, she considered how precisely she was going to phrase her first question to the Guard. When he came on the line, she said the first thing that came to her.

'Is Detective Leo Woods a real person?'

# 2

---

Fog. Outside the window. Inside his head. Another sleep-less night on Serpentine Crescent. Detective Inspector Leo Woods let the inch or two of raised blind fall. He'd grown used to these insomniac bouts, the fatigue they induced in him. Tiredness was the least of his troubles when the insomnia hit. The long nights were endurable but the days were a nightmare. A sour nicotine taste in his mouth, a dispiriting weakness in his limbs, the swamp fever of sensory overload. In the dim room Leo searched for a glimmer of consolation in his misery. To his surprise, he found some. It was Sunday morning. He didn't have to go to work.

He had no idea how long the DVD had been paused. Truffaut's 1960 classic *Tirez sur le Pianiste*. The kind of film you didn't have to leave your brain on hold to watch. A light rail train shuddered past Serpentine Crescent and faded off towards the Sandymount stop. He looked around the bedroom. It might have been the store room for an Oxfam charity shop. Clothes dumped in one corner. Books in another. DVDs piled on top of the wardrobe, framed paintings and posters leaning against its side. Directly opposite the bed, an old wicker laundry box filled with his collection of wall masks. Some destroyed, some merely damaged, the rest intact. He still wondered how he had drifted so seamlessly from an almost obsessive tidiness to this disorderly indifference. That was the trouble with habits: the good ones were too easy to lose, the bad ones too easily drifted into.

Leo lay back on his pillow. He wiped some drool from the collapsed left side of his mouth, a leaking tear from the eye that never closed. Six months had passed since the burst pipes in the attic flooded the house during the Big Freeze. The repairs completed a fortnight before, only the clearing up and the repainting remained to be tackled. There was, he knew, no excuse for living in this self-imposed squalor or for confining himself to this bedroom alone as if it were some kind of squat.

Along the rails that were little more than fifty yards from the house, another train tick-tacked inwards from the suburbs, slowing down for the Lansdowne Road stop. He fished out a half-smoked joint from the ashtray on his bedside table. He lit up, smoked the joint down to his fingernails and waited for the mellowing. The mellowing never came. Instead, one of his two mobiles rang. Not the work one happily.

He picked up the old Nokia Classic, so old it was already post-modern. Superintendent Heaphy. His boss. At eight-fifteen on Sunday morning? It was work.

'Aonghus, you're up and about early for a Sunday morning,' he said.

'I'm always up and about early. Especially on a Sunday morning. Unlike some.'

Leo let the reference to his godlessness go. Maybe the mellowing was kicking in after all. The super's voice was slurred and lispy. Didn't have his new dentures in, Leo supposed. The Hungarian teeth experiment had failed, the ceramic slabs unscrewed from his jawbones and a new plate fitted. The unhealed wounds in his gums, however, had the poor bugger in agony every time he wore the dentures. Whenever he could, he left them out.

'So, what's the problem then?' Leo asked.

'Harry Larkin was shot last night. They found him in his car on Tandy's Lane. Nothing from the Technical Bureau people out there yet but it's not looking good for him.'

Leo sat up. Harry Larkin. A real blast from the past. A double-barrelled blast. Harry and Liz. An unwelcome reminder of those days when his life had fallen apart. The first time it had fallen apart. He wondered if they were still together, Harry and Liz. Surely not.

'I know Harry's not exactly major league but that's one for the Special Detective Unit, Aonghus. Or Organized Crime, right?'

'We may need to bring them in on this. But not yet.'

'Why not?'

The background hiss in Leo's unrested brain increased. It felt like a meteor was heading his way. It was.

'He wants to talk to you, Leo.'

'Why the hell would he want to talk to me? I haven't laid eyes on him for donkey's years.'

'I don't know, Leo. But you'll have to liaise with the Pettycannon boys on this. Detective Sergeant Martin Buck is on his way to the hospital as we speak. He'll be waiting for you at the goods delivery area out behind.'

Leo neither liked nor trusted Buck. Never had. Met him back in the good old moonlighting days when they'd soldiered together briefly as bouncers at a night club off O'Connell Street. Saw the stuff the guy was made of and it wasn't nice stuff. The kick-backs Buck took from dealers slipping in and out of the club proved the final straw. Leo had refused a share in the takings and packed in the after-hours security game. Buck was resentful. And worried. *Going to shop me, are you, Leo?* He hadn't, but made every effort to keep barge-pole distance between them ever since.

'Jesus, Aonghus, you know I can't stand the guy. Can't they send someone else?'

'Buck's been covering the Chapelizod area for a good number of years. He'll be up to date on Harry's activities.'

'I'm telling you, he's a bloody liability.'

'It's not my call, Leo,' Superintendent Heaphy said. He cleared his throat, making way for the real trouble to come through. 'Harry was one of your IRA informants back in the eighties, wasn't he, Leo?'

'He was one of *our* IRA informants.'

'But you were his handler.' The super hurried along past his little exercise in self-protection. 'Anyway, he's in intensive care and drifting in and out of consciousness. He's been talking a lot of gibberish – apparently there's a bullet lodged in his brain and he's—'

'They found a brain?'

Leo's laughter rang false in his own ears.

'This is no joking matter, Leo. Listen to me.' Heaphy's voice went softer, squashier, *nil dente*. 'Most of what Harry had to say was mad old nonsense. Apparently he's suffering from dementia and seeing film stars all over the place. I don't have any specifics yet but it seems he talked about a kidnapping.'

'Harry was always delusional. Always spoofing. We never got anything solid out of him.'

In the silence that Aonghus maintained, Leo thought he heard another train. It wasn't passing on the rails outside his house. It trundled in from the suburbs of his past, bringing ghosts.

'What?' he demanded.

'You never got anything solid out of him?'

'*We* never got anything solid out of him.'

'You sure of that?'

'We had no use for him after '83, Aonghus,' Leo said. 'Check the files.'

'It's what's not on the files that bothers me.'

'There's nothing not on the files.'

Leo's head spun. It was too early in the morning to deal with double negatives. Especially his own.

'So why would he look for you after all this time?'

'How the hell would I know?'

'Leo,' the super said, with all the pious insistence of a papal nuncio addressing a recalcitrant bishop, 'they'll be putting him into an induced coma at about twelve. So you've a few hours to get out there to the hospital and see what Harry's game is. Garda Dempsey's on his way to pick you up. And Leo? We don't want any unexploded bombs from the past blowing up in our faces. Are you with me?'

'What makes you think there are unexploded bombs, Aonghus?'

'Because I'm talking to Leo Woods. Because you got in deep with that lot, Leo. Deeper than you should have.'

'I was doing my job.'

'Listen, Leo. I'm in the running for a spot on the *CrimeLink* TV programme again. And I don't want you messing up my chances, do you hear me?'

'Fifteen minutes, is it?'

'It's a five-minute segment actually,' Aonghus, clearly not a Warhol devotee, asserted. 'But it'll be every week for the whole season. A major boost to my profile if I get it.'

What was it with people, Leo mused, that they so longed to slip on to the same TV screen they wasted so much of their lives gaping at?

'And, by the way, you still haven't got that photo taken for your new ID card. I'm getting major hassle from the chief on this, Leo.'

'The old one's fine.'

'You're the only Guard in the country going around flashing an ID from the last century. It can't go on.' Superintendent Heaphy's voice slipped down an octave marking, in his usual unsubtle way, the change to a milder, touchy-feely tone. 'Look, Leo, I understand very well that . . . well, you know, given your . . . your condition . . . that it isn't easy for you to—'

'Piss off, Aonghus,' Leo said and tossed his phone back on the bedside table.

He lay back on the bed and thought about Harry Larkin. Once a docker, Harry had been a block of a man with a ruddy complexion and a sandy crew-cut. Free with his bullying fists but never picked a fair fight. A coward beneath the huffing and puffing. They usually were. And filthy-minded to boot with his seedy tales of under-age seduction. A man with no positive quality in him that Leo could ever decipher. Not even loyalty to the violent Republicanism he loudly mouthed off about back then. Mother Ireland's distress had been nothing but a front for his sticky-fingered thievery.

All a bloody twist of fortune it was that Leo had ever met the guy. Or misfortune. Such was life. Accident, coincidence, contingency at best. Harry had been Detective Sergeant Blackie Shaughnessy's tout in the Republican undergrowth for a couple of years. When poor Blackie died of a heart attack at fifty-one, Leo inherited the fat tout. Full of bluff and bluster the big man had been back in those murky days. Knew this fellow, knew that fellow, knew nothing. Knew less than he thought about his wife-to-be Liz too.

Priority number one here, Leo thought, was to kick this into touch, over the stands and on to someone else's patch.

He got off the bed, raised the blind a touch and looked out through the gap. No sign of the fog lifting. Literally. Metaphorically. Metaphysically. He heard the impatient honking of a car horn. Get dressed, Leo, and face the past. In the squad car down below, Garda Dempsey stared disconsolately ahead of him, ignoring Leo's thumbs-up signal. Leo felt the manic joviality rise in him that always came when the shit was about to hit the fan in some unpredictable way.

Five minutes later he sat down on the passenger seat and almost demolished the young Guard's mobile phone. The graphic on the back of the phone depicted a modern-day warrior above the title *Call of Duty: MW3*.

'What's this?' Leo asked. 'A new game?'

Dempsey glanced over at him, shrugged, sighed impatiently.

'It's just a new skin.'

'New skin. Jesus, I could do with some of that myself,' Leo muttered. 'What's wrong with you? Didn't pull at Copper's last night?'

Leo had never been there, of course, but had heard all about the place. Copperface Jack's. The city-centre night club for rednecks. Country boys hunting down country girls and vice versa.

'I didn't go,' Dempsey grunted.

'What did you do? Stay at home playing games with yourself?'

'I watched a DVD.'

22

'Let me guess. Tarkovsky's *Stalker*, or maybe Fellini's *Amarcord*?'

'No,' Dempsey said with a dismal, conversation-ending finality.

Great, Leo thought. An insomniac and a melancholic heading to the ICU ward of a hospital early on a Sunday morning. In a fog.

# 3

As Garda Dempsey steered the squad car into the yard behind the hospital, Leo caught sight of Martin Buck sharing a cigarette break with a middle-aged nurse. Style-wise, the time-warped detective had given the nineties and the noughties a miss. Most of the eighties too. Snowy bouffant hair, arse-huggingly tight denims, leather bomber jacket, too many buttons open on his plaid shirt.

'Go and get yourself a coffee in the staff canteen while you're waiting,' Leo told Dempsey as he opened the passenger door. 'Never know who you might meet in there.'

The young Guard shook his lowered head. He hadn't been his usual entertainingly bluff self for weeks now. Putting on weight too, Leo noted, the rawly shaven double chin threatening to expand to a triple. The strain of introspection didn't invest Dempsey's features with the signs of maturity. It made him seem more than ever a bewildered boy trapped in a man's body.

As Leo got out of the car and headed across to Buck, the nurse ducked back inside, laughing out loud. He imagined the joke had been at his expense. Or maybe he was being paranoid. Insomnia did that to a fellow.

'Leo. The heavens opened and the NBCI gods appeared.'

Buck's jocularity came through gritted teeth as he leaned against the wall, the sole of one sneaker propped against it, striking a pose like some second-rate rhinestone cowboy on the sleeve of a seventies C&W album. 'Must be a pain in the hole having to slum it with the locals.'

'You're looking boyish as ever,' Leo said.

'Five days a week in the gym. Do you still work out yourself?'

Leo pulled out a packet of Consulates in place of an answer.

Buck peered in through the window alongside him. Checking out the talent, no doubt. Something else always on his mind. Always the same something. And always less with anticipated pleasure than with dark intent. Buck's desires seemed to Leo to be rooted in contempt, perhaps even in hatred; his tales of conquest, missives from behind the lines of a dirty war.

'Still on the John Player Specials then, are you?' Leo asked. The kind of cigarette they advertised on Formula One cars back in the seventies when smoking was harmless fun.

'Packed them in years ago. Still smoking that old menthol shite?'

'They're healthier,' Leo told him. He snapped the tip, dropped it in his pocket and lit up. 'What do you make of this business about a kidnapping?'

'The guy's raving. Some loopy shit about a film being made in the hospital. And we're supposed to take this seriously? I don't think so, Leo.'

'And who does Harry imagine's been kidnapped?'

'Don't have the details yet.' Buck hid a smirk behind his cigarette. 'Apart from the fact that you're the leading man in this film he's dreaming up.'

25

Leo changed the subject.

'Any thoughts on who shot Harry?'

'Not as yet.'

Two possibilities had already suggested themselves to Leo, both of which would rid him of the case. A territorial dispute for the Organized Crime Unit to investigate. A run-in with dissident Republicans could be passed on to the Special Detective Unit.

'Has Harry been involved in any turf wars lately?' Leo asked.

'Not that we know of,' Buck replied. 'The thing is, much as I hate to give the scumbag any credit, Harry Larkin isn't overly greedy and he's never crossed the big guns. Kept his distance from the young guns too. The Westies, all that trigger-happy lot. Plus he's been building up the legit side of his business for quite a while now. He's got three pubs, two of them leased. Has a debt collection agency too. And, get this, the old bastard has an apartment in Lanzarote. The whole bloody country's sinking and Harry Larkin's never had it so good.'

'What about these dissident IRA groups and their protection rackets?' Leo asked. 'Could they be leaning on him?'

'Unlikely. He's always kept his old Republican buddies sweet. Throws a few bob at them every now and then to keep them off his back.'

Judas money, Leo thought. Then again, who didn't have to pay Judas money for one thing or another? Leo's options for divesting himself of the case were closing down, but he persisted.

'I'm assuming Harry's not gone one hundred per cent legit.'

'No, he's still in the illegal cigarette trade. He got in early on that game. As you know,' Buck emphasized, and grinned in response to Leo's warning glance. 'Counterfeit stuff from China, the Philippines, Slovakia. And brands you've never heard of. Regal, Imperial, 821 Reds. Cheap Whites from the Ukraine and Poland. Ever smoke them?'

'No,' Leo lied. Got them from his supplier Dripsy Scullion once. Never again. 'And that's it? Gets all his off-radar cash flow from cigarettes? What about drugs?'

That disbelieving grin again. Leo was getting tired of it.

'Cannabis, Ecstasy tabs, that kind of thing. But small-scale, and Harry never dealt in hard drugs. As you must know better than—'

'Listen, Martin, let's get this straight. I was Harry's handler for a few years in the early eighties before he decided there was no money in the patriot game and transformed himself into an Ordinary Decent Criminal. And, yes, I know his first wife died of a heroin overdose. But, no, I haven't followed his career. If he published an autobiography, I obviously missed it. He didn't come up on my radar when I was on the organized crime beat in the mid-nineties. We had bigger fish to catch. And that's it, right?' Leo dumped his cigarette. 'We should go find Harry.'

They went inside, flashing badges and asking directions along the endless corridors and stairways.

'Beats me how anyone got to Harry though,' the leather-jacketed detective said. 'He's had The Armenian covering his rear end for years now. Baz MacDonald, the West Belfast Armenian. Know him, do you?'

'I've heard the name. But do me a favour, Martin, don't call him The Armenian. Give these guys a fancy moniker and you're giving them some kind of perverse credibility. Call them what they are. Low-lifes.'

Buck didn't appreciate the lecture. The old resentment flared up in his narrowed eyes.

'Well, the Special Detective Unit gave him some credence. They thought he might be offering his services as a hitman when he came down from Belfast after the Good Friday Agreement. Seven similar MOs. Back of a motorbike. Two, three shots close in. Clinical stuff.'

'That's a pretty generic type of MO, Martin.'

'Yeah, but always the same type of gun. First-generation Glock 17. Semi-automatic.'

'But not always the same gun?' Leo said, making no effort to hide his scepticism.

'The PSNI up North are sure he had access to a stash of those Glocks,' Buck insisted. Doggedly. Wanting to bite but afraid he'd be beaten with an old stick if he did. 'Four of these shootings were in Belfast, pre-Good Friday Agreement. After that there were two in Dublin and one in Cork. The last one was in 2001.'

'So he's with Harry, what, seven or eight years?'

'Since 2002. Worked security around town before that. These days he's supposedly running the debt collection agency but actually covering the old bastard's tail. Until last night, at least. Maybe he saw his chance to take Harry's crown.'

'You think there's a chance this Baz guy turned on his master?'

'Absolutely. They were close, but then again that doesn't mean much in their world. The word is that Harry had more time for Baz than he had for his own two sons. Which is hardly surprising. One of them's a deaf dummy and the younger lad's—'

'Don't call him a deaf dummy.'

Leo couldn't remember the silent kid's name but remembered well the frightened little eyes in the rear-view mirror of Harry's car staring out at the mist thickening over the fields on Tandy's Lane all those years ago. And there was more – the car suddenly infused with the smell of urine, the older man swinging a backward fist and catching the child on the cheekbone. Leo had bollocked Harry but left it at that. Never followed up on the cry for help in that kid's eyes. The boy would be, what, thirty-five or thirty-six now?

'Show some respect, would you?' he told Buck. Passing on the blame. Some of it. 'What's his name? The deaf son.'

'Kevin,' Buck said, his tone flattened with tamped-down fury. 'The younger guy's Gary. A small man with big no-tions.'

A young nurse ducked into a lab unit under the indelicate probe of Martin Buck's stare. Leo saw a sign for the ICU ward at last.

'Is Harry's brother still in the picture?'

'Jimmy, yeah. Still the accounts man. Launders the cigarette money through their businesses. Once a shipping clerk, always a shipping clerk.'

'And the second wife? Is she still with Harry?'

'Liz, yeah,' Buck answered disinterestedly as he peered in through the porthole of the lab unit.

How had she stuck it out all these years? Leo wondered. And, for Christ's sake, why?

Beside the staff entrance to the ICU ward was an office whose door stood open. Buck took one look inside and left the talking to Leo. The grey-haired woman wore horn-rimmed glasses and with an irritated frown snapped Leo's proffered ID.

'But this isn't . . .' she began.

A closer examination of Leo's face softened and sweet-ened her. Leo didn't want to think why. He introduced him-self.

29

'Detective Inspector Woods, National Bureau of Criminal Investigation. I—'

'Eveleen's expecting you,' the woman said with the kind of lopsided smile she presumably reserved for the sadder cases. 'Eveleen Morgan, the senior ward nurse. You'll find her in the third room on your right.'

'Thanks,' he said.

He escaped along the corridor and knocked on the senior ward nurse's door.

The chestnut-haired woman's tag read S/N E. Morgan. She was neither petite nor svelte nor conventionally pretty. Instead there was an attractive fullness to her, a directness in her green-eyed gaze uncomplicated by impressions of Leo's hang-dog appearance. He extended his hand.

'Detective Inspector Leo Woods. And this is—'

'So you do actually exist then?' she said, a husk of tiredness in her voice.

'Apparently,' he replied, and she smiled broadly, getting the joke. Intelligence in a woman had always been an aphrodisiac to Leo. Trouble was, the intelligent ones had invariably sussed him out too soon. 'And this is Detective Sergeant Martin Buck.'

The hungry-eyed detective grabbed his share of the doorway.

'Pleased to—' he began but the nurse had already turned away.

'I took some notes of what Mr Larkin said, Inspector,' she said as she went to her desk and fished among its contents.

'What time was he admitted?' Leo asked.

'Quarter past three this morning. We've had a pretty hectic night. A hit-and-run only twenty minutes after Mr Larkin arrived and another patient took a serious turn for the worse.'

'How's Mr Larkin doing?'

'Not very well, I'm afraid,' Eveleen said, pushing back a lock of hair from her forehead as she searched. 'He was already quite a sick man. Obese, a smoker, and he'd had a quadruple bypass last year. Ah, here it is.'

Martin Buck had moved swiftly to her side. He reached for the sheet of paper but she held on to it. His lust-lorn features reflected too accurately Leo's own foolish longing. Eveleen scanned her sheet, looked up at Leo. Her eyes were speckled green. She had a late-night radio kind of voice, unhurried, companionable; it dispelled the constant static in Leo's brain.

'This is a list of the actors he mentioned,' she said, handing him the sheet. 'And the films I connected them with.' Old Harry's taste in film came as no surprise to him. Three shit movies. Well, in fairness, Liam Neeson was in one of them. Two and a half shit movies then. Buck peered in over Leo's shoulder.

'Whitney?'

They turned to Buck.

'I presumed he meant Whitney Houston,' Eveleen said. 'She was in that film with Kevin Costner, *The Bodyguard*.'

'Harry's got a teenage daughter called Whitney,' Buck told them.

The old sucking sand sensation dragged at the soles of Leo's feet.

'Has the family been in to see him yet?' Leo enquired of Nurse Morgan.

'They're in the ICU waiting room right now. No daughter with them though. I'm quite sure of that.'

'The Armen— Baz MacDonald's there too,' Buck added. 'Last I heard. But Gary hasn't arrived yet.'

'Is there a CCTV camera in there?' Leo asked. There was.

'Martin, we should probably get one of our officers up to the Security Control Room and see if the girl shows up.' Another thought occurred to him. 'They need to watch out for any signs of conflict among the family. Arguments, recriminations, whatever.'

'At your service,' Buck said. His thin smile couldn't hide his irritation at taking orders in the presence of a prospective conquest.

'And we need to ring the SDU and OCU desks. See if they can throw any more light on who'd want to shoot Harry or kidnap his daughter.'

Leo turned his better profile to the chestnut-haired woman. With a slight bowing of the head and a hand gesturing towards the door, he invited her out.

'Can you take me to see Mr Larkin now, please?'

Beside him, Buck snickered at his colleague's old-fashioned manners and pathetic hopefulness. Snickered again at her gentle but firm rebuff as she brushed by Leo.

'Wait here,' Eveleen said. 'I'll call you as soon as he comes to. It may take a while, I'm afraid.'

It did.

# 4

Ten minutes into the game against Peamount United and Detective Sergeant Helen Troy had already been through the pain barrier. Twice. A stitch in her side. Her calves rock solid with cramp. The air out west of the city in Newcastle seemed as rarefied as the upper reaches of the Himalayas and every breath she sucked in felt like it had less disposable oxygen in it. Around her, girls half her age zipped along in a different dimension from the one she inhabited. At thirty-four, six years out of the game was too much, even if she had been training since January.

Atletico Glasnevin were 2–0 down. The first and, possibly, the second goal had been down to her failure to rein in the carrot-haired kid who was her opposite number in midfield. All of which was bad enough but the same kid had just now grinned in bare-faced cockiness at her as they awaited a kick-out. *Time you hung up the boots*, the grin suggested.

Helen's early morning optimism back at the apartment had vanished. All those hopes and plans. The money from the sale of her father's house would soon materialize. The rent in Glasnevin would be affordable. She'd buy a small second-hand car. She'd hook up with some of those friends she'd lost along the way to Ricky's possessiveness and her own ambition. Dress up, live and dance in the world again.

Or, more likely, fall on her arse in yet another vain attempt to tackle the redhead.

The Atletico Glasnevin keeper kicked out the ball, long and high towards the middle of the field. Helen got herself in front of her ginger tormentor. As she rose to head the ball on, she shipped a knee in the back, an elbow in the neck, and landed on her forehead. When she looked dizzily up, the kid was waltzing away with the ball at her feet. Helen stayed on the ground, glad of the rest. She gathered whatever reserves of strength she had left and passed a silent verdict on the redhead. *You're dead, Rusty, fucking dead.*

Quarter to twelve but it still felt like blue o'clock in the morning in the windowless ICU ward. His third visit to the bedside in as many hours, Leo had twenty minutes at most to hear Harry Larkin out before the anaesthetist arrived. If he succeeded finally in whispering the guy awake.

Harry still had the wide girth but he'd lost most of his hair and his neck had grown scrawny since Leo had last seen him. The flesh on his arms had gone to loose folds. On the right arm, a heart-shaped tattoo shrivelled like some logo on a left-over balloon bore the name Brigid. Harry's first wife, victim of guilt and heroin. No prizes for guessing what Liz, the second wife, thought of the tattoo.

Behind his oxygen mask, Harry made emphysema noises that spooked Leo. He'd been especially wheezy himself recently from smoking too late into the night. He didn't know which was the worse prospect, dementia or emphysema. Dementia definitely, he thought. Your darkest thoughts, words and deeds spilling out in front of strangers. Though maybe dementia wasn't all bad. Maybe it was better to approach the big dark void imagining that you were walking off some film set and that beyond the cameras and the lights up there on their dollies there was another film waiting for you to star in.

'The bruises on his neck,' he said, trying to distract himself from his dire imaginings. 'What's the story there?'

'Can't say for sure,' Eveleen told him. 'But we often get that in shootings. The instinctive reflex when you're being shot at is snapping your head away. It can actually cause quite a bit of damage in itself.'

He watched her demonstrate the action. Or watched her sleek throat, the soft curls at the back of her swept-up hair.

'Of course, it might be disease rather than injury,' she added. 'Diabetes, for example.'

The need to keep his voice down ramped up the frustration Leo felt.

'Harry, can you hear me? It's Leo.'

Eveleen stroked the big man's hairy arm and watched the screens above the bed as though to measure the effects of her touch. The shake of her head was pessimistic. Harry, she'd already told him, hadn't woken when the family had been in to see him. Now they were wondering why they weren't being allowed to stay with him, complaining, suspicious. The wife especially, Eveleen reported.

Leo wished he could just slap Harry awake. The nurse's instincts were keener.

'Tell us about Whitney, Mr Larkin,' she said, and Harry's heartbeat picked up.

She lifted the oxygen mask. Beneath it lay the volcanically collapsed mouth of a toothless man.

'Did someone take your daughter, Harry?' Leo asked. 'Has Whitney been kidnapped?'

Harry's eyes didn't open. Instead, the lids tightened and tears formed. His lips moved but all they could hear was the scratching of his lungs. He nodded slowly.

'Why, Harry? Why was she kidnapped?'

On the screens, graphs soared, numbers increased exponentially. Harry moved his head from side to side. The gesture might have meant he didn't know or simply meant he couldn't take any more of whatever the embedded bullet was doing to his brain.

'Who took her, Harry? Who were you meeting on Tandy's Lane?'

Leo wasn't ready for the hand that seized his forearm, for the rasping attempts at words or for the general unco-ordinated alarms coming from the screens. Eveleen wedged back the fingers of Harry Larkin's left hand. Leo's relief proved short-lived: Harry's right hand shot out. Tubes and needles came undone. He pointed a finger at Leo. A finger of blame it felt like, of condemnation. Leo felt the knife of premonition twist in his own gut.

'Out!' Eveleen ordered and called for assistance. 'Sarah! Olive! Now!'

Leo staggered back until a bed end halted his fall. Further off, in a glassed-in isolation unit, a tragic Egyptian mural took shape. A startlingly tall grey-haired man and a long-featured angular girl with red dreadlocks stood, both in profile, hollow-eyed and motionless. Below them, a young man lay like some dead or sleeping pharaoh. A diminutive dark-haired woman in blue crouched low beside him.

Leo fished a tissue from his pocket and dabbed at the open well of his bad eye. His tears were yellowing. Infected again, he guessed. He strode out from the ICU ward doing the Eric Cantona straight-backed walk but leaving out the upturned collar bit. Sometimes you had to pretend to be

36

purposeful before you could figure out what the hell to do next. He found Martin Buck sitting near the ICU office where they'd first checked in and giving every impression of nursing a hangover. On the pooch in some late bar last night, Leo concluded. Enviously.

'Have you rung the SDU and OCU yet?' he snapped.

'Relax, Leo, I made some calls. Did Harry talk?'

'He wasn't able to. Did you get anything?'

'Not a lot,' Buck said. 'There's been no report of this Whitney kid having gone missing. Not from the family nor from anyone else. They'll be sussing out their informants on the ground for anything that might be relevant.'

In the constant to and fro of doctors, nurses and orderlies along the corridor, Leo couldn't think straight. He couldn't find a way into this case, a kicking-off point.

'Listen, Leo. You know the story here.' Buck sighed, his Sunday morning gone, the rest of his Lord's Day looking doubtful. 'Those boys back at HQ spend their time on the shooters, the hard drugs merchants, the headline-makers. They've no interest in Harry Larkin. Haven't had for a long time.'

Leo's bad eye hurt. Late morning and already he was running out of tissues. And ideas.

'I need a smoke,' he announced, and they went searching for an emergency exit to the hospital yard.

Outside, the sun had emerged from behind the last of the fog. Leo turned his back to it. The heat soothed his neck but the cold breeze worked its way inside his suit. He followed the advice of Charlie Llunga, the old chief without a tribe in that UN refugee camp over in Angola. Not thinking so much as waiting for the thoughts to come. *Make a silence in your head so the answers can come sing themselves.* Even if you were tone-deaf? Leo thought. He popped another filter, lit up again. Smoke hit his sore eye like a bee sting. He dabbed away the poisonous tears.

'Tandy's Lane,' Leo thought aloud. 'So, Harry chose the meeting place.'

'How do you know that for sure?'

'When I was Harry's handler, we always met there.'

Imponderables and variables crowded into Leo's mind. If there was a kidnap, how long would the family hide it? Given their natural aversion to getting involved with the police, that might depend on how long the girl had been missing. Or maybe they knew what the kidnap was about? But if Harry chose the site, why the hell hadn't he set a trap for the kidnappers? Tandy's Lane was perfect for a trap. One way in and one way out, Leo knew, having chosen the site himself all those years ago. Or maybe Harry had been caught in his own trap?

'We need to get moving,' he said. 'I want to take a look at the crime scene and you—'

'Shouldn't we start talking to the family?' Buck suggested. 'Pull them in one by one and see what we can get from them? I can start with Jimmy.'

Buck was right. They needed to talk to Harry's brood. Which included Harry's golden boy, The Armenian. But not yet. Even the Larkins deserved a few hours' grace in the circumstances. Which didn't mean that nothing of interest could be gained in the interval. The CCTV camera in the ICU waiting room came to mind. A strategy advanced slowly towards Leo out of the cigarette smoke. He told himself that this strategy wasn't just some excuse to avoid a little longer having to meet Liz Larkin. He almost believed himself.

'All in good time, but we can't justify piling in on them right now. I'll be back from Tandy's Lane by, say, three. And presuming good old Harry hasn't popped his clogs, we'll start talking to the royal family then.'

Body language, Leo thought. That was where he'd start with the Larkins. The CCTV camera was too remote, too empty of emotional atmosphere to really give a sense of the Larkin family dynamic. The gestures, glances, tones of voice that reveal who loves who and who hates who. The clues that indicate how a family divides up into opposing factions because every family does in a crisis. If he and Buck went barging into the ICU waiting room, all of this would be lost.

What Leo needed was a presence in the waiting room. Not someone whose big shaved redneck head had Garda written across the forehead. No, he needed someone who looked so normal they couldn't possibly be mistaken for a Guard. Detective Garda Ben Murphy might have fitted the bill if he wasn't a couple of thousand miles away at an FBI training course in Quantico. No matter. He wouldn't have been Leo's first choice anyway. That honour went to his steady and reliable detective sergeant.

'Name?' the referee demanded, wavering between the red and yellow cards in her notebook.

'Helen Troy. That kid's been getting away with bloody murder. Where was your little black book when she levelled me?'

She'd forgotten what it was like to be at the receiving end of officialdom. Forgotten the Golden Rule: don't provoke them. Now she paid the price. The ref chose red. Stabbed the card in the air like she was sticking it to a wall.

'Off,' she said.

'Ah, for f—' Helen began but saw the redhead stretched on the grass getting treatment for the gash on her knee. The kid was actually crying like a child. And she was just that. A child-girl. Bold and chipper but hardly deserving of the punishment Helen had meted out.

'Sorry,' she told the kid but got an unforgiving glare for an answer. 'Oh, grow up, would you?'

Another false dawn, Helen told herself as she started the long walk to the sideline. She hadn't kick-started her life as she'd hoped. All she'd done was kick a child. In the dressing room, she dumped her jersey on the table and sat for a while in her sports bra, elbows on grubby knees, hands tight in her hair. She stank of mud and sweat, and her leg muscles were setting in concrete. The effort of taking a shower was beyond her. The clock on the dressing-room wall told her that half-time was ten minutes away. She didn't want to face the others. She threw on her green track suit. Irish Universities Women's Squad – 1997, the crest read. Last century, she thought, and bailed out.

The bus-stop should have been a ten-minute walk away along the Lucan Road. Twenty minutes today, she reckoned, as her legs stiffened. It was going to be a long day. Nothing to do. She wished it was Monday. At least it was open country out here and the sun, warm on her shoulders, cheered her somewhat as she went. She fetched her mobile from the track-suit pocket, hoping that if by some chance she had a text message, it wouldn't be from her brother. Or from Ricky, her ex-partner. She had two missed calls and a message. All of them were from Leo. Work. Thank Christ. She could always depend on Leo. She rang him.

'Where are you, Helen?' Leo asked.

'I'm at a bus-stop across the road from Peamount Hospital.'

'Oh. I hope—'

'I was out here playing football.'

'You play football?'

'It's in my personnel file, Leo,' Helen told him. 'And my personnel file's been on your desk in Harcourt Street for months.'

'So it is. But I don't like to delve.'

'It's a personnel file, not a *personal* file.'

'Yeah, well, you know me and paperwork. Listen, I've a job for you. Some undercover work but nothing too dangerous, mind.'

Leo filled her in on the background, passed on some broad descriptions of the Larkins and Baz MacDonald he'd got from Martin Buck.

'The girl is small for a seventeen-year-old,' he added. 'Hair dyed black apparently. That's all Buck could give me on her. Anyway, it'll be obvious who she is if she shows up.'

He followed with a general outline of what he wanted from her in the way of observations and apologized for the vagueness of the task. He told her he'd be back at the hospital from the crime scene by mid-afternoon.

'Who's this MacDonald guy?' Helen asked.

'The Armenian, they call him, but we won't be gracing the scumbag with a title,' Leo explained. 'Besides which, he's not actually Armenian. Baz MacDonald's from Belfast. The story is that his mother was a bright spark and went to study at the Sorbonne in the seventies. She met up with an Armenian guy there. Apparently he was part of a guerrilla movement called The Justice Commandos of the Armenian Genocide.'

'That was against Turkey, right? The Turks denied there was any genocide.'

'Spot on,' Leo said. 'So, they started taking out Turkish diplomats in Paris and Vienna. But this Armenian guy got himself shot shortly before Baz was born. A few years later, mother and son came back to Belfast. Fast forward to 1992 and Baz joins the Provos. Earned himself a reputation beyond his years apparently. When he came down South, there was some suspicion he might be working as a hitman but nothing was ever proved. That's about all I have on him for now.'

'Sounds interesting.'

'The man or the job?' Leo said, veering into that lightness of spirit she so often induced in him.

'Both,' she said without hesitation and they laughed – but, for Leo, laughter was always the beginning of something darker.

'I'm relying on your instincts, Helen. And if those instincts tell you they've sussed you're a Guard, get out of that waiting room sharpish.'

'Will do,' Helen said, the sun brightening her world and shooting Vitamins A to D directly into her veins. 'I'd better go and call a taxi. I'll be there in half an hour.'

'That game must've started at some unearthly hour if it's over already.'

'It's not over.'

'You were subbed?'

'Red card.'

'My Dark Rosaleen,' he said, and she laughed.

# 5

Tandy's Lane hadn't changed much since Leo Woods had last met Harry Larkin there all those years before. Not once you got into its narrow, tree-cloistered depths. Out on the dusty edges of Lucan, it was a looping country road of two miles or so. Back then it had passed through open farmland a few acres of which had survived the more recent depredations of the developers. Along the lane, a handful of cottages and bungalows, each one separated by a discreet distance, spoke of a more civilized and private way of life. A rose-tinted glimpse of the past. Until they came to the white plastic tape marking the scene of Harry's shooting.

Garda Dempsey pulled the squad car into the margin by a cottage front wall. They'd barely exchanged a word on the half-hour-long drive. The young fellow's sighs had become ever more audible as they went. He clearly wanted to be asked what the matter was but Leo wasn't good at heart-to-hearts. In any case, his thoughts lay elsewhere, in a past that had not a hint of rose to it. His wife, Iseult, in those last days of their two-year marriage. *You've been with someone, Leo.* He blushed at the memory of his old denials. *I can smell her from your shirt.*

'Wait here,' he said.

'I wasn't going anywhere,' Dempsey said, dour as a winter rain shower. 'Sir.'

'You don't want to rub me up the wrong way today, Dempsey,' Leo warned, and when the young Guard made to answer, he cut him off: 'Don't.'

With a pucker of the lips, Dempsey turned away. Leo slammed the door and went in search of the Crime Scene crew. The shadowy lane felt colder than he'd expected. He was sorry he'd left off the thermals a few weeks back in his foolish adherence to seasons that no longer followed the old order. Then again, May had always been something of a schizophrenic month in Ireland. The Gaelic calendar, still in use, deemed it the first month of summer though the Met Office insisted it was the last month of spring. No wonder, Leo thought, the May sky didn't know whether to rain or shine.

Up ahead, Leo saw the white Crime Scene van. He recognized the man in whites at its opened rear doors.

'John, how's it going? Nice day for it.'

'We're just packing up here, Leo.'

He was a small fellow, not far above five feet. His dark eyes had a neutral detachment about them. Went with the job, Leo supposed.

'Can I take a look at the car?'

'No problem. Follow me. I've a few bits and pieces to pick up over there.'

'Should I suit up?'

'No need. We're done here.'

They moved along the sun-dappled lane, an incongruous pair given Leo's height. The breeze that funnelled along the lane caught his throbbing eye. He fished around fruitlessly in his pockets.

'Have you any tissues, John?'

The Crime Scene operative handed him a few, glanced up at him.

'Looks infected, that eye,' he said.

Harry's car was parked driver's side out at a rusted old gate leading to a wide green field. Same gate Leo and Harry had held their clandestine meetings at. Same field. Same abandoned construction, the grey blocks of the house still reaching waist height and no further. The house Harry had been building for his first wife before she'd died.

The car was a dusty old Audi 90, grey in colour with too many indents left carelessly to rust. Twenty years old, give or take. No flash with this Harry. No drawing attention to his bank balance. All four doors and the boot of the car were propped open. A carpet of shattered glass covered the ground below the driver's side.

'Car stationary when the victim was attacked,' John explained. 'Engine might not have been running but the battery certainly was and he had the heat on full blast. Can't say for how long. He was getting out of the car or getting back in. His right foot was still on the ground and propped the driver's side door. The window on that side had been opened. Hard to tell whether it was already down before the perp arrived or after.'

'So if he'd let the window down before going for his gun, we have to consider the possibility that he knew the shooter.'

'Yeah.'

Leo looked back along the lane and then forward. Two half-hidden bungalows two hundred yards apart and this the midway point.

'Did anyone hear the shots?'

'Silencer. But the victim fell against the steering wheel and set off the car horn. Actually, he may have been reaching down below his seat when he was hit. We found a Glock 17 semi-automatic tucked in there. He never got to use it.'

'First-generation Glock 17?'

'Yeah. Significant?'

'Might be. How many shots were fired?' Leo asked as he stooped to take in the interior of the Audi.

'We've picked up six spent cartridges, Nine by nine point nine millimetres,' John said and nodded towards the three figures in white still on their hands and knees by the gate on the other side of the car. 'There may be more. And, coincidentally, the Glock 17 fires the same cartridge. Not the only gun that does, of course. And there are plenty of Glocks out there. Maybe it doesn't mean anything much.'

'As the great football-philosopher often said, John, everything means something or if it doesn't it should.'

Clotted blood everywhere, blobs, strings of it. A party of bluebottles buzzing in feastly celebration made a Damien Hirst installation of the car's innards. Leo noted the opened glove compartment, the contents scattered on the seat and floor below. Ransom money, it occurred to him, in an envelope or package there? Or did Harry just forget in that blind moment of panic where he'd stashed his gun?

'What's the story with the glove compartment, John? Was Harry reaching across before he was shot?'

'Difficult to tell. But the passenger door was open too and we've found footprint traces on the inside verge. Won't get a lot from them anyway is my guess. Nike, size nines, but we'll have to confirm that. Mister Average basically. Only a couple of hundred thousand fits in the country.'

'The perp or perps were searching for something,' Leo said. 'So maybe there *was* a bloody ransom.'

'A ransom?'

'We're told his daughter may have been kidnapped.'

'Ah, the kid in the photo.'

'You found a photo?'

'Under the victim,' John said. 'I've got it bagged in the van if you'd like to—'

'Not yet,' Leo said too hastily. He wasn't ready to see it, didn't allow himself to think why. He switched tracks. 'No mobile, no?'

'Not a sign.'

'So, the shooter. Means of transport?'

The diminutive investigator bent down on to his hunkers. With a biro in hand, he indicated some details Leo couldn't differentiate in the shade of the roadside trees.

'Motorbike tyre tracks here. Bridgestone is my guess but very common treads, I'm afraid.'

Leo covered his streaming eye to focus on the light trail left in the shattered glass and loose pebbles.

'We found acceleration markings further up the road and at the junction out on to Adamstown Drive.'

'A perfect getaway. Long stretch over to Newcastle Road. No houses, factories, nothing.'

'They knew the territory,' John said.

'Every bit as well as Harry did.'

As they walked back to the Crime Scene van, Leo imagined the lane in the night fog. The motorbike's light emerging to the rear of Harry's car. He considered the options. Had Harry seen or heard the motorbike coming or not? The biker might have cut the lights but Harry must have heard the engine on this quiet road in the dead of night even had his window been closed. And unless he'd dropped off to sleep, he must have had plenty of time to get a hand to the gun under his seat. Or did he think that someone he knew and trusted was on the bike, someone he stepped out of the car to speak to? Someone he was setting up a trap for the kidnapper with? Someone such as Baz MacDonald, the man with the motorbike MO?

The Crime Scene operative climbed into the back of the van and emerged with a small clear plastic evidence bag. He handed the bagged photo to Leo.

'That's your girl,' he said. 'Our photographer had a look at it while he was here. He reckons it was taken on an old 35mm camera, probably eighties vintage. Might take some time to verify that.'

At first, all Leo saw was the blood. Harry Larkin's dark, clotted blood. It covered the entire bottom half of the photograph and was sprinkled liberally across the rest of it. He took the package across to where the sun's rays sprinkled through the roadside hedging. The left-side edge of the photo had been torn off along the vertical. He looked closer. A figure emerged from beneath the pointillist spray of blood.

The bikini-clad kid posing precociously in the photo was hardly more than eight years old. So the snap was taken when? 2001 or 2002? The top half of the white bikini was grotesquely padded. The high point of a green-and-white hooped shoulder was all that remained to be seen of the figure behind her. A Shamrock Rovers jersey? Or Glasgow Celtic? Close behind the girl was a backdrop of anonymous green vegetation, and on the grass below her a black and white terrier of doubtful pedigree dozed in the sunlight.

The dark pupils of her eyes, the pertness in the nose, the pencil-black eyebrows below the blonde hair convinced him that she was unmistakably Liz Larkin's daughter. Bright orange fake tan covered her arms to the elbow and her legs to mid-thigh. Her hair was piled high. Her lipsticked mouth mimed a kiss. And for all that, her eyes shone with guileless naivety. The eyes, it seemed to Leo, of a victim.

The photo left him feeling nauseous. This case wasn't about gangland turf wars or IRA extortion rackets. A family matter, he suspected, and it would take him to even murkier depths than he'd expected. Back in '82 he'd warned Liz straight up not to marry the fat tout. *He'll treat you like shit, Liz.* Her answer gutted him as much now as it had back then. *And you haven't?* Now he'd have to face her again, descend into the dank and dingy Larkin vaults.

The prospect of yet another dark domestic depressed him. Domestics were all that ever seemed to land on his desk these days. He longed for the wider horizons of his UN days, the sense of being part of world events and not just sniffing around some shady corner of a small island off the continent of Europe.

'There's a suggestion of the photographer's shadow on the bottom half where the blood is thickest,' the CS operative explained. 'It's a long shot but it might give you something to work on. May take a while to clean up though and we'll have to hope the blood's not been absorbed below the surface of the print.'

Leo squinted at the shot but saw nothing of the shadow.

'Someone's written on the back,' John added, and Leo turned the photo over.

A child's big-lettered scrawl. One word: Ludo. Followed by half a dozen enthusiastic if uneven Xs.

'The dog's name, you reckon?' the white-clad operative suggested.

'Yeah, probably. Send me a copy of this, John. Both sides. Today, if you don't mind.'

'No problem. I hope you find her.'

'Yeah,' Leo responded, though he felt nothing even remotely resembling hope in his heart.

This, he feared, might very well be a child who was lost in such a dark, unspeakable way that she would never be found.

# 6

The ICU waiting room was a magnolia nightmare of terrible ordinariness. Not the kind of place to wait for a loved one to die or not to die with its unforgiving white light, its bench seats, its wall-hung muted TV displaying a constant loop of news images that didn't matter much inside these walls. In here, no news was good news.

Detective Sergeant Helen Troy watched surreptitiously the others in the room. She wished now that she'd showered out at Newcastle. Dried sweat goose-bumped her flesh and her scalp tingled with imaginary nits of uncleanliness. Still, she told herself, this dishevelment of hers probably made the right kind of impression, appearance not being a priority when a loved one lay in the ICU ward.

Since she'd arrived ten minutes before, she'd identified two of the Larkins and their West Belfast Armenian minder. The smallest of the three men was clearly Harry's brother, Jimmy. Late sixties or early seventies and an old-school dresser, he wore a green and blue tartan jumper, yellow shirt and brown tie over brown trousers. His steely grey hair was swept straight back wetly. Behind thick-lensed glasses, his eyes were alert to every sound and movement in the waiting room.

Beside him sat the deaf son, Kevin. A big, thick-set man in his mid-thirties and carelessly dressed. Stained old denims; an oversized and not especially clean shirt, absent-mindedly unbuttoned halfway down his chest, the sleeves dragged rather than rolled up. He had plenty of greying brownish hair but had done nothing with it but let it grow. His features were puffy and his lustreless skin suggested an indoors life.

A few feet away from the Larkins sat The Armenian. Baz MacDonald. Unlike his pallid companions, the dark-featured man was impeccably dressed. He had on a grey-green Brooks Brothers-style suit, a subtly shaded grey shirt and a narrow tie that picked up the grey and green in its thin stripes. His hair was tight, black and curly. His sallow looks were striking in a brooding, Southern Mediterranean kind of way.

The three men eyed one another occasionally. Only Kevin betrayed signs of emotion, his eyes bloodshot and tearful. He engaged MacDonald in hand-signed exchanges which Helen couldn't follow. His gestures were deft and darting, The Armenian's less assured, though he did seem to be offering whatever reassurance the deaf man sought.

The door of the waiting room stood open. Whenever footsteps were heard from outside, all eyes turned to it. Expectant breaths were suspended until the figure, instead of entering the waiting room, passed to or from the ICU ward. Usually it was a nurse, sometimes a doctor or an orderly. A short, round-faced doctor with dark slick-backed hair and glasses and wearing an oversized white coat had looked in twice, a notebook laptop under his arm. Not a doctor, Helen decided. An intern, mid-twenties at most, with the nervous eyes of a school swot at sea in the grown-up waters of social interaction. His colouring was a shade darker than The Armenian's and belonged in a warmer climate.

For a while, no one came, and Helen wondered if her presence was the cause of the heavy silence among the Larkins and their companion. She felt vulnerable. She was running out of celebrity magazines to flick through. Besides which, the ubiquitous photos of Victoria Beckham were making her stomach protest its hunger. A shuffle of footsteps reached her ears. Someone was hurrying out from the ICU ward.

A small woman in a three-quarter-length designer blue raincoat paused briefly in the corridor. She looked towards the waiting-room door. Only Helen could see her. Manic eyes, Size Zero shape, she was very beautiful but in a disturbingly fragile way. Too young to be Harry Larkin's wife, Helen thought, and looked sharply away as the woman's coat fell open. The undoubtedly expensive gold lamé dress beneath hadn't been buttoned all the way up. A bare nipple was visible in the naked corridor light. As suddenly as she'd appeared, the woman tottered away on her high-heeled navy shoes, the little gold bows on them flashing.

Soon, the doorway had filled up again. Mrs Liz Larkin. Helen could tell because Jimmy Larkin stood up the instant she appeared. Her daughter, Whitney, wasn't with her. She carried a large Marks and Spencer bag, the cord of a dressing gown hanging over its edge. She wore autumn colours in a style that was a little young for her. Whatever good looks she might have possessed had weathered badly. Too much sun and too much alcohol to judge by the purpled flush and broken veins beneath the bronze. The wrong genes too. Some people simply aged in this cracked leathery way no matter the lives they'd led. Kept her figure though, Helen thought. Mrs Larkin didn't acknowledge The Armenian's nod of greeting nor did she look at Kevin.

'Is there any news?' she asked.

Even in the lower register her voice had a raw directness to it.

No one answered. She sat on the far side of Jimmy from the other two. A couple of chairs separated Liz and her brother-in-law. She clearly didn't like the small man any more than she liked the others.

'Where's Gary?' Jimmy asked. 'Is he all right?'

Helen waited for him to ask about Whitney. He didn't. Liz handed the shopping bag to him.

'He's on his way. Give these to the nurse, will you?'

Jimmy's walk was short-sighted and mincing as if he could barely see beyond the next step. Liz stared up at the TV when her brother-in-law left. Her absorbed expression seemed too immersed in calculations to pass as mere worry over her husband. Or perhaps that was an unfair conclusion, Helen thought, remembering her own veneer of tearless neutrality as her father lay close to death. Remembering how her brother and her ex saw heartlessness in it.

'Who do you have in here, love?' Liz asked Helen.

Her stomach tightened.

Leo had given her only the sketchiest of cover stories to fall back on. *You probably won't need it anyway*, he'd asserted. Wrong, Leo.

'My cousin,' Helen said. She didn't have to try too hard to sound timorous.

'What happened to her?' Liz followed up, her gaze fixed on the TV where countless thousands filled Tahrir Square in Cairo and despots continued to tumble across the Middle East.

'She's in a coma.'

The others stared at Helen. She blushed and a new wave of perspiration rolled in.

'Was it an accident or what?'

'No, she . . .'

A young man rushed into the waiting room. Short, pudgy, a prematurely aged baby-face on him. His hair, shaved tight on the sides, sported a greasy fullness on top with a gelled loose strand hanging stiffly over his forehead. A style popular with footballers of the narcissistic and not especially bright variety. He looked like he'd been to the Glasgow Celtic shop and bought everything he could lay his hands on. In the Junior Schoolboy section. Padded jacket, hoodie, jersey, track suit. All of which made him seem top-heavy. A cocaine head on him – his red-rimmed eyes were wide and unfocused. He stopped in the middle of the room but his limbs stayed busy. He needed to sit down but didn't know how to do it.

'Jesus, Ma?' he said. 'Who did this?'

'Gary . . .' The Armenian made to stand up.

'I didn't ask you,' he snapped. 'Where were you? Why weren't you with him?'

'Gary,' his mother told him, 'sit down.'

She tapped her palm on the bench alongside her. The cracking of her rings on the hard plastic sharpened the summons. Her son wasn't impressed. A stand-off threatened. Liz caught a glimpse of Helen's interest.

'Please, Gary.'

He sat. With reservations.

Jimmy returned from his errand, crossed the room and patted Gary's shoulder.

'He'll make it, Gary. That man is as strong as an ox.'

The young man looked slowly up at him.

'Yeah,' he said, his locked jaw grinding hard. The prospect

seemed to please him less than the prospect of revenge might have done.

The thundercloud of emotion in the waiting room didn't pass but lurked in the silence awaiting further expression. Gary eyed Baz with growing contempt while his constant foot-tapping irritated his mother. Kevin watched everyone from under hooded eyes more remotely than before. The new eruption wasn't long in coming.

'You've no right to be here, Baz,' Gary spat, his fists clenched but too small to impress. 'You're not family.'

The Armenian stared without emotion at Gary. Then his gaze moved dismissively on to Jimmy. Harry's brother gave a noncommittal shrug. Baz looked at Liz. She feigned absorption in the freedom-seeking hordes on the silent TV screen. Kevin seemed in a world of his own filled with a bleakness the others didn't share. The Armenian smiled at Gary and got up to leave.

'I'll go grab a coffee,' he said, his West Belfast accent a serrated knife.

His movements as he left weren't quite hurried but gave the impression of having a purpose. The hapless young intern who'd looked in earlier picked the wrong moment for a third reconnoitre. Gary's anger found a new target.

'Bleedin' asylum seekers,' he fumed and pointed up at the muted TV screen where the momentum of the Arab Spring was becoming unstoppable. 'Why don't you shag off back up there where you belong?'

The intruder peered up at the screen in confusion and back at Gary. He thought better of protesting, chose to be merely offended, and left.

'Everywhere. Everywhere you look they are. Taking our jobs. Sniffing around our—'

'Leave it, Gary,' his mother said.

He turned his attention to Helen. He seemed to be searching for reasons to hate this young woman with her sweat-spiked hair and green track suit. The waiting-room door was further away from Helen than she wanted it to be. She stirred, chucked away the magazine she'd been pretending to read, took out her mobile phone and acted out the sending of a text message.

'You're not allowed use that in here,' Liz informed her. 'See the sign?'

The leathery-tanned woman, still watching the TV, indicated the panel of X-crossed images above the door. No smoking. No eating. No mobiles.

'Sorry,' Helen said, sensing she'd been sussed. 'I didn't—'

'Your cousin,' Liz cut across her. She was the watcher now. 'What happened to her?'

Time to go for the Oscar, Helen thought. An emotional I-can't-talk-about-it performance, then head for the exit. Liz was too quick for her.

'Is she the woman with the brown hair in there?'

A trap, Helen supposed. All four of the Larkins waited for an answer. She threw them the one scrap she'd got from Leo.

'She took an overdose is all I know,' she said.

'I'm sure I saw that woman before somewhere,' Liz insisted. 'Is she from Lucan?'

It was time to move. Helen stood up and, to her consternation, Gary did too. She told herself she was in no immediate danger here. There were four uniforms stationed out by the lobby and front doors, she remembered. But the lobby was a long way off.

'Can you please leave me alone?' she said, and headed for the door.

'I've a good memory for faces,' Liz asserted loudly as Helen reached the corridor.

She followed the exit signs of which there were too many and which were too far apart. She felt certain that Gary Larkin was following her. Felt his eyes on her back and on her bottom so vividly that her walk became stilted and awkward even as she hurried. Don't look back, she warned herself, but the further she walked, the clearer her mind became. It didn't matter if she was forced to flash her ID at the young man or run to the uniforms out front for protection. The Larkins would know she was a Guard soon enough anyway. Assuming Leo kept her on the case. Assuming he wouldn't make too much of her foolish error with the mobile back in the waiting room.

In the main hospital building, afternoon visitors busied the corridors. The squeak of sneakers she'd imagined trailing her all the way from ICU was drowned now in the general footfall. Helen breathed more easily. Up ahead she saw the sliding front doors and two pairs of officers. She glanced back. No sign of Gary Larkin. She took out her mobile phone as she reached the doors. About to call Leo, she paused.

The hospital's smoking area twenty yards away to the left was an anachronism. A small timber structure resembling a bandstand that belonged in the middle of a park, it stood instead on a strip of waste ground reserved for some extension that had never been built. Among its bedraggled inhabitants, one smarter-looking couple stood out. The woman in the blue raincoat. And Baz MacDonald.

The dark couple neither looked directly at one another nor exchanged gestures. They sat five feet or so apart and didn't appear to speak but Helen felt that they were somehow together. The woman trembled visibly, her cigarette smoke rising erratically before the breeze took it. MacDonald let his cigarette burn away between his fingers. Helen was tempted to go and eavesdrop. Undecided, she hovered by the sliding doors, feeling an odd sense of teetering on the brink.

All at once, the air was rent by a fledgling cry from the lobby area behind Helen. A lanky teenage girl, dreadlocks swirling, rushed by and the sliding doors emptied her out into the bright day.

'Mum! Oh my God, Mum!' she called as she went, an undercurrent of anger in her desperation. 'He's gone! David's gone!'

The woman sprang up from the bandstand bench and ran towards her daughter. They rushed by Helen and on down into the labyrinth of hospital corridors. Back on the steps to the bandstand, The Armenian stood and watched, frozen in mid-stride.

The sliding doors opened before Helen again. Jimmy Larkin walked by her and stepped outside, squinting through his bottle-thick glasses, his head darting bird-like from side to side, searching.

'Jimmy?' The West Belfast accent sliced through the air.

The older man moved forward until the sliding doors closed behind him. He paused, shook his head, turned the palms of his hands up briefly in a gesture of acceptance and loss. The Armenian tossed his cigarette on the waste ground and walked away towards the carpark. If Harry Larkin was dead, Helen thought, there was every chance his minder was even now setting out to take revenge. She followed MacDonald along the curving, canopied walkway. At the carpark entrance, he strolled nonchalantly past the two Guards on duty and descended the steps towards the basement floor most of which was visible from where they stood. When Helen reached them, she tried to stay hidden beside the taller of the two Guards. She didn't know him. She flashed her ID.

'Radio one of our cars to follow that guy, OK? And keep me posted.'

'No problem, Sarge,' he said.

She heard the beep and clack of a car opening and peered around the tall Guard. The Armenian stood beside a sleek blue Mercedes sports coupé. Watching her. Smiling. Shaping his index finger and his thumb into the shape of a gun.

# 7

'Harry Larkin's clinically dead, right? So, how long does it usually take before the families pull the plug on old buggers like that?' Detective Sergeant Martin Buck asked of Nurse Eveleen Morgan. 'On average, like?'

Three was a crowd in the senior nurse's office. There were four of them there. Leo and Helen exchanged a wry glance as the nurse glared at their colleague. Buck's pulling strategy was of the Hate/Love variety. *Rub them up the wrong way,* he'd once told Leo, *and they'll rub you down the right way.*

'We don't *force* these decisions on people,' Eveleen said. 'We help them to accept the inevitable.'

Buck shrugged. 'Same thing.'

Appalled by his choice of words, Eveleen looked to Leo to rescue her.

'We're going to have to leave the family alone today, Martin,' Leo said.

'Right. And let them hide behind this decision? They could stall us for days.'

Helen had met a few real dickheads in the force but this guy had to be the most obnoxious yet. Earlier, he'd listened with a skin-crawling mixture of voyeurism and scepticism as she'd told Leo of the interactions she'd observed in the

61

ICU waiting room. She'd felt stupidly self-conscious under his leery gaze. Now she just felt annoyed. With herself. With Buck.

'You heard what Nurse Morgan said,' she insisted. 'The ICU consultant is with them now. And whatever our opinion of Harry and the Larkins might be, they're still a family faced with a terrible decision.'

'Are you kidding me?' Buck threw a leg over his knee and leaned back, his button-bursting chest to the fore. 'They're all the same, these people. Screwed-up dysfunctional families every last one of them. Believe me, they'll be glad to be rid of the old bastard.'

Martin Buck's breezy lack of self-awareness never failed to astonish Leo. The guy had left three wives and a clutch of children in his feckless wake. Leo wondered whether Buck had to pay alimony and, if he did, how the hell he survived on what was left of his detective sergeant's pay.

'Human relations are a bit more complex than that, Martin,' Leo remarked.

Buck stood up, all nonchalance and creaking leather jacket. He yawned.

'Not in my experience,' he said, and readied himself to ride into the sunset.

'Are the Larkins still living out in Chapelizod?' Leo asked.

'Yeah, Harry and Liz live in St Laurence Villas. Jimmy, appropriately enough, has a small house in Maiden's Lane.' Buck chuckled. 'Kevin – you know, the deaf . . . the deaf guy. He lives above their pub on Main Street. Jinky's. And Gary has an apartment across the river.'

'And Baz MacDonald? Does he live in Chapelizod too?'

'No, Sandymount. That's your neck of the woods, isn't it, Leo?'

The revelation left Leo uneasy. He wasn't quite sure why

it should do. Even leafy Sandymount had its share of dodgy types. Dodgier types even than himself. In any case, there was nothing to stop Leo from talking to this MacDonald guy. After all, he wasn't *family*. Helen's observations seemed to indicate that Harry's family didn't think so.

'Do you have an address for him?'

'Strand Road,' Buck said. 'Bayview Apartments.'

'Any word on where this MacDonald guy is headed, Helen?' Leo asked.

'Still waiting on a call from the squad car. Hopefully, they haven't lost him.'

Leo sat in the chair vacated by the rhinestone detective, who'd left them with a cowboy wave goodbye. His eyes were bleary, threatening to get teary, but his search for a tissue proved fruitless. Eveleen handed him one. She watched him too closely and he kept the collapsed side of his face averted from her as best he could. Tiredness swept over him and he knew that some variation on bitter-sweet longing would soon follow. Helen helped him out.

'That boy who died,' she asked of Eveleen, 'was he admitted before or after Mr Larkin?'

'Twenty minutes or so after.' She checked her papers again. 'Yes, three thirty-five.'

'What was his name?' Helen asked.

'David,' Eveleen said, as if she'd known him for years. 'David Goode. You know, most of the time, the sadness of it all doesn't get to you. But there was something about that boy.' She shrugged, turned to Leo. 'These kids and their motorbikes. They'll never learn, will they?'

Leo and Helen watched one another travel the same mental paths. On motorbikes.

'Where did this young fellow have the accident?' Leo enquired.

'It was a hit-and-run actually. In Kilmacud.' The nurse seemed uncertain. 'Or no, beyond Kilmacud, someone said. Stepaside I think was mentioned.'

Wrong end of the city, Leo thought. Still, it was at least the first cousin of a coincidence.

Helen's work phone rang. The squad car trailing Baz MacDonald had something to report.

'He's in Sandymount?' she said. 'And he's definitely gone inside? Great. Thanks, Mike. You'll let me know if he moves on? Thanks, I appreciate it.'

The two police officers stood up to leave.

'Right then, Helen,' he said. 'They'll be setting up an incident room at Pettycannon Garda Station and we need to grab some pews in there. Can I leave that with you? Better ring Martha. She'll help you sort it.'

Helen nodded. Eternally youthful, Sergeant Martha Corrigan was as efficient and companionable as she was beautiful. She wondered what she'd look like herself at forty. Nothing like the ex-Rose of Tralee, that was for sure.

'And see what you can get from Kilmacud station on this hit-and-run case, OK? Probably no connection with the Larkin shooting but better safe than sorry.'

Leo turned his better side to Eveleen.

'Thanks for all your help, Nurse Morgan. And for the tissue, of course.'

'Eveleen,' she said.

'You've had a hell of a long day, Eveleen.' The name had too nice a flow to it. 'Shouldn't someone have taken over from you by now?'

'She rang in sick.' Eveleen shrugged and came round from behind her desk.

To his and Helen's astonishment, she approached Leo and placed her hands on his cheeks. His skin tingled. Old synapses stirred in his brain, firing up memories of tactile tenderness even as the handsome woman lowered the lid of his bad eye.

'You haven't been using the lubricant for your dry eye,' she concluded. 'Now it's infected. Sit down, Inspector.'

'Eveleen,' he said, 'I really have to—'

'It won't take long.'

Leo sat down and placed himself in her hands. He could almost smell the salt of the day's exertions from her skin. And the acid from his own tired flesh.

# 8

Life looked different to Detective Inspector Leo Woods. His newly acquired eye-patch somehow reduced and squeezed into a tighter frame the dimensions of the world. Brightness and contrast were lessened too so that there was an odd leaching of colours, like a watercolour left too long in the light. Keeping focus on everyday objects that appeared to have lost their solidity was a real problem. He felt as though he were suspended between night and day, between the past and the future. Which was, he had to admit, pretty much the story of his life.

Garda Dempsey turned the squad car on to Strand Road as the evening light fell across Sandymount Strand and made a corrugated sheet of the bay water. Along the footpath and down on the dark sand, walkers took their constitutional with varying degrees of intent. He closed his one seeing eye and rested the muscles in there that had been carrying double their weight since Eveleen Morgan had fitted the eye-patch a few hours before.

'Bayview Apartments,' Dempsey muttered disinterestedly and swung the car on to the tarmacked drive.

Fronting the road was a two-storey pastel copy of a Georgian house, as unconvincing as a portrait painted from a photograph. The courtyard behind held three four-storey blocks with railed balconies that were more decorative than functional. Dotted about the place were planted boxes, well tended but still awaiting the flowers of May. In the parking spaces, none of the cars was more than two years old. A few Mercedes, a couple of Audis and a blue Mercedes coupé. Whatever his true role in Harry's little empire, Baz MacDonald was doing well for himself.

'You can head away now,' Leo told the young Guard. 'I'll walk it home when I'm done here.'

'You don't need me?' Dempsey said needily.

'Go get some rest.'

'Thanks, boss.' Dempsey waited for Leo to bail out of the car before adding, 'Thanks for nothing.'

'What's wrong with you, Dempsey? You're not yourself so long now, you'll have to think about changing your ID.'

'Like you care.'

The young Guard was clearly depressed over something. Or maybe just depressed, full stop. Leo hoped not. Strange, he thought, how depression seemed almost noble in beautiful and intelligent people but pathetic in those who were less bright and attractive. He shut the door on the young fellow.

On the bank of buzzers at the third block he tried, Leo found Baz MacDonald's name. He tried the buzzer a couple of times, shortening the intervals, insisting.

'Yeah?' a voice crackled.

'Mr MacDonald?'

'Yeah, who wants to know?'

'Detective Inspector Leo Woods. I'm here about Harry.'

'No problem. Been expecting you. Number eight. Second floor.'

The glass-panelled door clicked. Leo found a lift, got

himself in and pressed 2. The lift door closed and opened instantly. He was about to press 2 again when he realized he'd already reached the second floor. There had been no sensation of ascent. He hated these interludes of absence from his own life, these voids that time had forgotten to fill.

Apartment number eight stood directly opposite the lift. When Leo was about to knock, the door was swept back too quickly and, instinctively, he retreated a step. MacDonald appeared and it was the younger man's turn to be surprised. Or so it seemed to Leo. His reaction to seeing Leo didn't come within the usual parameters – revulsion, pity. Instead, what Leo briefly observed in Baz MacDonald's eyes was the seed of recognition.

'Come in,' he said, gesturing away the obsolete ID Leo prepared to flash.

'Nice place you have here. Good address. Must've cost a fair whack.'

'I'm a tenant. This pad's not in my league.'

'But the coupé is?'

'A repaired crash job. Push it over one hundred K and it's a rattling tin can. It didn't cost a lot.'

'And how much did your motorbike cost?' Leo asked.

'Don't keep one.'

'Prefer travelling as a pillion passenger?'

'I don't make a habit of placing my life in anyone else's hands, Inspector.'

Loose-tied, his shirt tail hanging, MacDonald wasn't drunk but the air was suffused with the astringent fragrance of gin. Every room had a mood and Leo was beginning to get a sense of the mood in this one. Downbeat, pessimistic, exhausted. A bit like the feel of his own house.

One-eyed, he scanned the apartment, the swivel of his neck exaggerated with the effort to take it all in. It was tidy and minimalist with retro pre-Wende kitsch furnishings. There were none of the usual Republican mementoes on the walls. The St Brigid's Cross of reeds made in the H-Blocks. The photo of Bobby Sands. The Easter 1916 Proclamation. Instead, three large prints hung there. He looked closer. Good quality prints, expensively framed. Each one depicted the same mountain and the same biblical tale. The Great Deluge and its survivors, Noah and his nameless wife, in their Ark.

'Mount Ararat, right? It's in Turkey, isn't it?'

'Yeah, but you can see it from Yerevan. It's the national symbol of Armenia,' the man from Belfast said.

'Not a great symbol for a country, is it? Something you want but can't have. I like the frames though.'

'Came with the prints. I bought them in Yerevan last year.'

'Go over there a lot, do you?' Leo asked and picked up a small framed photo from the shelf beneath the prints.

A seventies revolutionary couple straight from central casting. Big careless black hair on both of them, a thick tash on the man. Heavy woollen polo necks and wide flares. The woman was small and pretty though she'd probably have shot you if you'd told her so. The man's resemblance to MacDonald was apparent if you looked hard enough at the grainy old shot.

'I go once or twice a year. Strictly pleasure.' His thin smile wasn't real. He nodded at the photo. 'My folks. I expect you know all about them.'

'I don't actually. Not everything,' Leo said. 'Is your mother still alive?'

'She died two days before the new millennium. Not that it matters when but . . . I don't know, it seemed important at the time. Sit down, Inspector. Take a drink?'

Leo accepted the offer of a seat but passed on the gin. He'd expected to be stonewalled from the off by the ex-Provo. Instead, he was getting butter on both sides. Sad orphan story plus the offer of a gin. He didn't like butter on either side.

'Why don't we skip the pleasantries, Mr MacDonald.'

'Baz.'

'Baz. Who shot Harry Larkin, Baz? What was he doing out in Tandy's Lane?'

'I've no idea,' MacDonald said, and sat back in his faux-leather armchair. 'On either count.'

'Aren't you supposed to be his bodyguard or whatever?'

'I run a debt collection agency for Harry. Do some other bits and pieces for him too. But a bodyguard? No. Harry didn't need . . .'

He looked up at Leo, acknowledged his slip with a wry smile.

'But you were good pals, right? Harry looked on you as family, didn't he?'

'I'm not family, full stop,' the young man told his drink. 'I work for Harry. He threw me a break when I was on my uppers. But pals? Family? I don't need all that.'

'Harry threw you a break? Why would he do that?'

'His first wife and my mother were first cousins,' Baz said. 'When I came down to Dublin after Mam died, he gave me some work.'

'And now that Harry's gone, who will you work for?'

'For whoever takes over the debt collection agency.'

'And the cigarette smuggling.'

Leo's hand dipped instinctively into his jacket pocket. The over-full ashtray on the floor by Baz's chair brought Harry Larkin's emphysemic cough to mind. He desisted.

Baz put his glass on the polished ply coffee table as

though he'd had enough of it. He stayed at the edge of his seat and continued his silent conversation with the glass. Leo's good eye was tiring and the ex-Provo began to seem more like a hologram than a real man.

'So, who takes over the business? Jimmy? Gary? Or maybe this is your bid for power and glory, Baz?'

'No way.'

'Gary seems to think you should've been with Harry last night.'

The Armenian needed to think that one over. He tried Leo's one available eye for a hint of where this nugget had come from. Then he tried the glass of gin for inspiration and found it.

'Ah, the girl in the green track suit,' he said. 'Good-looking wee thing. For a Guard, like.'

Leo didn't rise to the provocation though his stomach tightened. He wondered if he should keep Helen out of harm's way. In other words, drop her from the case.

'So, why weren't you with Harry last night?'

'He rings me when he needs me. Last night, he didn't ring.'

'What did you and Harry talk about when you last met?' Leo asked. 'You talked about Whitney's disappearance, maybe?'

Baz sussed out Leo's good eye again but to no avail. A new tetchiness arose in him.

'Whitney's not disappeared. She's done one of her runners. She'll be back soon as she hears what's happened.'

'That's not what Harry told me.'

The double-take was beyond Baz's control and he couldn't hide its traces entirely. At last, Leo thought, a punch had cleared the Belfast man's guard and connected. He followed through.

'Told me someone's taken Whitney.'

'Harry's brain-dead. He can't have—'

'I talked to him in the ICU ward this morning.'

Baz MacDonald wasn't lounging any more. Stiff-backed, alert, he got his guard up again.

'Baz, we know the shooting is linked to Whitney. We found an old photo of her in the car. She's seven or eight, something like that. Someone had torn himself out of the photo. Or maybe Harry had torn this someone out of the photo? Or Whitney herself had? That someone wouldn't be you, would it, Baz?'

Puzzled calculation wrinkled Baz's forehead. So far as Leo could tell, his confusion was genuine.

'Like I said, you won't find me in the family album, Inspector.'

'Why would he go out to Tandy's Lane alone, Baz?' Leo went on. 'Why would he leave you out of the loop? Or maybe you double-crossed him. Pretended to set up a trap for the kidnappers only it was for poor old Harry all along.'

'Should've asked Harry when you had your wee chat,' Baz parried. 'Except there was no wee chat, was there?'

'You're right,' Leo said. 'It was more a monologue than a dialogue. Old Harry's mind was rambling but he was clear about Whitney and clear about wanting me to find her.'

'You?'

'We go back a long way, me and Harry,' Leo said, and watched to see if this was news. He couldn't tell for sure. Then he switched tack. 'Tell me about Whitney. She's got to have friends, right, schoolmates?'

'She doesn't go to school. Left on her sixteenth birthday.'

'What kind of kid is she? You say she's done a bunk before. Why? Doesn't get on with the folks?'

Baz picked up his glass and downed what was left. It

wasn't enough. He poured some more. This time he didn't offer Leo a glass. He patted his pockets for a cigarette packet but found none. Leo didn't oblige. As he checked the iPhone that was precariously balanced on the rounded armrest of his seat, disappointment prevailed in The Armenian's morose features. Leo's eye needed a rest but he couldn't afford to close it just yet.

'There's no easy way to put this, Inspector, but I've always kept my distance from Whitney. She's a troubled kid. Needy.'

'Tell me more.'

'I live by instinct, and my instinct has always told me to keep her at arm's length,' Baz told him. 'I can tell you that she's one of these, what do you call them, these goths. Drove Harry crazy, all that black-eyed misery. I told him it was just a phase.'

'Can't be easy to make yourself scarce if you're a goth, can it? I mean, you'd stick out like a bruised fingernail, wouldn't you?'

'I suppose.'

'How long has she been gone?' Leo asked. Baz shook his head, did the empty hands thing.

'First I heard of it was Friday.'

'So where have you been searching for her?'

'I haven't been searching for her.'

'That's not what we're hearing,' Leo said, testing the waters with a reasonable assumption.

Baz took his time answering, fiddled with his iPhone.

'Yesterday I checked some of the pubs around town where these goth kids hang out. She used to go in there Saturdays. Sometimes.'

'And?'

'I headed down to Cork.'

'Why Cork?'

'The Southern Gothic Music Festival,' Baz explained. 'A few of the goth kids I talked to mentioned it. I thought maybe Whitney had gone there but I didn't find her. I texted Harry again.'

'And what time did you get back from Cork? That'd be, what, a three-hour drive?'

'Four in the morning, half past.'

'Can anyone verify that?'

The Armenian shook his head.

A one-eyed sweep of the room offered Leo no indications of a second, even if temporary, occupant.

'You live alone?'

'Yeah. Obviously.'

Leo deployed some silence, hoping to draw out another irritated response from the ex-Provo. No new point of attack suggested itself to him. Apart from the one he'd been avoiding until now. He delayed it a little further.

When he stood up and his legs took his weight again he regretted having sent Dempsey away. Serpentine Crescent was little more than five minutes on foot but he'd never walked it with one eye before.

'We'll talk again, Baz.'

'No bother,' he answered and climbed lazily to his feet. He looked at his watch. A gold Rolex. 'Not so late next time, hopefully.'

He went by Leo and opened the door. Only now did Leo notice that the inner panel was reinforced with metal.

'Been a lot of break-ins along here lately, Inspector.'

'Really? I live just up the road and we've had no trouble.'

'Yeah, I've seen you around. Didn't recognize you straight off with the eye-patch,' the ex-Provo said, then moved swiftly, wryly on. 'Course they're not going to break into your gaff, are they?'

'Too right,' Leo said. 'I've had intruders in the past. Some of your Provo predecessors, actually. They're both dead now, God rest them. Of course, you've put your Provo past behind you, haven't you, Baz?'

'Yes, I have.'

'No one puts the past behind them. Not when there's blood all over it.'

The dark-haired man shrugged.

At the lift, he helpfully pressed the down button. The lift door opened. Leo stepped in, let Baz breathe a sigh of relief. Then he stepped back out again.

'One last question, Baz. Are you aware of any, let's call them inappropriate sexual relationships in the Larkin family? You know, between Whitney and . . . well, any of them.'

'No way,' Baz said. 'Whatever this is about, it's not about . . . that kind of stuff.'

'You seem pretty sure of that. Would that be because you know what it's actually about?'

The ex-Provo wasn't willing to share his thoughts on that one. Back in the days when he knew Harry and Liz, Leo's next move would have been a dig in the ribs. That was then. Now, a lot of water had flooded over the bridge and a lot of middle-aged fat over his belt. He was in no shape for a scrap with Baz McDonald. He stepped back into the lift. He paused for effect, touched the G button, and as the doors slid together said:

'You'll be seeing a lot of me.'

But Baz was quick. Before the doors had shut he answered:

'Just as well I'm not wearing an eye-patch then, isn't it?'

# 9

In the night-quiet, a one-eyed man bustled through Sandymount village. The shadows in the silvery street light were too dark and deep, his vision choppy and urgent as the view from a hand-held camera. On the other side of the street, a black dog chased a sweet wrapper sucked away by the breeze whenever it seemed within reach. The whispery rustle of trees around the small park on Sandymount Green hurried him on. He couldn't see into the park but he imagined the bust of W. B. Yeats in there nodding sagely on its plinth, muttering. *This is no country for old men.* I'm not that old yet, Willie.

A haunted urgency infected Leo. He was a man going down into Hades but it wasn't some wifely Eurydice who was waiting for him there. It was Liz Larkin and her daughter. A daughter, he wondered, every bit as damaged as Liz herself had been in her own childhood? How many times had he seen it in his years of police work, that bloody awful cycle of abuse within families from one generation to the next? Had he abandoned Liz to a fate worse than the bullying and beating from Harry he had imagined for her back then? Had her daughter's been a worse fate still?

And yet, Leo found no way to fit a kidnapping into this scheme of things. Baz MacDonald's assertion that Whitney had done a runner as she'd often done before made more sense. Maybe this time she'd made a clean break from the family. She was seventeen after all. Old enough to start a life of her own. One way or the other, Leo felt a deep sense of responsibility towards the girl. A responsibility that required his full concentrated attention and focus. Without sleep that would prove impossible. Tonight, Leo decided, he had to get some at all costs.

Back at Serpentine Crescent, he sat on the side of his bed and stared across at the rail line. High hedging masked the lower floor of the red-bricked houses on the far side and, in the shimmering leaves, Leo divined the faceless spectre of Whitney Larkin, the ghost of the undead Harry Larkin, the pale remembered face of the younger Liz Larkin. He wished they'd stayed out in Chapelizod where ghosts had thrived since the days of its resident nineteenth-century Gothic writer Sheridan Le Fanu. His weary brain summoned an image from an early silent film. A quill in candlelight, a shaky hand penning a posthumous addition to its *Ghost Stories of Chapelizod*.

Leo popped a filter, lit up and rang Dripsy Scullion.

'Erik.' The limping dealer delivered Leo's code name in his usual smoked-brain drawl. 'You woke me up, man.'

'Where are you?'

'I'm . . . Hold on a sec there while I take a gander out the . . .' Scuffling noises filled Leo's ear. 'I'm in Ringsend. But I'm fucked if I know why.'

'I need some high-voltage sleepers,' Leo said.

'Did you try the rail tracks in front of your house?'

Before Leo's expletive emerged a thought beat it to the gap.

'Do you know Chapelizod? As in, do you know anyone out there? Such as the Larkins?'

'The cigarette people?'

'Spot on.'

'Don't know them personally.'

'OK, listen, Dripsy,' Leo said. 'Harry Larkin was shot last night and he's not going to make it. See what you can suss out on it for me. And see what the word on the street is on who's taking over the business. There's a guy called Baz MacDonald works for Harry and he may be—'

'The Armenian?'

'Know him?'

'No, but I've heard enough not to ask questions about him.'

'Don't ask, just keep your ear to the ground.'

'Yeah,' Dripsy said glumly. 'And hope my head's still attached to the rest of my body when I'm done. Jesus, man, when do I get free of you? Haven't I delivered enough all these years?'

'Freedom's a delusion, Dripsy. And as Eric Cantona once said, the only freedom is the freedom from delusion.'

# Monday 2 May

# 10

Pettycannon Garda Station was a pleasure to look at but a pain in the arse to work in. A mid-nineteenth-century structure, its lower storey was faced with limestone blocks, its upper with subtly greying red brick. At each end of the three bays, a polygonal tower obtruded. The front doorway was capped with a radial fanlight. Inside, the rooms were too small. The veneered chipboard with which the place was decked out gave the station a temporary feel at odds with the sturdy exterior. Still, Leo reflected as he waited for the Incident Room to fill up, it was better than working in some Legoland construction that felt like it had been idly pieced together by a five-year-old on Ritalin.

Leo's one-eyed view had, at first, exaggerated the sense of claustrophobia. Fortunately, the ceiling was high and looking upwards helped to alleviate his discomfort. The vivid presence of Sergeant Martha Corrigan at his side helped too: there was a mid-morning alertness about her that he tried to channel.

Detective Sergeant Helen Troy sat at the far end of the table, dark circles under her eyes and a dark look for anyone who threatened to engage her in conversation. Including Leo. Her sullen mood was, in reality, down to the after-effects of yesterday's exertions on the football field.

Among the last to arrive, Detective Sergeant Martin Buck perked up when he saw the ex-Rose of Tralee at Leo's side. He tried a macho see-what-I've-got-for-you stare on her which she swatted with an indifferent smile. By way of bitter consolation, he latched on to Leo's black eye-patch.

'*True Grit*,' he called from the other side of the room.

'The John Wayne version or the Jeff Bridges?'

'Definitely Jeff Bridges. He looked way more wasted.'

'Thanks, cowboy,' Leo said.

Outside the long sash window behind them the sun had come out but it was a cold northern sun. There, Leo reflected, only to remind us Celts of the warmth we were missing. He stood up and went over to the long whiteboard. To its left an Ordnance Survey map had been attached. Wide red circles marked the crime scene location on the spur of Tandy's Lane and Harry Larkin's house in Chapelizod. Alongside, the Larkin family tree hadn't quite reached full bloom. There were the photo of the child Whitney and two mugshots featuring Harry and Jimmy in their prime. As yet, there were no shots of Liz, Gary or Kevin. The branch line leading to Baz MacDonald's mugshot was a broken one.

'Right then,' he said, calling the gathering to order. 'You all know the story here. A double-track investigation. Track one: the attempted murder, soon to be upgraded to murder, of Harry Larkin.'

He filled in the details of the shooting, of Helen's observations on the Larkin family dynamic.

'Track two,' he continued, 'is the possible disappearance of Harry's daughter Whitney. Whether voluntary or involuntary. OK, Exhibit A. Harry had this photo of Whitney with him while he waited in Tandy's Lane. It's pretty blood-spattered but we may get a cleaner version. You've all got copies, right?'

'We don't have a more recent shot?' one of the local detectives asked.

'Not as yet. That'll be one of our priorities for today obviously,' Leo responded. 'So, Harry's gazing at this photo of his daughter. Why? There are two possibilities here. Whitney's been kidnapped or she's run away from home. The supporting evidence for a kidnapping, such as it is, goes like this. Harry told the senior nurse in ICU that Whitney had been taken. Unfortunately, he was suffering from dementia caused by the bullet lodged in his brain which throws more than a little doubt on that claim.'

'More than a little doubt?' Buck said. 'It's fantasy football. Full stop.'

'Probably, yes. But we do have the fact that the glove compartment of Harry's car had been emptied out which might indicate a ransom package was to be handed over. In any case, Whitney's the only member of the family who hasn't shown up at the hospital yet.'

There was no escaping the next item on his agenda. He had to bring up his old association with Harry Larkin. The slow-motion billiard balls of last night's ineffective sleepers rolled around his bloodstream, thickened his tongue.

'So, a quick, eh, summary of my . . . my previous dealings with Harry Larkin. In the late seventies when he was a half-hearted Provo, we turned him.'

He could see the others' interest had been stirred. *Turned.* By fair means or foul, they knew. And knew that the legends surrounding Leo had begun back then. Some approved. Some didn't. Leo himself was among the latter.

'I took over the running of Harry in 1980. We used to meet in Tandy's Lane where he was shot early yesterday morning. He seemed a promising informant. Traded on the fact that he'd been interned in 1957 during the IRA's Border Campaign when he was still a teenager. In 1975, he married into Republican royalty: Brigid Cullen, who along with a couple of other women formed the bait in a honeytrap where four off-duty British soldiers were murdered in a Belfast apartment. She came down to Dublin after doing her bit for the cause.'

'Close your eyes and think of Ireland,' Buck put in. No one laughed.

'She had a son with Harry later in '75. Kevin, a deaf kid. But she went off the rails and died of a heroin overdose in 1979. After she died, we began to get some reliable hints that Harry blamed the IRA for what happened to his wife. Well, he wasn't going to blame himself for her death even though he was a violent, bullying piece of shit.'

His sudden vehemence surprised Helen. She'd decided earlier that the eye-patch suited Leo quite well. Now, added to the references to his murky early days in the force, it made a darker impression.

'Anyway, he was caught setting up a post office robbery in 1979. He'd served a four-year sentence in Mountjoy in the early seventies for similar offences. Couldn't hack another stint in there so he, eh, cooperated. We got a few bits and pieces of info from him over the next three years or so but nothing of real substance. After he married his present wife Elizabeth in 1984, he drifted away from the last of his old Republican pals but we'd already lost interest in him by then. Detective Sergeant Martin Buck will tell us about Harry's career path since then.'

The cowboy detective took the floor and did his solo. The strain of peeking out at the world with one eye had become wearying for Leo. He put a hand to his forehead and savoured a moment of blindness. Something in his brain wobbled. With a start, he realized that what had wobbled was time itself.

'Sir?' Helen's voice bore a weight of concern. 'Leo?'

'Sorry, got distracted there. Are you finished, Martin?'

'I've been finished for five minutes.' Buck grinned. 'What were you up to last night, Leo?'

'Oh, shut it, would you?' Helen told him.

Buck's ogling of her ever since he'd entered the Incident Room and his ribald interventions had somehow made the photo of the young Whitney before Helen seem even more sexually distasteful. What kind of mother dressed her child in a padded bra and let her pose like that, she wondered, while a couple of latecomers squeezed in at the back of the Incident Room and hid themselves from Leo's view.

'Now, it's too early to rule out either a hit by some business rival or a dispute with some dissident IRA mob, for that matter,' Leo continued. 'We all know about their protection rackets, though it seems Harry kept his old buddies onside. In any case, the Special Detective Unit and the Organized Crime Unit will be keeping an ear to the ground. So far, we've got nothing on either front. All of which leaves us with the strong possibility that this might be a family dispute with Whitney at its core.'

'You think one of the family might have shot Harry?' Helen said.

'It's a possibility we have to consider, yeah.'

'What about The Armenian?' Buck asked.

'Baz MacDonald,' Leo reminded him. 'He's family too. Harry certainly regarded him as such even if the rest of the Larkins think differently. I talked to MacDonald last night and he doesn't have a verifiable alibi. Not unless they had CCTV at the Southern Gothic Music Festival down in Cork.'

'The what?' someone asked.

Leo explained, asked one of the local men to contact Anglesea Street Garda Station in Cork to locate the precise venue and access any relevant footage. The goth hang-outs around Dublin would have to be checked too and a couple of detectives were chosen for the task. A second team was allocated the house-to-house enquiries detail: along Tandy's Lane for any clues to the shooting, around Chapelizod village for recent sightings of Whitney.

'And we need to track her phone if we can,' Leo continued. 'We don't have a number yet but we can try the service providers. She'll have to have registered with them.'

'Not if I know the Larkins,' Buck drawled. 'There'll be dozens of disposable phones floating around in that house. Any up-to-date Androids they use will have been stolen goods bought under the counter. That's how these people work.'

'You may well be right but it's worth a shot. What we're trying to establish here,' Leo told the teams, 'is the last sighting or contact with the girl and how she seemed. You know, her state of mind. Was she behaving normally? Was she distressed? That kind of thing.'

His last sighting of the girl's mother came to mind. Behaving normally? No. Distressed? Big time. The papers on the table before him seemed to float on choppy water as the muscle of his good eye struggled to cope with its workload. He wondered whether he should ring the super and bail himself out of the case altogether. Maybe even take the retirement package that was on offer in the latest cost-cutting exercise.

And do what? Curl up in Serpentine Crescent and wait for the last, the fatal, moulting?

'I'm not sure if this is significant,' Martha said, 'but the gun in Harry's car, the Glock? I ran a check and it may have come from the Libyan shipments to the IRA in '86 or '87.'

Probably not significant, Leo thought, since a major proportion of IRA arms had come from the Botoxed Gaddafi. But that hadn't been the point of the ex-Rose of Tralee's intervention. She was pulling him out of the fire. Again.

'We already know Baz MacDonald had access to these Glocks up North,' Buck said, avenging his earlier dismissal by Martha. 'He brought a few down with him. He gave one to Harry somewhere along the way. Full stop. It doesn't matter where they came from originally.'

'Everything matters,' Leo corrected him. 'Right then, let's get moving on this. We talk to the Larkins today. Separately if possible. Can someone check if they've gathered at the hospital again?'

'Done, sir,' one of the locals piped up. 'Mrs Larkin and Jimmy are at the hospital. The sons haven't shown up yet.'

'I'll take Jimmy,' Buck offered.

'Aren't you meeting the SDU guys in Harcourt Street this morning?'

'Yeah but—'

'The hospital detail's mine,' Leo insisted. 'OK then, the eldest son, Kevin, is deaf so we'll need to get someone in to help us on that. Martha, can you—'

'I can take that one, sir. My sister says I could sign before I could talk.'

Heads turned, Helen's so quickly that the bones in her neck cracked. From the phalanx of uniformed officers at the back of the room, Detective Garda Ben Murphy stepped forward. She'd never seen him quite so casually dressed before. Casual for him was suit and shirt with no tie. Now tieless and unshaven and sporting a slim-fit plaid shirt, he looked like an Indie singer-songwriter.

'Aren't you supposed to be on the other side of the Atlantic?' Leo asked.

'Had to cancel, sir,' Ben said, and averted his eyes to stave off the obvious follow-up question.

'Right, Kevin's yours then. And if Gary's still in Chapelizod when you've finished with Kevin, you can take that interview too, OK?'

The stubble-faced detective nodded.

Helen waited tentatively for an assignment. She tried to catch Leo's eye but all she caught was his eye-patch. He dismissed the class, but not before adding, 'Ben? Helen? A word?'

The two young detectives swam against the tide of their departing colleagues and reached Leo's side. He could tell that Helen had a lot to say and Ben very little. She dived in quickly.

'If you're taking Jimmy and Ben is taking Kevin, I could interview Mrs Larkin.'

'No, I'll do the talking with Liz later,' Leo said, attaching too much familiarity to the name.

'Well, I'll take Gary then. Or I can do the liaison with SDU. We share the same building back at HQ, don't we? So why send Martin Buck in there?'

'We have to keep the natives happy, Helen,' Leo said. 'Make Buck feel important. That kind of thing. And it keeps the guy out of our hair which we need to do because he's a bloody waste of space.'

'But there has to be something I can—'

'Helen, there's a problem with your staying on this case.'

'I know they sussed me yesterday in the ICU waiting room but—'

'These are pretty nasty people. I'm trying to protect you is all.'

'Because I'm a woman? Because I'm still a little girl as far as you're concerned?'

'Ah, for fuck's sake, Helen, you know I'm not like that,' Leo said.

She did, but she wasn't going to admit it. Leo looked to Ben Murphy for assistance. The young detective shrugged.

'She won't be alone,' Ben said. 'We can look out for one another.'

'OK, OK,' Leo said.

He drew closer to the two young detectives and waited for the last of the stragglers to leave the Incident Room. They looked at him expectantly as he tried to formulate an approach to the subject of abuse. He struggled to do so. It seemed to him that his secret knowledge of Liz's past was the only solid indication that abuse might be an issue in the case. Knowledge that would have to stay secret.

'This photo of Whitney,' he began. 'We may be looking at a possible kidnapper's calling card here. So, what's it telling us? I mean, it's not your usual family album photo, is it? A half-naked, inappropriately dressed child . . . that padded bra . . .'

'Which might be down to poor taste at worst,' Ben said, flushing lightly. 'And not the child's poor taste. The mother's, I'm guessing. And peer pressure, no doubt. On the child and the mother.'

'True,' Leo said. 'But I think we have to consider an abuse element here. Agreed?' They both nodded their assent, one with less vigour than the other. 'Better get going then. And no heroics, right?' Leo wagged a finger at Helen. She didn't like it but she didn't kick up.

'I don't do heroics,' she said.

'We all do heroics. It's the human condition. If we didn't want to be heroes so badly, we wouldn't be so bloody disappointed with ourselves,' Leo countered, his tongue loosened by his soporific brain. He changed tack. 'Everything OK at home, Ben? The kid?'

'Millie's good, thanks,' Ben said and left it at that, and so did Leo. As men do, thought Helen.

'Let's go find the Larkins then.'

# 11

Main Street, Chapelizod bisected a slope that rose from the River Liffey to the lower end of the Phoenix Park. The two sides of the street couldn't have been more different. On the higher side to the right stood a gap-toothed array of two- and three-storey buildings, some close to dereliction, others resigned to it. Across the newly constructed central plaza, the old had been swept almost entirely away. A stretch of generic shopping spaces and the front block of an apartment complex formed the new streetscape. Most of the light seemed to fall on this side. A steady flow of traffic passed through the village but the footpaths were empty apart from an ageing pony-tailed street-sweeper in a hi-viz jacket. Harry Larkin's pub stood halfway along the darker side of the street. It looked like a kip.

'Jinky's,' Ben Murphy said and swung the unmarked car into a kerbside parking space. 'Strange name for a pub, isn't it?'

As she unlocked her seat belt, Helen knew her colleague was merely trying to make up for his reticence on the drive from Pettycannon. He needn't have bothered, she thought. If he wasn't going to tell her why he hadn't gone to Quantico, she wasn't going to ask.

'I've seen stranger,' she said, and took out her work mobile. Nothing from the Technical Bureau yet on her request to have the motorbike tyre treads from the Kilmacud hit-and-run and the Tandy's Lane shooting compared. Still, her sense that the death of David Goode and the inevitable demise of Harry Larkin were somehow connected was an itch she couldn't stop scratching.

She got herself out of the car stiffly. Her leg muscles hadn't yet loosened up and a darting pain burrowed insistently into her lower back. She put her mind to the task at hand. Most of her mind consented. She scanned the upper windows of the dilapidated pub, wondering if the deaf man was inside.

Painted a deep unsightly green, the three-storey building was the narrowest on the street. Two small windows above stairs, their curtains closed, suggested a minimal and shabby living space. Kevin Larkin clearly didn't live the life of a high-flying career criminal. The blind in the larger window of the ground floor hadn't yet been raised for the day. There was no bell to ring just a heavy rusted old knocker that had forgotten what metal it was made of. The plywood sheet covering the door of the derelict house alongside had rotted with damp and come loose at the right-side edge.

'Any luck with the tyre treads?' Ben asked as he rapped the front door of the pub with the knocker.

'No.'

'What do we know about the guy on the motorbike?'

'David Goode. Nineteen. Lived with his parents in Wellington Road. They used to run an art gallery in Temple Bar until they went bust last year. He played hockey for his province at under-sixteen level and schools rugby. Did his Leaving Cert. last June and was on a gap year before heading to an American university on some kind of undergraduate science scholarship. Spent the time working for a charity that fixes up old computers to be sent to Third World countries and teaching pensioners how to use computers. That's about it.'

Even as she spoke, the guy became less and less likely to have had any possible connection with a crime family, even of the ordinary decent variety. She gestured ill-temperedly at the pub door.

'How the hell are we supposed to do this? I mean, he's deaf. He's not going to hear you knocking, is he?'

'He'll know I'm knocking.'

Ben tried the knocker for another minute or so. Kevin didn't know Ben was knocking after all, Helen thought with a satisfaction that felt churlish.

'My guess is he's already on his way to the hospital,' she said.

Ben raised a finger to his lips. He moved side-on to the door, listening. A couple of cars brushed noisily by on Main Street and he grimaced in irritation, blocking his outer ear. The street quietened again. Helen listened but heard nothing.

'It's a machine of some kind, going on and off in short bursts. Somewhere at the back end of the building, I think.'

Helen couldn't be sure if the faint punctuations in the silence she now heard were real or down to his having mentioned them.

'Maybe it's coming from further off?' she said.

'No, it's in there, whatever it is. And there's no lane out the back so—'

'You know Chapelizod?'

'Used to,' he said and left it at that in his usual gnomic

way. 'We could try the churchyard out back and get in over the wall there.'

'Or we could push this in,' Helen said, pointing at the warped chipboard hoarding next door.

She kicked at the board, hoping it would fall in one piece. It didn't. It broke into more pieces than she could count.

'Shit,' she said. He was looking at her like she'd lost the plot. 'Time of the month. The door's open. We might as well go in.'

It was one of those photogenic collapsed interiors that spoke clichés of memory and loss. Old portraits behind smashed glass among the rubble. Dust motes swirling in slices of light. A naked doll, one arm raised, deftly lashed eyes opened on nothingness. And deathly cold. A fallen coat stand toe-tripped Helen. When she steadied herself against the wall, she felt the vibration from next door in the palm of her hand. What was he doing in there?

'That smell,' Ben whispered. 'Can you get it? Petrol and some chemical, something like—'

'Aerosol spray?'

The back door at the end of the passage stood open. They went out into the litter-strewn yard. By the stone wall next to the pub a roughly hewn timber shelter four foot or so high proved easily mounted. One to each side, they made it to the view from above at the same moment. In the yard of the pub below them, a heavily built man crouched. The nozzled hose he held was attached to a small generator. Ben and Helen looked at one another.

Kevin Larkin was spray-painting a motorbike. A dark green like the shade on the front of the pub. The sudden stiffening in the musculature beneath his off-white shirt told the detectives that he had become aware of their presence. Helen reached for her gun but didn't yet draw it. The generator spluttered to a halt as Kevin turned his head. A mask with filters like insect eyes covered the lower part of his face.

As Ben and Helen prepared to jump the eight-foot drop into the pub yard, the big man was on his feet, kicking back the rear paddock stand and making for the back door of the pub with the bike. The two detectives hit the concrete and skipped off light-footed in chase. Larkin got the door closed when they were within a hand's reach of it. They heard the slide of a bolt and then the wild, hollow bark of the motor-bike's engine starting up in the confined space of the pub. Ben threw himself again and again against the heavy door. Timbers cracked but held firm. The motorbike growled again, whined to be let loose.

Out on Main Street, pony-tailed Nev Dunne swept the footpath philosophically. The Sisyphus of Chapelizod, he mused, sweeping the litter up the street so the wind could blow it back down again. He spat out the loose tobacco from another of those crappy Chinese fags Kevin sold under the counter, wished they'd get those little Chinky bastards to pack the things tighter. Regal, my arse. He heard the howl of the motorbike in his former local, Jinky's. It didn't surprise him. Nothing much had surprised his burnt-out brain for years.

The green door of Jinky's blew out into the street and an unmanned green motorbike shot out and into the air above the footpath and the street that sloped down below it. Kevin Larkin sat on the ground where the door used to be, looking bemused. As you would, Nev thought. The fuel tank took the brunt of the fall on the concrete slabs of the plaza across the way and the green motorbike exploded. Holy shit. Nev

Dunne closed his eyes. Opened them again. Yeah, exploded. Holy shit.

He ducked in off Main Street and scuttled up the incline of Park Lane. Accidents will happen, he sang to himself.

# 12

The six-bed hospital ward had been closed from lack of staff or money or a coherent service plan. No one was quite sure which. In any case, Leo had found a use for it. An interrogation room. He'd sent Garda Dempsey to fetch Jimmy Larkin from the ICU waiting room. While he waited, Leo recalled what he could of Harry's brother, the perennial number two in spite of being the elder lemon of the family.

Jimmy had never harboured any Republican convictions. Until the late seventies he'd harboured no criminal ones either. He was the white sheep to Harry's black. Then he'd been let go from his job as a shipping clerk down the North Wall after thirty years. He went on to use his inside knowledge of Dublin's docks to good effect. Or bad, Leo mused, depending on your perspective. Harry had run the heavy-lifting and the brute force wings of the cigarette smuggling operation. Jimmy did the sums.

The ward door opened. Garda Dempsey towered above the thick-spectacled man. Momentarily dazzled by the sunlight, Jimmy Larkin paused. His face scrunched up to get a better view of the room. Leo let him work at it, said nothing. From this distance, Jimmy didn't look much older than he'd done thirty years before. More grey in the slick-backed hair; a half stone lighter in weight maybe. Still bought his clothes in the same shop though. Or they were just the same clothes. Sleeveless tartan, nylon trousers, necktie big as a cravat.

Dempsey waited by the door as Jimmy stumbled forward.

'Thanks, Dempsey. I'll take it from here.'

'When you're finished, sir,' the young Garda said, his tone sharp with hurt, 'Nurse Morgan in ICU wants to see you.'

'Sure, no problem,' Leo said, and Dempsey left in a huffy twirl.

Eveleen. Music didn't work for Leo with his punctured eardrum and his tin ear. Still, there was music in that name, and it sang to him. But then the chorus kicked in. *Don't kid yourself, Leo.*

'Jimmy,' Leo said. 'Take a seat.'

'Leo, long time no see,' Jimmy said and moved to where the voice had come from.

He found the chair with his left hand, held out his right, drawing Leo into his narrow range of vision. His hand was cold and damp. His hail-fellow-well-met smile faltered, his surprise genuine.

'Jaysus, Leo,' he said, not without some relish. 'Did you have a stroke or what?'

'Bell's palsy.'

'What's the story with the eye-patch? Are you gone half blind as well? The half blind leading the blind.'

'You're looking fresh yourself, Jimmy, for a man of seventy.'

'Seventy-two. Can't complain. No point. Sure, who'd be bothered listening to old codgers like us anyway.' Jimmy swept off his glasses, breathed on them and cleaned them with a hankie. 'Still soldiering in the Special Branch, are you?'

'No, I'm with the NBCI now.'

'What's that?' Jimmy chuckled. 'The National Council for the Blind of Ireland, ha, ha!'

The small man's salt-of-the-earth demeanour, his rare-old-times Dublin drawl, his gas-man wit got under Leo's skin sooner than he'd expected. He sat, waited for Jimmy's rear end to find the seat of the chair opposite, and fast-forwarded to the business end of the conversation.

'Where's Whitney?' he asked.

'Where's Whitney?'

Same old technique from thirty years before, Leo thought. Repeat the question. Back in those days, he'd hassled the Larkin brothers relentlessly and very publicly in order to cover the true nature of his relationship with Harry. Jimmy was out of the loop, of course. Still was, Leo presumed. A man would hardly confess to his brother that he'd been a police tout. Leo lobbed a speculative grenade.

'Your niece is missing. Your brother was about to hand over a wad of cash and got himself popped. Where's the girl?'

Jimmy sat back and folded his arms. Behind the bottle-tops, a glazed look descended.

'We can talk about this at the station if you prefer, Jimmy,' Leo said and proffered an A4 enlargement of the blood-spattered photo showing the child Whitney, the dog and the shoulder clad in a green and white striped football jersey. 'Have a gawk at this.'

Jimmy took the sheet. He brought it slowly to within inches of his face and more quickly away. He clearly hadn't expected to see the photo. Which meant, Leo deduced, that The Armenian hadn't forewarned him. Why?

'Did you take this shot, by any chance? It's from an older camera. Antique. Like yourself, Jimmy.'

'Don't go in for the photography myself. Is that . . . is

that Harry's blood all over it?' Jimmy asked, his pallor gone corpse-grey.

'No, I spilled a tin of red paint over it.'

'Bastard.'

'We found this in Harry's car,' Leo persisted. 'What's that about, Jimmy?'

'No idea.'

'There's more, Jimmy. Your brother told us yesterday that Whitney had been taken by someone.'

'Yesterday? Harry wasn't able to talk to us yesterday.'

'He asked to speak to me. Wanted me to find Whitney.'

The small man was suffering from an overload of new information. Baz MacDonald hadn't told him about Harry's ravings either. Leo wondered if The Armenian had simply been too cagey to contact the Larkins, given the Garda presence. Or if he'd wanted deliberately to drop them in the shit.

'Why would he ask me to find the girl? You'd been searching high up and low down and couldn't pick up a trace. I know that for a fact.' The hint of a flinch in Jimmy Larkin, an almost imperceptible dart of the eyes in their bottles. 'Was Harry pissed off with the lot of you? Or maybe he didn't trust any of you? Was that why he went out to Tandy's Lane alone?'

'Bullshit, all of it,' Jimmy said. 'This isn't the first time Whitney has vamoosed and it won't be the last. She'll be back when the money runs out. That's how she is. Always was. A handful from day one, that young one, with her crazy stories and her—'

'What kind of crazy stories?'

'She wore Harry down with her antics,' he continued. 'Like, there was this time at school – and I'm talking secondary school, I'm talking thirteen or fourteen years old – and she goes and tells her teacher in front of the whole class that her father has three days to live. Mad stuff. Course, she's sussed out right away, and what does she do? Runs out of the school and they can't find her anywhere. Took us most of the day to find her inside in town. Is it any wonder Harry's heart was wrecked?'

'Ah, blame the victim. That's the strategy here, is it?'

'You're a Guard. You'd know all about blaming the victim. Nothing like the old Hillsborough option to get youse lot off the hook.'

Leo let the aspersion pass. Mainly because he knew the man in the tartan jumper was right on this count at least. If the South Yorkshire Police had their Hillsborough stadium, the Garda Síochána had their Donegal fiasco cover-ups. Among others.

'So, when did you become aware of the fact that Whitney had gone AWOL?'

'I don't live with Harry's family. I don't see them every day or even talk to them every day. First I knew of it was Friday lunchtime.'

The sudden helpfulness put Leo on his guard.

'Very specific of you, Jimmy.'

'Specific, yeah, because I call to Jinky's every Friday lunchtime to sort out the till for the weekend. Make sure there's enough change, all that. That's what I do, see? Do the accounts for Harry's pub and—'

'And the debt collection agency and the moneylending and cigarette businesses.'

'I do the accounts for Harry's pub, end of story. It helps top up my old age pension,' Jimmy said, and off-handedly added, 'Kevin told me she was gone again.'

'But Kevin doesn't live with the family either, does he? So, who told Kevin?'

'Don't know.'

For Leo, this was one of those moments when you know you've stumbled on something important but you don't yet know why it's important. All he could do was file it away under 'Timeline'.

'Take another squint at the photo, Jimmy,' Leo said, but the older man had grown obstinate. 'The original has been torn along the left. Someone's removed himself from the picture. Or been removed. That wouldn't be you, would it?'

'Never seen this shot before in my life.'

'Do you recognize the location?'

'No.'

'The dog?'

'What dog?'

'There's a dog in the photo, Jimmy.'

'I didn't . . .' Jimmy raised the sheet to his face again briefly. 'Didn't notice it.'

Which made Leo wonder if the impact of seeing the girl had distracted Jimmy from seeing anything else in the photo. Why? Shock, guilt, fear? Leo tested his theory. It expanded, as theories often do, even while he spoke.

'You know what this photo is telling me, Jimmy?' he said. 'It's telling me that what we have here is a squalid little family squabble. Dark undertones here, aren't there, Jimmy? A naive and vulnerable child. A tarted-up innocent custom-designed for a brood of amoral vultures. And Harry's the darkest, the most corrupted of you all.'

'My brother's not dead yet and you're already pissing on his grave.'

The rouge of embarrassment or rage or both spotted the high points of the little man's cheeks. There was something almost priestly about his offendedness. Leo switched the point of his attack.

'Do you follow the football, Jimmy?'

'That could be anyone torn out of the photo. Half the bloody country supports Celtic.'

Correction, Leo told himself. Jimmy hadn't been distracted enough to miss the jersey.

'Including Gary? And Kevin?'

'Including all of us. We run a Glasgow Celtic Supporters Club at Jinky's and—'

'Ah, Glasgow Celtic Supporters Clubs. Where bar-stool Republicans go to let off steam.'

'You don't have to be a Republican to support Glasgow Celtic.'

'I wondered why the pub was called Jinky's,' Leo said, shifting to softly-softly mode. 'The one and only Jinky Johnstone, right? Number seven in '67 when they won the European Cup. Some left foot that man had. Some control.'

He feigned a sigh of reminiscence. Jimmy Larkin slipped more naively down Memory Lane. For the first time he looked his seventy-two years, and more.

'Not a player to touch him in the game these days. Bleedin' Lady Godivas, the lot of them. That's what they coach them these days. Teaching kids to cheat. We never done that.'

'You did some under-age coaching yourself?' Leo asked, lulling the old guy, softening him up.

'I did,' Jimmy sighed. 'I did, indeed.'

It occurred to Leo that back in the day when Jinky Johnstone patrolled the left wing for Celtic, Jimmy Larkin was still more or less a decent, honourable citizen. He wondered if elderly misgivings over a misspent life bothered the former shipping clerk. He let the memories take a stronger hold of Jimmy before cutting in with a slice of reality.

'Who shot Harry?'

If Leo thought he was catching the small man off guard with a wide shot from left-field, the reply came from another field entirely and Leo was the one left reeling.

'I don't know. But it was a blessing in disguise.'

'For who? For you?'

'The brother wanted to die, Leo,' the older man said. He raised the edge of a flat hand to his chin. 'He'd had it up to here with all this shit.'

'All what shit?'

'Life, Leo, life,' Jimmy said. 'Ever since the bypass operation he's been going downhill. His heart was so bad, they weren't going to go ahead with the op. They shouldn't have bothered. Couldn't drink. Couldn't smoke. Couldn't stay awake through a DVD. Hardly stirred out of the house and most days he was too weak on the pins even to try. How he got himself out there to Tandy's Lane I'll never know.'

Jimmy let his stunted gaze drift around the hospital ward. Leo couldn't decide whether or not to believe in this melancholic turn in the conversation. Always good at the play-acting, the ex-shipping clerk had been. Leo wondered if the trick actually lay in the man's very myopia. If you couldn't see whether your act was having the desired effect or not, then you could focus entirely on your performance and not be distracted by doubt or lack of self-belief.

Jimmy stood up, fixed his bulbous tie, made himself even tidier than he already was.

'Bleedin' clowns, whoever shot him. They only had to wait a few months and Harry would've been gone anyway.'

He checked the big dial of his faux-leather strapped Hong Kong watch.

'We have an appointment with the ICU consultant in five minutes.'

'Pulling the plug?'

'That's Liz's call.'

'We'll find his killer, Jimmy.' A statement rather than a reassurance. 'And we'll find Whitney.'

The small man made his way to the door. He turned on cue.

'You fellows. Youse couldn't find shit in a sewer.'

# 13

The back door of Jinky's gave way at last. Helen and Ben, their semi-automatics raised, flung themselves inside. When they saw the big man at the front of the pub, dazed and floundering, they realized that the guns were unnecessary. Ben reached him first. He grabbed a fistful of Kevin Larkin's shirt and the deaf man cringed as though expecting a blow. The burning motorbike took all of Helen's attention. The tyres, she thought, as the thick black smoke carried off their rubbery substance to the heavens.

Ben took out his ID and lowered it to the deaf man's line of vision. Kevin's expression was composed of worry and wonder at the quicksilver fluency of Ben's hand-signing. He answered with panicked fingers. The silent exchange added fuel to Helen's frustration over the burning motorbike.

'Tell me what you two are saying, for Christ's sake. Don't just bloody sign.'

'He said it was an accident.'

'He said what was an accident?'

'The motorbike, the door, I presume.'

Kevin followed Ben's upward glance. She could tell that he'd recognized her from the ICU waiting room.

'Ask him why he tried to do a runner. He could've bloody killed someone out there.'

'I already did.'

'And?'

'He thought we'd come to kill him.'

Over at the plaza, a small crowd had gathered. From one of the shops at the far side of the street a middle-aged man in shirtsleeves had run out with a miniature fire extinguisher.

'Oh, for Jesus' sake. That bloody thing wouldn't douse a match,' Helen barked.

The man tried to unleash the extinguisher's contents but the foam merely dribbled on to his shoes.

Helen punched the wall with the heel of her fist. A text message rang in on her personal phone. Might be Leo, she thought, realizing she'd left her work mobile in the car. She checked it. Her ex. *Can we talk? Ricky.* Simple question, simple answer: no. She turned on Kevin Larkin.

'Who did you think was going to kill you?'

Ben translated. The answer was slow in coming but hand-delivered quickly when it did come. Ben spoke for the deaf man.

'The same people who shot my father.'

'And you know who these people are?'

Kevin answered with a shake of the head and lowered his eyes.

'You're lying,' she said. 'You know what this is all about, don't you?'

Ben hand-signed, but the answer was the same. The big man's wariness had returned and he watched Ben's hands like they were tarantulas.

'Why were you spray-painting the bike?' Ben asked, then spoke the answer:

'It's not spray-painting, it's custom painting. I put on the base colour and then I do designs. Airbrushing. It's my hobby. Graphics. I did all these.'

Only now did Helen notice the murals the deaf man pointed to around the walls of the pub. A more than average talent, she thought. The 1967 European Cup-winning Celtic team. The Lisbon Lions. Billy McNeill, Bobby Murdoch, Jimmy Johnstone – *Jinky* Johnstone. She knew all the names because her father had so often told her how he'd seen them play Waterford forty years ago. *Like watching the gods it was*, he'd told her.

'But why this morning?' Ben went on. 'Because it had to be done in a hurry? Because you wanted to disguise the bike?'

'I started work on it this morning because it has to be ready for the cup final,' Ben translated, continuing to relay the big man's lines as well as speak his own.

'Which cup final?'

'The Scottish Cup Final. Celtic and Motherwell. Gary's bringing it over to—'

'It's Gary's bike?' Helen interjected. Ben conveyed the question and then the answer.

'No. What I mean is yes, but he keeps it here and he lets me use it sometimes.'

'Did he use it on Saturday night?'

'No. He wasn't here on Saturday night.'

'Did you use it on Saturday night, Kevin?'

No, he hadn't, his gesture indicated. His shifty expression wasn't entirely in synch.

'Where were you on Saturday night?' Ben asked.

'Here in the pub. I work here and I sleep upstairs.'

'And you live alone, so you can't prove you were here all night?'

Kevin shrugged. The fug of exhaust fumes inside and the thick smoke drifting from the motorbike on the plaza were getting to Helen's sinuses. She pulled out the A4 sheet from inside her zip-up jacket, unfolded it and thrust the enlarged photo of the young Whitney before Kevin's eyes. He pushed her hand away but she forced the sheet on him again. He tried to raise himself and Ben pressed him back down. His face twisted itself into an attitude of pleading.

'This is what it's all about, isn't it? Ask him, Ben.'

That shake of the head again for an answer. To her disgust, she found herself silently cursing his deaf bloody dumbness that was too easy to hide behind, too easy to play-act with. She needed to calm down, disengage for a bit.

'Talk to him, Ben,' she said. 'But tell me everything he says. Everything, right?'

'Why would I not?' Ben said, and he looked at her as though he knew what it was she'd been thinking just a moment before about the deaf man.

He began to hand-sign again, speaking their dialogue.

'Where was this photo taken, Kevin?'

'In the garden.'

'Whose garden?'

'My father's garden. In St Laurence Villas.'

'When was it taken?'

'Her First Communion day. But I wasn't there. I never saw this photo before.'

'If you weren't there, how do you know it was her First Communion day?'

'Her hair. And the fake tan. I saw some photos that were taken in the churchyard.'

'How come you weren't there?'

'I was sick. The flu. I didn't want Whitney to catch it.'

'Take another look at the photo,' Ben signed.

Reluctantly, the big man glanced at the A4 sheet that Helen proffered. And glanced again, but more furtively. Something had caught his eye, Helen felt sure. Something that sobered him.

'This was found in your father's car. Why do you think he had it with him?'

'How would I know?' Crouched in the pub doorway, her back to the street, Helen felt the ache in her legs go up a notch.

'When did you last see Whitney?' she demanded, mouthing the words exaggeratedly.

'Tuesday or Wednesday, I don't remember which. She doesn't call here every day.'

Kevin wasn't looking at her as Ben interpreted his words. He was looking beyond her and giving the impression of heeding a sudden warning. Before she could think why, she felt why. The blow to the back of her head pitched her down on top of the deaf man. He broke her fall with his big fleshy hands. Ben sprang up and swung a fist at her attacker. Gary Larkin. Dazed, Helen lay across Kevin's lap. He gazed at her pityingly. Above them, carrot-haired Jinky Johnstone looked down from the wall, strangely life-like, almost seeming ready to speak. Helen felt spooked.

Out on the footpath, Ben grappled with the younger Larkin. He landed a blow or two but Gary kicked and twisted his agile little frame and somehow got in behind Ben, got an arm round his throat and squeezed until the detective loosed an elbow and sent it crashing into Gary's ribs. Spots of vividly fresh blood stained the smaller man's Glasgow Celtic jersey as he lay pinned beneath Ben. Apart from the blood, something else about Gary's appearance had changed but Helen couldn't quite figure out precisely what.

'Enough, Ben!' she shouted as she rolled away from Kevin and reached for the Flexi Cuffs on her belt.

From his prone position, Gary caught sight of Helen, recognized her, appraised her body. He sneered through bloodied lips. A new Mohawk hairstyle, Helen thought, that was the change. His father's brain-dead and waiting for the plug to be pulled and this guy goes and gets a haircut?

'Bitch,' Gary spat with misogynistic venom. 'How's your fucking cousin, bitch?'

Ben dragged him to his feet, turned him face to the wall. They got the cuffs on. Tight. Very tight. All the while they kept an eye on Kevin. They didn't need to. He hadn't moved except to bury his head in his hands. Helen called in for back-up and some cars to bring Gary to Pettycannon station. She hoped they wouldn't have to wait too long. They needed to tighten the screws on Kevin and search his little lair. Even if the throbbing in her head continued worryingly to worsen.

Over at the plaza, the crowd had melted away. The motorbike tyres, on the other hand, hadn't finished melting yet.

# 14

The labyrinth of hospital corridors led Leo back to ICU. He flattened the spring of his salt-and-pepper hair, straightened his tie, prepared himself for the pain of vicarious pleasure. The door swung open as he raised his hand to knock. Nurse Eveleen Morgan, her head turned to the side to catch the time on the wall clock, walked directly into Leo's midriff. Startled, they both retreated, watched to see how the other had taken it. And laughed, apologized, took the blame in the same breath, the same rhythm, almost the same words. They laughed again.

'Come on in,' she said. 'How's the eye? Any better?'

'Scratchy, you know. Can't get used to the eye-patch though. Never could.'

'Let me take a look.'

Leo sat and gave in to a restfulness that he knew could only be brief. The anticipation of her touch was sweet, the touch itself sweeter still. Eveleen lifted the eye-patch.

'I ordered up some eye ointment from the pharmacy,' she said as she extended and examined the well of his bad eye.

'You shouldn't have.'

'You're going to have to stick with the eye-patch for a few more days, I'm afraid, Leo.'

'They tell me it suits me. Some do anyway.'

'It does actually,' she agreed. A frank statement rather than a good-doggy reassurance. 'You asked me to get in touch if anything else occurred to me in relation to Mr Larkin. Well, I'm not sure if this is relevant, but yesterday, as you know, was pretty hectic in here. And we, the staff nurses and me, didn't get to talk much before they went off duty. So, this morning, one of the girls told me about something that happened while I was dealing with the Goode family.'

'The hit-and-run kid who died,' Leo said, and felt the sting of the ointment in the raw lower lid of his eye.

'Yeah. His poor mother, Frida, she really lost it in the isolation room,' the green-eyed nurse recalled. Brown flecks in there too. Hazel. 'Happens all the time, of course. She was lashing out at her husband, and I mean physically. And screaming . . . We hear it all the time with these hit-and-runs. The driver would never be caught and, if he was, all he'd get would be a few years off the road and a slap on the wrist.'

She replaced Leo's eye-patch, leaned back to appraise it, and made some adjustments before sitting back on the edge of her desk.

'Anyway, while all this was happening, one of the girls, Olive, was on the ward. She'd drawn the screen around a patient a few beds down from Mr Larkin's. She heard him moaning and it was very agitated. So she took a peep from behind the screen and Mrs Larkin was there. She'd put her hand near his and when he tried to take it, she'd pull it away. She seemed to be actually taunting him and Olive had to ask Mrs Larkin to stop. And got a tongue-lashing for her troubles.'

'Interesting.'

'People react differently, I know. But Mrs Larkin doesn't

behave like a woman who's about to lose her husband.'

'I suppose not.'

To Leo's disappointment, she went back round her desk, sat down and began to finger some files. It felt like a gentle nudge towards the door.

'I'm sticking my nose in where it's not wanted, aren't I?'

'Christ, no. I need all the help I can get with this investigation, believe me . . .'

He wanted to say her name but couldn't let himself. He knew how easily, how hungrily, he might have lapped up the illusion of some intimacy between them. She swept a lock of chestnut hair back from her forehead and her wry smile lifted Leo again.

'As a matter of fact, I'm doing some investigating here myself, Leo. I could do with a few tips from a pro.'

'I'm no pro,' he said, wishing his name didn't roll off her tongue so carelessly. 'But if I can help . . .'

'Oh, it's just something that came up yesterday while we were up to our eyes here. I probably overreacted and now Immunology are getting the hump.'

'Immunology?'

Eveleen leaned forward, her elbows on the desk. Leo knew he had to get back to work but he wasn't going anywhere while she worked the muscles of his one good eye so effortlessly.

'The Immunology Department,' she explained. 'See, yesterday this guy, an intern over there, kept showing up in the ICU ward. He'd just wander in, check some charts and disappear again without a word to any of us. So I confronted him, asked him who'd sent him over. He wouldn't give me a straight answer but I got his name from his ID and told him not to come back without some authorization. I was being a bitch, I know, but it was a heavy day.'

'These young fellows,' Leo said, for no particular reason beyond a desire to draw out this opportunity to be near her. 'They can get carried away with themselves, can't they?'

'Oh, I don't know. We all have our off-days, I suppose.' Eveleen was clearly the forgiving type. Leo's type. 'But the thing is, the really odd thing is that Immunology are insisting that this guy wasn't on duty yesterday. In fact, they're telling me he's not due back on duty until the weekend. They're also adamant that he wasn't sent over here to ICU by anyone in Immunology. It's a mystery.'

They both stood up. Leo clung desperately to the last vestiges of their conversation. He remembered the woman he'd been trying to forget all morning. The woman he could no longer avoid meeting. It didn't require much imagination to know how Eveleen would feel if she knew how he'd treated Liz Larkin all those years ago. Not very forgiving after all, maybe.

'What's this intern's name?'

'Mahmoud Maguin.' Her pronunciation of the Arabic seemed unusually authentic.

'Where's he from?'

'According to his personnel file, he's Libyan born but grew up in Ireland. When his parents went back to Libya, they sent him boarding to Clongowes Wood. Got himself an especially plummy Dublin 4 accent.'

'I'm D4 myself,' Leo said. 'Old D4, of course. The accent hadn't drifted out into the mid-Atlantic when I was growing up.'

Her right hand busied itself with her hair. Not so much a nervous gesture as one that focused her thinking, her assessment of the matter at hand. Foolishly but irresistibly, Leo wondered if he was the matter at hand. She green-eyed him.

'There's a coincidence, I live in D4 too. I'm just a blow-in, of course.'

'From?' Which wasn't the question he really wanted to ask. *Where exactly in D4?* was the question he'd wanted to ask.

'Galway. Salthill, do you know it?'

'Nice spot.'

They'd come to a standstill. It was time for both of them to move on. Eveleen sat back down at her desk, Leo moved towards the exit.

'Well then,' he said, talking his way distractedly through the grasping of the door handle, the opening of the door. 'Let me know how the investigation goes, won't you? And thanks again . . .'

'Eveleen,' she said.

'Eveleen.'

# 15

In her student days in Cork, Helen had done voluntary work for a while with the Simon Community. That was before she'd met Ricky, who had no interest in helping anyone but himself. More than once in the intervening years she'd chided herself for not sticking with the work in spite of him. Same with the football. Same with all the friends she'd let slide away. Instead, she'd let herself become his pet project – a working-class naif mentored by a bourgeois layabout. In any case, she'd never forgotten the men and women she'd visited, their storied lives. What she had, until now, forgotten was the smell that invariably clung to them. An admixture of defeat and unwashed sweat, of apology and bad luck. Kevin Larkin's rooms reeked of it.

The big man led Ben and Helen through a kitchenette. A sinkful of delph encrusted with mouldy gunge, a small Formica table whose surface had served as a breadboard for some time without having once been cleared of crumbs. The living space was an improvement only in the sense that little of the waste was of the food variety. Magazines and comic books whole, ripped or clipped littered the floor. *The Magazine of Fantasy and Science Fiction, Judge Dredd*

*Megazine*, *2000 AD*. On a bulky and muted old TV, the Arab Spring continued apace. Beside the TV stood a blank-screened PC of a similarly ancient vintage. In the far corner, a spectacularly steep stairway led to an attic bedroom.

Kevin sat on the only available armchair without bothering to clear it off. He let the two detectives fend for themselves. They remained standing. It seemed the more comfortable option. The back of Helen's head still ached fiercely from the blow it had taken and Ben continued to let his concern for her show too keenly. She knew the drill. She should have been undergoing a medical check, not ploughing on with the interrogation. But enough time had already been wasted. Their search of Kevin's equally chaotic bedroom had yielded no results. The photograph of the half-naked child had begun to haunt Helen. Every lost minute seemed like another minute taken from Whitney's life, another minute closer to her death.

The questions she relayed to the deaf man through Ben led them around in circles once more. Only one thing was clear: behind his caution lurked fear. There were no prizes for guessing who he was afraid of. Gary, his little runt of a brother. So, no, he had no idea where Whitney was. He couldn't say if she'd run away from home before. He knew nothing of a kidnap. He didn't know if she'd planned to attend a goth music festival in Cork. So it went, until Ben tried a new angle. Helen wasn't sure where it was leading but she let him take over. She found a section of wall that wasn't too unclean to lean dizzily against as he talked her through the conversation.

'Who's the best signer in your family, Kevin? I'm guessing it's Whitney. Am I right?'

'People find it hard to learn signing . . . it's not always because they don't want to . . .'

Kevin joined his hands to stop them talking.

'But Whitney is the only one who really talks to you, isn't she?' Helen asked. 'The others can't be bothered. Why is that, Kevin? Why have they dumped you here to fend for yourself?'

'They haven't dumped me. I live here because I'm thirty-six, and I'm deaf, not mentally deficient.'

Helen cut off the outlet he'd found in his show of assertiveness. Ben conveyed her message.

'I saw how your family treated you in the ICU waiting room, Kevin. Your stepmother and Gary completely ignored you. Your Uncle Jimmy barely looked your way. You're nothing to them. Your father was the same, I bet. He treated you like shit too, didn't he?'

Kevin shook his head. His hands tried to expand on his answer but the instructions they waited for didn't come.

'Did he treat Whitney like shit?' Helen asked.

No response to Ben's signing.

'Did he give her good reason to run away?'

Again no response, apart from a wary glide of the eyes from her to Ben's fingers and back.

'Did your father mistreat Whitney?'

Big locked fists wouldn't let Kevin answer.

Helen readied herself for a quick retreat should her next question push him over the brink. Her feeling of unwellness had turned to a vague sense of panic. She held on so firmly to a chair-back that her arms shuddered.

'Did your father have an inappropriate relationship with Whitney?'

Ben wasn't happy with the question. When he put it to the big man, it seemed more lengthy, more hedged about than her own abrupt formulation. Kevin's hands were suddenly busy again, dizzying her, stirring a sea-sickness in her stomach. She wondered if Ben was embellishing the deaf man's signs, aggrandizing his language so that she'd feel even worse about herself than she already did.

'We're scum to you, aren't we? Everything about you says you're dealing with the lower orders here so you feel free to jump to all sorts of offensive conclusions about us.' Ben waved aside Helen's attempted intervention. 'My father wasn't like that.'

Ben cast a silent, worried query towards her. She ignored it.

'Baz MacDonald makes an effort to sign, doesn't he?' she said. 'Which means that you get on well with him. So, would I be right in thinking that he was the one who told you Harry had been shot?'

'He texted me and said something had happened to my father. Then he came over here and told me and drove us to the hospital.'

'What time did he text you?'

The deaf man took his Smartphone from his trouser pocket and scrolled. He held up the mobile.

'Baz. Six-fifteen a.m.,' Ben read aloud.

A man without secrets, Kevin's gesture suggested. He dipped his head and came up with a deep breath and a confession. An honest man.

'I took the bike out on Saturday night. I went to the twenty-four-hour Tesco in Lucan. I often go there at night. I prefer to shop late.'

'The Lucan Tesco is just across the N4 from Tandy's Lane, isn't it, Kevin?' Ben said, signing.

The room fell so quiet they could hear noises from the cordoned-off street below. The pounding in Helen's head was becoming unbearable. She told herself to stop looking at the vertigo-inducing attic stairs.

'Why is he telling us this?' she asked of her colleague.

The deaf man had lip-read the question that hadn't been intended for him. Ben read the deaf man's signs.

'I told you because you'll probably find out anyway. But all you have to do is ask them in Tesco. They know I often shop there after I close up here.'

It was easy to imagine Kevin Larkin among the deserted aisles of a white-lit, early-hours supermarket. Alone, shuffling self-consciously, his expression composed in equal measure of loneliness and stifled intelligence. A sudden sense of utter bleakness hit Helen. She couldn't remember why her head hurt so much.

'Do you have a recent photo of Whitney?' she asked through Ben.

'Are you all right, Helen?' Ben asked.

'Just ask him, OK?'

Kevin's reply came unsigned. A shake of the head.

'Any photo would help,' Ben told him. 'It doesn't have to be recent.'

'I don't have any photos of her.'

'You don't have even one photo of your sister? Isn't that a bit odd?' Ben probed. 'What about the PC? Surely there's a photo of—' Ben stopped as Kevin's hands were already darting out a reply.

'Switch it on if you like. My password is jinkyjohnstone67, lower case. You'll find nothing.'

'You weren't so close after all, then, were you, Kevin? You and Whitney. In fact, this suggests the very opposite, doesn't it?'

Kevin Larkin's disagreement lacked vehemence. He shifted his bulk forward, leaned his elbows on his knees, clutched the greased strands of his bushy hair before he let his hands speak.

'Whitney hated having her photo taken. The Guards know that already.'

The two detectives moved forward with perfect synchronicity. One step. Then a double-step to a halt. Unlike her colleague, Helen didn't remain stock-still. She teetered. The room began slowly to journey through the cosmos. Helen didn't know where it was taking her. She wondered why Ben kept talking to himself aloud.

'How would we know that, Kevin?' Ben asked, and the deaf man blanched.

'The court case last year. The one about the mobile phone photo.'

'Someone took her picture on a mobile phone and she, what, she flipped?' Ben suggested.

Helen felt herself fade, heard something fizzle away in her brain.

'Yes. And Whitney had to do ninety days' community service last summer. But she was the one being bullied. Do you call that justice? And now all this. Poor Whitney, she didn't deserve . . .'

Kevin Larkin's hands stopped signing and shot forward to break Helen's fall.

# 16

Earlier, Garda Dempsey's silence had suited Detective Inspector Leo Woods' mood. Now it irritated him, left him too much with his own thoughts. Liz Larkin and her brother-in-law had left the building before he'd got to the ICU waiting room. There had been nothing for it but to head out to Chapelizod. He felt as if he'd foolishly conceded the neutral venue of the hospital and would now be playing an away game.

'What the hell's wrong with you?' he asked. 'Spit it out or you'll be back on the beat chasing gurriers along O'Connell Street.'

'It's personal.'

'It's always personal. Tell me.'

'I've a wedding coming up,' the young Garda said. Funereally. 'My sister.'

'And?'

Dempsey scouted Leo's face for sincere engagement with his dilemma. He didn't find what he was looking for.

'And nothing,' he said, returning his watery-eyed attention to the road. 'You'll just take the piss like everyone else.'

'You don't want her to get married, is that it?'

'No.'

'She's younger than you and you're pissed off that it's not you getting married?'

'No.'

'You wanted to be best man but she found a better one.'

'See?' Dempsey said fiercely. 'I knew you'd only take the piss.'

'Just tell me what the bloody problem is,' Leo said, his patience snapping. 'I can't help you if I don't know what the hell is up with you.'

'I don't need your help. I need a woman.'

'Join the queue, Dempsey,' Leo said but softened when he saw the big boy's moist eyes. 'You're young, son, you'll meet someone, but not if you stay in watching DVDs all weekend.'

The young Garda wasn't listening. He stared ahead like a man on the road to nowhere.

'I only need her for the day, like. This is my third sister to get married and I was on my own for the first two weddings. Everyone was laughing at me. Imagine what it'll be like this time.'

'Things never turn out as badly as you imagine,' Leo said. Not true, he told himself, not always. 'Have you someone in mind to ask?'

'Yeah, but I can't bring myself to ask her.'

Dempsey was right. Leo couldn't help him. He played the éminence grise instead.

'Just do it. Walk through the fire, Dempsey, there's no alternative. You can't slip under the flames or fly over them or duck to the side of them. You have to walk through the fire.'

'I'll remember that, boss,' the young fellow said. 'If I ever join the circus.'

'You're already in one,' Leo said and, giving up on him, checked his phone.

Four messages. Three from Detective Sergeant Helen Troy. One from Detective Sergeant Martin Buck. He read Buck's first. *Some choice nibbles here at SDU!! Ring me.* It wasn't only the prurient nature of the message that annoyed Leo. Exclamation marks in texts always got to him. Especially double ones. Life wasn't that amusing or exciting. He pressed the green phone icon.

'You have something for me, Martin?'

'Yeah,' Buck said. 'Seems Gary Larkin's got a buddy with a big mouth.'

'As in?'

'As in this guy's been telling his pals over in Lucan that when Gary takes over the Larkin empire, he'll be the right-hand man. An SDU informant heard him bullshitting at a party a few months back. "This time next year I'll be a player" kind of thing.'

'So Gary has an accomplice in his bid for power and glory.'

'I'm not so sure. The SDU guys think this fellow's just as flaky as Gary.'

'Who's Gary's pal then?'

'Derek McCarthy. He's a cougar trainer in the Step-Up gym over in Lucan.'

'A cougar trainer?'

Buck chuckled. 'A personal trainer specializing in middle-aged women, Leo.'

'Let's pull him in then and see if we can teach him to jump.'

'No problem. Got a little something on Baz McDonald too,' Buck continued. 'Seems Harry brought him in when one of their cigarette deals went pear-shaped. Back around 2000, the Larkins made contact with a Slovakian manufacturer and set up a new channel of supply which worked out fine until June or July of 2002, when they got stung by the middle man for major money. Fifty thousand euro, the story goes.'

'Do we know who this middle man was?'

'Young Slovakian guy,' Buck explained. 'He lived in Lucan for two years or so. Name of Anton Bisjak, but the SDU discovered later it was a fake ID. So, basically, they've no idea who this guy really was. Anyway, Harry went ballistic. He thought Gary had let himself be used by this guy. Apparently, Bisjak joined their Glasgow Celtic Supporters Club and got very pally with Gary, so pally he was like a trusted member of the family.'

'So, Harry called in Baz MacDonald to go after him?'

'Yeah, toured the city with a couple of thousand euro in one hand and a Glock 17 in the other. Had every Slovakian in the city shitting his pants. Went on for weeks apparently, this hunt.'

'And they didn't find him?'

'Harry claimed they never did and SDU say the guy never showed up again. Seems MacDonald stayed on Harry's payroll full-time after that. All of which probably means Gary and our Armenian friend were never best buddies, to say the least.'

It was good stuff but a bad vibe rang through it. Leo put the vibe into words.

'All this info on McCarthy and Baz, you knew nothing about it before SDU told you?'

'Fuck you, Leo. Harry wasn't on your radar in the nineties and he wasn't on ours in the noughties,' Buck said, and cut the call.

It was too late for regret. Leo chastised himself anyway. The guy had a dodgy past but who didn't? He opened the three texts from Helen. *We're taking Gary Larkin in 2*

*Pettycannon on officer assault charge. Helen.* Officer assault? Somewhat guiltily, he hoped it was Ben and not Helen who'd been hit. Leo stared at the second text. It was the same as the first but sent ten minutes later. He moved on to the last message. Same wording again, sent a few minutes after the second one. A network problem? Maybe, but it didn't feel right.

He rang Helen's phone and got her voicemail. He rang Detective Garda Ben Murphy.

'Sir?'

'What the hell's going on there, Ben? I've got the same message from Helen three times. Is she . . . ?'

'She's in hospital, sir. Concussion.'

'Who hit her?'

'Gary Larkin,' Ben replied. 'They're going to keep her in overnight as a precaution. The tests are clear. There's nothing to worry about. She's a tough nut.'

Alongside Leo, Garda Dempsey's large jaw was beginning to drop. He leaned forward to focus on the road and pretend he wasn't listening.

'He came at us from behind. I should've reacted quicker.'

Leo resisted the temptation to bollock the young detective. Instead, he withheld the reassurance Ben was clearly seeking.

'So, tell me what happened and why and what, if anything, you learned from this fiasco.'

'It was far from a fiasco, sir.'

'Just shut up and tell me,' Leo snapped, and Dempsey emitted a mirthful grunt which Leo cut off with an elbow to the pudgy driver's paunch.

Leo's insomniac brain struggled to retain the details that came so thick and fast he almost suspected the young high-flyer was putting him to the test. The mental notes he made were written on sand and the tide was coming in fast. Ben Murphy reached the end of his account.

'So what's this aversion to having her photo taken about?' Leo asked.

'It might just be that she's, you know, self-conscious about her appearance, or . . .' Ben hesitated.

'Or it might have some connection with that lurid photo in Harry's car?' Leo suggested.

'I suppose,' Ben said.

'OK, Whitney was in trouble last year so we have a photo on file, yeah?'

'Martha checked on Pulse, there's no photo,' Murphy said. 'It was a minor assault case and she pleaded guilty. Got a community service order.'

'And the motorbike tyres are a write-off?'

'Looks that way, yes. We might get a make but not a match.'

'And Kevin knows more than he's admitting to?'

'Definitely. And knows more than Gary wants him to admit,' Ben added. 'Kevin's on the point of breaking down with every mention of Whitney. He knows something's happened to her. Whether he knows precisely what, I can't say. My gut feeling is that Gary knows damn well what's going on here.'

The abuse scenario came to mind again. Wild speculations followed. Gary abuses Whitney. Takes dodgy snaps of her. Whatever. She threatens to out him. He kills her. Pretends it's a kidnap. Sets up Harry. Et cetera, et cetera. He was beginning to feel like a dirty old B-movie hack with the DTs and a looming deadline. He changed the script.

'I wonder if our Gary has launched a pre-emptive strike?'

'In relation to?'

'The battle for succession,' Leo said. 'We know Harry

didn't have a high opinion of Gary. We also know that Baz McDonald was the golden boy. We know that Harry has been sliding downhill for quite a while so succession had to be in the air chez les Larkins. Apparently, Harry didn't have more than a few months left in him at best. Plus Gary may have had an accomplice in his ambitions to take over from Harry. One Derek McCarthy.'

Dempsey steered the car on to Usher's Quay. The dead water of the River Liffey lay masked beneath bright, dazzling ripples that hurt Leo's good eye. He told Ben what he'd learned of Gary Larkin's links with McCarthy, asked him to get a team out on the streets of Lucan to locate the man. And pronto. His first instinct had been to head straight to Pettycannon station himself and grill Gary. He knew, however, that this first instinct was merely a further excuse to put off the showdown with Liz Larkin.

'Take the interview with Gary and lean heavy – heavy as you can this side of legal,' Leo said.

'I'm not sure I can trust myself on this one. I've already hit him a few shots more than I should have.'

'Don't worry about that, Ben, he's only a little bollocks anyway,' Leo said, and felt the kind of mixture of pride and shame a father might when he'd seen his son win his first street scrap.

'Got Whitney's phone number from Kevin, by the way,' Ben said. 'I'm not sure how long we'll have to wait for a result from the service provider. Tomorrow at the latest, I should think.'

'Good stuff. And, Ben? Tell Helen I'll be in to see her later. Tell her I . . .' Viciously, he wiped some tears that had escaped below the eye-patch. 'Ask her would she prefer flowers or a bottle of Lucozade.'

'No problem,' Ben said.

Leo ended the call. Jesus Christ, he told himself, wasn't it just as well he didn't have a daughter all the same? Or a son, for that matter.

'Is Helen all right?' Dempsey asked, a tremor in his gruff tone.

'Yeah, she'll be fine,' Leo said, and closed his good eye.

'It wouldn't have happened if I'd been there. I'd have boxed his—'

'Yeah, like Superman,' Leo answered, letting himself spin and float in the darkness behind his good eye and his eye-patch. 'We all think we're Superman, don't we? Until we hit the wall and we don't crash through it, we crash into it. No wonder Nietzsche broke down in front of that poor horse in Turin.'

'You're pure weird,' Dempsey said.

'Took you long enough to figure that out, son.'

Leo looked out at the city. The unmarked car crossed Island Bridge, turned left on to Conyngham Road, the long stone wall and high trees of the Phoenix Park to the right. Where once he went a-courting. With a woman who wasn't his wife. With a woman who was barely yet a woman.

# 17

Leo hadn't been out in Chapelizod for years. He felt the keen disappointment of return, the suburban village looking the worse for wear. Never go back, he thought. But you always did, didn't you? As a young man, he'd always liked the place, its sense of refuge from the city, the literary associations that appealed to his early pretensions. Joyce's impenetrable *Finnegans Wake*. Sheridan Le Fanu's *Ghost Stories of Chapelizod*. And there was Iseult's fascination with it, her paintings of the ill-fated lovers Tristan and Iseult, said to be buried beneath an old ruined chapel in the village. Which was pretty bloody ironic, given that Chapelizod was also the burial ground of his marriage. Thanks to the Larkins, among others. And, in fairness, to Leo himself.

On the river side of the narrow stretch beyond Chapelizod's Main Street and St Martin's Row stood St Laurence Villas. Handsome and well-established, the two-storey terraced houses were set back five yards or so from the road. Twelve in all. The numbers, however, ran only to eleven. The final pair, made into one, was the seat of the Larkin empire; the last door had no number. Harry Larkin's new address, Leo mused. Nowhere, Chapelizod.

There wasn't room to park so Leo had Dempsey drop

him there and go find a parking space back in Main Street.

He got himself across the forecourt paving without pulling out his cigarettes though he fidgeted with them as he rang the bell. Beneath his eye-patch, a healing itch had started up. The door opened a sliver and then another. For a few short moments, neither one recognized the other. Then the past flooded in and the damage that life and time had done to both of them provoked a tsunami of surprise, regret, self-consciousness. Nothing left standing but the wreckage.

Liz Larkin found her voice before Leo did.

'Leo?' It wasn't a question. Or at least not a simple question.

'Liz,' he said, and waited for the onslaught. It didn't come.

The gap in the door hadn't widened any further. They looked at one another. She was wearing pink rubber gloves and a pink apron over a cream Lycra track suit. Her once pleasing face had begun to collapse inwards, the skin compromised by sun-worship and from letting the good times roll for too long. Or the bad times. Cruelly, the word *tsantsa* came to Leo. An Ecuadorian shrunken head. He tried to remember who it was who'd said that the eyes never change. That other French philosopher, Derrida. Liz Larkin's eyes had changed. They were sharper, darker, pickled in bitterness. Got that one wrong, Jacques.

'Can I come in?' Leo asked.

'Why?'

'You know why, Liz. I've a job to do.'

'Where have I heard that line before?' she said. 'What happened to your face?'

The old bluntness was still there then, but it didn't arise out of naivety any more.

'Bell's palsy. It's a long story.'

'Pierce Brosnan had that too, hadn't he? There's hope for you yet.'

She pulled back the door and stepped aside to let him pass. Inside, the décor was flowery. Very flowery. Lilies everywhere and none of them real. Embossed on the wallpaper, woven into the carpet, etched on the decorative hall mirror. The air was astringent with cleaning chemicals. Leo wondered if she'd been trying to rid the house of the last traces of her nearly-departed. She showed him into the sitting room. More lilies on the curtains and on the couches and a pair of plastic ones in a long slim vase on the mantelpiece. Two walls were entirely shelved with DVDs. Another wall held a vast TV screen and surround-sound speakers. No wonder old Harry retained his obsession with films even after his brain had been scrambled.

Indicating the armchair behind him, she pulled off her cleaning gloves and turned to the mirror above the mantelpiece. He sat, waited as she undid her apron, took out his cigarettes. Lycra track suits didn't take prisoners but she'd kept her shape. Working out, Leo wondered? At the Step-Up gym in Lucan?

'We don't smoke in the house,' her mirror self told him.

'You gave them up?'

'I gave up a lot of things that were bad for me.'

'But Harry was a smoker, wasn't he?'

'Harry gave them up too when his heart started acting up, Gary never smoked and Whitney's asthmatic so she . . . Look, I know why you're here. So before you ask, yes, Whitney's gone. And not for the first time. She's taken her passport and her laptop. And that's not a first either in case you're wondering.'

She moved too quickly towards him and his one-eyed view screamed collision. He dropped back further in the armchair. She stood over him, hands on hips, defiantly brusque.

'Her passport?' Leo said. 'Is she gone to your apartment in Lanzarote?'

'She doesn't like Lanzarote.'

'When did you last see her?'

'Wednesday.'

'So she's been gone, what, five nights? Is that usual for her?'

'Yeah.'

'And you don't feel at all uneasy about her absence?'

'You know nothing about how I feel. You never did,' Liz said.

'Have you rung or texted her about Harry?' Leo asked. 'Look, we're tracing Whitney's mobile as we speak, so we're going to know if you're being straight with us.'

'I tried,' she said. 'Gary tried too. We texted her, left voicemails, told her about Harry, but she didn't answer.'

'That seems pretty extraordinary, doesn't it? She knows what happened to her father and still she doesn't come back?'

'You don't know Whitney. She's . . .'

Liz clammed up, though Leo could see she was delivering a silent tirade against her daughter.

'You say it's not the first time she's done this. Where has she gone in the past?'

'You really think she'd tell us where she takes herself off to?' Liz said. 'You know what seventeen-year-olds are like, don't you, Leo. Remember?'

'You were more than seventeen.'

'Checked my birth cert, did you, before you decided to make your move?'

'I didn't decide. It happened.'

Liz laughed at him. She retreated to an armchair oppo-site Leo, dropped herself lightly down among the lilies. He remembered that laugh. A late-night laugh, a naked laugh. It used to resonate too deeply in him. Now it grated on his ears.

'Right,' she said. 'So it was my fault as much as yours?'

'No.'

'And it was my fault that I ended up spying on my hus-band for two years?'

He might have split hairs on this point. Technically, she and Harry hadn't been married at the time. But what was the point? Leo thought. And how the hell was he going to get to the real purpose of his visit if she kept dredging up the past and he kept sinking in it?

'Listen, Liz . . .' The itch in his infected eye became a scratch and he pressed the eye-patch hard into it. 'I talked to Harry at the hospital and he asked me to find Whitney. Why would he do that if there's no connection between her . . . OK, let's call it her absence, and the attack on him?'

'Well, first of all,' Liz began, 'you might have talked to Harry but he didn't talk to you. He talked to that bloody cow of a nurse. Which, by the way, she should have told me at the time. And, secondly, Harry was hallucinating as you know damn well because of the bullet in his brain. Which I did manage to drag from the bitch. If she crosses me or any of us again, she'll regret it.'

Her venom didn't shock Leo. Its target did. He'd needed to be goaded. Now he had been.

'Do you have a recent photo of Whitney? I'm told she's not keen on having her photo taken.'

Her right hand remembered its old cigarette habit, came to her lips, descended and, in the space of a breath, came back up again. When her hand dropped to the armchair rest again, she'd figured out where the information had come from.

'Kevin,' she said, coldly dismissive.

'Do you have a photo or not?'

'You don't need a photo. She's not missing.'

'Don't have me force the issue.'

For a moment, it seemed Liz Larkin was about to follow the double-entendre route again. She reconsidered.

Halfway to the door, she said, 'The last photos I have were taken nearly two years ago. She doesn't even look like that any more.'

'That's OK,' Leo said, making to stir from his seat.

'Wait here,' she told him.

While she was gone, Leo looked along the DVDs on the shelves beside his chair. Rubbish mostly. Movies rather than films, flights of shallow escapist fancy. Love and war of the lite, happy-ending variety. Romcoms for the girls, zombies and explosions for the boys. On the lower shelves were the box-sets. Some good stuff here. *The Godfather* trilogy. *The Sopranos. Boardwalk Empire.* He wondered if Harry and Gary ever actually got the moral in these morality tales. He wondered if Liz did. Or maybe they found some comfort in the myth of family values prevailing in spite of the carnage.

On a dresser in one of the fire-block alcoves stood a display of framed photos. None of the shots included Whitney. Most of them included Gary. An entirely un-expected Gary. Leo couldn't believe his eye. He lifted the patch. He couldn't believe the other eye either.

Young Larkin, it seemed, had been on stage and screen in his boyhood. In one photo, Gary posed with the actor Ga-briel Byrne. In another, he danced with a troupe in what was clearly some Christmas pantomime. Was that the Olympia stage maybe, or the Gaiety? How had Harry felt about seeing his son sporting ballet tights? Not the fat man's scene by a long shot. As Leo examined the photos more closely, Liz returned.

'Gary was a child actor?'

'He tried to be,' Liz said, her features pinched with anger. 'He worked so hard at it and never got a break just because of who we were.' A long-held grievance, and it took flame, burned in her. 'He was up for one of the lead roles in that film with Gabriel Byrne, *Into the West*. You should've seen his screen test. Only seven and he was a natural, but all he got was a bit part.'

She looked beyond Leo, beyond the sitting room, beyond the present moment. He wondered if she was imagining the life she and Gary and perhaps all of the Larkins might have lived had he got that break.

'But he stuck at it for a while?' Leo said, nodding towards the photos.

'He did,' Liz replied. 'Knock after knock but he kept on going to his acting and dancing lessons. He got a few lines in *The War of the Buttons* after that. Did the Gaiety pantomimes for years. But the last film he went for finished him. He was fourteen. He couldn't take it any more. Who could blame him?'

'What was the film?'

'*The General*. That broke him.'

Leo raised the good eyebrow. The film had depicted the life and death of a well-known Dublin criminal. Known to Leo and, perhaps, even to Harry himself. And yet Liz betrayed not a hint of self-consciousness or embarrassment as she spoke of it.

'He was perfect for the part. Everyone said so. Everyone,' she repeated. 'But they gave him a Mickey Mouse part with a handful of lines and we told them to stuff it.'

'What did Harry make of the singing and dancing lark?'

'He knew it was all part of the process,' she said sharply.

'But if I know Harry, he didn't like it very much, did he?'

She thrust a couple of snapshots into his hand and turned from him. The setting was a pub or a club. Low-rent, teeming and messy. A lot of red-eye in the shots and focus wasn't the photographer's strong point either. Brain-dead Harry had already begun to go blurry. Gary raised a pint of lager like a trophy. Twisted, maybe stoned. Jimmy was on shorts, whiskey or brandy. Inscrutable, his thick spectacles reflecting the camera's flash. Beside her brother-in-law, Liz laughed and fingered the red ruby centrepiece of a silver necklace. Of Whitney, there was little to see. Her long blonde hair fell over much of her face and you could tell she didn't want to be there.

'What was the occasion?'

'Our twenty-fifth wedding anniversary,' she said. 'We had a great night.'

Leo knew what the defiance in her voice was about. Twenty-eight years ago he'd all but pleaded with her not to tie the knot with Harry Larkin. All but. If he'd loved her he might have pleaded but lust and affection didn't add up to love. Nevertheless, he'd cared about what might lie in store for her. She'd be marrying another, scarcely milder version of her father. And, for Christ's sake, hadn't she cried often enough on Leo's shoulder, telling him what that old buzzard with his glass eye and his stale Guinness breath had done to her? Now she was trying to tell him he'd been wrong. He didn't believe her, but neither did he believe that he had any right to say so.

'You took only two photos?'

'We took plenty. She's not in the rest of them. You can look if you want to.'

'What was her problem about having her photograph taken?' he asked. 'I'm told she got herself a community service order because of it.'

'She's like any kid her age. She's plagued with acne, the poor thing. It bothers her a lot, you know.'

'Who took these two shots?' Leo asked. 'Kevin?' Liz stared him down. 'Ah, Kevin wasn't invited, was he? Did Baz MacDonald take them?'

Her eyes narrowed contemptuously at the mention of the ex-Provo.

'He wasn't there.'

Leo examined the photos again. He didn't know what else to do. In the hazy background, a group of young guys stood laughing and drinking pints from raised and seriously tattooed arms. A couple of teenagers among them prompted a thought.

'A boyfriend would have her photo, surely, wouldn't he? Does she have a boyfriend?'

'Not that I know of. Not that she'd tell me if she had.'

'Or friends? Some of those goth kids? Can you give me their names?'

'I don't know any of them. She doesn't bring them home. She doesn't bring anyone home.'

Leo reached into his pocket for the dog-eared A4 photocopy of the photo from Harry's car. He took it out but couldn't make himself show it to her, stained red as it was with Harry's blood.

'Harry had a photo of Whitney on him when—' he began.

She was ready for the revelation. Which probably meant that Jimmy Larkin had warned her what to expect.

'I never saw that photo in my life. I wasn't there when it was taken.'

'You weren't there for her First Communion day?'

'I was in the house getting stuff ready. You know what it's like on a day like that.' She watched him closely. 'Chaotic. And you know what kids are like when they're hyped up. Bouncing off the walls and . . .' She sat back with unconcealed satisfaction. 'You don't have any kids, do you?'

'No.'

'Did you ever marry? After Iseult, I mean.'

She was avenging herself on him, twisting the knife, pulling his teeth out one by one.

'No,' he said. 'Your daughter isn't fully dressed in the photo. Can you explain why Harry had it with—'

'Did you ever find your father?'

'I didn't try. Tell me about the photo, Liz.'

'I never saw it,' she insisted, though she still mined Leo's one eye for pay-dirt. 'She never came back, did she? Iseult?'

'Someone's standing near Whitney in the shot,' Leo went on, shaken and stirred but not spilled. Beads of sweat begged to be wiped from his forehead. He left them there, hoped they wouldn't trouble the one decent eye he had left. 'Someone wearing a Glasgow Celtic jersey. Who is he? Why was he torn from the shot?'

'Could be anyone. We had people calling all morning that day.'

'They were all wearing Celtic jerseys?' he asked, sour as he needed to be now, pissed off, almost tempted to unfold the A4 sheet and force her to look.

'As a matter of fact, most of them were wearing jerseys,' she said. 'It was the weekend of the Scottish Cup Final. Celtic versus Rangers. Go check it if you don't believe me. There was a gang of them going over to the game that morning and they called in before they left.'

'So who tore the photo and why did Harry have it with him when he was shot?'

'How would I know?'

'Did he tell you where he was going last Saturday night?'

'I didn't ask him.'

'You didn't ask him? Jimmy tells me that Harry was struggling to get about of late. And you tell me he went out in the early hours and you didn't think to ask where he was going?'

'I'm a heavy sleeper. Remember?'

She laughed at him again, provoking him, though not to desire as in the past. Time to pull the pin from the grenade and be done with it, Leo thought. He opened out the A4 sheet, held it out towards her. She dragged her eyes away from it, once, twice and again. The colour drained from behind the tan papyrus of her skin.

'Bastard,' she said.

'So, Harry's out there on Tandy's Lane in the middle of the night with this photo in his lap. Is he waiting to pay a ransom?' Leo tested another theory which expanded as he spoke. 'Or blackmail money? Actually, I very much doubt it's a ransom. And if it's blackmail, who exactly is being blackmailed? Who's got something to hide? Harry or that little runt of yours, Gary?'

'Don't you dare talk about my son like that,' she hissed, turned venomous, her hard raw core exposed at last.

'I'm told Baz McDonald was Harry's favourite. That must've pissed Gary off big time.'

'McDonald worked for Harry, full stop.'

'Takes after his father, Gary does,' Leo went on, poking. 'He's just assaulted one of my officers. A female officer. Put her in hospital, he did.'

'It was a misunderstanding,' Liz insisted. 'Gary's not like

that. You have no idea what Gary's like. What he's been through.'

'Been in trouble with the law, has he?'

'Once. Ever. And it was self-defence.'

'When was this?'

'Years ago. Ten years.'

A harmless enough record, Leo thought, for the crown prince of an illicit empire.

'Was he here on Saturday night when Harry set off for Tandy's Lane?'

'Gary doesn't live here,' she said. 'He has an apartment across the river.'

'I'm well aware of that. But was he here on Saturday night?'

'No, he wasn't.'

'So, let's test the blackmail hypothesis. Let's say someone sent Harry this photo of his half-naked daughter by way of reminding him what he'd done or maybe was still doing to Whitney. Or what Gary had done to—'

Liz jumped to her feet and the A4 sheet fell from Leo's hand. When she came towards him, she planted one sneaker on the paper. He didn't think this was deliberate but he couldn't be sure.

'What did you say?' Her breath came punched. 'Are you suggesting . . . that my husband . . . my son . . . abused . . . just because I was . . .'

Her hand came swinging from his blind side. The slap had more sting than power in it. The real humiliation came when the slapping hand she drew away became entangled in the cord of his eye-patch and swept it off. She took a step back, stared down in disgust at the raw well of his collapsed and infected eye.

'Look at you. You filthy, ugly bastard. You look just like him.'

'Like who?'

'You know damn well. My father with his disgusting glass eye.'

She lowered her left eyelid with a finger, mimed the popping out of the eyeball into the palm of her hand.

'I tried to help you with that,' Leo said. 'I told you I'd trace him over in England and protect you if you took a case against him.'

'You ran for the fucking hills when I confided in you,' she said. 'I was damaged goods to you.'

'It wasn't like that. I was a mess. I was no good for anybody back then.'

'Too bloody right, you weren't.'

Liz went to the mirror over the mantelpiece. She hid her reflection from him.

'Harry had his faults, but what you're accusing him of . . . He was nothing like my father. He loved his daughter.'

'Do you?' Leo asked, the question emerging before he had time to reconsider it.

Where precisely this line of enquiry was going escaped him for the moment. Sometimes you went in blind and hoped that something came to hand. If only to help you keep your balance in the storm.

'Only a man without children could ask a question like that,' she said. 'She doesn't make it easy for us. Everything we do for her she throws back in our faces. Treats us like dirt, she does.'

'In what way does she treat you like dirt?'

'Just . . . generally,' she said, and it was a drawing back. 'It's how teenagers are, I suppose.'

A rebel in a crime family, Leo thought. Rebelling against what precisely? Against the life of crime itself? Against living on the wages of her father's sins? Or against something more sinister still? He needed to know more about the girl. He reached down and picked up his eye-patch from among the lilies of the floor carpet. As he rose, he stuffed it in his pocket. A tentative relief smoothed out some of Liz Larkin's sun-baked wrinkles, but not for long.

'Can you show me Whitney's room?'

'There's nothing to see in there,' she said and, to Leo, it almost sounded like a confession, like she was admitting to having cleared the room of any evidence. Liz came to the same conclusion. 'Oh, for Christ's sake, follow me then.'

# 18

A soft, golden light welcomed Detective Sergeant Helen Troy back into the world before her eyelids had parted. Memory hadn't quite kicked in yet. The late sunlight and the radiator's heat were two separate realities but, for a few slow minutes, she imagined they were one. She yawned so hard the joint of her jawbone cracked, and that was the end of the beautiful illusion. She sat up with a start. A hospital bed? The door of the semi-private ward stood open as though someone had just left in a hurry. She couldn't remember how she'd got there but her head ached. Somewhere in the muffled distance, her work mobile was ringing.

No. Muffled but not distant. As she reached down to the locker by the bed, she felt a cool breeze along her spine, her bottom and on the backs of her legs. She was wearing a backless hospital gown. She pulled the covers about her and reached further down but the phone had stopped ringing.

The scene in Jinky's pub in Chapelizod recalled itself, though not quite in its details. The scream of the motorbike's engine; the blow to the back of her head; Kevin Larkin's grieving face above her – the last thing she remembered.

She eased herself out of the bed, knelt on the floor and

emptied the bedside locker of her possessions. The phone rang again. She found it in the pocket of her zip-up. The Technical Bureau.

'John. What's the story?'

Her voice echoed back to her, distended and deeply unsettling. She told herself it was nothing but the vagaries of technology, the strange loops of feedback.

'I'm out in Wilkinstown,' John said, 'near the Meath/Monaghan border. Bogland mostly. We've got a corpse in a white Ford Transit van. Shot in the back of the head, execution-style.'

'There's a connection with the Harry Larkin case?'

'No. The kid on the motorbike. David Goode.'

Beyond the ward door a bulky nurse strode by, reversed and looked in. Helen's eyes were just above the parapet of the bed. The nurse was about Helen's age but sounded matronly.

'Get back into bed this minute,' she told the young detective. 'And put away that phone. They're not allowed in here.'

Helen pressed the phone into her chest and gestured the nurse away.

'This is important police business, right? It won't wait.'

The nurse wasn't having any of it. She stepped into the ward but didn't make it very far. Helen was on her feet and, when the sway in her brain steadied itself, barked, 'Get out of here. Now.'

'You can't speak to me like that.'

'I just did. Out.' While the nurse fled, Helen lifted the phone to her ear. 'Tell me more, John. What's the connection with David Goode?'

In the hospital gown, her rear end froze but the rest of her heated up with anticipation. She fished around for her underwear as John spoke.

'I'd just finished examining the kid's motorbike when this call-out to Wilkinstown came,' he said. 'Bottom line is, I found evidence of a minor collision on the van. Then I realized the paint markings on the van matched the colour of the motorbike and vice versa.'

'Vice versa?'

'There were traces of white paint on the bike. This is a preliminary conjecture, of course. The paints will have to be analysed. But I think we're looking at a match here.'

'And the victim, was he shot with a Glock 17?'

'Looks like it,' John said. 'The guy in the van had a gun too. We found it beside the body.'

'Not another Glock?'

'No, an FN Five Seven. Made in Belgium. A semi-automatic delayed blowback pistol. Don't know much about them but I'll do some checking for you. It's a serious weapon though.'

Helen stood there with her back to the window, her underwear in her hand. She'd forgotten the cold, or her brain was too preoccupied to register it.

'Any ID on the victim yet?'

'Not yet. The exit wounds are – well, extensive would be an understatement. Twenty-five to forty age range, I'm guessing. Height and build I can't judge yet because of the body position. Well-dressed. Olive-skinned. Possibly North African origin though he could be French, southern European, American even.'

Helen's heart missed a beat, almost missed a second.

'Or Armenian?'

'I really don't know. There's not an awful lot of his face left.'

'Thanks, John, I appreciate the call.'

At the ward door, three nurses and a middle-aged doctor

had appeared. Oddly, they weren't looking at Helen but beyond her. She turned and looked out the window. A ground-floor window. With three workmen smoking and enjoying the view to the rear of her hospital gown. Exposed, she thought of the child Whitney, the girl who grew up to despise having her photograph taken. She hated this sense of sexual threat that had lingered in her since she'd first seen the shot of Whitney. It smacked of weak-mindedness and of a helplessness she refused to submit to. She fished her ID out from among her clothes and turned to the workmen. She got the window open and flashed her card.

'You've just been ogling the tail-end of a detective sergeant,' she shouted. 'Next time you see me, it'll be in court, you arseholes.'

The men scattered, leaving three smoking cigarettes on the ground in their wake. Then, amid the protests of the nurses and doctor, Helen began stiffly to dress herself.

'You really should not leave,' the Indian doctor said, his intonation mild and musical.

'I'm grand,' she insisted, and just then noticed the plastic-wrapped bunch of lilies on her bedside table. There was a card but it had been left blank. Some mistake surely. She left them there. She hated lilies anyway, hated how they masked the scent of death by exaggerating the ugly sweetness in the scent of decay.

In the corridor outside the ward, Helen readied her phone for action. She stopped, looked back at the doctor who'd returned to checking someone's file at the ward station. She remembered the foreign intern who'd appeared again and again at the door of the ICU waiting room the day before. North African? Very possibly, she thought.

'What about the flowers?' the heavy-set nurse called

sourly after her. 'We're not here to provide a disposal service, you know.'

'They can't be mine.'

'Yes, they are. Special delivery half an hour ago. For Helen Troy.'

'No one sends me flowers any more,' Helen said, too busy to stay surprised for too long.

In the girl's room, adolescent pessimism prevailed. Walls painted black, the ceiling too, though it had been decorated with a thousand minuscule stars. A couple of teenage vampires pouted toothily on the wall. Below them were hundreds of CDs, neatly shelved, along with a dozen or so books. The band names left him cold. The Cure, The Cult, My Chemical Romance. The books bore titles short, sharp and spare as penknives. *Cut. Impulse. Burned.* One visual image repeated itself among the CDs and books. A pale crescent moon face, androgynous and curtained with stylized black hair. A mask of sorts for those who had much less to hide than they darkly imagined.

The contents of the wardrobe were black too with an occasional glimmer of pink. On the desk by the window, a redundant wireless mouse sat on a pad. Leo checked the drawers below. They were too neat. He knew they'd been tidied up, emptied of any clues to Whitney's heart and mind or her whereabouts. Nothing was out of place, and that was a problem. Incongruities offered the best clues. Here, there were none. On all fours, he looked under her bed. Not a crumb, not a dust ball, not a spidery thread.

Leo stood up. The room told him nothing he didn't already know and that wasn't much. He looked at the ceiling, switched off the light. The luminescent stars lit up a little too greenly at first but then surprised him with the infinite perspective of a real night sky. Hand-painted, he decided, and subtly done. The primal wonder of starlight filled his heart briefly. Oddly, the lettering on some of the CD spines lit up too. He plucked one from its shelf and a cascade of CDs followed, falling around his feet. A couple of plastic cases crackled under his feet as he stepped across to the light switch.

The expected shout from below didn't come. He switched the light back on and began to pick up the pieces. As he tried to put the splintered cover back on one of the cases, he paused. On the floor to his right lay a CD with Arabic lettering on its front above a pencil sketch of a short-bearded singer who was clearly no goth. Leo picked up the CD. On the back, all of the lettering was in Arabic too. Apart from the last tiny line: 'Produced in Libya'. Among the other CDs, he found nothing remotely similar. The incongruity triggered a tenuous connection. Eveleen Morgan's mysterious Libyan intern. A coincidence maybe but one worth pursuing when there was little else to pursue.

His work mobile rang but aware that he was being watched, he let it ring out. Liz Larkin stood above him. On one knee, Leo held up the CD and asked, 'This isn't her usual taste, is it? "Produced in Libya"?'

'I don't know. How the hell would I know?'

'You're her mother.'

'Which is why I don't know.'

'She has a Libyan friend maybe?'

'No way,' she said a little too quickly. 'Will you please leave me alone.'

'I'm sorry, Liz. But these questions have to be asked.'

'Stop calling me Liz,' she cried, and she was briefly her less self-possessed younger self again. 'My name is Elizabeth. Mrs Larkin to you.'

'Why did you stay with Harry all these years?'

He knew he didn't have the right to ask but sensed that he had to understand the nature of Liz and Harry's relationship if he was to get to the bottom of this case.

'He gave me everything,' she said. 'This house, a place in Lanzarote, everything I wanted. There was nothing he wouldn't do for me. Or for Whitney.'

Unconvinced, Leo stood up, stared at her. Another unwelcome theory surfaced in him.

'If you're involved in Harry's shooting, tell me now. Please,' he begged. 'I know what he was like. I know you had every reason to—'

'You knew him thirty years ago. People change. Some of us do anyway.'

Leo regretted the hurt and dismay he'd wrought in her pinched expression. He desisted but Liz didn't.

'You want to make a monster of him but you're the monster here. Thirty years and you're still the same unfeeling bastard. Now, get out of my house.'

When he made it to his feet, his work phone rang again. He was talking to Helen before he reached the front door. She didn't have time for the niceties of his concern. She gave him a corpse, possibly North African. He gave her the Libyan CD and the mysterious intern. Then she gave him the possible paint matches on David Goode's bike and the dead man's van.

'So, either we're looking at a bunch of odd coincidences here or the killings of David Goode and this guy in the van might somehow be connected to the attack on Harry Larkin,' Leo said.

'Which means we need to look at this new crime scene out in Wilkinstown. I can head out there right now.'

'What? No way, Helen. You've been concussed and—'

'I got the all clear. I'm perfectly fine.'

'We've got to get clearance from Navan station before we invade their territory anyway and that might take—'

'So I'll come back into Pettycannon first and we'll take it from there.'

'Jesus, Helen, my bare arse will be up on the dartboard if anything happens to you.'

'I'll confiscate the darts,' she laughed. 'One last thing, Leo. Someone sent me a bunch of lilies in the hospital. Who the hell knew I was there besides—'

'I asked Ben if you'd prefer flowers or a bottle of . . .'

'Leo . . .'

Whatever it was she had to say was drowned in what sounded embarrassingly like a sniffle.

'Thank you so much, Leo.'

'For nothing at all,' Leo said. Literally, he thought.

Still, it felt good to get something right for a change. Even if it was by accident. Fair dues to you, Ben, he thought. Have to thank the young detective when he got to Pettycannon.

As he rang Martin Buck, he wondered if Ben had made any progress in the interview with Gary Larkin. Probably not. He'd have rung or at least texted if he'd come up with something. When the country and western detective eventually answered his phone, Leo issued the same summons to Pettycannon.

Walking back to find the car, Leo picked up his pace as he went by a three-storey Georgian house whose grey dash was a yellow excrescence in the street light. Blocked cellar windows below the spiked rails completed the forbidding picture. Up behind, Leo knew, was a small church and graveyard. That old Gothic novel *The House by the Churchyard* had been written here. Le Fanu himself might still be *in situ*, such was the chilling aura the house exuded.

*Sleeping Dogs*

Chilling too was the memory of the book's premise. The burial of a murder victim throws up the skeleton of a more ancient killing. And if any family had skeletons in the cupboard, it was the Larkins.

# 19

The music was synthetic. The production values poor. Vaguely oriental string sweeps, a tinkly keyboard, a heavily persistent gut-resounding beat. The voice was the best part, hovering between song and speech – punched, throaty Arabic delivered with passion. Helen couldn't tell if the bearded man sang of love or misogyny, social disparity or the gold-tap pleasures of fame.

She watched the work mobile Leo had placed on the table, willing it to ring. They still awaited clearance to head for the Wilkinstown crime scene. Her own work mobile refused to ring too. She'd asked Martha Corrigan to send a car to Sandymount and check if Baz MacDonald was at his apartment. Whatever incomings she got were on her personal phone – three irritating texts from Ricky.

The others in the Incident Room were equally un-impressed by the music. Leo pressed a finger to one ear. Martin Buck held his head between the vice-grips of his hand and popped some effervescent tablets into a glass of water. Ben winced, shook his head damningly but, as usual, took copious notes. It wasn't Easy Listening time in Pettycannon Garda Station.

The disc itself and the insert had offered little by way

of explanation. The music had been burned to a generic and unlabelled blank disc. The cover art and liner notes they examined were photocopies, the originals dispatched with the CD jewel case to Forensics. The script remained indecipherable to them: the Arabic interpreter Ben had rung and texted hadn't yet returned his call.

The first track ended. Leo pressed the stop button.

'Thank Christ for that,' Buck said, still clearly smarting from Leo's insult to his competence earlier in the day. 'Why are we listening to this irrelevant shit anyway?'

'It's a loose thread, Martin, and that's what we do. Pick at loose threads no matter how small.' Leo turned to Helen. 'Any thoughts on the music?'

'Well, it's hip-hop. Certainly wasn't done in a big studio and might even be a garage job.'

'It was made in a garage? How would you know?'

'As in it's probably home-made,' Ben told Leo and, to Helen's surprise, went into fine technical detail. 'Judging from the poor mixing, the uncomplicated drumbeat, the timbre and the time envelope on the instrumentation, it was probably done with a pretty basic music software package. The sound quality is poor too, certainly not lossless or anything like it.'

Leo looked at the two young detectives. It was bad enough not understanding Arabic but this new techno-English left him feeling utterly obsolescent.

'So, technicalities aside,' he said, 'I think we can safely assume that this CD wasn't bought in any shop, right? So someone may have given it to her. An acquaintance. A friend. Maybe even a boyfriend. Possibly someone of Libyan extraction.'

'At the ICU waiting room, Gary launched into a totally xenophobic attack on this foreign intern who kept showing up,' Helen added. 'So, he wouldn't be well disposed to Whitney's having a Libyan pal.'

'True. And, by the way, I'm told this intern guy wasn't actually on duty last Sunday which is curious to say the least.'

Leo stood up and went to the whiteboard. At its centre, the two photos of Whitney. Alongside, the bubble chart of the Larkin family line had been filled out a little more. A photo of Gary, not a recent one, with some details below it. Three convictions. Not quite the *once ever* that Liz claimed. Two cautions for possession of small amounts of illegal cigarettes at some outdoor markets in Dublin, 1998 and 1999. Three months in juvenile for assault in 2001.

He drew two outlying bubbles to the right of the Larkin one, labelled them. *Body in van – North African – Libyan?* Further right, another bubble. *David Goode.* He drew a line from one bubble to the other. Then he drew a broken line from the Libyan bubble to Whitney Larkin. Along its rails he wrote *Libyan hip-hop CD?* Between the new bubbles he placed another. *Foreign intern.* Only yesterday he'd baulked at the prospect of yet another seedy little domestic. And a domestic it might well yet prove to be, but not a simple one and not one confined entirely to some suburban village on an off-shore island in the cold Atlantic.

'OK then, let's say Gary's outburst at ICU is connected to his having seen some foreign guy with Whitney. If that's so, then surely others must have seen them together too. I mean, a goth kid with a North African – it's not exactly a common sight around Dublin, is it?'

'Can someone tell me what the hell any of this has to do with the Harry Larkin shooting?' Buck interrupted, his fingers pressed to his temples.

'Anything that leads us to Whitney Larkin matters,' Leo

said. 'We find Whitney or explain her absence, we get closer to why Harry was shot. I'm sure of it.'

Leo's infected eye hurt. He'd dolloped on the ointment earlier. If it was having any effect, it was a case of things getting worse before they got better. The story of his life, he thought. Except that things never really got that much better. He dug out the eye-patch from his pocket and put it back on.

'I take it we haven't tracked Whitney's phone yet, Ben?' he said.

'It's not showing up on the system. Which means the GPS has been disabled or the battery's run out or been removed. Tracking the phone's history will take a little longer and—'

'And it'll get us nowhere.' Buck again. 'Like I already said, the kid's probably got a disposable phone. She's a Larkin, right? She's learned the tricks of the trade.'

'It's looking that way,' Leo agreed. 'OK, Helen. We put the word out to all stations on Whitney and a possible Libyan boyfriend.'

'But we're assuming this friend is male,' Helen said. 'It could be a girl or a young woman.'

'Good point. Let's keep that in mind then. In any case this Libyan friend, if it's a he, is unlikely to have been this mysterious intern, Mahmoud Maguin. Somehow, I don't see him swapping CDs with Whitney.'

The others agreed. Then Ben Murphy changed his mind.

'It's a long shot,' he said, 'but maybe Whitney's been in that hospital for treatment recently?'

Martin Buck placed his mobile on the table and studied the young detective sceptically. A nasal chuckle or two later, he spoke as though he was explaining the facts of life to a child.

'First off, there's the age gap. She's seventeen, these

interns are generally mid to late twenties; the foreign guys tend to be even older. Second, there's . . . let's call it the socio-economic gap. Basically, can you see a hospital intern hanging out with a skanger from a dodgy crime family? And Whitney's not exactly Miss World material, is she?'

At first, Leo wondered if the rhinestone detective knew of that long-ago liaison with Liz and was taking a dig at him. Buck's attention, however, remained fixed on Ben. Maybe it was a simple case of locking horns with a rival for the doe's attention.

'We'll check the hospital records for anything on Whitney,' Leo said. 'I'll take that. I need to head over there and check out this intern anyway.'

'And meanwhile, this fake Armenian's out there planning his next hit for all we know,' Buck protested. 'He's our man. We pull him in and sit on him. Full stop.'

'We've nothing to pull him in on, Martin,' Leo said. 'Listen, we're just testing the waters here. See what floats, see what sinks.' He turned to Helen. 'So, the white van out at the Wilkinstown crime scene. What do we have on it?'

'Stolen early last week near the city centre. Smithfield. And that's about it. The Technical Bureau are dusting for prints and last I heard the pathologist hadn't arrived yet.'

A silence fell on them. Maybe Buck was right. Maybe they were letting themselves be sidetracked. Maybe this stuff was all noise and no signal. But the constant hiss in Leo's head went on unabated, dissipating his concentration into rivulets of alternative scenarios.

'Same van knocks Goode from his bike on Saturday night, Sunday morning,' he speculated aloud. 'And now possibly contains the body of Whitney's Libyan friend. Therefore we have to consider the possibility that the Larkins and maybe Gary in particular were involved in both incidents.'

'We don't have a time of death on the body in Wilkinstown yet,' Helen said. 'Gary might already have been in custody when it happened.'

'But his friend Derek McCarthy is still out there,' Ben said. 'Gary says he doesn't know where he is. We're trying to track him down but no joy so far.'

'What did Gary have to say about his sister?' Leo asked.

'He says she's not missing, that she often leaves for days at a time. Never saw the photo before either, he claims.'

'So, basically, all of the Larkins are singing from the same hymn sheet on this?'

'That's how it looks. An agreed party line and everyone toes it.'

'I know Whitney left school a year ago,' Helen said, 'but we might get something from her classmates and maybe her teachers. We've a couple of local officers on that but we haven't heard back from them yet.'

'Check that out, Martin,' Leo said. 'Put the skids under them.'

Buck threw him a glowering look.

'What's Gary's story for last Saturday night and Sunday morning, Ben?'

'He says that he and his mates were heading over to Glasgow early Sunday morning to a game. First they went drinking in town until midnight with their various girlfriends. He doesn't have any, by the way. Not at the moment, he says. So then they bought a slab at an offie and played poker at his place, the apartment in Chapelizod, until they left for the airport. All of which, of course, his friends will verify.'

'So, he was at the airport when he heard about Harry?'

'Yeah. They were to catch a nine o'clock flight and got to the airport, he claims, at half past six or so. Then he gets a call from Jimmy at seven, half seven. The others, apart from Derek McCarthy, take the flight. Gary doesn't show up at the hospital until after twelve. Which leaves a gap of four and a half to five hours. He says he had to wait half an hour for a taxi which, in his own words, was driven by "a fucking black pygmy" who got lost and took almost an hour to get to Chapelizod. Which means he's still left with three hours to account for.'

'And what's his explanation?'

'Grief basically. He couldn't bring himself to go to the hospital. I don't believe him.'

Leo's mobile rang. It was Navan station. They were OK with NBCI taking a look at the crime scene. Outside, the light had begun to fade. The clear sky already had a moon and a couple of stars in it. A perfect night for viewing a corpse in a County Meath bog. If you were into that kind of thing. Leo decided he wasn't. He left that kind of thing to poets and junior officers.

'Right then,' he said. 'We'll have to take a look at the scene out in Wilkinstown. Can you do that, Ben?'

The young detective glanced down at his phone. Checking the time, Leo supposed.

'I'll take it,' Helen said.

'Jesus, Helen,' Leo remonstrated, 'you're not even supposed to be at work. You know the score with concussion.'

'If the body turns out to be this intern's, I'm the only one who's actually seen him.'

'I'll go with you,' Buck said, almost lurching forward as he spoke. 'Wouldn't want you out in the bog all on your own.'

Leo was undone by Helen's mask of desperation. And by Buck's mask of pernicious lechery.

'OK, you and Ben head out to Wilkinstown. And keep me updated.'

'Thanks, Leo,' she said, and in her overly grateful expression Leo could see that she was thanking him for the flowers again too.

He'd have to come clean on that, Leo thought. That and a lot of other stuff maybe.

'And, Martin, get an alert out to the ferry ports and airports,' he told his disgruntled contemporary. 'Apparently Whitney's taken her passport with her though I somehow doubt she's gone abroad. See if she's shown up on their radar and ask them to watch out for her, OK?'

'So your little protégés get to scope the crime scene and I get to chase shadows?'

'Who better to chase shadows,' Leo said, unable to resist the one-liner. 'Than a man without substance.'

Buck didn't appreciate the joke.

# 20

They passed through shuttered night-towns and sleeping villages. Drove by isolated houses, darkened cottages, floodlit haciendas. Here and there, across the dead of night on the flatlands, their headlights momentarily caught the flashing eyes of cats and other creatures of the shade. At the wheel, Ben Murphy stared straight ahead. Silent, reflective. He leaned forward, towards the steering wheel, wiped away a patch of condensation.

'Those lights up right,' he said. 'That's got to be it.'

The usual mix of trepidation and anticipation shivered along Helen's spine. The CSI tent came into view, a few hundred yards from the main road. Fright jumped in with the ringing of her mobile. Not the work mobile. Ben glanced across at her. He knew it wasn't the work mobile. She checked. Ricky. She hadn't answered his earlier messages. Maybe her brother was in trouble again. Maybe there was a problem with the house sale. She took the call.

'Yeah?'

'Hey, love, it's Ricky. How's it going?'

'Leave out the four-letter words, would you?' she said.

Beside her, Ben gestured with a left turn of both hands and mouthed *Will I pull in?* Helen shook her head, frowned.

'What's the problem?'

'There's no problem, I've got something to tell you.'

'About Jamie?' she said, keeping her voice even.

'It's about me, Helen.'

'Always is.'

The CSI tent was clearly visible now. Two TV crews had already set up camp at the turn-off. A tired-looking female reporter sorted her hair, worked up a concerned expression for the camera. The tick-tock of the indicator ratcheted up the tension in Helen.

'I've moved to Dublin, Helen,' Ricky said. 'It's better for the band, like.'

'Both of you?'

'No.' Ricky paused. 'Jamie left the band.' Another pause. 'Things have got kind of complicated down there.'

'Hold on a second,' she said.

In a laneway jam-packed with cars, hooded and masked figures, ghostly white, mingled with uniformed and plain-clothes officers. Ben parked behind the last car and unbuckled his seat belt. She gestured at him to go. He got out and went round to the boot. Helen took advantage of her privacy.

'Listen, Ricky, I don't give a shit whether you're in Dublin or New Delhi, I don't want to know. What's this complication then? The house? There's a problem about selling the house?'

'Sort of . . . Jeez, Helen, you need to ask him about all that shit.'

'Tell me, Ricky, or get off the frigging phone.'

His delay in answering infuriated her, and when it came it wasn't an answer anyway.

'Could we maybe meet up for a—'

'Ring me back when you've decided to tell me the truth for once in your life.'

Helen cut the call and checked the new message that came in on her work phone as she got out of the car. Martha Corrigan. *The car heading to MacDonald's apartment got sidetracked to an assault in Leeson St. Will get back to you. Martha.* Bloody hell, Helen thought, didn't they know the difference between a street-fight and an execution? She went to the back of the car where Ben was suiting up in the NBCI blue gear. Her scalp tightened. Why the hell do I put myself through this? she asked herself as she imagined what lay in store for them in the CSI tent. In the cavernous dark beyond the crime scene, the lights from the nearest houses were so minuscule and distant they might have been stars at the far end of the sky.

'Pass me the blues,' she said.

Detective Inspector Leo Woods and Senior Nurse Eveleen Morgan walked down the aisle. There were two witnesses. An old man in a dressing gown and a young woman in tears. Confetti wasn't allowed inside chapels these days. The couple didn't hold hands but their expressions spoke of the pleasure they already took in one another's company.

Leo wasn't dreaming. Eveleen had explained that the hospital's chapel was a short-cut from ICU to the Security Control Room. As they left the hallowed precincts, she told him of the real Mahmoud Maguin. He hadn't yet told her of the body in the van.

'He definitely wasn't on duty for the last few days,' she explained. 'Apparently he's big into hill-walking and is gone down south somewhere. Kerry they think but they're not sure. And he's not due back on duty until Friday.'

'Has anyone tried to contact him from the hospital?'

'One of the secretaries in Immunology has but got no answer. But actually that isn't so unusual, Leo. These guys work horrific hours and sometimes, well, they see a call from the hospital when they've got time off and they ignore it for as long as they can. It's hard to blame them.'

Leo held yet another door open for Eveleen. He kept her to his right, his better side.

'How long has it been since the first call to him?'

'Early afternoon. So, eight hours or so.'

'An unusually long time for him not to have responded?'

'For this guy, yes,' Eveleen said as they neared the Security Control Room. 'They tell me Mahmoud's a very conscientious type. And he's certainly not out getting tanked up in some Kerry shebeen. He doesn't drink and keeps very much to himself. We can get his ID up on the system.' This time it was she who held the door open. 'Here we are.'

The grey-skinned man gazing up at the array of monitors wore a uniform that had begun to outgrow him. He raised a hand but didn't turn from the screens. He looked like a man who wouldn't know what to do with himself when he no longer had all these lives to snoop on. The room smelled of coffee and solitude. Not unlike Leo's house in Serpentine Crescent.

'Ev,' the man said, a decibel above a throaty whisper as though not to alert the people on the CCTV screens to his presence.

'Gus. This is Detective Inspector Leo Woods. Leo, this is Gus Ewart.'

When the man turned briefly and nodded, Leo saw the circular plastic valve on his Adam's apple. He felt that unfair but instinctive revulsion he so often discerned in others.

'Can you give me a screen, Gus?' Eveleen asked. 'I need to get Mahmoud Maguin's ID up before we look at the CCTV images.'

'No problem, Ev.' The wheeze of the security man's plastic voice-box terrified Leo. Gus pointed to the central screen in the bottom row of five. Slid his swivel chair sideways so she could work the keypad. She typed in a password. Then she typed in a name. Mahmoud Maguin. The young doctor's image appeared on the screen. A broad face, deeply pockmarked. Forehead, thick and furrowed, lending his expression a serious, preoccupied look. Black hair combed slickly back, heavy-framed glasses. It was hard to tell for sure but he seemed slight and oddly hunched. Eveleen applied some zoom to the personal details and Leo learned that the twenty-six-year-old Maguin was five-five in height and weighed in at one-forty pounds. Under the heading 'Medical Conditions' he learned more.

'Scheuermann's Kyphosis?' he asked of Eveleen.

'An orthopaedic condition. Curvature of the upper back, basically.'

'And this would be immediately apparent, would it?'

'Not necessarily,' Eveleen replied. 'He's young. It'll become more pronounced as he ages.'

If he ages, Leo thought.

Helen and Ben stepped in under the glare of the arc lights. A night shoot, Helen thought. She spotted John, the diminutive Technical Bureau operative, over at the blue Crime Scene tent. The murmur of voices exaggerated further the bleak remoteness of the place. She was glad to hear John's matter-of-fact call. It was as if some normality had been restored to the night.

'Line up here for the viewing, ladies and gentlemen,' he said, and held up the flap of the blue tent with one hand. In the other was a bagged item.

'What have you got for us, John?' Helen asked when they reached him. 'What's in the bag?'

'Another bag. Empty, I'm afraid.'

He raised it towards them. A green canvas shoulder bag, the kind you might carry textbooks in. Medical textbooks? Or some thick wads of ransom money?

'Not an awful lot more to report as yet,' the operative told her. 'One shot, it seems. Victim fell, head down, from the passenger seat and, well, he's sort of jammed beneath the steering wheel. We can't complete until the pathologist gets here. So, no TOD yet but certainly late last night or early morning.'

Helen stepped inside the tent. Here the arc light was more intense and it burned her eyes. In that first instant, the windscreen of the small white Ford van appeared to her to be splattered with a black treacly substance. Then she saw it was congealed blood staining the inside of the windscreen. Ben walked by her and went to the passenger door which, like all the others, was opened out. He looked in and looked away, took a hard swallow and looked again. Helen followed him. She went through the same routine. Her stomach settled but it was a compromise. It wasn't promising not to throw up later.

The body lay crossways and downwards in a semi-foetal position. In the mess that was the head, propped against the gear stick, an exploded side-face had been shorn of all features. The man's bulk was exaggerated by the heavy overcoat he wore. Beneath the coat was the kind of expensive suit Baz MacDonald wore, though not the one Helen had seen him wear. Could a hospital intern afford such luxuries? Helen asked herself. Maybe, if he came from a well-off family as many foreign interns must do. The FN

Five Seven pistol lay in the well below the passenger seat. No empty cartridges were to be seen. Unlike the attack on Harry Larkin, this was precise, dispassionate. And, therefore, a different shooter?

'Do you reckon it's MacDonald?' Ben asked.

'I can't tell for sure,' Helen said and checked her work mobile again. Nothing from MacDonald's apartment in Sandymount. 'The clothes fit the picture but he doesn't seem tall enough and he looks heavier. Or maybe that's just the coat.'

'Or the bullet-proof vest?' John chimed in from behind them.

# 21

Leo watched the intern walk backwards through his life. No great trick in that, he thought. Insomniacs did it every night of the week. The young man kept his head down most of the time as he hung around the lobby area between reverse trips to ICU. More stockily built than Leo had expected from the ID photo, he seemed below average height. Then again, the CCTV view from above tended to foreshorten every passing figure. The collage of clips that Gus Ewart had put together of the man's movements wound its way back towards the sliding doors of the entrance. Not once in his three visits to ICU with that folder under his arm had Mahmoud Maguin reversed to the Immunology Department.

'You haven't told me what this is about, Leo,' Eveleen said. 'Do you think something bad has happened to Mahmoud?'

'We've got a body in a van out the country and I'm afraid the face is . . . well, not recognizable. We suspect it might be Mahmoud.'

She put a hand to her mouth and turned to the screen bearing the young intern's image, seeing it in a darker light.

'You want me to keep it going back?' Gus asked.

Behind them a photocopier started up, buzzed and whirred, delivered the photo of Mahmoud Maguin.

'Yeah, thanks,' Leo said.

The young man reversed out by the sliding doors and back towards the carpark. Along the way he passed by what looked like a bandstand where three or four people sat. Leo caught a quick glimpse of the West Belfast Armenian and the dark-haired woman, David Goode's mother there.

'Can you go back to the bandstand?' he asked.

The couple didn't appear to be speaking or making eye-contact with each other.

'OK,' Leo said. 'Let it run again.'

The thin controller obliged. Leo watched the intern back-pedal into the carpark. Something flashed a little way off but the vehicle remained hidden. The intern lowered his right arm, pocketed his keys. Leo leaned closer. The man disappeared behind a wide pillar. A text alert rang from Leo's work mobile. He searched himself, got the phone among the cigarette tips and balled tissues. But he couldn't take his eyes from the screen to read the message.

'Leo?' Eveleen said.

He didn't look back at her. On the screen, a wispy puff of exhaust fumes emerged from behind the pillar.

'Sorry, yeah? Pause it there, Gus,' he said and turned to the nurse. 'What is it, Eveleen?'

'I think I've found something that might identify Mahmoud,' she said, pointing at a screen that gave more extensive details of the young intern. Leo came to her side. 'See here under "Comments"? It reads, "Dr Maguin's orthotic brace is not considered to be an impediment to his practice or—"'

'What's an orthotic brace?'

'A kind of padded support,' Eveleen said. 'It's wrapped around the thoracic area in cases of kyphosis. Sometimes the brace covers the entire upper body.'

'And he'd be wearing it all the time?'

'Possibly. Depending on the severity of his kyphosis.'

'Do we have an address for him?'

'Oak Lodge Apartments, Castleknock,' Eveleen read aloud.

Leo watched the screen. Gus moved things back. A pair of full-on headlights reversed towards the security barrier. It wasn't a white van the intern was driving. It was a red Toyota Corolla.

'Do you recognize that as Mahmoud's usual car, Gus?'

'Yeah,' the controller said and reeled off the number from memory as he scanned the other monitors before him.

Leo watched the red car recede into the distance beyond the hospital carpark. He read Helen's message. Bullet-proof vest equals orthotic brace, he thought. It seemed like they had a match for the corpse in the van. Mahmoud Maguin wasn't just reversing into the city of Dublin. He was reversing into the Kingdom of Heaven.

'Thanks, Gus,' he said, and turned to Eveleen. 'I've a couple of phone calls to make. Won't be a . . .'

'That's OK,' she said. 'I'm coming off shift in a quarter of an hour so I'd better get back to ICU and tidy up. See you again, then. Bye, Gus.'

'Did you sort your car out, Ev?' the controller asked.

'Still in the garage. Bloody thing is an old wreck. Like myself.'

She was already on her way as she spoke. Gus raised a hand but kept on watching his screens. Leo hurried after her.

'Eveleen?' he called, his voice too loud in the quiet night-corridor. 'Can I offer you a lift?'

'That'd be good,' she said with a backward glance and a flash of those green eyes. 'Twenty minutes, at the front entrance, OK?'

Leo watched her walk the entire length of the corridor. Even as she pushed through the doors at the far end, he stood rooted to the spot. Then his right hand reminded him that it held a mobile phone. He rang Sergeant Martha Corrigan. The irony wasn't lost on him. She'd been the last woman he'd given a lift to outside of work. History, so ancient it was pre. He asked her to send a car to Mahmoud Maguin's apartment building, see what could be sussed out.

Then he rang Helen. He told her about the orthotic brace. He listened as she called out to John if the victim might be wearing a brace rather than a bullet-proof vest. The CS operative couldn't say for sure until the pathologist got there and the body could be moved.

'Was the victim wearing glasses?'

'They may be under the body,' Helen said. 'And, by the way, Baz MacDonald isn't our victim. I sent a car over to Sandymount and his blue coupé's there. Lights on in the apartment too.'

It was late. Leo could no longer think clearly and, besides, he didn't want Helen out there in Wilkinstown half the bloody night after the day she'd had.

'OK then,' he said, 'we'll wrap it up for tonight. Seems Whitney was never a patient in this hospital by the way, but I've got someone in here who'll check with the other Dublin hospitals. Unfortunately, they've all got separate systems so it may take a while. So, listen. First thing tomorrow, take Ben with you and talk to the Goodes and suss out what you can on David. I'll tackle Gary, see if I can spook him. That sound OK?'

'No problem.'

From down the phone line, Leo heard the rush and bustle of an ill-tempered wind starting up.

'Get yourself home out of that God-forsaken place, will you, before you catch your death? And, Helen? If you get a headache tonight or you're feeling sick . . .'

'Jesus, Leo, I got a wallop,' she said. Her lightness of tone was pitched a little high. 'It's not the first one I ever got and I'm sure it won't be the last. Have to go now. Ben's waiting for me.'

He put away his mobile. Eveleen was waiting for him.

'Lee Marvin.'

'Yeah, right.'

'No, really. Ever since you put on the eye-patch, I've been trying to think who you reminded me of.'

In the darkened interior of the unmarked car, Leo felt relaxed enough to chuckle at Eveleen's suggestion. The half-hour wait while she finished up had been worth it even during those first awkward moments of the journey. Things had lightened up since then. Big-time. He wished the journey was a longer one.

'Would that be the suave dark-suited version in *Point Blank*,' Leo chimed, 'or the alcoholic gunslinger in *Cat Ballou*?'

The Lee Marvin film that had first come to mind was Fritz Lang's fifties film noir *The Big Heat*. Marvin, a young punk in a square-shouldered suit, tosses boiling coffee at the face of ditzy Gloria Grahame and disfigures her. At the end, she returns the favour.

'*Point Blank*, of course.'

She laughed, and the ruined faces vanished from Leo's mind. Hers was the most natural of laughs and she put no impediments in its way. She lay back in the passenger seat, perfectly comfortable, at ease with herself. Beside her, Leo felt puckishly adolescent. She released something in him, freed him in some kind of subtle way.

'Didn't he wear an eye-patch in *The Comancheros*?' Eveleen wondered aloud.

'Or was that the John Wayne character?'

'You could be right. You know your films.'

'I'm more into European cinema really. Early Truffaut, late Fassbinder. That kind of thing.'

'Oh, excuse me,' she said. 'You're one of these subtitle snobs then, are you?'

'I don't need the subtitles actually. Not for the German and French anyway.'

The words were out before he heard the idle boast in them. That was the trouble with freedom. Some people didn't know what to do with it. Apart from screw it up.

'Not much use to me in this case I'm dealing with, unfortunately,' he continued. 'Arabic is what I need and I don't have a bull's—'

'I can read Arabic,' Eveleen said. 'Though I'm a bit out of practice.'

'Really? Maybe you might make sense of this for me.'

Leo scrabbled about in his pockets as he drove. The photocopy of the CD cover and insert came to hand only after he'd spilled a handful of balled-up tissues and cigarette tips.

'Worked over there, did you? In the Middle East or North Africa, I mean.'

At first, her silence suggested she'd judged the question intrusive. Then she leaned forward towards the windscreen, and he saw she was engrossed in the task of decipherment.

'Can I switch on the light for a sec?' she asked, then added off-handedly, 'Yeah, ten years. Saudi. Dubai. A short stint in Kuwait. This is a protest song, Leo.'

'Is it? As in Arab Spring protest?'

'Yeah, an anti-Gaddafi song. It's called something like "Fallen Palaces". As in, you know, derelict.' She scanned the script again. 'The first verse is printed here. It goes "Your palaces have fallen in on themselves", meaning the interiors have collapsed. "Your doors are barred, your windows are . . . covered, blocked up. The place you thought was safest is now your tomb."'

Leo looked out on the quiet tree-lined Haddington Road. Red-bricked houses hunkered down for another century of more or less uninterrupted peace. A world away from the mayhem prevailing in Libya these days. Leo wondered if some remnant of the conflict had washed up on the shores of Ireland. And if it had, what connection it could possibly have with David Goode or Whitney Larkin.

'This was recorded only two months ago,' Eveleen told him. 'In Benghazi. Which is the centre of the revolt against Gaddafi.'

'Did the file on Mahmoud Maguin say where his people are from? Which city, I mean.'

'Tripoli. I noticed because I was there once.'

They'd reached Bath Avenue. Her place was a few minutes away. He didn't want the night to end. Not this part of it at least, he thought, knowing that for the insomniac, nights neither began nor ended.

'Do we know who the singer is on this CD?' Leo asked.

'Let's see,' she said, and repeated a phrase complete with glottal stops that was incomprehensible to Leo. 'Barh lej lel hhurr. The free man? Not an actual name. A – what do you call it? – a stage name. The Free Man. As in a new Libya. If it ever comes to pass.'

'But Gaddafi's a goner, isn't he?'

'Probably. But I wouldn't put money on peace and freedom after he's gone.'

'A case of *après moi le déluge*?'

'I'm afraid so.'

He flicked the indicator and turned the car into Vavasour Square.

'I'm up here on the left, near the end,' Eveleen said, gathering her things.

A cul-de-sac of single-storey russet-bricked houses surrounding a small tree-lined park, the place had a self-contained and unpretentious air about it. Much like Leo's present passenger.

Former passenger. He'd pulled in. She had the door open like a woman in a hurry. Leo gazed up at the great glass-panelled ovoid that was the Aviva Stadium, its overbearing modernity not altogether spoiling the Victorian square. Halfway out, she paused.

'You haven't told me where you live exactly, Leo.'

'Far side of the stadium. Serpentine Crescent.'

'We hear the same trains in the night then, don't we?'

'Yeah,' Leo said, and his brain told him to leave it at that but his tongue didn't get the message. 'I hear all of them, every night.'

'Thanks for the lift,' she said, checking her mobile as though indicating that, unlike him, she had a private life with other people in it. 'See you, then.'

'Yeah, see you.'

Her face was perfect to behold under the pale street light. He beheld it until she was gone. And for a little while after, until his work mobile rang. The squad car out in Castleknock. Mahmoud Maguin wasn't in. The couple in a neighbouring apartment had seen him leave the complex on Sunday evening. He hadn't returned since.

*Tuesday 3 May*

# 22

After the rush-hour headache of Baggot Street and Pembroke Road, broad Wellington Road was a breath of expansive, if expensive, air. Peaceful surroundings came with a price-tag. Helen wondered how the Goodes, their art gallery gone bust, could afford to continue living among these long terraces of two-storey Edwardian houses set back grandly from the tree-scaped footpaths.

'Here we are,' Ben said and swung in by an open gate on to the gravel forecourt.

Three cars were parked there. A red Porsche and a pair of those new Volkswagen Beetles – a black and a blue – that Helen loved. From a distance. Helen couldn't afford a car, full stop. And wouldn't do for some time, she suspected, now that a question mark lay over the sale of her father's house. She'd stayed up half the night waiting for her brother Jamie to ring or at least answer her texts. He hadn't done. Her future remained paved with negative equity.

'Three new cars and a house on Wellington Road,' she said. 'Who wouldn't want to be bankrupt?'

They got out of the car and crossed over to the bank of steps leading to the front door. Down in the well of the basement entrance, two green retro bicycles complete with front baskets stood like props in a BBC period piece. At the top of the steps, however, the script changed. Hidden at the turn of the front door architrave was a panel of buzzers and nameplates, five in all. One of them was blank. The Goodes were at number three. She pressed the buzzer.

'Yes?' a voice answered.

'Mr Goode? Detective Sergeant Helen Troy here. Can we have a word?'

'Have you caught someone?'

'Not exactly. It's complicated. Can we come in, please?'

'Up the stairs, first right,' the voice said and, with a hollow click, the speaker went dead.

A wide hallway signalled the careless anonymity of shared rental property – empty, its walls not quite clean, the worn carpet ridged and bumpy, a smell of damp predominating. The steps of the stairs had the springiness of loosening timbers. From the first landing they saw the door to number three had been left slightly ajar. Before they reached it, a spectacularly tall man emerged from another apartment. Prematurely grey, he had a fixed, dumbstruck look about him. He buttoned up his shirt as they went by him.

'Anthony Goode,' he said, and held out a long-fingered and very cold hand.

Helen took it.

'Sorry, I thought . . .' she said, looking to the door of number three.

'The apartments are small so we've got two. My brother in the States owns the house. We grew up here, you know.'

Anthony Goode bore the typically abstracted expression of the bereaved. An expression that suggested the present no longer existed for him. His tone had that ever so slightly anal-retentive quality of genteel superiority. He was a thoroughbred but not an overtly arrogant one.

'This is Detective Garda Ben Murphy,' Helen said. 'We're very sorry to intrude at a time like this but I'm afraid it can't wait.'

They stepped inside apartment number three. The place was tiny. A short, dark passage had two doors to the left, one to the right. Goode brought them into a bright but cramped room that seemed to serve as a kitchen, sitting room and dining room. The generous ceiling height made more of the space than it deserved.

'Frida will be with us shortly,' he said as he tidied away some cups and plates from the coffee table. 'She's been prescribed some very heavy sedatives. So, please understand if she's not quite . . . with us.'

'Of course.'

The man's air of desperate gentility moved her. He was a large quiescent animal cruelly caged. She imagined him negotiating these small spaces, an adolescent clumsiness about him.

'Do sit,' he said, and plumped up some cushions on a leather sofa.

He picked up a bundle of magazines from the coffee table. Helen could see the man was doing all he could to avoid the purpose of their visit.

They heard the creak of a door in the apartment.

'We're in here, Frida,' he called.

The tall man tossed the magazines behind a second leather sofa at the opposite side of the coffee table. They fell with an unexpected softness. Helen noticed the protruding edges of some pillows and a sleeping bag. As he waited for his wife's entrance, Anthony Goode didn't seem to know what to do with his large hands.

Frida Goode had the fragility of a perfect miniature. Everything she was made of seemed precisely sculpted.

MARK O'SULLIVAN

Black hair drawn tightly back, coal-black eyes, pale ceramic skin, the mole an inch or so above the right edge of her upper lip. She wore a pale gold nightdress. Her ultramarine kimono-style dressing gown provided more cover than the blue raincoat had done back at the hospital. She addressed her husband but looked at the two detectives.

'Who are these people?' she asked in a sedated drawl, the pupils of her eyes rolling upwards, showing the frighted whites. Her voice was lazily honeyed and moneyed.

'Garda detectives, Frida. They have something to tell us.'

When Frida walked by her husband, the difference in their heights became absurdly apparent. Physically, she was the child to the man. In every other way it seemed that he was the child to the woman. She sat, her legs folding under her body in slow motion. He sat on the same sofa but they weren't sitting together. Frida took out a cigarette packet and lighter from her dressing gown pocket and, tremblingly, lit up.

Bothered by the cigarette smoke, Helen's mind blanked and, instead of returning to the present, arrived at that terrible moment twenty-six years before when she'd learned of her mother's death in a hit-and-run accident. She remembered the matronly face of the middle-aged Ban Garda verging on tears.

'There's been a development in your son's—' Ben began.

'You've traced the car? The driver?' Frida's impatience with her own slow voice was apparent.

'We've found the van that may have knocked your son from his motorbike,' Helen said. 'In a place called Wilkinstown in County Meath. A bogland area about an hour from the city.' She knew how important details were to a victim's family. Every last fragment. 'A Ford Transit van. White. 2007 registration. It had been stolen from the Smithfield area.'

'Have you got the driver?' Anthony asked.

'This is why we called to you in person,' Helen said. 'We have to tell you that we've found a body in the van. It may be the man who knocked down your son.'

Anthony Goode stared at the two detectives blankly. The news took its time travelling towards the processing area in his wife's brain. When it did, she uncoiled herself, sat upright. Some chemical stronger than the sedatives had temporarily rescued her from drowning. Her eyes were wide, joy in them, vengeance aflame on her cheeks. The long coil of ash on her cigarette fell into her lap. She didn't notice.

'I'm glad,' she said.

Her husband turned to her, stupefied.

'Don't pretend that you're not glad too,' she insisted. 'He killed our son and couldn't live with it.' She turned to the two detectives. 'That's the story, isn't it? Suicide.'

'I'm afraid not, Mrs Goode. He was shot,' Ben said. 'And we can't assume he was the one driving the van when your son was hit.'

The couple were silent but in different ways. Anthony stared at his great, useless hands. His wife stared at the sky outside the window, finding things there that intrigued her, made her think perhaps more clearly than she'd done since her son's death.

'You realize this killing has certain implications for our investigation,' Helen told them. 'It's unlikely to have been coincidental.'

'David's death might not have been an accident?' Anthony asked.

'Possibly,' Helen said.

At her husband's side, Frida had become lost again in her narcotic haze. Her eyes rolled back, only the whites showing briefly before her head dropped forward again and found some equilibrium. Her cigarette burned precariously close to the skin of her fingers.

'This is just one of several avenues we're exploring,' Helen assured Anthony Goode. 'But, unfortunately, we do have to look at it very closely and, so, there are questions we need to ask.'

Frida had re-emerged from her stupor. Her hand circled the ashtray until she willed it to stop and stubbed out her cigarette only to light another.

'David murdered? It isn't even remotely possible. You have no idea what he was like,' she drawled. 'Goode by name, good by nature. So many people used to say that. It was a family joke. When we actually *were* a family. Until you ruined it all.'

She glared at her husband. The accusation was clearly an old one. Helen suspected Anthony had an answer for it but wasn't going to divulge it in the presence of others. She wondered if Frida referred to their bankruptcy or to something more personal. She couldn't bring herself to delve further just yet. Instead, she began a roundabout journey towards the Libyan connection.

'Has David been in hospital at any time over the past, say, three months?'

'No,' Anthony replied, puzzled.

'Even as an out-patient, a follow-up visit? Say for an immune system problem or—'

'No, he was perfectly healthy. I don't understand what you're getting at.'

'The man we found may have been of Libyan extraction,' Helen explained, 'and may have been an intern at the

Immunology Department in the hospital where your son
. . . Does the name Mahmoud Maguin mean anything to
either of you?'

It didn't. She wasn't sure where to go next. Beside her, Ben
Murphy completed yet another page of notes and picked up
the slack.

'Do you have any Libyan friends or any business contacts with Libyan nationals?' he asked. 'Clients, your social
circle?'

'We don't have clients any more,' Frida slurred. 'And as
for a social circle, no one wants to know us.'

'We don't have any Libyan friends, no,' her husband confirmed.

Testing theories on this grief-sundered couple felt like
some cruel psychiatric experiment but Helen, aware of
how little progress she'd made with the Goodes, drew the
scalpel. She addressed Anthony but kept his wife in the
corner of her eye.

'I'm aware that you've filed for bankruptcy, Mr Goode.
And that you're likely to have left some debts unpaid. Have
you experienced any, let's say heavy-handed efforts to pay
these debts? Any aggressive debt collection agencies, for
example? Or maybe there were debts owed to you that you
tried to call in? Or hired some agency to collect?'

As she hammered away with her repetition of debts, debts,
debt collection, Helen observed Frida's lack of reaction.

'What in heaven's name does my financial situation have
to do with David's death?' the tall man asked.

Frida Goode slowly rose and began to totter away towards
the door. Her husband made to guide her. She brushed
him aside, almost catching him with the lit cigarette end.
To Helen she spoke with a slow deliberation as though
translating her thoughts from a foreign language.

'I am going to be sick but I will be back.'

'Really, there's no need—' Helen began, but Frida stayed her with a raised hand and lurched out of the room.

'These drugs, they may anaesthetize the pain but reason goes out the window, I'm afraid,' Anthony said, attempting a wry smile. He had too serious a face for wryness. 'This is not my beautiful wife, I can assure you.'

'It's perfectly understandable,' Helen said. 'I have to ask you, Mr Goode, whether you'd noticed any change in David's behaviour of late. Did he seem worried or troubled maybe? Had his habits changed, for example? Late nights, that kind of thing?'

'I can't honestly say I saw any difference in him. But even if there had been, David wouldn't have let it show. Whatever it was that happened to David, it happened because he was too good,' he insisted. 'I'm certain of that.'

The sound of Frida's empty retching reached them. Ben Murphy broke its nauseating spell.

'Did David have many friends? I mean, a particular group he might have hung around with, that kind of thing?'

'He had so many,' Anthony replied. 'He was into computers but he wasn't at all one of those geeky loners. Far from it, in fact. Everyone loved him. You'll see when we hold the memorial service. And when we bury him. Whenever that might be.'

Helen and Ben exchanged looks of puzzlement. The tall man elaborated.

'He gave his body to medical research,' the tall man explained. 'It may be some time before there's a funeral. But we'll hold a memorial. Soon. When Frida is . . . you know, up to it.'

David Goode's generosity of spirit had, it seemed to Helen, a downside. His parents' grief process would be delayed perhaps for months, their son's ghost hovering in some netherworld. A netherworld that was rapidly filling up. Harry Larkin, David Goode, the man in the van. And Whitney?

'These friends. Can you give me some names, addresses?' Helen asked.

'Why would you want to drag his friends into this?'

'You know how it is with kids, Mr Goode. Sometimes their friends know more about their lives than parents do.'

'This is true,' he conceded. 'And our present arrangements mean I know even less. You see, David and Georgia more or less occupy the other apartment. That's where their friends call and often we have no idea who's coming or going. But we've always been . . . hands-off that way.'

'Georgia is your daughter?' Ben asked.

'Yes. She's eighteen. She's devastated.'

Only now did Helen take note of the framed photograph on the mantelpiece. Taken, she guessed, three or four years back. A holiday snapshot. A happy family of four in some sunny, blue-skied place. The fragile impermanence of normality of which Helen was only too well aware. She recognized the tall girl whose mass of red hair was more pre-Raphaelite than Rasta when the shot had been taken.

'We'll need to talk to Georgia,' Ben said. 'Is she in the other apartment right now?'

'She's staying with friends, over in Ranelagh.'

'Georgia knows more than she's telling.'

Frida Goode had returned so quietly that her intervention startled all of them. She stood behind the sofa Helen and Ben sat on. Her eyes rolled back again and she swayed. They could tell that more was on its way though she was having great difficulty articulating it.

'She's hiding something. She has to be.'

Anthony Goode's patience snapped.

'Please stop this nonsense, Frida.'

His wife responded in kind: 'She *has* to be hiding something.'

'Who isn't? Who isn't hiding something?' Anthony pleaded.

It was time to move on, Helen decided. She got to her feet. Ben followed.

'We'd like to see David's room, if you don't mind,' Helen said.

'Of course,' the tall man answered.

He looked like he was glad of the excuse to hide from his wife.

# 23

It was an old trick but sometimes it still worked. Leo stood outside the door of the interview room in Pettycannon Garda Station turning the handle but not opening the door. He left off for half a minute or so and repeated the trick. He waited, twiddled it one last time, paused, then burst into the room. Gary Larkin's chair went into reverse with a screech. The brakes were applied when he saw Leo's face. The ex-child actor's expression ran the gamut of emotions from A to B. Abhorrence to bemusement. The absurdity of Gary's brush-head hairstyle almost made Leo laugh. The Least of the Mohicans, he mused.

'Jesus,' Leo said as he slammed a file on the table, 'I've seen you before. You were in that film . . . what was it called? The one about the Travellers and the horse.'

He felt a little embarrassed with his philistine pose. Then again, you didn't always get the part you were hoping for in life, in work.

'*Into the West*. Which end of the horse were you, Gary?'

'Fuck you.'

Half the night, Leo had been dogged by visions of battering the hell out of the little guy for what he'd done to Helen. The other half was spent reminding himself of the damage this might do to the investigation. In neither half of the night had the tablets kicked in. He was on a sleep-deprived high. Which, he knew, was actually some kind of upside-down low – like poor old Laika, the first dog in space who went up and never came down.

'You were a dancer too, I hear. I bet Harry came to all the gigs, did he, son?'

The young fellow struggled to find the mood of the role he'd cast himself in. Grace under pressure, stoicism, Pyrrhonian Scepticism, that kind of thing.

'He didn't think a lot of you, did he? Compared to The Armenian, like, he thought you were a complete waste of space.'

'We'll see who the waste of space is.'

'You're going head-to-head to take control of Harry's empire then, are you? Gary Larkin versus Baz MacDonald? The bookies won't even bother to call the odds on that one.'

Leo took the First Communion day photo of Whitney from the file.

'Take a look at this, Gary. Your father had it on him when he was shot. That's your shoulder there, isn't it? The one with the Glasgow Celtic jersey.'

Gary Larkin worked hard not to appear disconcerted by the photocopied shot.

'No,' he said.

'Someone's torn you out of the shot. Harry maybe?'

'It's not me. I don't know who it is.'

'But you were there.'

'Course I was there but it must be nine or ten years ago. Whenever. There was a shitload of people there.'

Leo knew what was coming next. The agreed Larkin family story. He let it run anyway to see if it had got any more threadbare.

'All wearing Glasgow Celtic jerseys?'

'Most of them, yeah. The most of them were heading over to—'

'The cup final, yeah,' Leo said. 'Which of you cooked up that story, Gary?'

'You don't need to cook up the truth.'

'Actor, dancer, philosopher. Is there any end to this man's talents?'

Leo let some silence settle over them. It wasn't real silence. Gary shifted about on the plastic chair, the brush of his denims deepening his own unease. Leo almost felt sorry for him. Felt sorrier for his mother though. Major emotional investment going down the drain there, he thought. Yet another.

'Was your Slovakian pal there?' he asked. 'The guy who ripped you lot off. Remember? When Harry had to bring in Baz to sort out the mess? Anton Bisjak, right?'

The two halves of Gary's Mohawk skull reddened. Some gristle and a couple of popping veins showed in his neck. He wanted a fight but he didn't want a fight with a big ugly man.

'No.'

'He'd already scammed Harry by then?'

'No.'

'What about Derek McCarthy?'

'We didn't know Derek back then.'

'So where's Derek now? What's he up to?'

'I don't know.'

'Sure, you know. He's out there stalking Baz MacDonald, right? Does he have a death wish or what?'

Gary tugged at the collar of his Glasgow Celtic jersey, puffed out his chicken chest.

'Derek can take care of himself. I can too.'

Leo laughed, and resentment clouded Gary's pint-sized features. He'd been laughed at before and often. And, if Leo's instincts were right, by his father. And often. It was time, Leo reckoned, for another leap in the dark.

'Tell us about Whitney's Libyan friend, Gary,' he said. 'Couldn't have been happy about that now, could you? Your sister hooking up with one of those lads.'

Caught off guard, Gary stared at his inquisitor. His twitching lips waited for a delivery from his brain. It didn't come.

'You need to cooperate with us here, son.' Leo drew out an A4 sheet from the file. 'You assaulted one of my officers yesterday, right, and resisted arrest? Here's a couple of sample verdicts on similar assaults for you to mull over. Galway District Court, eight months – and that was just a dig in the ribs. Cork Circuit Court, three years. Clonmel Circuit Court, ten years. That last sentence was for an assault on a female officer, by the way.'

'I didn't know she was a bleedin' Guard,' Gary said. 'I didn't even know she was a she. That short hair and all. I thought someone was attacking Kevin and I jumped in to defend him. Like any brother would.'

Leo leaned closer to him. Gary couldn't come to terms with the one-eyed man whose collapsed side-face spoke to him of emotionless aggression.

'Right, you and your brother are dead close, aren't you?'

'We're Larkins. We look out for each other.'

The claim was half-hearted. Leo moved closer still to the young man.

'You weren't looking out for him. You were warning him not to talk. Not to talk about what, Gary? Whoever it was shot your old man arrived on a motorbike. And Kevin says it was your bike that went up in flames in Chapelizod. Very

194

helpful your brother was. Couldn't stop him talking, my officers tell me.'

'He can't talk.'

Leo shot a hand out to the back of Gary's neck and drew him close.

'We have a rule in here, son. I tell the jokes. Now tell me about this Libyan guy before I use your arse for kicking practice.'

'We never laid a finger on that fucking Arab,' Gary said. 'We warned him off. Full stop.'

At the door of the second apartment in the Wellington Road house, Anthony Goode paused, raised a knuckle as though to knock. He seemed to have forgotten that no one was inside. He opened the door, stood back and let the two detectives through. Removal boxes of varying sizes crowded the corridor. Through an open door, Helen saw a room solely given over to storage. Anthony reached above her head and pushed in the next door.

'David's room,' he said, struggling against the tremor in his voice.

To the left of the door stood a sofa bed. The bedclothes and pillows had been folded neatly away at one end. A low table contained two laptops, a printer and a neat stack of A4 pages. Left and right of the one long window, deep floor-to-ceiling shelving was curtained off neatly. With a glance, Ben brought Helen's attention to the wall right of the door. It held narrower shelves of books, CDs and DVDs. A Libyan hip-hop CD among them, perhaps? Ben began to scan the shelves.

'These laptops, Mr Goode,' Helen asked. 'Do you know if we can get into them? Passwords, I mean.'

Her neck hurt whenever she looked up at him, the pain of yesterday's blow stirring itself again.

'They're not David's. He had a silver Mac. I'm told it may have been stolen from the scene.' The tall man shook his head. 'These ones here he'd been fixing up for a Third World charity. He had his own laptop with him when . . . carried it in a canvas shoulder bag. That's missing too. Along with his iPhone.'

Helen and Ben shared a surprised glance. The guy in the white van had taken the laptop and then what? Had it taken from him? Why? In any case, it was hardly the act of a killer bent merely on revenge for a young boy's death.

'Do you have any idea why he'd have taken his laptop with him? Isn't that a bit odd considering the incident took place at three o'clock in the morning?'

Anthony Goode mussed his grey hair, looked about his son's room as though seeking there an answer to the petite detective's question. He shook his head. Beyond him, Ben Murphy appeared to have been frustrated in his search through the CDs. He turned his attention to the lower shelf of DVDs.

'David may have been visiting one of his elderly clients,' Anthony said. 'Not *clients* exactly, of course. He taught them how to use computers on a voluntary basis. He'd set up internet, email, Skype. That kind of thing. Make it simple for them.'

'But so late at night?'

'It probably sounds desperately irresponsible of me but I've no idea what time he left the house.' The tall man sat on the window sill. He blinded himself for a moment or two with a thumb and forefinger. 'He might have called on one of these elderly people earlier and then gone . . . I don't know, to meet some friends or . . .'

'What about your wife? Might she know what time David went out?'

Anthony shook his head.

'Or your daughter?'

'Georgia wasn't here. She's been staying at a friend's house for the past week or so. In Ranelagh, as I said. Marlborough Road.'

'But she was with you when you got to the hospital, wasn't she?'

'I picked her up in a taxi in the city centre. She'd been out with this friend.'

'Why was Georgia staying with her friend?'

'Oh, the usual,' he said. 'A difference of opinion with her mother. They're a temperamental pair. To say the least. Mothers and daughters tend to be like that, don't they?'

'And this difference of opinion, what was it about?'

'The evils of materialism more than likely,' he replied. 'Georgia thinks my wife is a dupe of the consumer society. I've always been bemused by how different they are from each other.'

Anthony shrugged, raised the palms of his hands. There had been so many clashes between his wife and daughter, his gesture suggested. Inconsequential clashes, his half smile added.

'Were they close, David and Georgia? Or did they clash too?' Helen asked.

'Very rarely. David was so level-headed it was almost impossible to have a disagreement with him. Even for Georgia. He was our peacemaker.'

Helen crossed to the low table and appraised the laptops there. On each of them a Post-it sticker contained a list in a tiny hand-written script of perfect precision. Most of the items had been ticked. *Hard Drive Clean-up. Disc Defrag. System Optimization. Malware Removal.* The list went on. The header on the stickers read *PCDonors.ie.*

'It's an Irish charity,' Anthony said, anticipating her question. 'All above board, I can assure you. And all voluntary. You'll find more behind that curtain. He was at it day and night.'

Helen went and swept back the curtain. On the shelves were a few more laptops, some fax machines, a dozen or so computer mini-towers, some of them quite ancient, five flat-screen and three more bulky monitors. And a further shelf of CDs. Ben was at her side in an instant. She got a quick glimpse of the album covers as he slid out each CD one by one and slid them back in again. David Goode's taste was indie. Shoegaze, Indie pop, Indietronic. Suddenly, Ben raised a CD aloft.

'Bingo,' he said. 'And there's an inscription.'

# 24

'She probably wasn't even with the guy,' Gary Larkin insisted. 'I mean, as in going out with him. Another one of her fake boyfriend stories.'

'Ah, so you and Uncle Jimmy are working to the same game plan,' Leo said. 'Rubbish the victim.'

'She's not the victim. My father's the one who got plugged here.'

The emotion was real, though Leo suspected it arose less from grief than from Harry's rejection of his ex-child actor son. Leo knew damn well that when it came to father–son relationships, the son would always be a child no matter what age he'd reached. And the child would always take the blame for the father's failure to respect him. Which didn't mean, of course, that the child was blameless.

'What's this Libyan guy's name, Gary?'

'I don't know. I don't know anything about him, where he lives, what he does. I only saw him the once.'

'With Whitney?'

'Yeah. And, yeah, I warned him off because Whitney had no sense. You've no idea how gullible she was.'

'Was?'

'*Is*. I mean *is*,' Gary fulminated.

'When and where did you see them together?'

'Last year . . . I don't know . . . July or August I think it was. He gave her a lift home from Tallaght. It probably wasn't the first time but, for sure, it was the last.'

'This Libyan guy wasn't driving a white van by any chance, was he?'

'I don't remember.'

'But you'd remember whether it was a van or a car, wouldn't you? Even if you didn't remember the colour.'

Gary shrugged. 'Might've been a van, yeah.'

The guy was throwing him a bone to run after, Leo thought. Problem was, the bone might or might not exist. Dogs fell for that trick every time. Leo went sniffing elsewhere.

'So, Whitney was working in Tallaght, was she? What did she work at?'

'She did a community service order over there. Washing off graffiti and stuff. He was serving an order too.'

As astonishing revelations go, this one was up there with the best. Orange veering towards red on the alert scale.

'So, you warned him off?'

'Yeah, we did.'

'We?' Leo said, then found the answer himself. 'Ah, your missing pal Derek McCarthy.'

'Just 'cause you clowns can't find him doesn't mean he's missing.'

A hint of smugness entered young Larkin's features.

'Tell me about Whitney's so-called fake boyfriends.'

'There's nothing *so-called* about it. She was weird that way. Always making up stuff.'

'Such as? Come on, Gary. Cooperation, right? We haven't written up your charge sheet yet and you don't want us writing it up in a bad mood now, do you?'

The decision-making process that Gary Larkin mimed wasn't going to win him any Oscars but he put his heart and soul into it and there wasn't a dry eye on his face.

'I know most of it was harmless but it was hard on Mam especially.' He paused, held the shaved sides of his head in his hands. 'Like, you know all this goth shit? You know how that started? This is, like, nearly two years ago. She comes home one day in hysterics and Mam is trying to find out what's wrong. So, eventually, Whitney tells her that her boyfriend's committed suicide. And, of course, there was no boyfriend. No one ever saw her with anyone. Then she gets thick when Mam doesn't believe her and she goes and stays over in Kevin's for a few nights pretending she's disappeared. She actually left a freaking suicide note. Not for the first time either. Mam was going apeshit until Kevin had the cop-on to tell us on the QT that she was in his place.'

'So Kevin is the one she turns to when she's in trouble?'

'Sometimes.'

The prospect of confronting the deaf man seemed even more uninviting than meeting Liz again had been. Had to be done though, Leo thought, and soon. Kevin had clearly been the closest of the Larkins to Whitney. And Kevin had as much if not more reason to despise his father as his stepbrother. Leo had seen the evidence of that all those years ago – a child gaping with equal terror at the unfinished house in the misted fields, at his father, at Leo. If Leo couldn't forget it, he doubted Kevin could.

'When am I getting out of here?' Gary demanded. 'Just charge me and let me out, right?'

'You'll be out of here by lunchtime, maybe late afternoon,' Leo said. 'But, one way or the other, it'll be sooner than is good for you, Gary. And hear this: we don't have the time, the resources or the inclination to keep you under surveillance. So you'll have no protection out there if you decide to go to war.'

'I don't need your protection.'

'I bet you've watched lots of Harry's DVDs,' Leo said. 'The *Godfather* films, *The General*.' Gary eyed him testily. '*The Sopranos*. Doesn't it ever occur to you that they all get blown away in the end? These are morality tales, right? Guess what the moral is, Gary.'

The young man sat up straight, brushed the palms of his hands along his shaved temples. An accident waiting to happen. No, an incident waiting to happen.

'I'm ready for whatever comes,' the undersized Mohawk said.

'No one's ever ready for what comes,' Leo told him.

Helen and Ben had moved on to Georgia Goode's room. The name inscribed on the CD inset had meant nothing to Anthony Goode. *Thank you my rebel friends, Hadi.* Helen believed the claim because he had admitted that it spoke poorly of a father to have known so little of his children's lives. The mess he'd made of his own finances, he'd told her, had distracted him unforgivably.

Unlike her brother, Georgia seemed to have a let-it-lie-where-it-falls policy on everything from clothes and toiletries to books. Open wardrobe door, open drawers spilling their contents. The stale smell of unchanged bedsheets prevailed in the windowless space. From the walls, Che Guevara and Hugo Chavez presided over the rebellious contents of the room. It occurred to Helen that this might be more than just a careless mess. Maybe it was someone leaving in a hurry.

'Is it always so untidy?' Helen asked.

'I've seen it worse, believe me,' Anthony said. There was a

new alertness in him, an acerbic change in his tone. 'I didn't think it was possible, but then I suppose three grown men can do a lot more damage than a young girl.'

'Three men?' Ben asked.

'Three of you people.'

'Georgia's room has already been searched?' Helen put in. 'When?'

She wondered if some Kilmacud detectives had already visited and, if so, why they'd trashed the place. Che and Hugo's features seemed to have taken on a new, more offended hue.

'Last year. But surely you already know that?'

'I didn't actually,' she said.

Overcoming his scepticism, Anthony relented. His head sagged slightly forward, the stoop returning to his upper back. He leaned against the door jamb.

'Georgia was our rebel. David believed in good works, she believed in action. Which is how she got herself arrested and charged with assaulting a police officer.'

'What were the circumstances of this assault, Mr Goode?' Ben asked.

'It was a protest outside the Israeli Embassy back in January of last year. A peaceful protest. But when Georgia was leaving, a Guard demanded to know her name, address and such. She told him to mind his own business. The usual bolshie teenage nonsense. But he persisted and she was foolish enough to place a hand on this fellow's chest.' His tone had turned to disbelief. 'They put her through the courts. A seventeen-year-old girl with a social conscience.'

'Was your daughter issued with a community service order by the court?' Helen asked.

'Yes, she was. She spent eighty days – can you believe that? – eighty days removing graffiti out in Tallaght.'

'When did she serve her order?'

'Last summer.'

Which, Helen knew, was when Whitney had served hers. A tenuous link or mere coincidence? Only one way to find out, she thought. Talk to Georgia. They had to get to Marlborough Road. But the last thing she needed was a wasted journey.

'Can you ring your daughter and tell her we have to speak to her? Like right now, if you don't mind. We'll be over in Ranelagh in five minutes.'

'There's no point.'

'What do you mean?' Ben asked. 'She's not there?'

'Oh, she's there all right. But she won't answer the phone to me. Nor to my wife.' He was clearly flailing himself again. 'I could ring Angela, I suppose. Sarah's mother. Sarah being Georgia's friend.'

He took out a mobile phone from his pocket, a set of reading glasses from the breast pocket of his shirt. Helen and Ben stepped out into the corridor cum storage vault. To their right, an open door led into the kitchen. On the other side stood a door not yet opened. Ben tried the handle. The door was locked.

Anthony Goode's suddenly raised voice reached them from the girl's room.

'Are you quite sure?' he said, and the volume went down again, though Helen and Ben could still hear what he had to add: 'And last week?'

They waited for him to appear. When he did, he looked ill.

'Georgia's not there,' he said. 'And she hasn't been there all week.'

'Do you have any idea where else she might be?' Helen asked.

204

'She's probably with another friend. I'll make some calls.'

'We'll need a recent photo too, if you don't mind.'

'Of course, yes.'

Behind them, Ben tried the locked door again.

'That one's for storage only. There's nothing of David's or Georgia's in there.'

The ex-gallery owner's naivety was painful to watch. He couldn't have made it more obvious that he had something to hide.

'Do you have the key?' Ben asked, though Helen wondered if they were merely wasting time here. 'We need to check everything, you understand.'

From his trouser pocket, Anthony retrieved a bunch of keys. He got the wrong key into the keyhole a couple of times before the door finally opened. He hadn't been lying. The room was entirely given over to bed-ends, mattresses, more boxes. And leaning against one wall, stacks of framed paintings, empty frames and long hollow tubes containing, Helen supposed, prints or posters.

'They help to pay the bills,' Anthony sighed. Then he added dismally, 'I have a confession to make.'

The two detectives turned from their perusal of the stacked paintings.

'Technically, these works should still be in our gallery in Temple Bar. The Porter Lane Gallery. Technically, in fact, they're no longer mine to sell. But I do sell them occasionally to friends and on the internet.' Guilt sent a wave of irritation across his features. 'I might easily have taken the best pictures. It was difficult enough to take even these few.'

'Let me get this straight,' Ben said. 'Do you own the building where the gallery is housed?'

'I used to. At first, I rented the gallery space. Then – and this was my big mistake – I took out a loan and bought the building and both neighbouring ones. We had a beautiful design for the place. A gallery and printing works. But the banks took the buildings. Our house too, of course.'

Helen's mind was elsewhere. On the Probation Service. From her previous job in the Garda Vetting Office she knew someone who might help confirm that Georgia and Whitney had done their community service work together. Betty D'Arcy, a senior probation officer in the Dublin region. She reached into her jacket for her mobile. It wasn't there. Nor was it in the pockets of her denims. Must've left it back in the first apartment.

'Be back in a minute,' she said, gesturing to Ben – mimed a phone to her ear, indicated the other apartment with a backward jerk of the thumb.

At the open door of number three, Helen paused. Somewhere inside, Frida Goode was on the phone. Something disturbingly sexual resided in the woman's tone like those feral cat cries you sometimes heard in the night, chillingly incoherent and ambiguous in their meaning. Helen stepped inside the apartment. The voice was coming from behind a half-opened door to her left. Powder blue walls, navy and gold curtains, a gilt-framed painting that was a patchwork of blues. Besides the blues, there were the shoes. Dozens of them, all piled carelessly together. Frida was a spender. Or had been. Until the banks moved in.

As Helen went by the door, she caught a quick glimpse of the woman's bare feet at the end of the single bed in there. Frida's strange song went suddenly off air. Helen kept moving. As she'd guessed, her mobile was on the coffee table where they'd sat earlier. She pocketed it, took a deep breath and plunged towards the corridor.

Frida's voice stopped her in mid-track.

'Are you spying on me?'

She was kneeling on the bed. She'd been crying, the pupils of her drugged eyes great vacant discs.

'I'm sorry,' Helen said and held up her mobile. 'I left my—'

'I've been arranging David's memorial service. Do you have a problem with that?'

'No. I . . . I'm sorry.'

Her heart pounding, Helen made her escape. Anthony and Ben stared at her when she reappeared. Blame in the taller man's expression, concern in her colleague's. She ducked into the storage room that had been unlocked. Out of view of the others, she rested against the wall. Her head ached. This case was kicking the shit out of her. She felt harassed, bullied, assaulted. Felt exactly as Whitney Larkin must be feeling. Keep digging, she told herself. But for what? She scanned the room. Did a double-take. She saw, hidden in the well behind where some framed paintings leaned, the inner moulding of a mask. Its shape aroused her curiosity though she didn't quite know why. Some empty picture frames stood in her way and she began to move them. Out in the passageway, Ben scrutinized Anthony Goode again.

'When you say you might easily have taken the better paintings, you mean you still had access to the building after the banks moved in?'

'They've changed the locks. All but one.'

'And you have the key?'

As she listened, Helen reached in to where the mask lay. It was a stretch but she was almost there. The bunch of keys in Anthony Goode's hand tinkled as he searched through them. And searched further. And again. Helen got a hold of the mask and drew it out. Meanwhile, Anthony turned to Ben.

'The key to the gallery is gone,' he said.

'Ben,' Helen called, and held up the mask for him to see.

All three of them shared a frozen moment. All four of them if you counted the face on the mask.

# 25

In the carpark behind Pettycannon Garda Station, Leo found a small rectangle of sunlight and propped himself against the bonnet of a squad car. He snapped the tip from a Consulate cigarette and lit up. The sleeping tablets that hadn't worked last night were insisting on getting their job done now. Wearily he considered the arbitrary nature of people's lives. Gary's, Liz's, Whitney's too perhaps. Lives that might have been utterly different if they'd had one lucky break. The trajectory of every life was deflected by whim or by bad luck or by some unfortunate misunderstanding. Nobody was, in the end, who they really wanted to be. Maybe that was why people needed the movies, needed their reassurance, their delusory escapism. Maybe that was why everyone wanted to be someone other than themselves.

He took out his mobile phone. Three callers to answer. He'd leave the best wine until last. Eveleen. The most urgent he'd return first. Helen. The other call he might not bother making at all. Superintendent Heaphy. If it was important enough, Aonghus would ring again. He scrolled Helen's number and rang.

'Leo, I hardly know where to start. OK, first we found another copy of the Libyan hip-hop CD, in David Goode's room. Plus, we now know that Whitney and David Goode's sister, Georgia, were handed community service orders. Georgia served hers in Tallaght and—'

'Whitney served hers in Tallaght too and some Libyan kid was there at the same time,' Leo interrupted. 'Gary Larkin just told me. Says he doesn't know the name but there can't have been too many Libyan kids on community service orders last summer.'

'His name is Hadi. I've asked a contact in the Probation Service to check the files for me.'

'Christ, this is beginning to sound like some Enid Blyton adventure. What the hell were these kids up to?'

'I think we know what at least one of them was up to,' Helen said. 'David, that is. We found a mask at his apartment. The Anonymous mask, you know, the *V for Vengeance* one.'

Leo wasn't altogether in touch with the modern but he knew the history of masks. He remembered the Guy Fawkes masks that came free with the comics every autumn back in the sixties. The Anonymous mask was a rip-off of the illustrator Alan Moore's more stylized version from the eighties.

'David Goode was one of these computer hackers?'

'There's a good chance he was. We've discovered that an empty shoulder bag found in the white van was probably David's. He carried his laptop in it.'

'So these people were after David's laptop?'

'We can't be one hundred per cent sure yet, naturally,' Helen said. 'But, let's say our body in the van is this Libyan intern. Well, I remember reading a piece in the newspaper about Libya a few months back. Gaddafi had shut down the internet because of cyber attacks on government sites.'

'Sounds like you got it in one, Helen. What did Georgia have to say for herself?'

'She may be in hiding.'

'But why?'

'No idea,' Helen said. 'We think she may be in an art gallery the Goodes ran in Temple Bar but lost in the crash. We're heading there now.'

'Be careful, Helen. And keep me posted.'

His mobile was ringing even as he cut the call. Superintendent Heaphy.

'It's about time you answered the phone, Leo.'

The man's false teeth were in and they were hurting. Leo could tell from the agonized falsetto.

'Hold on a minute.'

A series of shuffling sounds followed, then a door was slammed, metal twisted against metal. More shuffling. The super had locked his office door. And taken out the false teeth. He sounded vaguely like a reasonable man again.

'Right, question number one,' he began. 'Why is your team investigating a hit-and-run accident while we have the Larkin saga on our hands? And why are you getting yourself involved in this murder out in County Meath?'

'Because we've discovered a link between all of these cases,' Leo answered. Instinct told him to hold back on the rest for now.

'You have? But how in God's name could this business of the Larkins have any connection with . . . with . . .' The wobble in the super's voice confirmed his instinct. Aonghus was fishing but he wasn't dishing.

'With what? Is there something you're not telling me, Aonghus?' Leo asked, knowing there was always something the super wasn't telling him. And always something Leo wasn't telling the super.

'I hear things.' Cryptic was the super's fail-safe mode in tricky situations.

'Jesus, Aonghus, you'd want to talk to a shrink about that.'

'Listen, Leo.' Heaphy was whispering now and in code, his tongue clicking wetly against his bare gums. 'I'm told the higher powers are meeting an attaché from a certain, eh, friendly world power today.' America, Leo deciphered. 'And they'll be discussing some so-called diplomats from a certain North African dictatorship' – Libya? – 'who've been expelled by a certain friendly minor world power.' Britain? 'There's a suggestion that one of these fellows was running agents in the UK and may have had an agent here in Ireland too.'

'We've got a Libyan Secret Service agent on our hands?' Leo said, dumping the code book.

The superintendent began to dodge and fudge and rummage his brain for words that said something and nothing at the same time.

'No, it's just a possibility, a theory. What I'm saying is that this element of your investigation might be better steered clear of for the moment. Chances are that today's meeting will change the perspective on this incident out in Meath. It'll probably be handed over to the Special Detective Unit since there's an international element to it.'

'Aonghus, I'll follow wherever the investigation leads me.'

A fluster and bluster or two later, the super was back on the line. The false teeth were back in, his voice pained again.

'Listen, Leo. I'm going for the *CrimeLink* audition tomorrow afternoon and the last thing I need is you flying solo out there, do you hear me? There's talk of a Chief Super vacancy coming up and I want this *CrimeLink* job on my CV. So, if they tell us to pull out of this Libyan business, we pull out. And that's an order.'

There was only one way to keep the super onside for the

moment, Leo thought. Aim your fire at his ambition.

'You're looking at this through the wrong end of the telescope, Aonghus.'

'What do you mean?'

'Your profile will go through the roof if we get to the bottom of these cases,' Leo continued. 'Think about it. Think about marching into that interview for Chief Super and slapping three big files down on the desk. Harry Larkin – sorted. David Goode – sorted. Libyan Secret Service agent – sorted. Game, set and match.'

'Mmm.' The air lightened at the far end of the line. 'Maybe you're right.'

'You know I am,' Leo said, moving deftly on. 'OK, you need to know that Gary Larkin will be released over the next couple of hours and there's a pretty decent chance that he and Baz MacDonald may have a go at one another out there.'

'The National Surveillance Unit have no interest in the Larkins. And overtime's out of the question. We're under serious pressure on our budget from the Minister.'

'Don't say I haven't warned you, Aonghus. If this kicks off and some innocent bystander gets shot in the crossfire, your arse will be on the line not mine. But it's your call.'

'It's not my call,' the super insisted. He sounded a bit like Eichmann at his trial in Jerusalem. Like Leo's father that one and only time he'd met him in adulthood. In 1982, the year of Leo's fall from grace.

'Ich war nur Befehle befolgt,' Leo muttered.

'What was that?'

'Nothing, boss.'

'I have to go now. I've a budget meeting in a few minutes. But one last thing. What's the problem with Ben Murphy? Why didn't he go to that FBI course in Quantico?'

'I've no idea, Aonghus.'

'I bent over backwards to get him on to that course, Leo, and he let me down with a bang,' the super went on. 'Tells me he couldn't go because of a family issue. And when I asked him if there was some problem with the little girl, he told me he couldn't go into details. Surely to God I deserve a better answer than that after all I've done for him? Is he not cut out for the job or what?'

'He's cut out for it all right. But maybe he has the good sense not to want it.'

The thought surprised Leo, emerging as it did only as he spoke. He wondered if he'd hit the nail on the head. But he didn't wonder about it for long. There was already more than enough to wonder about with the Larkins and the Goodes and the Libyans and, now, the Americans and the Brits.

'And, Leo? Day after tomorrow. Four p.m. I've booked you in to have your new ID done. No ifs and buts.'

'But I'm in the middle of—'

Heaphy ended the call. There wasn't time for Leo to work up a head of heat. Think, he told himself, think. He felt like a juggler with too many balls in the air. A juggler with an eye-patch. A first, surely. OK. David Goode was a hacker. The Libyans had shut down the internet because they were being hacked. So, they discovered David was one of the hackers? How? And why were the Americans interested? Had young Goode also been involved in hacking American government sites or the sites of major American companies? Leo knew that Anonymous did that kind of thing all the time. He'd heard whispers back in the Harcourt Street HQ that some Irish kids were suspected of involvement. Was David Goode one of these kids? He called the ex-Rose of Tralee and put her on it. She knew everyone at SDU because everyone wanted to know her.

Leo popped the tip from another cigarette, lit up, fixed his tie and prepared himself to ring Eveleen. He felt nervous as a teenager in love. His index finger lingered tentatively over the call button.

Temple Bar was a maze of narrow one-way streets and alleyways. Pubs, restaurants, small shops and galleries squatted down together there as though to fend off the worst of the recession. Late weekday mornings like this one, the place looked like it was losing the struggle. At the weekends, Helen knew, the battle became a hell of a lot rougher but more lucrative. For the pubs and clubs, at least. This morning, backpack tourists and arty types prevailed in the cobbled warrens the two detectives rushed through.

They'd abandoned the squad car just off Dame Street. In two minutes flat, Helen and Ben were at the entrance to Porter Lane. No more than a dead-end passageway filled with second-hand daylight and permanent shadows, the place had a damp, sinister chill to it. From both sides, three-storey buildings faced each other, their dank, depressing proximity like an inescapable marriage. Halfway along the left-hand side a faux-antique quill-and-scroll sign was to be seen. Porter Lane Gallery.

'Is there a back way out of these buildings, do you reckon?' Helen asked.

Ben showed her the GPS map on his mobile.

'Doesn't seem so. But I'm not sure how accurate this map is. Most of this area doesn't show up on Google Street View.'

They moved in along the alleyway. The few shops they went by were shuttered. The front window of the gallery was shuttered too. On each side of the window stood a door. One appeared to lead directly into the gallery space and advertised *Original works and prints – Framing service available*. The second, Helen supposed, opened in on the stairway to the upper floor. Tentatively, she pushed a shoulder against the gallery door. Too well secured to give way, she guessed. Ben had moved to the other door. A frailer piece of work, it shook when he touched the timber. Silently, he asked her assent to push on through. She gave it. He jostled the door and it was sucked inwards as though by some collapsing vacuum and banged loudly against the wall of the vestibule.

Ben listened to the building. All Helen could hear were the sounds from the street at the end of the alleyway and the usual city-centre bustle further off. A sharp turn of Ben's head alerted her to a dripping noise, slow and distant at first. He climbed the claustrophobically narrow stairs, step by careful step. Helen followed. Then he put his weight on the wrong spot in a stair and his left foot was swallowed as though by quicksand. Only louder. Much louder. The crash of plaster below set off a crash of glass above, a muffled scream.

Ben struggled to release himself from the trap of broken timbers and in his struggle blocked Helen's way. She didn't get by him until he leaned flat against the wall and even then it was a tight squeeze. She bounded upwards. The room from which they'd heard the breaking glass was directly ahead. She shouldered the door. Which hurt. A lot. Then she tried the handle. Which worked.

The far window of a room, larger and more blindingly bright than Helen expected, had been raised and most of its glass rectangles smashed. Apart from a few bloodied shards. The building opposite the window was a mere few yards away. Another lane then, after all, narrower still than Porter Lane. She ran to the window and peered out. A door lintel below offered a precarious but negotiable jumping-off point to the ground below. The lane itself, comprising only back entries, was empty. Georgia was gone.

She got her phone out, rang in an alert for all city-centre officers. By way of description all she could think to say was *tall girl running and bleeding*. It sounded like the title of a murder ballad. She surveyed the alleyway all the while as though this might bring the girl back.

'Christ, look at this,' Ben said, and she turned from the window.

He was standing at the door, his left foot bared and blood-soaked.

'You'll need to have that seen to, Ben.'

'No, it's just a scratch,' he said and, indicating the contents of the room with a wide sweep of his hand, repeated, 'Look at this.'

She looked around the room, saw for the first time what it actually contained.

'Holy shit,' she said.

# 26

'Leo.' Eveleen Morgan's voice delighted him and then, in an instant, disappointed him. 'Gus Ewart asked me to ring you.'

'Yeah?'

'You know, the guy in our Security Control Room?'

'Yeah . . . good. And?' They weren't words. They were tired, crestfallen things.

'Are you OK, Leo? You sound . . . odd.'

'Yeah. Both.'

'Pardon?'

'Both OK and odd,' he said, and she laughed. That was something. To someone who had nothing. 'Gus has something for me?'

He sighed. Deflation didn't seem so bad when you'd reached the bottom of a sigh. He began to idle around the carpark behind Pettycannon Garda Station. It felt like he was walking somewhere with her. If only virtually.

'He's been going through the tapes for last Saturday night and he came across something that might be of interest to you. It's to do with Mrs Goode.'

Leo found himself in a corner of the carpark where the sun didn't reach.

'I'm sure the poor woman is under enough pressure as things stand,' Eveleen continued. 'This probably isn't even relevant and might even be intrusive but I know I can trust you to treat this information sensitively.'

'Of course.'

'Well, it seems Mrs Goode didn't arrive at the hospital with her husband and daughter. Gus showed me the tape of Mr Goode and his daughter getting out of a taxi and running towards the main door. And, well, she's not with them.'

'So, she arrived separately?'

'Yes. Gus picked her up on a different camera further back on the entrance road.'

'Someone dropped her off there?' Leo said. Helen's suspicions about Frida Goode and Baz MacDonald came to mind. 'Was it a blue coupé?'

'No, a black Honda Accord. The licence plate is partly obscured but I've got some of the digits here. 08 is the year. No county ID, I'm afraid. But the third digit of the next number is three and . . . do you have a biro to get all of this down?'

Leo fumbled around in his pockets with his free hand. He knew he wasn't going to find a biro but he kept on searching anyway. He was always doing that kind of thing. Looking for what wasn't there and finding something different. Or nothing.

'Can you text it to me . . . Eveleen?'

'Will do,' she said. 'And, Leo?'

'Yeah?'

'Mrs Larkin and her brother-in-law had another meeting with our consultant this morning. They've just left, in fact. The thing is, we're really under pressure for space now and—'

'And Mrs Larkin refuses to make a decision?'

'Yes. It probably sounds awfully cruel to you but we have to prioritize in here. Mr Larkin's brother agrees. We're hoping he can bring Mrs Larkin around.'

'Has he told you he'd try?'

'He understands the situation.'

Which might mean, Leo thought, that Jimmy was merely acting the hail-fellow-well-met again and telling the nurse what she wanted to hear. Or it just might mean that Jimmy wanted his brother dead. Why?

'I can see where the woman is coming from,' Eveleen continued. 'They've obviously been married a long time, reared a family and all. That kind of attachment goes deep. You're staring at the void when you lose that.'

Leo wondered if she was speaking from personal experience. In any case, he couldn't make himself believe in some happy-familied *Darling Buds of May* scenario for Liz and Harry. They were the wrong kind of Larkins.

'Are they still at the hospital?'

'Mrs Larkin's here but Jimmy left twenty minutes ago,' Eveleen said. 'He'll be back later. I'm hoping we might have a decision by then.'

Leo searched the musty store room at the back of his brain for some further reason to keep her on the line. He blew the dust off an old thought.

'Anything from the other city hospitals on Whitney Larkin?'

'Not as yet,' she said, stifling a yawn as she spoke. 'The major hospitals don't have anything and with the smaller ones it's more difficult to find fully digitized records. Then there's the ones that have closed. So it's a slow process, I'm afraid.'

'You sound tired,' Leo said, the pot calling the kettle burnt-out.

'Not especially. I yawn when I'm nervous. Just get a fit of it.'

'Something at work?'

'No, it's more . . . well, more personal. More . . . Oh, to hell with it, I'm too old for this farting around. What are you doing tonight, Leo?'

He found a sunny patch of wall to lean against. He dumped his half-smoked cigarette. Time was away and somewhere else. Eveleen broke into the silence.

'You're probably all tied up with this investigation at the moment.'

'No. Well, naturally I'm busy but I do try to keep the old work–life balance in mind.' As in 99 per cent work and 1 per cent life, he told himself. The 1 per cent being something of an exaggeration. 'So, yeah, I'm . . .' Available? Wrong word. Free? Worse word. Up for it? Get down, Leo.

'How do you feel about dinner at my place at, say, eight-thirty?'

'Honoured, surprised, delighted,' he said. Terrified. 'Should I go on?'

'Probably not,' she said. 'Half eight then?'

'Half eight it is. And thank you, Eveleen.'

'Ev.'

'Thank you, Ev.'

In the upstairs room of the Porter Lane Gallery in Temple Bar, two single mattresses lay side by side on the floor. Tossed, careless bedclothes covered both. There were no pillows just rolled-up sheets. Scattered between the mattresses were empty take-away cartons, Coke cans and a squashed cigarette packet. The few clothes strewn around – denim jeans, two blouses, a long woollen cardigan – were all, Helen guessed, women's clothes. And black. With latex-gloved hands, she checked the tags. She was only slightly wrong. Extra Small. Teenage sizes really. Smaller teenagers than Georgia Goode.

Beside her, Ben crouched, his mobile clamped between his ear and the point of his shoulder as he scanned the area around the mattresses. He'd kept the line open, hoping for a sighting of Georgia. Or of a new-look Whitney Larkin. So far, there'd been none. For now, all they could do was wait for the Technical Bureau team to arrive. Helen had already sent a squad car to patrol the streets of Chapelizod on the off-chance that Whitney might turn up there.

Helen returned to the small sink in the corner opposite the mattresses. When she'd first been startled by what she'd found there, a wave of relief had risen in her. Whitney was alive, her first thought. Now she realized that her optimism might have been premature. Whitney had certainly been here though not necessarily this morning and perhaps not for days if the encrustations of food in the take-away cartons were anything to go by.

The stained enamel sink was filled almost to the brim. Blocked. On the surface of the water, little logjams of snipped black hair floated. Very black hairs. As in goth black. Propped on the rear sink edge was a box of hair dye labelled Deep Blonde. Alongside, the little dyeing brush had hardened with its treacly load. In the uncovered space beneath the sink was a plastic bag of shorn black hair. Whitney had a new image. Short hair, probably short blonde hair. Helen looked at the bag and at the box of dye again. Very short. Very blonde.

'Helen?' Ben called, and she caught his eye in the mirror above the sink.

He was holding some small white objects in his hand. She turned, approached him.

'Inhalers,' he said. 'The pharmacy label's got Whitney's name on them.'

'Empty?'

He shook his head and bagged the inhalers. Helen looked around the squalid, damp-walled room and thought how bleak but cruelly appropriate a place it might be for a troubled kid to spend her last days in. Her colleague picked up the empty cigarette packet and began to unfold it from its mashed state. The brand wasn't one Helen was familiar with. Not that she was an expert on cigarette brands.

'Regal? Never heard of them,' Ben said. 'I wonder if they're illegal?'

'Maybe.' Helen was doing a sum in her head. The answer wasn't clear but had to be significant. 'We can't rule it out but Whitney is hardly a smoker. Given the asthma and all. And the Goodes. The apartment the parents shared stank of cigarette smoke. But I'm pretty sure there wasn't a whiff of it in David or Georgia's rooms.'

'Which means that they had a visitor while they were here. Someone who stayed a while.'

'One of the Larkins? Or one of their crew?' Helen speculated.

'Do we know which, if any, of the Larkins are smokers? I'm pretty sure Gary isn't.'

'How can you know that?'

'I was a smoker myself,' Ben explained, 'so I'm kind of hyper-sensitive to that smell from smokers' clothes. Makes you wonder what the hell you smelled like yourself when you smoked.'

'So, you'd have noticed if Kevin was a smoker?'

'I honestly can't remember for sure,' he admitted, disappointed with himself. 'The exhaust fumes from the motorbike might have masked the smell or—'

'Leo might know if Mrs Larkin or Jimmy are smokers. But there's one I'm certain of: Baz MacDonald. I saw him in the smoking area at the hospital.'

Echoes of activity began to fill the alleyway below and soon the place filled up with techies. From the top of the narrow stairs she could see John open the carrier bag draped over his shoulder.

'Got some bits and pieces for you here, Helen.'

She glided down by Ben, who was fishing beneath the broken stair-board for his shoe.

'Some information on the FN Five Seven,' John said, indicating the first page. 'The make of pistol we found in the white van? You mentioned Libya, right? Well, the Libyan military use these pistols if Wikipedia is to be believed. Only don't tell anyone I Wikied it.'

'Libyan military? Christ.'

'Belgian, French and Spanish police use them too though. And the American Secret Service.'

Speechless, Helen leaned against the door frame. She looked up at Ben. He'd retrieved his shoe from below the broken stair timbers but held it in mid-air now as though he'd forgotten which foot was shoeless.

'The ECTFs,' he said. 'The European Electronic Crimes Task Forces. They're based in Rome and London but it was the American Secret Service that set them up and works alongside them.'

'Chasing down hackers,' Helen told herself aloud.

Beside her, John cleared his throat to remind her of his presence – and, his gesture towards the stairs suggested, his desire to get on with his work.

'Sorry, John,' she said, her mind filled with dark-suited men wearing Ray-Bans and white-wired earpieces.

'It wasn't an orthotic brace, by the way,' he added. 'You'll find the details in there. It was a bullet-proof vest. And we found no glasses when we lifted the body.' Helpfully, he removed the top sheet of paper and pointed to the one below. 'Prelim report from the pathologist. Time of death between one and four o'clock yesterday morning. As you can see there, he's done a match-up with Mahmoud Maguin's data from the hospital. He's almost one hundred per cent satisfied the body isn't the intern's. You seem disappointed.'

'No, John, baffled,' she said, and looked up at the blue strip of sky above the dark alleyway. 'If it's not Mahmoud Maguin, then who the hell is it?'

Descending the stairs, newly shod, Ben Murphy added another question to the catalogue: 'And where the hell *is* Mahmoud Maguin?'

'We have to get a look inside his apartment today,' Helen said. 'Ben, see if you can muster up the management company for the estate.'

'And if we can't?'

'We'll find our way in.'

# 27

The mid-afternoon traffic on South Circular Road moved more slowly than Detective Inspector Leo Woods might have wished. In the driver's seat, Ben appeared to share none of Leo's irritated impatience. Then again, the young officer wasn't the one making the decisions on how to proceed in this labyrinthine case. In the Kingdom of the Blind, he reflected drily, the one-eyed man is the Inspector of Police.

Helen, no doubt, shared this jaundiced view of him right now as she headed out with Martin Buck to Clondalkin in search of the Libyan boy. Her contact in the Probation Service had come up trumps with Hadi's surname and address. More than that, she'd confirmed that Whitney Larkin and Georgia Goode had been in the same team as Hadi Al-Baarai while working their community service orders. Meanwhile, Helen had told Leo, a management company rep was waiting to let her and Ben in to Mahmoud Maguin's apartment in Castleknock.

Leo, however, needed Ben with him in Chapelizod so he could talk to Kevin Larkin. They'd visit Jimmy too. See for himself how the two men reacted to the discoveries in Temple Bar. Besides which he preferred to keep her focused on the Libyan and David Goode elements of the case. The need to feature Martin Buck in at least a co-starring role on the investigation also forced his hand. She understood, right? He hadn't got an answer to that. Or not in words.

He hoped Buck was behaving himself. To Leo's surprise, the cowboy detective had offered to pass on the outing with Helen and take the interview with Jimmy Larkin instead. Leo declined. He wanted to poke around the relationship between Whitney and her uncle some more. Have a snoop around his bachelor pad while Ben sneaked an off-the-record peek around Gary's apartment across the river.

He looked at his mobile. Nothing back from Sergeant Martha Corrigan yet on the cyber crime meeting at HQ. He got a glimpse of the time on his phone. Half past three. In five hours he'd be at Eveleen's. He hadn't been on a date since the last century. Anxiety clawed at his gut. The temptation to ring his dealer grew with every passing second. He was glad to be busy.

'The Mosque,' he said, indicating the refurbished Presbyterian church to their right with its lumpy cut-stones and its austere lines. 'We should contact all of the mosques. See if anyone knows of Mahmoud Maguin's whereabouts.'

'Done, sir. Might take time though. Quite a big Muslim population here now. Surprised me actually.'

Should've known Ben had it covered, Leo thought, not best pleased to be reminded of his own slowness of mind these days. Too many pills popped, too many banned substances inhaled. Couldn't be good for a man. Though better possibly than facing reality twenty-four hours a day.

'How many Muslims do you reckon live in Ireland?' Ben asked.

'Haven't a bull's.'

'Sixty thousand or thereabouts. Hard to imagine the country has changed so much, isn't it?'

Silence fell again in the unmarked car. Leo knew he was going to have to come down heavily on the deaf man and it bothered him to be stepping into the shoes of the bully Larkin. Still, what choice did he have? Whitney turned to Kevin when she was in trouble so the guy had to know more than he was admitting to.

They'd reached a freer stretch of road within sight of Islandbridge and picked up speed. It didn't last long. More traffic lights went against them. They were caught in the red traffic-light loop.

'How many deaf people would you say are in Ireland?' Ben asked. 'I mean born deaf.'

'What the hell is this? *Who Wants to be a Millionaire*?'

The young detective laughed more heartily than Leo imagined he could. Leo cut him a cold glance. It occurred to him that Ben didn't look so flashy any more. What was it? The suit. He wasn't wearing a suit. In need of a shave too. Or maybe he was going for the chilled-out look? No, he wasn't just going for that look. He actually was more chilled out than usual, not so eager to please or impress.

'Just give a guess,' Ben said. 'Wouldn't you intuitively imagine there were at least as many deaf people as Muslims in Ireland?'

'I suppose.'

'And you'd be way out. Only seven thousand deaf people.'

Leo hated to be wrong about anything. It came, he knew, from being wrong about most things.

'Does this conversation actually have a point? Or is it some Tarantino *Le Big Mac* interlude?'

'Sorry, I've just been thinking about Kevin Larkin,' Ben said. 'I talked to my sister about him.'

'She knows Kevin?'

'No, not personally. But like I said, it's a relatively small group of people and there's a pretty strong sense of community. So it's a five degrees of separation kind of thing.'

'You mean six degrees of separation.'

'No, it's more like five now. In fact, I've heard Facebook have analysed their site and it'll come out at something like four-point-eight degrees of separation.'

'Yeah, in the virtual world,' Leo said dismissively. 'Your sister knows someone who knew Kevin?'

'More like someone who knows someone who knows someone. But the bottom line is that Kevin was a very bright, quiet kid. Won some kind of national children's art award at primary school level and then went off the rails soon after. Actually, he still paints. He did some really good murals in the pub. And there's the airbrushing on the motorbike, of course.'

'And a starry sky in Whitney's bedroom. From before he was banished to Jinky's, I'm guessing.'

'A starry sky? He's done one of those in his bedroom above the pub too. I noticed it when I searched his place yesterday.'

'Which might imply that Whitney was a pretty regular over-nighter there,' Leo said. 'How many bedrooms are there over the pub?'

'Just the one.'

'You say Kevin went off the rails but he doesn't have a record, does he?'

'No, but when he was eight or nine years old he began to turn into a pretty vicious bully. So much so that the school couldn't handle him. He quit when he was sixteen. Had to.'

Eight or nine years old, Leo thought, which would have been – what? – 1984 or 1985 at a guess. And Liz had married

Harry in 1984. The young deaf boy's presence was one of the last-gasp arguments he'd put to her while warning her off marrying Harry. *I'll deal with him*, she'd said. Angrily. Then again, everything she'd said by then was tinged with anger.

'How vicious are we talking here?'

'As in beating up on kids his age and younger,' Ben said. 'My sister reckons his behaviour came from frustration. It seems he didn't get the kind of support he needed at home. People engaging with him, signing, encouraging him to get involved in the wider deaf community. That kind of isolation is difficult to cope with.'

What a bloody battle life must be for the deaf, Leo thought. A battle some of them at least must lose. A battle, in Kevin's case, that ended with collateral damage? Such as with the shooting of a violent, unsympathetic father? And might there have been other victims of the deaf man's pent-up frustration? Victims even more vulnerable than himself? Whitney? It felt wrong to think Kevin Larkin capable of such carnage but to a detective everyone walked under a cloud of suspicion.

'We're going to have to hit Kevin low and hard, you realize that, don't you?' Leo warned. 'If he's innocent, we'll be doing him a favour in the long run. That's how this game goes. Most people like to be liked, Murphy. Detectives don't have that option.'

'Yeah. I understand.'

'And, by the way,' Leo added, 'thanks for sending those lilies to Helen for me.'

'What lilies?' Ben asked.

On the drive from the city centre to Clondalkin, Detective Sergeant Martin Buck's attempts at conversation grew increasingly embittered. The water he drank from a small bottle curdled his lips. Or more probably, Helen guessed, it was the fizzing headache tablets he'd surreptitiously snapped and slipped into the bottle. He'd tried her musical tastes, her social life, her marital ambitions. When nothing took root, he ventured into sarcasm.

'I hear you play ladies football,' Buck said, taking one last sour swig from the bottle.

'Women's football.'

The turn-off to Monastery Lane came into view. Helen flicked the indicator.

'That'd be mainly lesbians, I take it?' Buck ventured.

'Yeah, but I'm sure that would all change if you showed up in the dressing room,' Helen said. 'Check out the numbers on your side, will you?'

Quiet and tree-lined and well-maintained, the street was more respectable than upmarket. A pleasing and varied mix of houses had more breathing room around them than was common these days. Detached and semi-detached dormer bungalows stood in silent repose on this May afternoon, the sun bringing out the best in them. Helen spotted the house number they were looking for. On the short driveway by the unfenced front lawn, no car was to be seen. Her spirits sank. She parked the unmarked car on the street.

'Doesn't look like anyone's home,' Buck said.

He hadn't bothered to loosen his seat belt even as Helen's whipped back to its base. Over at the house, all the blinds were down. Some advertising flyers hung undigested from the mouth of the letterbox on the front door. Buck was probably right.

'I'll go check,' she said and the retro detective sighed, untied himself and followed her to the house with his C&W lope. He lit himself a cigarette as he reached Helen's side.

No answer came at first to her triple buzzing of the door-bell. Short, short, long. It was the family carillon in the Troy household when her family was still complete and long after her mother had died. Her anger shifted momentarily from Martin Buck to her brother Jamie. Not a word from him yet. She tried a double ring and another. Through the small single pane of frosted glass on the door some movement was visible. The letterbox opened, spilling its half-eaten meal of flyers.

'Who is it?' A woman's voice; hushed, foreign, frightened.

'I'm a policewoman, Detective Sergeant Troy,' Helen answered, stooping down to catch a glimpse of the hooded eyes on the other side. 'Are you Mrs Al-Baarai? Hadi's mother?'

The dark eyes worried in Helen's direction.

'I am Mrs Al-Baarai. You have a man with you.'

Martin Buck laughed aloud.

'My husband is not here and there are no other men,' Mrs Al-Baarai said more distinctly now. 'Please come another day.'

'I'm sorry, Mrs Al-Baarai, but this is extremely urgent. It can't wait.'

'This man you have, can he stay outside, please?'

'Ah, for Jesus' sake,' Buck muttered. He sucked on his cigarette and flung it on the lawn. 'Open up now, missus, or we'll push the door in.'

Helen stood up from her crouch at the letterbox. She faced Martin Buck. It was easy to see why the woman inside had no wish to encounter this particular specimen of the male gender. The hair, the leer, the attitudes from yester-year.

'I'll take this,' she said firmly.

'The fuck you will.'

'You know the drill on ethnic diversity, right? We have to accommodate people whenever possible.'

'I'm going in there,' he said and made to pass by her, ready it seemed to put his boot to the door. 'The woman could be bullshitting you. Christ knows who the hell is in there.'

'Let's see what Leo thinks,' Helen suggested. Buck stopped up short, looked down at her, stepped in closer so that he was looking even further down on her. Helen took out her work mobile, scrolled for Leo's number.

'Ah, good old Leo. Go for the old father-figures then, do you?'

The shock flummoxed her. He turned, swept back his bouffant blond hair and walked back towards the un-marked car. When he got there, he swung the driver's door open and cast a cynical eye on her.

'You'd be his type too. The little-girl look, you know?' he intoned. 'Take a peek beneath his pseudo-intellectual bullshit and ask yourself why he's so obsessed with this abuse lark.'

Behind her, Helen heard the slide and turn of two, then three locks. The door opened. The middle-aged woman standing before her wore the long black chador but her olive-skinned face was uncovered. A tear-stained face, desolate.

'Have you come to tell me that my son has been killed?' she asked.

# 28

On Main Street, Chapelizod not a parking space was to be found. Instead, they improvised one in the narrow confines of Church Lane. Not quite legal but it would have to do. Below the churchyard, an ageing hippy-type in a hi-viz jacket swept the footpath. He called to Leo and Ben as they walked by.

'Wouldn't leave the motor there, guys,' he said. 'There's a squad car pooching around the village the last two hours. They'll have you, those cops will.'

'We *are* the cops,' Ben said.

Nev Dunne shook his head in bemusement while Leo popped the tip from a cigarette and, lighting up, proffered the packet.

'Time was when you could tell a cop a mile off,' he said, taking a cigarette and storing it in his hi-viz for later.

'Do you drink in Jinky's?' Leo asked.

'Once in a blue moon. Not a drinker, me.' With a shifty chuckle, Nev changed the subject. 'Paying them a visit? That'll be a first.'

'What?'

'Jinky's getting raided.' The slice of bitterness in the old hippy's voice had Leo wondering if the guy had been barred from the pub. 'Never happens. Not unless they get the word first.' Then, looking beyond Leo, he added, 'Ah, the posse.'

Back along Main Street and to their right, the squad car hove into view. Leo flagged it down. He recognized the driver – Garda Dempsey, pink with an optimism that had been missing in him for weeks. The driver's side window slid open. In the passenger seat sat a female officer who'd clearly never seen Leo before. He ignored her fascination with his face. It was the wrong kind of fascination. He wondered if the young Garda had got himself a wedding partner.

'Anything to report?' he asked of Dempsey.

'Not so far, sir.' Dempsey tipped Leo an uncoordinated wink. 'No movement at Mrs Larkin's house or at Jimmy's.' He nodded in the direction of Jinky's. 'They're putting in a new door on the pub.'

'Have you been across to the other side of the river? The apartment block where Gary lives?'

'Yes, sir. Nothing stirring there either.'

'OK then, stick around for another while and pick me up at Jimmy Larkin's house. I'll be needing a lift to Ballsbridge. And, Dempsey, remember the flames, right?' He lowered his head to catch the female officer's eye again. She seemed awfully young to him. 'One of my best men this fellow is. Listen and learn.'

The look she gave him didn't augur well for the big boy's chances. She might be young, it suggested, but she was well beyond the age of reason and pushing towards the age of cynicism. Leo patted the roof of the squad car and it drifted away, along with Dempsey's hopes. The two detectives moved on. From up ahead, they heard laughter. A single, barely audible voice emerged that sounded vaguely familiar to Leo.

'Sounds like the pub's open for business, door or no door,' Ben remarked.

Leo stopped up abruptly. He turned and looked back along the cars they'd just walked by. The blue Mercedes coupé was among them. The voice he'd heard was Baz MacDonald's.

'Our West Belfast Armenian's paying Kevin a visit. I wonder why?'

The pub lay twenty yards or so ahead. Leo took a last few pulls from his cigarette and dumped it.

'Looks like we have a breach of the smoking regulations here,' Ben said.

Leo bristled. He set about preparing a defence of the indefensible but couldn't get beyond the expletives repeating themselves in his head. Ben nodded towards the pub door by way of explanation. A blue-grey cloud hung above the lintel.

'The bastards,' Leo said. The hypocrite, the other Leo thought.

'They've replaced the damaged hoarding in the derelict house next door too.'

From the doorway of the pub, they observed the scene inside. A new, unpainted door lay flat across some low tables, shavings on the floor below one end. Two workmen in navy overalls turned from their high chairs at the bar counter, pint glasses suspended before open mouths, cigarette hands frozen in mid-air. Baz MacDonald was nowhere to be seen. The workmen lowered their glasses, wondered what to do with their cigarettes.

'Baz?' one of them said. 'Eh, customers?'

'We're closed.'

The voice seemed at first to have come from another room. Then Baz emerged from below the bar counter, step by upward step. A cellar, Leo guessed. The smile on The Armenian's face didn't entirely disappear when he saw them. In his mind, Leo added the laughter and the persisting smile and came up with a Baz MacDonald whose mood had changed radically since their first meeting.

'I can explain everything,' he said, jocular, leaning his elbows casually on the counter. 'Put out the cigarettes, boys.' He didn't look in the workmen's direction as he spoke.

They obeyed without demur.

Ben entered the smoke-filled space, waving an indignant hand before his nostrils. At the doorway, Leo scanned the murals along the side walls. They were better than average work. The Glasgow Celtic European Cup-winning team of 1967, each of their faces so faithfully rendered that he recognized every one of them. He was a kid again, waiting in mounting expectation for weeks to see the game live on TV. Never did get to see it. Not live anyway. The nuns in the care home had insisted that everyone had to walk in the Annual May procession.

'Regals?' Ben asked of the workmen, whose cigarette packets lay in plain sight on the bar counter. 'Where did you get these?'

'Bought them off a lad down Moore Street,' one of them answered, got stroppy. 'Who wants to know?'

'You're talking to a policeman, Mike, show some respect,' Baz said. He gestured towards the doorway, kept his smile all the while. 'Get back to work now, boys. Sorry about that, Inspector Woods.' Baz deliberately ignored the younger detective. Head-honchos only talk to head-honchos was the suggestion. Leo joined Ben at the counter.

'Kevin's upstairs,' the dark-haired man told him.

'So you're the new lord and master of the Larkin empire,' Leo said. 'Running the pub, fixing the door, keeping in with the neighbours with the new hoarding out there.'

'Wrong on all counts, Inspector,' Baz responded. 'Kevin runs the pub. He fixed the next-door hoarding himself and was trying to hang the new door until I called. That's a job for the professionals. So I rang my friends here to help out.'

'Smoke the Regals yourself, do you, Mr MacDonald?' Ben asked abruptly.

'No, they're bloody awful, so they are. I'm a Lucky Strike man myself.'

He took a cigarette packet from his pocket and held it out. His eyes never left Leo's. Ben took the cigarettes, examined the packet.

'Counterfeits? We can have them tested if—'

'Don't waste your time,' Baz cut in. 'I bought them in the shop across the street. Ask them, they'll tell you.'

'I bet they will.'

'Take a look around the cellar there, Ben,' Leo said. 'No problem with that, Baz, no?'

'Be my guest,' he said and stepped aside to let Ben through.

While the young detective descended, Leo sat up on one of the vacated high chairs. Only one way to go after Baz MacDonald, Leo decided. Fists flying, wild and speculative, hoping to land a knock-out punch.

'Tell us about your relationship with Frida Goode, Baz.'

'Sorry?' He stayed with Leo's single eye. 'Can't say I know anyone of the name.'

'You were in the smoking area of the hospital the other day. She was there too.'

'Her and how many others?' Baz said with a shrug.

'Three others. An elderly couple and a middle-aged woman wearing a dressing gown.' Baz smiled. He'd picked up on the hint. The CCTV footage had been reviewed. His mind did a slow rewind of those minutes, Leo could tell.

'Yeah, I remember the old boy,' he said. 'Bill Twomey. Had a wee chat with him on the subject of gall-stones. The woman in the dressing gown . . . don't know the name but she had emphysema. Can you credit it? Emphysema and she's out there smoking. I haven't been able to enjoy a bloody cigarette ever since. Thinking of trying these new electronic ones actually. Course they'll find some bloody problem with those too. What's a smoker to do, eh?'

He laughed. He was on a roll. But Leo wasn't ready to roll over yet.

'So, you sat within a few feet of Frida Goode and didn't speak to her. But you spoke to the old fellow even though he was at the other end of the smoking area.' MacDonald drew his elbows back from the bar counter and stood tall. A little cartoon bubble appeared above his head with a light bulb in it. That was the general idea anyway.

'Ah, this would be the woman whose son died,' he said. 'The one who ran back inside when her daughter called her, right?'

'How do you know it was her daughter?'

'She called her Mum. A dead give-away that.'

The ex-Provo's mobile sounded. A message. He left the phone in his pocket.

Ben appeared from behind him, brushing dust from his sleeves.

'No skeletons, Ben?' Leo asked, and the young detective shook his head. 'OK, Mr MacDonald, we'll head upstairs. We've got some new information to share with Kevin. More than some, in fact. You'd better come along too. Wouldn't want to leave Kevin's cousin out of the loop now, would we?'

Leo dismounted the high stool.

'I've business to take care of,' the dark-featured man said.

'Haven't we all, Baz?' Leo said. 'Lead the way.'

Almond eyes washed in the redness of weeping, Mrs Al-Baarai began to compose herself. Helen waited. She tucked her left foot embarrassedly behind her right. When she'd taken off her shoes at the door, she'd discovered an expanding hole in her sock from which her big toe was determined to peek. The room was almost entirely bare but for the sofas they sat on and some prayer-mats that had been rolled out on the floor. For the Al-Baarais, Helen presumed, the emptiness and lack of decoration left room for God. For Helen, it left room only for disquiet.

'Are you OK to begin now?' Helen asked.

'I'm sorry,' Mrs Al-Baarai said and drew in a sobbing breath. 'I live in such fear these days.'

'Why did you think your son might be dead?'

The question drew more tears.

'Hadi is in Libya for two months now. He is with the rebels.'

'He's fighting in the revolution over there?' Helen said, astounded.

'He travelled there in March. Two weeks ago he went missing in Misrata. Last week we were told that a body brought back to Benghazi was probably our boy. It's our home city and my husband has gone there but I have no news from him yet.'

'He got into Libya? But isn't it a no-fly zone?'

'Through Egypt. He flew to Cairo and was driven to the border at El Salloum.'

*My rebel friends.* Hadi's inscription on the CD wasn't just adolescent posturing then. It was the real thing. Or maybe it was both.

'Mrs Al-Baarai, I'm here because we're investigating the death, in what may or may not have been a hit-and-run accident, of a boy named David Goode.'

The question she had in mind didn't need to be asked. Mrs Al-Baarai covered her mouth with the handkerchief squeezed tightly in her trembling hand.

'You knew David Goode then?'

'He was Hadi's friend,' Mrs Al-Baarai said. 'He called here sometimes. A fine boy. I spoke to him on the phone only last week.'

'Why did he ring you?' Helen asked, sitting up, rigid with anticipation.

'He wanted to know if we'd heard from Hadi. He was such a kind, considerate boy.'

'And this was when exactly?'

'Early in the week,' the black-clad woman said. 'It is so difficult to remember the days with all this worry. Tuesday, I think. And again on Saturday.'

'And David's sister, Georgia, did you know her?'

'No. I heard Hadi speak of her when he served . . .'

The woman lowered her eyes.

'You understand these questions have to be asked,' Helen reassured her. 'Can you tell me why Hadi got a community service order?'

'The judge, he wouldn't listen,' Mrs Al-Baarai said, growing more impassioned as she spoke. 'My son endured insults and attacks for years from those boys. And once, only once he fights back and he is taken to the police station. My husband pleaded with them but one of these boys, his nose was broken and the police, they had no choice. And these attacks didn't stop while he served his sentence.'

She broke down again.

'The same kids beat up on him again?' Helen asked.

The woman shook her head.

'Hadi told us these were different people but I don't know.'

Helen's ears pricked up. Different people as in Gary Larkin and Derek McCarthy?

'Mrs Al-Baarai, is the name Whitney Larkin familiar to you?'

A new alertness entered the woman's grief-stricken features.

'You really need to be honest with me here, Mrs Al-Baarai. Whitney worked her community service order with your son.'

'I don't know this name.' The woman disengaged herself from Helen's stare. 'This is the truth.'

But not the whole truth, Helen thought.

'Did Hadi have a girlfriend?'

Mrs Al-Baarai's sudden interest in straightening out the creases of her handkerchief betrayed her. A new and, perhaps, too convenient flood of tears followed. Outside the window, Martin Buck was pacing up and down, his phone angrily clamped to his ear. Dumping on her, Helen assumed.

'There was a girl. I never saw her but my husband did and . . .'

'Your husband thought she was, what? Unsuitable in some way?'

The woman wept more genuinely now.

'They argued all the time because of that girl. Not only that girl but everything. Hadi and my husband, they are both stubborn. He was thinking that Hadi had gone wild. Never going to the mosque, staying out late, drinking. We could not believe it when he asked for our blessing to go to Libya. We thought this is just his wildness again and my husband refused. He tried to make Hadi understand that getting rid of Gaddafi in this way would solve nothing. Look at Iraq, he told Hadi, look at—'

'How long did Hadi's relationship with . . . with this girl last, Mrs Al-Baarai?' Helen cut in. 'Were they still seeing each other before he went to Libya?'

'I don't know. If I knew I would tell you.'

'Maybe they were still in touch until . . . Does Hadi have a computer?'

'He took his laptop with him when he left. He Skyped and emailed often until he reached the Libyan border. Then he sent messages through his . . . his fellow fighters who came out of Libya for medical treatment or to rearm. Sometimes he faxed. And then, all of last week, nothing. Nothing. Not one word.'

'So you last heard from him when?'

'On Sunday, nine days ago. *Nine days.*'

The pain of loss intruded again, doubling the woman over. The most heart-rending of moans emerged from deep within her, a dark echo of the cries of childbirth. Nine days ago, Helen thought. And Whitney had gone AWOL three days later. A girl with a predilection for fantasy. A fantasy that might extend to a trip to Libya subsidized unwillingly by the Larkin family?

Helen moved on to the last item on her agenda.

'Does the name Mahmoud Maguin mean anything to you?' she asked. 'He's a medical intern. His parents live in Tripoli.'

'I know this name. We go to the same mosque but we don't know him personally.' Mrs Al-Baarai heaved with sobs again. 'This was my husband's dream for Hadi. To study Medicine. But they fought each other over that too. And now there is nothing left to fight over.'

Helen left the woman alone with her distress. That was the trouble with martyrs, she thought as she closed the front door: the people they hurt most were invariably their own.

# 29

In Leo's monoscopic vision, the pub stairway topped by a half-open door recalled the queasy geometry of early German cinema. A Nosferatu shadow skulked on the wall above and to his left. Baz MacDonald's or Ben's? Or Kevin's? It was impossible to tell.

Leo put away his work mobile, digested the contents of Helen's call from Clondalkin that had delayed his ascent. A further bizarre twist of perspective. He wondered what kind of alchemy he was going to have to employ to meld the elements of this case together. Heat and a hammer was the best he could think of. He climbed the stairs.

Silent though the room had seemed from below, a lot of talking was going on. Of the signed variety. All darting hands and dancing fingers, Ben and Kevin smiled at one another. Until the deaf man saw the one-eyed man. Kevin's fingers fell out of the air and hung by his sides. He stared at Leo. The discomfort of the others became palpable but the big man's absorption in Leo's face was unrelenting. Ben cleared his throat.

'We were just talking about how I came to learn—'

Leo shushed him with a hand. He knew Kevin wasn't staring at him out of pig ignorance. These were the eyes of a man for whom real, regenerative sleep was an unachievable nirvana, Leo thought. A man who didn't have to sleep to find nightmares. He found one now. Leo was in it. A younger Leo. The 1983 model.

'You remember me, don't you? Sign that, Ben.'

The deaf man nodded before Ben had raised his hands. Leo had imagined that the downturn at the left corner of his mouth might make his lips unreadable.

As tall a man as Leo but broader, Kevin sat on a kitchen chair that creaked violently beneath his weight. The room about him was cluttered but not altogether untidy. Nothing like the mess Ben had described after his earlier visit. He wondered if Baz MacDonald was responsible for the clean-up. Then he wondered why he might be. The guy cared for his cousin? Or maybe he was just taking care of number two? Did Baz have one Larkin in his camp at least? And, if he did, what did that mean?

'You remember the day Harry hit you out on Tandy's Lane? Must be nearly thirty years ago now,' Leo asked, and Ben, surprised and disconcerted, signed. 'You were in the back seat. Late evening and the mist was crawling towards us, past the house that was never finished.' An unexpected thought delayed Leo. 'The house that should've been your home. Remember that evening?'

A low, pained sound emerged from the deaf man. He shook his head. Sitting on a lower step of the precariously steep attic stairs, Baz MacDonald watched with reluctant fascination.

'Yes, you do,' Leo said as Ben's hands moved fluidly. 'You wet yourself back there out of pure fear. Fear of the mist, fear of Harry for sure, fear of me too probably. And Harry swings a fist back at you. You were an innocent, frightened little child and he punches you. Right here, remember?'

Leo put a fist to the high point of his own sagging left cheek. Kevin's response was the same as before but different. Similar in its negative intent, different in the shame that burned itself into the deaf man's features. It wasn't the emotion Leo had been aiming for. Baz and Ben glanced at Leo and then at each other. The good guy and the bad guy in agreement. Leo was a bollocks.

'I was a bollocks, a total bollocks. Sign it, Ben. I saw this happen with my own eyes. I told no one. I let you down, Kevin. You deserved my protection and I didn't give it to you. We were all such careless people in those days but that's no defence, is it? I'm truly sorry. Can you forgive me?'

Out of the deaf man's fists, some signing eventually emerged. Ben turned them into words.

'Yes, I saw you before, but I don't remember where, and this punch . . . no, it never happened.'

Leo sat down on a battered armchair opposite Kevin. He could feel the sweaty heat emanating from the tousle-haired man. Baz got another text message. He didn't check it.

'Harry beat you. He probably beat all of you black and blue. But you especially because you had no one to defend you, right, Kevin?'

'Gary didn't have it easy either,' Ben responded for Kevin.

The deaf man was avoiding Leo's gaze now, staying focused on Ben's hands.

'Gary might have been a major let-down to your father but you, you were just a bloody nuisance to him, weren't you? So he dumps you out of your home. Lands you in this old shambles of a place.'

'I was twenty-seven when I moved in here. It was well past time for me to move on.'

'Your stepmother was never going to be a mother to you. And you had what? A couple of photos of your mother maybe. Some misty memories maybe of a better time. Some fantasies about another life in that house on Tandy's Lane that never got built. That was all you had to shield yourself from that bastard with.'

Kevin's hands shot quickly up and Leo's head went instinctively back.

'I can take care of myself. I don't need a mother. I have a mother. In here,' Ben snapped, his tone catching the punched rhythms of Kevin's signing as the big man stabbed himself in the heart with a thick forefinger.

'You have nothing, Kevin,' Leo said. 'You live in a shithole. You dress like a down-and-out. You smell. Sign it, Ben, and don't have me tell you again. No one gives a goddamn about you, Kevin, least of all your own family. And you don't give a goddamn about any of them. Including Whitney. Because if you did actually care about your sister, you'd tell us what was going on here. Because if anyone knows, you do. You're the one she turns to when she's in trouble. Or maybe she just uses you, touches you for a few bob when she's stuck, hides out here when she's playing out one of her fantasy scenarios. Or were you the one using her? You painted a night sky above your bed for her just like the one you painted in her room.'

Abuse of one kind or another might have been par for the course in the deaf man's life but Leo's tirade still struck home. Of course it did, he thought. Abuse never goes away, never gets easier to cope with. He knew that better than most. Over by the attic stairway, Baz had unfolded his arms, made himself tall.

'There's no call for that kind of—' he began.

'You shut your bloody mouth. This is a hell of a lot more polite than a fucking IRA nutting squad interrogation.'

A dart of pain in his infected eye left Leo wincing. A tear

trickled to the lower edge of his eye-patch. He searched his pockets for a tissue but found only cigarette butts. When he looked up again, Kevin Larkin held out a fresh tea-towel to him, the tag still hanging from it. Leo took it. He raised his eye-patch, gave the deaf man a good look at the raw, poisoned well. We are fellow sufferers of a kind, he wanted to suggest. Fellow wanderers in a world made for others. That kind of thing.

Kevin signed, Ben spoke.

'That was my bedroom when I lived in St Laurence Villas. The night sky was for me, not for Whitney.'

Leo believed the deaf man's reply because it was brief and simple. Lies were rarely either. Baz's mobile began to ring. He couldn't decide whether or not to take the call.

'Are you going to answer that?' Leo barked. 'Or would you prefer I dumped it out the window?'

Baz reached into his pocket and cut the call without taking the phone out. On his face, the third cousin of a smile said something like *Happy now?* Leo might have reacted but the irritatingly busy phone had brought to mind another line of enquiry.

'We've been trying to track Whitney's phone, Kevin, but it's gone off-radar.' He paused, waited for Ben to catch up with his signing. 'Does she have a disposable?'

The deaf man shook his head.

'Come on, Kevin. It's par for the course in your family's business, right?'

'In my father's business, yes. But not in mine. Or in Whitney's.'

If Kevin was lying it didn't show. What showed was pained isolation. The deaf man was an outsider, though not because he wanted to be.

'You've been dealt a rough hand, Kevin,' Leo tried. 'A

cruel father, a disappearing mother. I know how you feel.'

The deaf man's laughter came as a surprise to Leo. An oddly staccato laughter that couldn't quite trust itself to have free rein. The man's signing grew more leisurely, Ben's interpreting slowed.

'You know how I feel, do you? All my life I've been hearing that. My teachers at school. The school psychologist. The tears she cried for me. And, here in the pub, these late-night drinkers trying to soften you up for another pint on tick. The guy who sweeps the street out there. All love and peace, man, and passing little notes to me. I know how you feel, Kev, I'm an outsider myself, never had a break, Kev, can I get another pint on tick there? I threw the bastard out. You have no idea how I feel, Inspector, none. Nobody does.'

Don't ever bring your life into work with you and vice versa, some old codger whose name Leo had long forgotten told him in those early days on the beat. A blank page made out of stone is what you have to be, young lad. At nineteen, Leo already had an aversion to mixed metaphors. And to grey-haired wisdom. He still had.

'Ben, give us your notebook there,' he said, and the young detective handed it to him doubtfully. 'And a biro.'

He wrote: *I was eight years old. Learning to play the piano from my old man. Trying to. I didn't have a note in my body and no sense of rhythm and he'd already burst my eardrum with his fist. So one day he had enough of it and brought the piano lid down on my hands. Got all my fingers free just in time. Apart from this one.*

Leo tore the page from the notebook and gave it to the big man, gave him time to read it. Twice, three times, with growing disbelief. He held out his left hand towards Kevin, palm down, fingers splayed out flat except for one. The small one. Scarred, its oddly convex shape raising it from the plane of the others. Ben and Baz peered at his hand but only Kevin understood. Leo retrieved the page, stuffed it in his pocket. He wrote some more.

*For all I know, my old man might still be alive. Pushing ninety if he is. But I can't let myself go looking for him because if I found him, I swear to Jesus, I might kill him for what he did to me and my mother. The piano was just the tip of the iceberg. Believe me, I do know how you feel, and the feeling never goes away. Which is why I want to rule you out as a suspect here. You can read my face and, Christ knows, that isn't easy, but I can read yours too and your face is telling me you're holding back.*

Kevin took the second note, read it, handed back the notebook and bowed his head.

Baz had retaken his seat on the attic stairs, his hands gripping the outer edge. Leo drew out the packet of Regals he'd confiscated in the pub below. He took one, offered one to Kevin. The big man's need for a cigarette overcame his initial surprise. Leo lit them up. He'd let the man take one decent pull before he hit him with the news from Temple Bar.

Baz MacDonald's phone rang again. His hand was already in his pocket but he didn't move to answer the call.

'That's the second time it's gone off,' Leo said.

'Sorry,' Baz said, and the phone went dead.

'Don't let it happen again,' Leo warned, and turned to Kevin Larkin. 'We've found where Whitney has been hiding.'

He waited as Ben delivered the message. The smoke from Kevin's cigarette spiralled brokenly. He held his cigarette hand by the wrist, steadying it. Leo watched Baz for his reaction to the next revelation.

'We believe she was hiding out with Georgia Goode. Know her? She worked out in Tallaght with Whitney.'

Kevin's gesture of denial came hedged about with delay and uncertainty. Baz moved not a muscle. The ex-Republican was good but not that good. The bland stare remained in place but the focus, Leo suspected, had turned inward. The stare stayed bland when Kevin changed his mind. Just.

'Whitney talked about this girl and her brother. They were decent kids. Kind. They made her feel better about herself. Better than before anyway.'

'David Goode was taken into the ICU ward on the same night as your father. Maybe coincidental, maybe not. A hit-and-run victim. Maybe accidental, maybe not.'

A half truth was called for, Leo thought. Not a half truth actually, a possible truth.

'Thing is, Kevin, we haven't got the tapes in yet but we're pretty hopeful on some CCTV cameras near the entrance to Porter Lane where they were hiding.'

The Regals packet lay exposed in the palm of Leo's hand. He lowered it so that it swam into Kevin's view.

'They had a visitor while they were there, Kevin. A Regals smoker possibly. Or does Whitney sneak one every now and then in spite of the asthma?'

A shake of the head. The head sinking further down. Leo placed a hand on the big man's shoulder and felt the burn of body heat. When he spoke, Leo found himself trying to imagine what it must be like to feel the vibrations of a voice touch you but not hear the voice.

'We have to start joining the dots here, Kevin. I don't want to have to stick you in a cell for a couple of nights. But that's what happens next if you keep stonewalling us here, right?' He waited for Ben to finish signing. 'Tell me about

Whitney and Hadi Al-Baarai. The Libyan kid. You've heard of Hadi, haven't you?'

Leo saw the surrender in the deaf man's expression before the nod of admission arrived.

'Tell me more, Kevin.'

# 30

Oak Lodge in Castleknock was a gated community. Fenced in by manicured trees, the curvaceous landscaping had been trimmed to perfection. Neatly camouflaged in its nooks and hollows, red-brick semi-detached houses and four-storey apartment blocks hid discreetly. No one was ever going to work their community service order scrubbing away graffiti here, Helen thought. Not in the foreseeable future anyway. Then again, real estate futures hadn't been all that foreseeable of late.

At the steering wheel of the unmarked car, Martin Buck took the flower-bedecked roundabout too quickly so lost was he in sour self-absorption. He scowled at her as though she were to blame. Outside the second apartment block they encountered stood a young man she took to be the management company rep. His fair hair was too wavy, his suit too pin-striped and his exaggerated gesture of checking his wrist-watch too annoying. For once, the two detectives were in agreement.

'Little bollocks,' Buck said. 'I'll sort him out.'

He swept the steering wheel left and set them on a direct course for the preening rep. At the last moment he swung right and to a screeching halt. A hail of loose stones peppered the suit. Buck bailed out and Helen let the altercation play itself out. The cowboy detective returned with a set of keys while his victim ducked into a silver BMW and sank low inside.

'Bastard was insisting he'd have to come inside with us,' Buck said. 'Let's get this over with.'

They passed through a set of absurdly misconceived Doric columns at the entrance to the apartment house. Behind some tall, exotic potted plants they found a lift and ascended silently. In the mirrored interior, Helen saw too many versions of herself and way too many of Martin Buck. They both looked tired. She knew why she was tired. Buck, it seemed to her, hadn't exhausted himself with his notorious but, to her, unlikely midnight athletics. His exhaustion wasn't about physical exertion but worry. When he spoke as they reached the door of Mahmoud Maguin's apartment, her instinct was confirmed.

'Listen, Helen,' he said, his hand to a clearly aching head. 'I'm under pressure these times. Family issues, you know.'

Helen was tempted to ask which of his three families he might be referring to but let it pass as he tried ham-fistedly and without much success to fiddle the keys into the two locks.

'Christ. Did you ever have one of those days when the key never fits?'

Heated, his face lost whatever was left of its youthfulness and most of its menace.

'I've had a few.'

He handed the bunch over to Helen. She got the door open on her first try and stepped inside. Plush was the word that came to mind. And fluffy. And sparkling. Plush red curtains and carpet, fluffy white sofas and armchairs. Gilt-ridden mirrors and frames, candelabras. In the bathroom, gold taps added to the sparkle. Mahmoud Maguin liked his home comforts.

'Some pad for a single guy,' Buck remarked, genuinely impressed by the vulgarity. 'His father owns it apparently.'

At a long table before the sliding balcony doors, the older detective flicked through some medical textbooks, notepads. Helen pulled on some latex gloves. Buck took the hint and the extra pair she'd brought along. They went along the corridor that led out of the main sitting area and opened opposite doors. Their voices clashed. Same message, different words.

'Mahmoud's room,' Helen said.

'Sleeps here,' Buck said.

One of them had to be wrong. They looked at one another. The Libyan intern had had an overnight visitor. The detectives took a room each and began their search. Soon, it became clear to Helen that the room she'd chosen was Mahmoud's. A neatly pressed set of medical white coats on a shelf of the built-in wardrobe, a row of expensive suits hanging there. On the dresser, a stethoscope, some books on immune disorders.

'Bingo!' Buck called from the other room.

From the doorway, Helen watched as the older detective squatted by the side of the bed and fished inside a leather briefcase. When his hand emerged, he was holding what looked like a passport in pale green. He opened it, squinted at the photo.

'Our mystery man no doubt.'

'He's Libyan, right?'

'Yeah,' Buck said, handing over the passport then dipping into the briefcase again. 'Or, let's see, Moroccan. Or Italian. Italian? How did he think he'd pass as a wop?'

'Libya used to be an Italian colony,' Helen said and took the remaining passports from Buck.

Their corpse in the van was called Yusef Dorda. And Mohammed Al-Amir. And Ali Marrone. His face was thick-featured, heavy-browed and indented with pockmarks. His black hair was variously curly, slicked back from the forehead, and flattened with a parting at the side. As Yusef from Libya he wore glasses, but even then his features couldn't be mistaken for the more youthful lines of Mahmoud Maguin's.

'Anything else?'

'Notebooks, some documents.' Buck swept them out, scanned them, handed them over. 'All in Arabic.'

He went digging further under the bed and came up with a laptop. A silver Mac. He handed it to her, held on to the bed as though to steady himself from a dizzy turn.

'You OK?'

'Yeah, no problemo. Mahmoud Maguin's?' Buck speculated. 'Or his mystery pal's?'

'Maybe neither. David Goode had a silver Mac.'

She turned the laptop over. On the bottom right-hand corner was a small sticker. *PCDonors.ie.*

'It's David's,' she said.

In the flat above Jinky's pub in Chapelizod, Leo waited impatiently for Kevin Larkin's response. He still had to pay a visit to Jimmy before he headed back home and got himself ready to call on Eveleen Morgan. His stomach clenched whenever his mind fast-forwarded to her place in Vavasour Square but there was still time to get in touch with his dealer. Time to pop some relaxant that wasn't too relaxing, some upper that wasn't too up. And he had a more valid reason to ring Dripsy. The dealer hadn't got back to him on what the street was saying about the Larkins and Baz MacDonald. Not a reason, he thought, an excuse. If the man with the fake limp had got anything, he'd already have been in touch.

The deaf man began to sign. Ben began to talk.

'I never met Hadi but, yes, Whitney liked him a lot. Loved him, I suppose.'

Sitting back on his seat, Kevin sighed. His eyes closed briefly and he breathed evenly as though unburdened.

'Gary and Jimmy tell me that your sister is something of a fantasist,' Leo said. 'As in inventing romantic tragedies for herself to star in. Are you sure this relationship with Hadi was real and not all in her head?'

'It was both, I suppose. I doubted her for a long time. It wasn't the first time she'd fallen in love or thought she had. But I went along with it. Because she wouldn't be telling herself these stories if she didn't need them. Who doesn't? Who doesn't need their lives not to be so fucking miserable they're hardly worth living? Right, Inspector?'

Leo looked at Ben.

'Fucking?'

'Deaf people can curse too, sir,' the young detective said, not looking at him. Working hard not to, Leo thought. 'I left out the earlier ones.'

'Don't leave anything out.'

Ben scratched his stubble, the jaw tightening beneath. Kevin Larkin was signing again.

'When she told me that Hadi had gone to fight in Libya, I didn't believe her. I didn't say as much but she knew. So she showed me some emails he'd sent from El Salloum—'

'El Salloum?' Ben signed back. A few seconds later he delivered Kevin's answer: 'A border town between Egypt and Libya.'

'And Whitney told you he was missing presumed dead?' Leo asked.

The deaf man was too busy wringing his hands to use them for talking with. Instead, he nodded. Behind him, Baz MacDonald turned his attention to the door at the far side of the room.

'When did she tell you this?'

Ben signed the question, voiced the answer.

'Last week. Last Tuesday. And it was like I knew this was what she'd do with the story. You know, like some stupid film where you can tell exactly what's going to happen. And I—' Kevin's hands fell briefly mute and Ben stopped interpreting. They came up again. 'I said, Hadi's told you he doesn't want to see you any more or he's never coming back from Libya, hasn't he? And she got so upset I had to go along with her story. What else could I do? So she calmed down and I thought, this is going to be OK, this will pass. And it was OK. Until she came back a few hours later. Until she asked me for the money.'

They waited, all of them resisting the force that drew them physically towards the deaf man, their resistance doubling, tripling the tension in the room. Kevin's hands were tired. Slow fingers delayed Ben's transmission – a radio station drifting in and out of hearing. In the deaf man's expression was a plea for absolution.

'She wanted to go to Cairo. It was mad, completely mad, but she had it all planned. Fly to Cairo. Get a taxi to El Salloum. Four hundred miles, I said, in a fucking taxi? Taxis are cheap there, she said. But a seventeen-year-old girl alone? She had an answer for that too.'

'Which was?' Ben asked before continuing to deliver Kevin's responses.

'She said she wasn't going to be travelling on her own.'

'Who was going with her?' Leo asked.

'She wouldn't tell me. She didn't trust me any more. Not once I'd told her I didn't have the kind of money she was asking for.'

A bitter defeatedness darkened Kevin's brow. The defeatedness was his own to keep. The bitterness was for Leo.

'You were right, Inspector,' Ben continued for Kevin. 'I have nothing. Less than nothing when it comes to money. And on Tuesdays there's maybe a hundred or a hundred and fifty euro at most in the till because Jimmy collects the weekend takings every Monday morning or I drop them over to his place. I might have fifty or a hundred euro here in the flat at any given time but that's all. I showed her what I had.'

He held out the wells of his two palms, less than nothing in them.

'I pulled out every last cent I could find. I said, take it. But she walked out.'

Tears dampened his face but didn't soften the anguish there. He kept on signing, let the tears fall where they might.

'I was always good to her. I always tried to look out for her. I always have.'

Leo gave Kevin the tea-towel. He hadn't noticed the image on the fabric until that moment. Mount Ararat. A memento from Armenia.

He looked over at Baz MacDonald, who was still studying the door at the other side of the room, though absently. The guy had plenty of money stashed away no doubt and he was the perfect travel companion cum bodyguard. The only likely one from among Whitney's circle of acquaintances.

Baz looked like doors had become his new hobby, a hobby that was developing into an obsession. The door spoke to the West Belfast man but Leo couldn't hear what it was saying.

'Did you tell anyone else that she'd asked for this money?' Leo asked.

Kevin shook his head.

'Do you reckon she asked the others for the money? Your father, Gary, Liz? No? Or Jimmy?'

More silent negatives. Leo guessed he'd get another but tried anyway.

'Or your well-travelled cousin here?' he suggested. 'He seems the caring kind. Fixes your door. Tidies your room. Brings you gifts from far-off places.'

Kevin turned to Baz. Something equivocal in his consideration of the man, Leo sensed. The debt collector looked like he wasn't getting what was owed to him. The negative came in long after it was scheduled to. A weariness had entered Ben's voice, Leo noted.

'If she'd asked the others, they would have laughed at her. Baz wouldn't do that. But he'd talk her out of it. He'd convince her it didn't make sense. She knew he would. The thing is that, crazy as these adventures she dreamed up were, she actually knew deep down they were crazy. She wasn't totally deluded like my father was in hospital. She wasn't sick. She was . . . cursed, trapped. Whitney never had a chance with those people. Never. Not once I'd left home. My life, here in this shithole, is better than hers ever was. She couldn't break the circle, Inspector.'

'Which circle is that, Kevin?'

The one Leo had in mind was the circle of abuse, the one that led back to Liz Larkin. But how could Kevin possibly know about his stepmother's childhood horrors? The big man had a less specific circle in mind, as Ben informed the room.

'The kind you get in all messed-up families. The poison you breathe in from, I don't know, all that rough talk, all those cold-hearted, sarcastic put-downs. Those people had no idea how much they hurt her because they never understood her. They thought they knew what was best for her but they got it wrong every time. Every fucking time.'

Leo picked up the sliver of truth Kevin had dropped, made a knife of it, pierced the big man's heart.

'Why did you leave your sister to the mercy of *those people*, Kevin? Why did you abandon her? Why did you leave her to rot in that house?'

Open-mouthed, Kevin Larkin gaped at him, swallowed hard. Slowly, he signed. Ben couldn't bring himself to look at Leo as he spoke the deaf man's self-lacerating words.

'Because I was a coward.'

A gulping noise set off what might have been the beginnings of a small cry had he not staunched it with the locking of his jaws. Even if he'd wanted to say more, he wouldn't have been able to find his hands. They were wrapped in around him somewhere as he contained his great crouched bulk.

'For Christ's sake,' Baz MacDonald said, 'leave the man alone, will you?'

'We're done here, Ben,' Leo said, and glanced over at the debt collector. 'But we're not done with you, Bazzy boy. Anything happens to Gary after we release him from custody today, you'll be our first port of call.'

He stepped across to where Kevin sat huddled. He placed a hand on the heaving shoulder. The deaf man looked up, all the way back up from his childhood.

'Sign this, Ben,' Leo said. 'I'm sorry I had to push you so

hard, Kevin. I could give you the old eggs and omelettes line but the truth is I'm big and awkward and ugly. I'm all the things you imagine yourself to be but you're not. And, let me tell you something else. You don't have nothing like I said. I saw your murals downstairs, I saw your night sky in Whitney's bedroom. You have a real talent. You're an artist. I can tell. Me? I have a job. Full stop. OK?'

He offered his hand to the big man. The big man took it.

# 31

In its decline, the low sun filled the frame of the window in Mahmoud Maguin's kitchen. Ruddy molten light, reflected from the glass and stainless steel surfaces, blinded Helen at first. Rectangular holograms floated on her retina as she began her search. Her mobile rang. Betty D'Arcy, the probation officer.

'Betty, you have something for me?'

Methodically, she pulled open the doors of the kitchen presses as she spoke. Tumbling sounds and slammed doors from one of the bedrooms marked Martin Buck's less orderly approach.

'Yeah. I contacted the supervisor out on those Tallaght schemes to see if he remembered anything of interest about those kids you mentioned. And he did.'

'Terrific. So what did he tell you?'

'Well, there were eight kids on the scheme but this trio were very close,' the probation officer said. 'Georgia was the catalyst, it seems. She's big into causes, apparently. So Hadi gets some racial abuse and she's there backing him up. Then Whitney was picked on because she was . . . well, she gave the impression that she was slow mentally. Sullen too, very troubled.'

The kitchen presses reserved for delph and glassware and cooking utensils were full. The few reserved for food were almost bare. Three jars of instant coffee. A couple of packets of biscuits. Mahmoud didn't have to fend for himself. It was a privilege Helen had never had. Not since she'd left home for university at eighteen. She checked her personal phone as she spoke on the work one. Nothing from her brother yet. In Jamie's case, no news was bad news.

'Troubled as in . . . ?'

'As in she cried a lot. Some kids can be like that on these schemes, you know. They find they're not quite as worldly wise as they'd imagined. So Georgia and Hadi take her under their wing. To be honest, the supervisor thought at first that maybe she was supplying them with . . . well, you know, given her background and all. But no, these kids really brought her out of herself. It was like Whitney had become some kind of project for them, the supervisor felt. The three of them were inseparable by the time they'd finished out their community service. And Whitney was a different girl according to the supervisor.'

'In what way different?'

'Less confrontational,' Betty explained. 'Actually, this supervisor said something interesting on that. He sensed that for the first time in her life Whitney felt included, so to speak.'

The probation officer's revelations left Helen oddly irritated. She remembered how she herself had been taken in hand by Ricky back at college, right down to the kinds of clothes she wore. Middle-class interventions in the lives of the lower orders bothered her. What if Georgia Goode had set off some rebellious fervour in Whitney that had gone pear-shaped?

'There's another, maybe not relevant, detail,' Betty

continued. 'Apparently there was an incident on their first day at the Tallaght site. An accident actually. Not involving the kids but two of the parents. It seems that Georgia Goode's mother was very upset after dropping her off there. So upset she couldn't stop crying, and when she went about pulling her car out from where it was parked on the street, she clipped another car. Whitney's father's car, actually.'

'And there was some kind of altercation?' Helen asked, Harry Larkin's bullying reputation in mind.

'Not at all. The opposite, in fact. Seems Mr Larkin was very sympathetic. And the supervisor later discovered that he'd actually taken the blame though it clearly wasn't his. Not only that, but apparently Whitney's father paid for the repair job.'

'So Harry Larkin knew Mrs Goode?'

In the corridor leading to the bedrooms, Martin Buck had taken a sudden interest in Helen's phone conversation. His stare had lost its more unseemly elements. He turned away before Helen could tell for sure what had replaced them.

'It seems so, Helen,' Betty replied. 'I hope this helps.'

'It does,' Helen told her. And it doesn't, she told herself. 'Thanks a million, Betty. I owe you one.'

She rang Leo.

Helen's voice filled the unmarked car parked outside Jimmy Larkin's two-up, two-down terraced house on Maiden's Lane. They had her on speaker. Leo and Ben listened to the mystery deepen, its roots bifurcating further and further down into the damp, dark earth. The corpse in the white van was a real-life Libyan spy complete with fake passports, she told them. A spy who had in his possession David Goode's well-secured laptop. Then there was that unlikely meeting to report on. When Harry met Frida. When she'd finished, a doubled silence fell. In the car. In Mahmoud's apartment. A silence profound as the deaf might know, Leo speculated idly.

'Good work, Helen,' he said. 'OK then. First off, ring SDU and hand over the scene . . .'

'But this is our—'

'Listen, I talked to Superintendent Heaphy earlier and, in his usual roundabout way, he told me that SDU had information about some Libyan diplomat who was expelled from London a few weeks back. Seems he ran agents over there and may have had one in place here too. This presumably is Mahmoud Maguin's sleep-over pal.'

'And our guy in the white van.'

'Yeah,' Leo continued. 'Looks like he found out about David Goode's hacking exploits. But it appears that he might not have been the only one who knew that David was a hacker. Or, at least, knew there was a hacker operating from here. The super tells me the Americans are talking to our cyber boys back at HQ today. I've asked Martha to suss out what she can from the meeting.'

A curtain twitched over at the front window of Jimmy's house. In the driver's seat, Ben stirred and looked in Leo's direction for the first time since they'd left Kevin Larkin.

'How long have the Americans known about this Libyan guy?' Ben wondered aloud. 'Were they following the Libyan while he was following David? Was he wearing a bullet-proof vest because he knew he was being followed?'

Helen's voice intervened, a pitch higher, her imagination diving into the sea of possibilities and surfacing with the wildest one.

'You don't think the Americans killed this Libyan guy, do you?'

'It doesn't add up,' Ben decided. 'If the FN Five Seven in the van was American Secret Service issue, why wasn't it used and why was it left there?'

'Listen, Helen,' Leo said, 'we've no choice but to hand over the case to SDU now. We insist on staying in the loop, of course. And we dig wherever we need to dig to find Whitney, right? We've got nothing from the house-to-house enquiries and nothing from the ferries or airports so, as of now, we go public with her disappearance. Probably should've done before now even if the family did insist she wasn't missing.'

Leo hated the sound of his own voice when he was making excuses. It sounded like his father's had. *Es war ein Krieg kein Picknick.*

'And Georgia Goode's disappearance?' Ben asked. 'Do we publicize that?'

'Not yet, we don't want the kid more panicked than she already is,' Leo said. 'We need to put a team on that list of friends you got from her father. Also these protest groups she's been involved with in the past. Let's assume she went into hiding after David was killed because she knew he'd been sussed and maybe knew someone had been watching him. But why does she think she's a target too? And why in Christ's name was Whitney hiding out with her?'

Leo closed his good eye. The patch on the other kept out enough light to give a reasonable impression of darkness. He seemed to see Kevin Larkin's agile fingers flittering by like bats in a darkened belfry. The deaf man had told him more than Leo had yet deciphered. He felt sure of that. He tried to recall the conversation in more detail but Helen intruded.

'Shouldn't we at least finish the search here before we call in the SDU? See what else we can find?'

'Of course. But half an hour, forty minutes at most, and then you're out of there.'

She ended the call without answering.

'I'll go talk to Jimmy,' Leo told Ben. 'Dempsey's giving me a ride home.'

'You're not coming back to Pettycannon station?' Ben said, tossing a hint of mild surprise into the mix.

Leo didn't feel he owed the young detective an explanation but the explanation came anyway. Sounding like an excuse.

'I've an appointment at half eight.'

The look of concern he got from Ben surprised him. He wondered if the trepidation he felt whenever Eveleen came to mind was showing.

'Nothing serious, I hope?'

'Christ, no,' Leo said, a smile breaking naively across the side of his face that he still had, in theory, some control over. 'Meeting a friend. But my phone stays on so keep me posted, right?'

The young detective nodded, stroked his unshaven cheek with a hand whose real intention was clearly to cover a grin.

Leo got out of the car in a huff. He felt like an idiot. In the upper glass panel of Jimmy Larkin's front door, he caught his own reflection. He looked like an idiot. He needed to take his sweaty apprehension out on someone. The ex-shipping clerk would do. Do very nicely, thank you.

Helen opened another high press in Mahmoud Maguin's kitchen and all hell broke loose. All over the apartment. Ducking below a hail of falling cornflakes Helen heard, in the same instant, a hollow crash from the corridor. An incoherent shout. Martin Buck's. Something big, heavy and human fell on the kettle-drum floorboards of the corridor.

Bounding steps added a drum-roll. The banging shut of a door ended the solo.

Helen unholstered her gun and stepped across the kitchen floor, the cornflakes crunching beneath her Docs. She took a breath, turned the corner in the Weaver position. Legs spread shoulder-width, her firing hand pushed forward, support hand back to take the recoil.

Martin Buck lay on the ground, eyes half closed, a loose hand clutching at the bare floorboards for a hold on consciousness. Behind the prone detective, the door to a coat press stood open. Only the door into Mahmoud's bedroom remained closed. There were stirrings inside that might have been the breeze from an open window. Or someone was skulking about in there. Helen went down on one knee beside Buck, her gun still cocked. Blood leaked from a long gash on the back of his head.

'Is it Maguin?' she whispered.

'Don't know. Caught me from behind.' He looked down at himself, his portly stomach exposed. 'Where's my jacket?'

The middle-aged detective's eyes closed down and his face turned grey and elderly. His hand stopped clawing at the floorboards. He was out of it but breathing. With some difficulty, Helen moved him on to his side, bent his knees to prop him. She stood and got her back to the wall alongside the bedroom door. In her mind, she saw Mahmoud on the other side of the door, leaning back to back with her against the same strip of wall. She saw his face from the scanned hospital ID photo. But not his hands. Or what he might be holding there.

'Mahmoud?' she called. 'I'm a police officer. Detective Sergeant Troy.'

She listened for a response, voluntary or involuntary. None came. She got the work mobile out of her zip-up jacket. Quietly she rang for back-up. When the call ended, there were no signs or sounds in the apartment for Helen to interpret except what she felt in her gut. Whoever it was, he was still in the bedroom.

'There's no way out for you. The grounds will be surrounded in a few minutes.'

Helen heard a distant thud, a raking of pebbles. Her quarry was on the move. She tried the handle of the bedroom door. It wasn't locked. She placed both hands on the semi-automatic and kicked through. She ran to the open balcony doors at the far side of the room and caught sight of the man. She couldn't tell if it was the medical intern. Grey track suit, black baseball cap. He wasn't running freely. A limp on the right throwing him off-balance, delaying his progress. Helen appraised the drop. It was doable. Just. She slipped her gun back into its holster and climbed out over the balcony rails. Three or four inches of plinth between her and the fall.

Most of the way down it felt like controlled flight. The last few feet upset her body's calculations and the ground slammed into her left side. She stood up. Nothing broken, just a generalized battering that would soon turn black and blue. The man had disappeared from sight. She sprinted away in the direction she'd last seen him take. Sore as she was, her legs felt strong. Her training with Atletico Glasnevin hadn't been wasted. Not entirely.

Emerging from the hollow surrounding the apartment building, she saw him again. When he'd crossed into the hills and dales of the sweeping front lawn, a mere twenty yards separated them. She still hadn't seen his face nor redrawn her gun. Over at the main entrance, just as the first of the squad cars appeared, she launched herself at the man, taking him down low with a rugby tackle. There was no struggle which pissed her off because she wanted to hit him.

Mahmoud Maguin sobbed like a child humiliated in a schoolyard scrap. His concerns, however, were rooted in an all too adult world.

'I knew this would happen,' he cried. His plummy, adenoidal South Dublin accent surprised her. 'My family's dead now, totally finished. All of them. They're going to die.'

'You have to help us, Mahmoud,' she said as she watched the decision to clam up harden his sallow features. 'Or things can only get worse for you.'

'Worse than losing everyone?' the medical intern asked of the trees and the flowers and the carpet of grass in that artificial Garden of Eden. 'Everything?'

# 32

'Mammy.'
   The word, uttered respectfully by a seventy-two-year-old criminal, felt both absurd and oddly disconcerting to Leo. The woman in the framed photograph on the wall of Jimmy Larkin's hallway was broad, pug-ugly and mean-eyed. She was Harry Larkin in a frumpy dress and a cockroach wig.

'Fine-looking woman,' Leo remarked as he followed the thick-spectacled man into his parlour.

'Reared us on her own. Five of us.'

'Five?'

'The other three died when they were only chisellers. Rough times those were back then in the Foley Street tenements. One room we had.' Jimmy sat down at a blue Formica table by the lace-curtained window. His melancholy speech came over as a justification for a life of crime. A more reasonable one than the white-collar crooks ever came up with for their depredations, Leo had to admit. 'The young crowd these days, they know nothing about what the likes of us went through. Nettles for dinner. Imagine lobbing that on the table in front of them. They'd shit bricks.'

'Green bricks,' Leo said.

Jimmy didn't take kindly to having irony applied to his nostalgia. He fingered the lace doily on the table irritatedly. Leo hadn't seen a doily for years. Now that he'd absorbed his surroundings, he saw that the room might have been the set for some 1960s Dublin soap. Lace curtains, laminated surfaces, an orange sofa complete with crocheted antimacassar. A stack of old-style book-keeping ledgers at one end of the Formica table completed the time warp. Only the yellowing grey computer in an alcove by the beige-tiled fireplace seemed out of place.

The ex-shipping clerk reached for an ashtray on the window sill. And a packet of Regals. He lit up, didn't offer Leo one. He left the packet alongside the ashtray like a provocation.

'Tell me about the trip Whitney was planning to make to Libya. The one she asked you to stump up for.'

Magnified eyes were useful for the viewer who wanted to spot a break in the usual rhythm of blinking or a sudden dilation of the pupils. Leo spotted both.

'Me?' Jimmy chuckled mirthlessly. 'She wouldn't ask me for a glass of water if she was on fire.'

The spectacles had slipped down his nose. He left them there.

'She didn't like you?'

'She didn't like anyone who called her up on her bullshit fantasies.'

'That's the only reason she didn't like you?'

'You'd have to ask her that. I'm sure she'll come up with some mad story. That's her form.'

'Her Libyan friend, Hadi, wasn't fantasy,' Leo said. 'You knew about him, right? The kid she scrubbed graffiti with out in Tallaght.'

'Heard tell of him all right. Gary handled that.'

'Beat him up?'

'Warned him off.'

'Did Harry know about Hadi?'

Jimmy laughed, blew some smoke at Leo's eye-patch.

'Are you joking me or what? If Harry'd known, this Libyan kid wouldn't be able to walk never mind—'

'Never mind what?' Leo asked. Jimmy was doing his blind trick again, focusing on his inner self, giving his inner self a clip on the ear. 'Never mind fight with the rebels in Libya?'

'News to me.'

'Here's some more news for you, Jimmy. We found where Whitney's been hiding. An art gallery in Temple Bar. Ring any bells?'

The revelation didn't have quite the impact Leo had expected. Jimmy took a last luxurious drag from his cigarette and stubbed it on the ashtray. He sat back. Only one conclusion suggested itself to Leo: Jimmy had been forewarned. By Kevin? By Baz MacDonald? It was possible but instinct told him otherwise. And yet, he asked himself, who the hell else could have got the word to Jimmy so quickly?

Leo picked up the Regals cigarette packet.

'Whitney had a visitor who smokes your brand, Jimmy.'

'Well, that narrows it down to a couple of thousand people. You're getting there, Leo. You might even get there before they put you out to grass.'

'We're gathering CCTV material from Temple Bar. We've cameras looking right on to the entrance of the lane.'

'Drunken stags and hens is all you're going to find on them cameras, Sherlock. Kiss-me-quick hats and cider flagons.'

'Whitney was hiding out with a kid called Georgia

Goode,' Leo persisted. 'Whitney met her in Tallaght too, just like she met Hadi. Now Georgia's brother David is dead. A hit-and-run that was no accident. Same night Harry was shot. Do you believe in coincidences, Jimmy? I don't. Not where the Larkins are concerned.'

'The name Goode means nothing to me.'

There was one last detail that Jimmy couldn't possibly have been prepared for by Baz or Kevin. The little nugget Helen had delivered out in the car. When Harry met Frida.

'The name Goode means nothing to you. Interesting.' Leo narrowed his good eye, waited. Poured himself a cigarette from his own packet. Snapped the tip. Lit up. 'So Harry didn't tell you, then?'

Leo stood up. Fixed his tie, buttoned his jacket. Jimmy watched the detective's every move in spite of himself. Waited for the oracle to speak. Resisted momentarily and looked out by the lace curtain. The squad car had arrived to pick Leo up. Jimmy surrendered.

'Didn't tell me what?'

Leo strode across the room. He found himself standing before a sideboard covered with trophies and medals. Nickel-plated most of them, the sheen long lost and in its place an opaque, jaundiced reflection of the fading light. Above the sideboard were ten or twelve team photos. Under-age teams. Girls. Under-tens the youngest. Under-fifteens the oldest. 1995 the earliest year. 2004 the latest. Jimmy there in each one with more hair than now. His hands on their shoulders. A leer you'd arrest a man for in the circumstances. In the centre of the front row from 1998 to 2002, a little mascot. Whitney.

'Didn't tell me what?' Jimmy repeated.

'Whitney was your team's mascot for a while, I see.'

'Yeah, until she lost interest. What didn't Harry tell me?'

Leo turned to the small man, saw the white snooker balls of his eyes drop hurriedly out of sight.

'She lost interest? In 2002? That was her First Communion year, wasn't it, Jimmy?'

'She lost interest because she couldn't kick a bleedin' ball,' Jimmy blustered. 'She was uncoordinated that way too.'

'Why did you pack in the coaching, Jimmy?'

'Because the kids don't listen any more. Know it all, they do. And the parents are worse.' His voice tightened into a whine. '"Why didn't you pick my Mary? My Tanya is better than Celine."'

'And that's the only reason?'

'What other reason would I have?' The small man seethed, flushed. 'I know what's on your mind, all right. You're obsessed, you know that? I wonder why you can't get that shit out of your head.' He shot up from his chair. Still a lively little man, Leo thought. 'What's this crap about Harry? Harry didn't tell me what?'

Attack is the best form of panic, Leo mused. Put his musing away for later consideration. Globules of sweat had formed along the wrinkles of Jimmy's forehead.

'You keep the books for all these businesses, right?' Leo said, gesturing at the medieval computer and the book-keeping ledgers. 'So, you'd know of every payment Harry made.'

'Harry kept his own kitty.'

'But you'd know, for example, if Harry had an accident in his car last year, wouldn't you? You'd know he paid for the repairs. Not only for his own car but the one that hit him. Or maybe it was a favour from some dodgy mechanic pal of his?'

'What are you talking about? Harry didn't have a car accident for years.'

277

'Last July, when he dropped Whitney to Tallaght to start her community service order there was an accident,' Leo said.

Jimmy Larkin had just heard the best joke in his long lifetime. His laughter came all the way up from the pit of his stomach. It sang of relief and sarcasm and spit-in-your-eye triumph. Leo didn't like the tune.

'Last July,' Jimmy began, but hilarity overcame him again. He took off his spectacles, wiped them with the lace doily from the table. 'Last July, Harry was in St James' Hospital having heart surgery and then recuperating in a nursing home in Lucan. He never took Whitney to Tallaght. Not the first day. Not any day.'

Inside, Leo reeled.

'So, who brought her to Tallaght?'

'Not me, I don't drive,' Jimmy said. 'After that I can't help you. Much as I'd like to, Leo, my old friend.'

Whitney had been playing her fantasy games out in Tallaght too, it seemed. Her driver wasn't Harry. Nor Gary, because he wasn't old enough to look like Whitney's father. And hardly Kevin because it would have been apparent to the supervisor who'd witnessed the incident if a deaf man had been trying to communicate with Mrs Goode.

'Baz MacDonald brought her?'

'I haven't a bull's notion who brought her the first day.'

'But Baz did bring her sometimes?'

Jimmy's was a Judas shrug. He lit himself another Regal. The small man's smugness riled Leo.

'Soon as you people pull the plug on Harry, maybe sooner, MacDonald will take your cigarette money and everything else.'

'No, he won't. Baz is heading away.'

'To where?'

Another shrug, but a more abrupt one. A welling up in him that he swallowed back down. Then he looked up at Leo out of the magnified wells of his spectacles. Watery wells.

'If you'd seen Harry over the past few months, you wouldn't be so free with your allegations,' Jimmy cried. 'He was a broken man. Broken by that useless bloody family of his. Every one of them more trouble than the next. Sucking him dry, and not one iota of gratitude for all they had, for all he gave them.'

'Spare me the violins, Jimmy.'

'The last time I was up in that poor man's house,' he blubbered. 'The last DVD I ever watched with him . . . an old one, a Warren Beatty picture, *Bulworth*. This fellow's sick of life so he hires a hitman to kill him, only he changes his mind. And do you know what Harry said to me? Do you know what the poor man says? I wouldn't change my mind, he says. That's a broken man, Leo. And you want to make a devil out of him?'

'Are you telling me he hired—' Leo began, the name Baz MacDonald on his lips again.

'I'm telling you about a film we watched. I'm telling you he doesn't deserve to have his grave walked all over by youse lot.'

'He's not dead yet,' Leo said, provocatively, pushing for some more angry revelations. But they didn't come. Just one big grieving one.

'For your information,' Jimmy said, a catch in his voice, 'we're letting my brother go peacefully tomorrow. I'd ask you to leave us alone for a few days only I know I'd be wasting my breath.'

The small man sat and lowered his head to where

his arms rested on the table. He gave a pretty decent impression of a man grieving for a lost brother. Leo saw himself out of the room. He wondered whether the dispute between the Larkins and Baz MacDonald had been settled in some way. Or maybe it had been a fiction from the first-off. A fiction he'd been foolishly taken in by. Harry in drag looked grimly down at him from the photo in the hallway. *If there was no feud, no kidnap, ransom or abuse, then who the fuck shot me, Leo, and why – and where's my daughter?*

Leo closed the front door but the questions followed him outside where Garda Dempsey waited for him in the squad car. He rang Helen, filled her in on the possible Baz MacDonald/Frida Goode scenario, the deaf man's revelations about Whitney's Libyan fantasy and tomorrow's pulling of the plug on Harry. He threw in Jimmy's early retirement from coaching young girls for good measure. She gave him a diluted version of Mahmoud Maguin's arrest, his refusal to talk and a more vivid description of Martin Buck's hospitalization.

'That'll knock his one-track mind off the rails for a while,' he said and registered her surprise at his lack of sympathy for the cowboy detective. 'I mean it's just a cut and concussion, right?'

'Yeah,' Helen said. 'You coming in to Pettycannon now?' Leo's hesitation drew more vibes of surprise from her. 'You're not?' Left unsaid were profundities such as *Where are your priorities? Can you morally justify indulging in romance at a time of great crisis? Are your passions ruled by your head or your crotch?*

'I'm meeting a friend for dinner. I do have a life, you know. And my phone will be—'

'Relax, Leo,' Helen said. 'Have a nice evening.'

She hung up, and Leo couldn't decide whether she'd meant to be sarcastic or sincere. Good, old-fashioned Catholic guilt swarmed over him. Comes of having a nun for a mother, he told himself.

# 33

Daylight had begun to fade in the east-facing Incident Room at Pettycannon Garda Station. Helen sat alone there, the call from Leo deepening her sense of solitude. She was glad for him but no less sad for herself. The long day had exhausted her. Yet, she felt unwilling to turn on a light. That was how the night started and she didn't want the night to start.

She texted her brother again. Her message was less abrasive, veered towards pleading. To her surprise, the trick worked. Jamie rang her.

'Helen.'

'Jamie, what's the story with the house?'

'Yeah, I'm fine, Sis.' His sarcastic tone burned through her moderation like acid. 'Sorry, I misheard you there. Thought you'd asked me how I'm doing.'

'And you asked me?'

'I don't need to. You've got Ricky the Poodle back. Normal service resumed. Helen holding the leash.'

'I haven't seen him and I don't want to. You didn't answer my question.'

'Of course. You'll let him grovel for a while first.' Jamie's laugh was the cynical kind that always came before he hit you with something. 'I don't have to sell the house.'

'What about this guy you owe all the money to?'

'Sorted, Sis. Changed circumstances, like.'

It sounded like the usual invitation to walk into his personal quagmire. She stayed put.

'We agreed to sell the house. And I'm the one with power of attorney here, remember.'

'You want to throw us on to the street?'

'Us?'

As a singer, Jamie had Sinatra timing. Used it to good effect in real life too.

'Us?' she repeated.

Helen's heart kept the quickening beat and Jamie swung in when least expected on the off-beat.

'Me and Deirdre,' he said.

'Deirdre?'

'You wouldn't know her. And not forgetting the baby, of course. They tell us it's a girl. Want to guess what name we won't be giving her?'

Jamie was eight years younger than her but for as long as she could remember he could beat her up, make her cry, make her wonder why. He still could.

'I'm trying to pay the mortgage on an empty apartment and renting one here in Dublin,' Helen insisted. 'Most of my wages go into that bottomless pit. I have no savings. Not a penny. I can't remember the last time I bought myself a new fucking dress or went to a restaurant. Some days at the end of the month I actually don't have a dinner, and as for—'

'Helen, you made your own choices and now you want me to bail you out?' Jamie said. 'No one forced you to buy an apartment up in Tipperary or go running around the country trying to get yourself promoted. Meanwhile, I stayed home with Dad all those years you were gone, went through every last shitty day of his dying with him. Now his granddaughter's going to be born in this house and raised here in our home.'

At first, every response that came to Helen's mind felt weak or selfish or plain heartless. When she regained something of her equilibrium, she kicked back.

'How did you get this guy off your back? What did you do for him?'

That cynical laugh again.

'Worried about the old career prospects again, are we?'

'Answer the question.'

'You're the detective, Helen,' he sneered. 'If you figure it out you might even get yourself another stripe.'

Helen cut the call and tried to get back to typing up her report of the Castleknock incident but her hands shook with an emotion that was somewhere between rage and guilt. And guilt won out, as it always did, finding other reasons beyond Jamie's animosity to justify itself. Such as bemoaning her father's failure to dump him out of the house years back. Such as cursing her mother's carelessness, walking on the wrong side of the road the evening of the accident. She hated thinking such things. She got her mind back on the work.

Mahmoud Maguin languished in a cell somewhere below the Incident Room, terrified, silent. Insistently silent. She'd hoped to get something out of him before the Special Detective Unit took charge. She hadn't. Once the SDU people arrived she'd have to call it a night whether she wanted to or not. Long minutes passed until suddenly one of those minutes was shorted out with a sharp, furious perception. She was being watched. Ben Murphy stood at the far end of the conference table.

'What?' she said, her spiky defences shooting up.

Ben shrugged, sat in at the long table. His stubble had gone well beyond the designer look, exaggerating the leanness of his face, impoverishing it. He looked like a hungry prisoner. She went back to the report she'd been typing on the laptop screen. All the while she kept watch on her colleague at the periphery of her vision.

'You shouldn't have done that, you know,' he said.

'Done what?'

'Taken a chance like that. Gone chasing this Mahmoud guy. The squad cars were at the gates, for Christ's sake,' he insisted as he approached her warily.

'So I leave the arrests to the big boys, is it?'

'What I'm saying is he could've been armed. OK, he didn't have a gun that you could see, but he might have had a knife. Or, who knows, he might have had martial arts training or—'

'Or none of the above. I followed my gut and it worked. End of story.'

He was above her now, flushed and bleary-eyed.

'That's the problem, Helen, you don't think. And when you do bother to think you—'

She got to her feet, shouting to cut him off, their faces within touching range.

'You just do your own job and let me get on with mine, Mister fucking Mystery Man. I don't need an escort. This isn't Jane Austen.'

'No, but it's not *Wonderwoman* either.'

'Boys, girls, get back in your seats and behave yourselves.'

It was Sergeant Martha Corrigan. She looked from one to the other, amused. And arriving at ridiculous conclusions, Helen suspected. She might have said so if the auburn-haired woman hadn't waved a sheaf of pages at them and taken a place halfway along the table.

'Back to work,' Martha said, and ignoring Helen's dagger eyes added, 'I'll sit between you so you can't get at each other.'

Reluctantly they sat, focusing on the pages so neither one would have to surrender a look.

'Leo asked me to find out what I could about this meeting on cyber crime at HQ today,' Martha began. 'Is he about?'

'No,' Martha's sulking pupils answered as one.

'Well, I'm clocking off shortly so you can pass this info on to him.' She raised a couple of stapled A4 sheets from the file. 'OK, first off, this. I haven't shown you this, you haven't seen it and you don't talk to anyone but Leo about it, right?'

She placed the pages before her on the table so that both detectives could lean in and read them. Helen felt a frisson of excitement as she absorbed the details of the title page. *Secret and Personal . . . Top Secret . . . Delicate Source . . . UK Eyes . . . The Secret Service . . . Libyan Intelligence Activity in the UK and Ireland.* The emblem had a crown on top and below it the motto Regnum Defende.

'MI5?' Ben asked, the tiredness banished from his widening eyes.

'Obviously,' Helen said and flicked over to the next page, speed-reading as the ex-Rose of Tralee spoke.

'Basically what we've got here is a report on a high-ranking Libyan diplomat in London who ran their ESO operation over there. ESO – External Security Organization – keeps tabs on anti-regime Libyans abroad. This diplomat was over and back to Ireland since the late eighties and had contact with the Provisional IRA.'

Helen and Ben shared an accidental glance. Each knew what the other was thinking. Baz MacDonald, the ex-Provo with the motorbike MO.

Martha went on. 'So, late last year, MI5 informed our security and intelligence people that the guy might have an agent in place here, in Dublin. They didn't know his identity but our National Surveillance Unit have been monitoring a number of suspects and it turns out one of them is—'

'The man in the van?' Helen said.

'Yeah, Yusef Dorda by name,' Martha said. 'NSU weren't carrying out twenty-four-hour or even daily surveillance. The usual problem. Too much work, too few bodies. Besides which their main focus is on Al Qaeda links here in Ireland. So this Dorda guy was well down the priority list. Anyway, they've been checking on him more or less weekly since March last and—'

'At Mahmoud Maguin's place?' Ben interrupted.

'No,' Martha replied. 'Dorda lived in an apartment in Milltown. It's been checked out and he was last seen on Saturday evening. They reckon he went into hiding at Maguin's apartment after the hit-and-run incident.'

'But how did he discover that David Goode was an anti-Gaddafi hacker?' Helen asked.

'Nothing on that yet. But they've confirmed that Mahmoud Maguin's father works at a hospital in Tripoli. Whether the family are genuine supporters of Gaddafi, we can't yet say.'

'So we can't assume Mahmoud was blackmailed into helping this Secret Service guy to save his family?' Ben said.

'Not until the SDU digs deeper,' Martha told him. She passed some pages to each of them. 'OK, back to Whitney then. A summary of the reports we got from the various schools she's been to.'

'Took them bloody long enough to get this done,' Helen muttered.

'Don't knock the locals,' Martha said. 'As a matter of fact,

I'm told this file has been on Detective Sergeant Buck's desk since yesterday lunchtime.'

'Why would he sit on it?' Ben asked.

'Carelessness,' Martha told him. 'Apparently he's got a bit of a reputation for this kind of thing.'

Helen scanned the pages. Whitney had changed schools three times at primary level, twice at second. Learning disabilities had clearly hampered her progress. Poor concentration and well below average reading age scores were cited. From among a list of problems 'letter reversal' caught Helen's eye. The phenomenon, according to the writer, was mistakenly attributed to dyslexia and, in any case, had been self-corrected in Whitney's secondary school years. The phrase 'behavioural difficulties' abounded though the pages were short on specifics. Aggressive, uncooperative, disruptive were about as descriptive as the reports got.

Three psychological referrals were mentioned though it was clear that Whitney had changed schools before the results, if any, had come in. One comment attributed to the principal of Whitney's last school suggested that 'the child's parents appeared to have followed a strategy of moving her on once a psychological examination had been recommended'. The Larkins, it seemed to this woman, were unwilling to face the reality of Whitney's obvious learning and behavioural issues.

'Nothing new in all this,' Ben said, setting down the A4 sheets. 'Nothing unexpected at any rate.'

He pressed his fingers wearily into his closed eyelids.

Sensing she'd missed something, Helen went back to the first page and began to read more slowly through the reports. And found a line she'd scanned over too quickly first time around: 'A compliant, if somewhat timid and under-achieving child in Junior and Senior Infants classes,

Whitney began to show her troubled side towards the end of her Second Class year.' Helen read the line aloud as though the others weren't there. Ben dared a questioning glance at her. In between them, Martha produced another A4 sheet. An enlarged photo. Whitney in the Garden of Eden.

'This just came through from Forensics,' she said, and they leaned in closer. 'They've cleaned it up, removed all of the blood spatter, and they're sure none of it soaked through. No shadow of the photographer, but these marks you can see on her flesh . . .'

Helen's eyes widened. Her whole body ached at what she saw. The marks were nowhere else to be seen in the shot.

'Christ,' Ben said. 'She's covered in—'

'Bruises,' Helen gasped. 'Oh my God.'

They stared at the photo. It didn't make sense to them. The child Whitney posing cheekily as though altogether unaware of the appalling state of her pale shoulders and stomach and upper thighs.

'Second Class,' Martha said. 'That would be when Whitney made her First Communion, wouldn't it? I'm no expert on these things but I seem to remember my niece making hers at the end of Second Class.'

'And the First Communion ceremony would be near the end of the school year,' Ben said. 'The month of May usually.'

'So the abuse was well under way when this photo was taken,' Helen said. She pressed her temples as though that might stop the lurid scenarios playing out in her mind. 'I don't understand how the parents could've avoided all these psychological referrals. Surely the alarm bells were ringing around this kid from early on? So, how did they get away with it all those years?'

'You need to put this to Mrs Larkin,' Martha asserted.

Ben didn't seem quite so sure. He looked at the photo again, eyes damp in their deep sockets.

'There's always the possibility that Mrs Larkin was a victim in all of this too,' he said. 'If Harry Larkin was our perpetrator then he was the one calling the shots. My guess is that all of them were terrified of him. That's how it often goes in these situations.'

'All the more reason to confront Mrs Larkin,' Helen insisted. 'And right now. Catch her off guard.'

'The night before she has to let her husband pass away?' Ben asked.

Like a referee, Martha intervened – her hands raised, a look of mild reproof on her perfect features. All that was missing was the whistle.

'We should probably call Leo,' she said, and was taken aback when the young detectives spoke across one another though not at cross-purposes.

'Maybe not,' Helen said.

'Probably shouldn't,' Ben said.

'Why not?' Curiosity and concern vied with one another in Martha's tone. 'Is he OK?'

'He's, eh, meeting a friend,' Ben told her.

'Oh.' Martha began to gather her files together. A light flush brushed her cheeks. 'Good for him.' She handed one of the files to Helen. 'I've made a copy of all that lot for you.' She stood up to go, a question hovering around her full lips but failing to emerge.

They watched her glide away with her catwalk stride and a balletic twirl around to the left when she reached the door. If Helen had long suspected there'd been something between Martha and Leo in the past, now she felt certain of it. She wondered how far back it went. Before or after?

She got her jacket on and picked up the file, her mobile,

her notebook, looked for her biro. Ben stared at the far wall, seeming to see things that greatly saddened him there.

'Listen, I can take this myself,' she said. 'You probably need to get home to Whitney.'

'Millie,' he said before she had a chance to correct herself. 'No. She's . . . she's on a holiday.'

'I could do with one myself,' Helen said. 'When we get to the bottom of this bloody case.'

If we ever do, she thought.

# 34

At the lock gates below Portobello Bridge, a little girl danced delightedly between her parents as she threw bread crusts to the swans assembled there for her sole pleasure in the dusk of a cold, clear evening made golden by ordinary happiness and by the certain childish knowledge that she was, for this moment, the centre of a benign universe. Every kid had a right to a moment like that, every adult a right to a memory like that. Life didn't always offer such consolations. Not to Whitney and Kevin Larkin. Nor to Liz, for that matter. Nor to Leo himself. Maybe not to the brooding young Garda at the steering wheel of the squad car either.

Leo wished the traffic lights would turn green. The atmosphere in the car stank of failure. The damning failure in their fruitless search for Whitney Larkin. The inevitable failure that lay ahead for Leo in his latest bid for love, or at least companionship. The failure Garda Dempsey hadn't yet been able to bring himself to speak of. Leo opened the passenger side window a few inches. The breeze blew in and Dempsey blew up.

'Close the bloody window,' he seethed. 'It's bad enough

going to the wedding on my own without having a bloody cold as well—'

'Relax, Dempsey. She turned you down?'

'I thought she liked me,' the flush-necked man-child said. 'One night in Copper's, she told me I was a fine thing. She was a bit twisted, like, but she wasn't that twisted.'

'You reminded her of this charming tête-a-tête, did you?'

'Yeah.'

'And she wasn't impressed?'

'No. She got fair thick, so she did.' Dempsey shook his head, his grim gaze uncomplicated by insight. 'And it got worse.'

'What happened?'

'She punched me.'

Leo glanced across at the big boy. Tears coursed down Dempsey's cheeks. Big tears, hailstones, only hotter. The floodgates opened.

'Every night I watch the DVDs of my sisters' weddings. And now there'll be a third one and I'll be flying solo in that too.'

It was a little bit Chekhov and a whole lot Molière farce. Leo felt sorry for the young fellow but he had yet to hear the punch line. So to speak.

'Why did she punch you, Dempsey?'

'All I did was tell her there'd be no hanky-panky, like.'

They were on Merrion Road, a few minutes from Serpentine Crescent. Dempsey's buffoonery was having the wrong kind of effect on Leo. He imagined a similar hapless-ness overcoming him when he called to Eveleen's. The last of his confidence drained away and was replaced by an anxious vacuum that needed to be countered with chemicals. He unpocketed his personal mobile, found Dripsy's number, readied himself to ring as soon as he stepped from the squad car.

'I wouldn't mind,' Dempsey broke out operatically, 'but she wasn't even the one I really wanted to ask.'

Leo didn't ask.

Darkness hadn't yet quite fallen but the street lights had come on in Chapelizod. The grottier sections of Main Street had been transformed so that mere dereliction took on the sweet melancholy of slow decay as Helen and Ben walked to Mrs Larkin's house in St Laurence Villas. Her earlier undercover confrontation with the soon-to-be widow loomed large in Helen's thoughts.

'Are you sure you want to do this?' Ben asked. 'She's going to stonewall us from the off when she recognizes you.'

'She's going to stonewall us no matter who does the questioning.'

'Maybe we should give Leo a quick ring?'

'No. It's my call. The man deserves a night off.'

She rang the doorbell to cut off Ben's protests. She rang it again to banish her own misgivings. When the door was swept open, she stepped back. Gary Larkin stood there looking a little worse for wear after his overnight stay in Pettycannon station. Helen had forgotten he'd been released from custody earlier. Her skull reminded her of where he'd hit her. He'd changed his image again, shaved off the sweeping brush of hair. No longer a Mohican, he sported a dark suit and open-necked white shirt. All that was missing was the black tie. The squashed features of his baby face expressed annoyance. Inside the house an action movie was playing. Automatic gunfire, cries, screams and explosions. Someone was saving the planet from extinction again.

'Is your mother here?' Helen asked.

Gary didn't answer. He had the usual short man's problem with suit jackets. The hem hung halfway between his hips and his knees. It made him look too ridiculous to take seriously though Helen knew she had to take him seriously.

From behind him, Mrs Larkin appeared. She wore a black dress with veiled sleeves. She'd had her hair permed, the metallic smell of the hairdresser's shop still wafting from her. Dyed too, Helen thought, a shade too youthfully for her age. Her expression remained neutral but recognition resided in the dark eyes.

'Come to tell us how your cousin is, have you?' she asked. 'Helen.'

The young detective's weak smile felt like an inadequate mask for her unease.

'We'd like a word, if you don't mind. There've been some developments in the case we need to talk to you about.'

'At a time like this?' Gary snarled. 'You people, you have no respect for—'

'Back away, Mr Larkin,' Ben warned as Gary took a step towards Helen.

'I'm standing in our property, I don't have to back away.'

'Leave it, Gary,' his mother told him and, disappearing from view, raised her voice. 'Follow me.'

They passed along a wide hallway and into a brightly lit kitchen complete with island, butcher's block and every other desirable accessory. Unfortunately it smelled like a funeral parlour. The lilies did it. Bundles of them along the hardwood counters and in the vases that Mrs Larkin had presumably readied for the wake. I felt a funeral in my nose, Helen thought.

Beyond the kitchen was the conservatory – their destination it seemed. The lights hadn't yet been switched on there.

Mrs Larkin sat primly into a throne-like cane chair, knees together and to the side. The sense of calm radiating from her was real but as yet indecipherable. Things had changed in her world since that day in the ICU waiting room, Helen thought. Changed for the better. The two detectives sat. Their cane chairs crackled and popped.

'Sit down, Gary,' his mother said.

She was doing a benevolent matriarch impression but her son wasn't impressed. Ben had his notebook ready to go. Helen took the plunge. The shallow end first.

'You've probably heard that we found Whitney's hiding place in Temple Bar.'

'My brother-in-law told me.'

'We don't know how long she was there for. Possibly just for one night, maybe right up until—'

'Sunday,' Mrs Larkin said.

'Sunday?'

'Whitney went down the country on Sunday. I don't know where she is now but I know she's safe. That's all that really matters, isn't it?' she asked of Ben. Endearingly. And as if she'd guessed that Ben had a kid, Helen thought. Or already knew. 'I wanted her to be here for Harry's funeral but if she feels she can't hack it, well, I might not like it but I can understand where she's coming from. When he had the bypass last year, she couldn't visit him in hospital. She's never been good at dealing with, you know, reality.'

'You've been talking to Whitney?' Ben asked.

'She texted me.'

'When?' Helen asked, over the shock about enough to have become sceptical.

'A couple of hours ago.'

'We've tried to trace Whitney's phone and it's not registering. Is this a disposable that she texted from?'

'It's her phone, the one she's always had,' Mrs Larkin insisted. 'She obviously just leaves it switched off most of the time.'

'It'd still send out a signal then, wouldn't it?' Ben said.

'She's disabled the GPS and taken out the battery, Sherlock,' Gary told him. 'It's not rocket science. Not unless you're a cop, of course.'

'Did Whitney tell you where she is?' Helen asked Mrs Larkin, ignoring Gary's taunt.

'I asked but no way would she tell me,' Mrs Larkin replied.

'Did she talk about the girl she was hiding out with? Georgia Goode?'

'No.'

'Has she ever spoken about this girl? Georgia was in Tallaght on that graffiti cleaning scheme with Whitney.'

Liz Larkin shook her head. Her hands were a little more nervous than they had been.

'Or Hadi Al-Baarai? The Libyan kid your son here warned off?'

Gary examined his fingernails, or what was left of them. It seemed he'd been doing quite a lot of worrying.

'Weekend before last, Hadi went missing presumed dead in Libya,' Helen went on. 'Whitney found out a few days later. She was devastated. Surely that didn't escape your notice?'

'I knew something was wrong,' Liz Larkin said. 'But she never talked to me about anything any more.' She paused for a moment of what seemed like genuine regret. With a sigh she went on. 'Gary warned this kid off because I knew he'd use her and dump her. She's seventeen going on twelve. Back in March when she told me he'd gone to Libya, I didn't believe her. She never mentioned him after that. I thought she'd put it behind her. I mean, she doesn't even mention him in her texts. You can read them if you want.'

'You don't have to show these people anything, Ma,' Gary objected.

'Anyone could have sent those texts,' Helen said.

Mrs Larkin reached to the shelf below the cane coffee table and fished out her mobile from among the house and home magazines. She looked at the screen with an almost rapturous relief and proffered it to Helen. Keeping her distance. Just enough distance that Helen had to get up from her chair to take the old Nokia Classic mobile. She'd often joshed Leo for being the only person on the planet still using that museum piece. She looked sceptically at the older woman.

'I don't bother with all this new tech stuff,' Mrs Larkin said.

'Lots of new tech stuff in the kitchen,' Helen remarked, but Mrs Larkin glided by the implication.

'There's two texts from Whitney. Read them. The rest are my own business.'

Helen read the texts. *I'm sorry about Da. I'm so sorry he went in a coma before I came back. I'm ok so you don't have to worry. I don't want to see him dead or the cemetery. I'll be home soon sometime. I'm sorry. W.* The second text was briefer, less regretful. *Don't ask me where I am. I'm fine. I can take care of myself. I'm down here in the country since Sunday. No, I'm not coming. I can't that's all. W.* The texts had been sent at 18.34 and 18.52. They had something tangible to pass on to the service provider now.

She handed the phone to Ben.

'Anyone could have Whitney's phone,' Helen told the woman.

'You're accusing us of—' Gary began.

'You think we have it?' Liz Larkin chimed in with a laugh. 'Ring the number then. Feel free to walk around the house and listen. Go on, ring it. It'll be switched off but you'll hear her on the voicemail.'

Helen rang Whitney Larkin's number. She listened to the double beeps with growing apprehension as she realized she was about to hear the missing girl's voice. She felt like some vulgar tabloid hacker but she kept the phone to her ear. The fragile pitch of innocence rang in the girl's voice. *Whitney Larkin isn't here. Leave a message after the tone and she'll get back to you.* What, Helen wondered, did the girl's use of the third person imply? Her sense of being no more than an object?

'So, let's say she left on Sunday,' Helen said. 'How did she travel? Does she drive?'

'No, she can't drive. She probably took the train or the bus, whatever.'

'Down here in the country,' Ben read from Whitney's text message. 'Might that suggest she travelled south rather than north, Mrs Larkin?'

'When you live in Dublin, everywhere else is down the country.'

'True,' Ben smiled. 'But might she have gone, say, to Cork?'

'Why would she go there?'

'The Southern Gothic Music Festival,' Ben said. 'Baz MacDonald tells us he went down to Cork looking for Whitney on Saturday but didn't find her. Maybe he arrived a day too early?'

Ben's reference to The Armenian drew a surprising response from the Larkins. There was a smugness in their shared glance, something enigmatic too. Helen's first thought was that the conflict with MacDonald had been resolved in some way. Her second was to wonder precisely how.

'You've settled your disagreement with Mr MacDonald, I take it?'

'There *was* no disagreement.'

'He won't be taking charge of things then?'

'Baz has other plans now,' Gary said, to his mother's obvious displeasure.

'Baz always had other plans,' she corrected him.

'Such as?' Helen asked.

'You'd have to ask him that, love,' the older woman told her.

Helen drew out the photocopy of the cleaned-up First Communion photo and unfolded it. She placed it on the coffee table near Mrs Larkin.

'The photo's been forensically, eh, tidied up but it's clear that Whitney's body is covered in bruises. Can you explain?'

A greyness entered the woman's overly tanned features. In an instant, she withered visibly. Oddly, she looked inward rather than in Helen's direction for someone to blame.

'Bastard,' she muttered. She looked up at Helen, her head nodding some kind of confirmation to herself. 'So Leo didn't have the balls to come and show me this himself?'

Riveted, Helen and Ben found no answer to her rhetorical question. Gary too was silenced. He gazed open-mouthed at his mother. He might as well have had a question mark stamped on his forehead, Helen thought. All three of them might. A question mark with LEO in big fat capitals up front. Then the ring of the doorbell scattered the silence. No one moved.

'Aren't you going to answer it?' Ben asked Gary.

The doorbell rang again. Gary began to finger his mobile phone.

'Put the phone down,' Ben said.

The doorbell rang a third time.

'Let's go see who's visiting,' Ben suggested.

Liz Larkin remained surprisingly and obstinately quiet. She stared at the photocopied shot on the coffee table. A new uncertainty clouded the woman's bitter-almond eyes.

# 35

The tall young man at the Larkins' front door was a cross between Barbie's Ken and the footballer Ronaldo. Black hair greased back. Handsome in a gormless and yet slightly shady way. He was dressed for a different hour of the day and for a less northerly climate. A sprayed-on T-shirt outlined in precise detail his musculature. His arms were covered in tattoos like a disease.

'Deadly suit, Gary,' he said.

Then he saw Ben and, further off, Helen. His smile stayed in place even as he descended from high-spiritedness to deflation.

'Derek McCarthy?' Ben asked.

'Who's asking?' the action man said. His worried falsetto didn't quite match the physique.

'We've been looking for you, Derek,' Ben said. 'Didn't Gary tell you?'

He flashed his ID. Action man did a double-take. Then he looked down at Gary for inspiration. He wasn't good at reading the runes.

'No. I mean, yeah, but I didn't think it was, like, urgent.'

He was getting it wrong, wrong and wrong again. You could tell by his collapsing expression.

'Where have you been for the last few days? Keeping watch on Baz MacDonald?'

'No way, man. I was down at the brother's gaff in Wicklow,' McCarthy said, flushing naively. 'Bray. It's a ghost town, man. Ask the brother, he'll tell you I was there.'

Helen pointed at the open door from which the noises of playful war still emerged.

'Step in there, Derek. You can make your explanations to Detective Garda Murphy.'

The tall man dumbly sought Gary's advice. Gary gave him the nod and made to follow him into the front room.

'Not you, Gary.'

'I was going to turn off the telly. Do you mind?'

'Derek can do that.'

Helen led Gary back towards the conservatory. On edge, he glanced back towards the hallway, the front room. She wondered if she could tip him over a little as they went.

'You don't choose your friends very wisely, do you, Gary?'

'What?'

'Well, Derek's not the sharpest needle in the sewing box, is he?'

'Piss off, you dyke.'

'And what about that Slovakian guy who robbed you lot blind before he vanished into thin air. What was his name? Anton Bisjak, right?'

Gary paled. When he sat, the crackling of his cane chair expressed his unease. He couldn't make the crackling stop.

'You brought him into your Glasgow Celtic Supporters Club, I hear,' Helen continued. 'That was pretty dumb, wasn't it?'

'I didn't bring him in. He was a Celtic fan before he ever came over to Ireland.'

About to say more, he stopped himself short. Why would a Slovakian be a Glasgow Celtic fan? Helen asked herself. Maybe there'd been a Slovakian player with the club back then? She'd Google it later. See if anything came of it.

The photocopy sheet was scrunched up on the coffee table. In the long glass French doors she saw the reflection of Liz Larkin's return. An odd sensation of being approached by the same woman from front and rear unsettled her.

'Sit down,' Mrs Larkin told Helen firmly, a blue file in her hand.

Puzzled, Helen sat and Mrs Larkin dropped the file into her lap. In heavy black marker, the words *Whitney – Medical* were inscribed on the cover flap. Helen took out her notebook and biro. She looked up at the woman for some explanation.

'What you see on Whitney's body aren't the kind of bruises you imagine.' Mrs Larkin was beyond irritation or anger. She was telling a story she'd told too often before and she was tired of it. 'My daughter had a condition called Henoch-Schönlein purpura. The symptoms were internal bleeding, arthritis and she bruised easily. The school wanted to have her see a psychologist. They put a social worker on us and we could've lost her to foster care. These are reports from three specialists saying Whitney had HS. She recovered from it before she was ten. You can take it all with you but I want it back. Now, if you don't mind, I'm going to bed. I'm losing my husband tomorrow. Killing him, you could say. I wouldn't wish it on my worst enemy. Not even a Guard.'

When she had crossed halfway into the kitchen, she spun gracefully and fixed her newly permed hair. She stood in the soft spotlight coming from the hood above the kitchen island. Ten, fifteen years of sun and booze had been airbrushed from her face. Her looks were suddenly striking. And vicious.

At the far end of the kitchen, Derek McCarthy and Ben appeared.

'When you're talking to Leo, ask him if he's still into seventeen-year-olds,' Liz Larkin said. 'And ask him if he still sleeps with other men's wives. And tell him from me, I only wish to Christ it was him I was pulling the plug on tomorrow. Did you get all that, Helen, or should I repeat it for you?'

'No need,' Helen said, and couldn't say another word.

Over by the kitchen counter, Ben stared at the bunches of lilies. As she departed, Mrs Larkin's hand rested on McCarthy's tattooed arm like a butterfly in no hurry to leave.

To all appearances, Leo was a man out for an evening stroll. His heart, however, kicked and raced like a small dog on a leash as he circled the Aviva Stadium to reach Eveleen's house. Along the way he picked up two bottles of wine. A red and a white. To be sure to be sure. Now he wasn't so sure. What if she didn't drink wine? What if she didn't share his predilection for Nero d'Avola or Gavi di Gavi? And what if Eveleen didn't smoke? What the hell was he going to do with his hands, his mouth, his head if he couldn't drink or smoke?

He checked his mobiles. No text messages from his dealer or from work. No fresh developments in the case then. Thank Christ.

He crossed the junction between Haddington and Shelbourne Roads. To his left, a pair of pubs on opposite corners across the way provided a double measure of temptation. On his right was the long side wall of Beggar's

Bush barracks that now housed the National Print Museum he kept meaning to visit. Fate as usual lobbed in another ironic grenade. A dark cloud spread itself across the sky and headed towards him. He warned it off silently but clouds don't listen. Especially the dark ones.

On Bath Avenue, as he neared the end of the barrack walls, Leo drew to a halt. Prints. He remembered the Mount Ararat prints in Baz MacDonald's apartment, the quality and tastefulness of the framing. And remembered Helen's description of the store room in the Goodes' apartment, the stacks of empty frames under which she'd found David Goode's Anonymous mask. Had Frida Goode done the framing?

His personal phone began to vibrate in his pocket. Dripsy.

'I'm going to kill you, Dripsy, you little bollocks,' Leo said, a loud crowd in his ear.

'Hold on a sec, everybody's talking here,' the limping dealer said and found a quieter spot. 'Hey, man, what did I do now?'

'You didn't answer my texts. You didn't pick up when I rang. Where are you? Are you anywhere near the Aviva?'

'Not unless there's another Aviva in Galway.'

'Jesus wept. Why didn't you tell me the other night you were going to Galway?'

It had started to rain. Heavily.

'How could I know on Sunday that my brother was going to pop his clogs?'

'Sorry, sorry, Dripsy,' Leo muttered. 'Sorry for your loss.'

'No worries, Erik, the last time I met the guy was in Letterfrack when I was fourteen.'

'Letterfrack? As in the industrial school?'

'Yeah. Shit spot that.'

Leo had heard the most horrific stories of how the kids

were maltreated in that hellish place where no one had cried stop until the crying had long since stopped. Sometimes he wondered why he liked the dealer so much. Apart from the quality of the goods, of course. Maybe it was simply the fact that hell was just another four-letter word for guys like Dripsy. It could rain piss on them and they'd still come up smelling of rosy hope. Dripsy did.

'I'm hoping he might have left me a few bob,' the dealer said. 'He done well for himself after Letterfrack. Before he left he promised he'd never forget me.'

'But that must've been forty years ago,' Leo said. 'You never met him since then?'

'He lived in America but he wanted to be buried in Galway with the mother.'

The downpour destroying Leo's best grey suit didn't seem so bad after all. And when Dripsy came up with more quality goods, it didn't matter that they were neither inhalable nor ingestible.

'Baz MacDonald,' he began, and Leo allowed him the long Beckett pause. The guy deserved it.

'You got something for me?'

'He's heading off to Armenia.'

'Where'd you get this? I'm not asking names, but are they reliable?'

'Got it from two different guys, sound as a pound the two of them.'

'Any word on why he's going? Or when?'

'When? No. Why? Because he fell out with Harry Larkin.'

'Like, recently?'

'Yeah, very recently. Weeks. The usual story. Money, the word is.'

'Did he shoot Harry?'

'Jury's out on that one, Erik,' Dripsy said, and amid a

clattering of footsteps in the background he whispered, 'Have to go. They're closing the coffin.'

'I hope he leaves you thousands, old son.'

'Ah, no, thousands would be dangerous,' Dripsy said. 'Hundreds would be nice though. A fellow could survive hundreds.'

The call ended. Leo checked the time on his phone. Five past nine. Christ, he was late. Soaked to the skin, he hurried along towards Vavasour Square. Helen and Ben had probably headed home by now and, besides, it could wait until the morning, couldn't it? At Eveleen's door, he texted Helen. *Frida Goode may have framed the prints in MacDonald's apartment. Also got word from a source that MacDonald's leaving town. Talk tomorrow.*

It could wait. Couldn't it?

# 36

Windscreen wipers flapping furiously against the elements and the odds, they drove slowly along the endless stretch of Dolphin Road. At the wheel, Ben stared straight ahead. Beside him, Helen gazed at the canal to her left. The swollen waters lapped perilously close to the brink. She felt close to the brink herself, felt something very like grief. Maybe Martin Buck had got it in one with his father-figure jibe. She'd already known what it was like to lose a good father. Now she knew what it was like to lose a dodgy substitute.

Helen's stomach had turned when Leo's text message came through as they sat in the car in Chapelizod ten minutes before, still in shock after Liz Larkin's diatribe. In the one brief snatch of conversation they'd been capable of since then, they'd agreed that their working day hadn't yet ended. This apparent ceasefire between the Larkins and The Armenian had to be followed up on immediately. MacDonald's imminent departure too. And there was the question of his relationship with Frida Goode. Ben's earlier misgivings about acting without Leo's say-so had dissolved. They were headed to MacDonald's Sandymount apartment.

As they waited at the red light on the Dolphin's Barn junction, Ben ventured an opinion. It sounded like an offer of consolation.

'Mrs Larkin's just trying to throw a spanner in the works. At the very least, she's totally exaggerating things. OK, she probably knew Leo back in the past, but how could she know all that stuff? A man wouldn't tell things like that to a . . . a . . .'

'A teenage lover?'

'Why would you believe that woman? I know Leo had a bit of a reputation on that front but—'

'How would you know that? Locker-room talk?'

Ben didn't answer.

A lump of disgust had lodged in Helen's throat. She wanted to spit, to scream. She held it in.

'Anyway, that's not the point. The point is, Leo's totally compromised in this case. I mean, for God's sake, I'm trying to count the number of levels he's compromised at. He knew this woman. Intimately. He screwed her when she was the same age as Whitney is now. OK, give him the benefit of the doubt. Say she was eighteen, nineteen. It's still bloody appalling.'

'But Leo was young too. Twenty-five, twenty-six at most. If she was, like, nineteen or twenty, that wouldn't seem quite so—'

'For Christ's sake, Ben, he was a police officer. He was sleeping with an informant's squeeze and it obviously went on even after she married.'

'Not necessarily. She could've been talking about other, you know, other women he was . . . involved with.'

'We'll talk about all that later,' Helen insisted, needing more time for the emotion to drain away from the subject.

'What did Derek McCarthy have to say for himself? The Bray story is bullshit, right?'

'Yeah. He admitted that he's been doing the rounds of Harry's business acquaintances looking for a lead on who pulled the trigger. Which implies that they don't know who shot Harry.'

'Or it's meant to imply that they don't.'

'I suppose. Still, I'm inclined to believe McCarthy. He seemed too rattled to be spoofing.'

'The guy's a dope on a rope,' Helen said. 'They might easily have sent him off on that fool's errand just to give the impression that they don't know who the killer is. And if that's the case, I'm guessing Gary isn't the one pulling the strings. Mrs Larkin is. And that makes Leo's position even more untenable.'

'True,' Ben agreed.

A new thought grew wings in her, flew wild.

'What if she's behind her husband's killing?' she said. 'What if this stand-off with MacDonald was all a sham and she actually paid him to do it? She's in control. You can sense that in her, can't you?'

'Maybe so. But how does Whitney's disappearance fit into that theory?'

'I don't know,' Helen admitted. 'But she's dangerous, that woman. We need to keep this possibility in . . .'

He looked across at her and turned sharply away when she caught his glance.

'What?'

'The lilies.'

'In her kitchen? What about them?'

'The lilies you got at the hospital. I didn't have them delivered and Leo didn't send them.'

'You think the Larkins sent them?' she asked. Her dry tongue chafed against her palate when she recalled Mrs Larkin's addressing her by name, her antipathy at the ICU waiting room. 'You think *she* did?'

'It's probably just coincidence,' he said, 'Still, you need to be very careful, Helen.'

'I'm always careful.'

'I don't mean to pry but—'

'Don't,' she warned, but Ben wasn't for putting off.

'Do you still live alone?'

'Mind your own bloody business.'

'What I mean to say is, do you have somewhere you could stay until this case is sorted?'

'No,' she answered. 'I mean, no, I have no intention of letting anyone freak me out.'

The worst thing in life wasn't being alone, Helen thought. The worst thing was having no one you could ever fully trust to comfort you, protect you. She wondered how many bonds of trust Leo Woods had broken in his life, in his career. How many lies and half truths had he spoken? More than most, she guessed. It seemed absurd to feel so betrayed by an insignificant little lie over a bunch of lilies. But she did.

They were on Haddington Road. Ben clicked the indicator to the right. As they neared the junction with Northumberland Road, a no-right-turn sign came into view. Ben glanced at his colleague. She shrugged, nodded. It was just another rule that police officers could ignore. They turned right.

At Eveleen's door, Leo stood bedraggled. He did what he could to sort the mess the rain had made of him. His charcoal grey suit had turned black. Appropriately enough, he thought, in mourning for his chances to impress. She wore black too but brightened by a green and black shell necklace and her green-eyed smile.

'Come on in, Leo,' she said.

He followed her inside. The rooms were small though not suffocatingly so. Subtle colours prevailed, off-whites of varying degrees of warmth. The furnishing quietly belonged. In the dining room a table had been set for two. Above the table, an extendable lamp had been lowered. It gave off a perfectly dome-like and intimate light and was the heart of the room.

'We should get the business end out of the way first,' Eveleen said.

Wrong-footed, Leo nodded. She picked up on his confused misinterpretation and threw him a wry smile.

'The hospital records,' she said. 'I got a friend in Admin to do some more digging and she didn't find anything on Whitney. But she had these sent over. Some files on another of the Larkins.'

'Which of them?'

'Kevin.' She handed over two sun-bleached green folders. 'Fractured jaw. Head, neck and upper body badly bruised but no serious damage. Must've been in a scrap. Seems the fracture happened at least two days before he showed up at the hospital.'

Leo scanned the files. Kevin's address – St Laurence Villas. Still lived with the Larkins then. When? He found the date: 4 June 2002. Which had to be, he reckoned, a week or so after Whitney's First Communion. A realization dawned. Kevin hadn't moved out of the Larkins' house until he was twenty-seven, he'd told Leo. And he was born to Harry's first wife in 1975. Leo had known that all along. Why hadn't he copped it straight away? Kevin was twenty-seven in 2002.

'Everything's more or less ready to go,' Eveleen said. 'Would you like to sit?'

'Sure.'

'I'll take your jacket then. You're soaked through. I'm afraid I can't offer you a change of wardrobe.'

'No problem. I'll dry out soon anyway.'

'Be back in a sec,' she said and looked at the files in Leo's hand with the unspoken insistence that he set them aside before she returned.

While Eveleen moved about the kitchen, he took one last quick scan through the pages. Was there some connection between the Communion Day photograph, Kevin's fractured jaw, his permanent departure from St Laurence Villas? What the hell was happening in that house back in 2002? What the hell were those people up to? With a skip of the heart, Leo had at least one fragment of an answer. The Larkins and cousin Baz had been out a-hunting. The SDU report was somewhat vague in details but had described the Larkins' so-called search for the Slovakian as having occurred between June and July 2002.

'Duck spring rolls OK?' Eveleen asked. 'Leo?'

'Sorry, yeah. Great. Lovely,' he faltered. Christ, he told himself, I should be at work.

Shouldn't I?

# 37

In the forecourt of Bayview Apartments in Sandymount, the parked cars basked fluidly in the light from the street outside, the rain having just given them a free car-wash. Baz MacDonald's blue Mercedes coupé looked especially pleased with itself. By way of compensation for her own poverty-stricken state, Helen pressed the buzzer to his apartment, left her finger on it. A call came from above.

'Oi! Leave it aht, you lot, or I'll call the police.' A cockney accent out of deep bellows.

They looked upwards. The naked top half of a full-breasted and round-paunched man hovered in the heights. Longish greying hair feathered back in the breeze, the top of a bath-towel visible at his midriff.

'We are the police,' Helen told him.

'Yeah roigh'. An' I'm Jesus Christ. Get aht a here.'

'More God the Father than Jesus Christ, I would've thought,' Ben remarked, and Helen almost chuckled in spite of herself.

'You wha'? Roigh' then. You two don't make yourselves scarce before I get down there, I'll 'ave you both.'

The god retreated into his heaven and they waited. When the front door shot back, Helen felt like the referee in last

Sunday's game as she flashed her ID in the big man's face. It was a nice feeling. Too nice. The man stepped back, held on firmly to his bath-towel.

'The guy's obviously not bloody in, is he?' he complained.

'You know Mr MacDonald?' Ben asked.

'No, I don't. He ain't gonna win any Friendly Neighbour awards, that's for sure.'

They went up in the lift with the toga-tugging Londoner. When the door slid open, he pointed directly ahead.

'Number Eight,' he said and went to the door alongside.

'Sorry we had to disturb you, sir,' Helen said.

'It's all roigh',' he said and, suitably mollified, added, 'His light's on but I really don't think he's in there, you know. Straight up.'

'You're probably right. Thank you, sir. Just one last check.'

She knocked on the apartment door. The half-naked man had begun to shiver but didn't step into his apartment just yet. Something on his mind. Helen's glance held a question and he answered it with a shrug.

'I saw him leave a few hours ago.'

'But his car's still outside,' Ben said.

'Well, he's taken a taxi then, ain't he? Whatever. I'm pretty sure he hasn't been back because I haven't had to listen to Charles fucking Aznavour all evening long. "She". I never want to hear that song again.' He smiled at Helen. It was a more pleasant smile than she'd expected. 'It's an old one. Long before your time, love.'

'No, I know it. Elvis Costello did a version back in the nineties.'

Ben cut across their musical tête-à-tête: 'Did he leave alone?'

'No, had his lady friend with him. The "She" in his life, I reckon.'

'Small, black hair, mole on her cheek?'

'Yeah.'

'She's been here before?' Helen asked.

'Not so often of late but, yeah, she's been a regular these past few months.'

'Were they here last Saturday night?'

The man's heavy breasts shivered as he made a stab at recollection.

'I hit the town Saturday night,' he explained. 'Hit it hard. But, yeah, I seem to remember they were here when I left at eight or so in the evening. I got back at two, maybe three. I heard them leave during the night, but what time? No idea. You know what alcohol does to the clock, right?'

'I've heard,' Helen said.

'Better get myself back inside before I catch a cold. Awright? And 'ere, don't tell him I've told you all this. I can do without trouble from the neighbours.'

'Sure, thanks for your help,' Helen said, and waited for the door to close behind him. She turned to Ben. 'So Baz MacDonald and Frida Goode are an item after all. And this supposed trip to Cork was bullshit.'

'Yeah,' he said, and they both fell silent, each of them scrambling through the files in their minds, trying to square this new knowledge with what they already knew of the case while they went back down in the lift.

When they stepped out into the vestibule below, they were met by a curiously strong breeze from the short stairway to their left. A door banged out an occasional rhythm somewhere lower down. They followed the sound.

At the end of the steps they found the banging door. It led outside to the rear of the apartment building. A much-trodden trail through the wet grass took the two detectives to a gap in the crispy brown beech hedging along the boundary. Helen looked back along the trail and realized that it was hidden from the forecourt. They went through the gap, raindrops from the crackling leaves spraying their faces, and found themselves on the wide turn of a laneway. Between a black Honda Accord and a green Skoda Octavia was an empty parking space. She stopped up short.

'The night the Libyan was shot, we sent a car over here to check if MacDonald was home,' she said. 'They saw the coupé, they saw the lights on in the apartment, and saw them switched off. So we presumed he was inside.'

'You think he might have one of those remote control lighting systems? You can do it directly from your mobile phone these days.'

'Exactly.'

'And if he used this exit, our guys wouldn't have seen him from the forecourt. He may even have had a second car parked here.'

'Which means he could've shot the Libyan. And we know for sure now he had motive. He's having an affair with Frida Goode. So he avenges her son's death. Maybe she asked him to.'

They looked along the puddled lane. Both of them imagined a car turning in from the street, imagined the headlights and the dim shapes of Baz MacDonald at the wheel and Frida Goode in the passenger seat. Or vice versa, Helen thought.

'Maybe they went out in Frida's car?' she said.

'Christ, yeah. Leo's source says MacDonald's leaving for Armenia soon. What if she's going with him? What if they've already set off? We should check the airports and the ferries.'

'I suppose,' Helen said. 'But she won't be leaving. Not

now. At least, not until they hold that memorial service for David. I can't believe that she would.'

'Should we wait and see if they come back here tonight?'

'I don't see that we have any other choice,' Helen said.

# 38

A silent hour had passed since they'd moved the car to get a better view of the lane behind Bayview Apartments. They were glad when the rain came again. Thick drops pelted against the car roof and filled the self-conscious vacuum left by the lack of conversation. Helen sank low in the driver's seat, let her eyes close. Disconnected images swirled through her mind. Baz MacDonald hand-miming a gun. Two notches on it. A green and white hooped Glasgow Celtic jersey with Anton Bisjak's name on the back but no number. And lilies. A great mound of them. And she knew that beneath them lay Whitney. She dived through the lilies, the noxious sweetness of their perfume sickening her, and fell against Whitney's body . . . She woke with a start, her head on Ben's shoulder.

'Sorry,' she said, pulling herself back embarrassedly. 'How long have I been asleep?'

'Half an hour, give or take,' he said. 'It's been a long day. Too long.'

His beard appeared to have thickened even as she'd slept, or maybe it was just a trick of the light. He looked drawn, a little haggard, a man tortured into wakefulness. He stared out through the streaming windscreen.

'Way too long,' he said.

'I can get another officer here if you—'

'No. Helen, there's something I want to tell you.'

He hesitated. Helen was tempted to cut off the conversation but she hesitated too.

'I'm no mystery man, Helen. My life got complicated way before time, that's all.'

'You don't need to tell me any of this.'

'But I do. I've made my decision and I want you to hear it from me before—'

'Decision?'

He turned towards her. He spoke as though he'd been rehearsing while she slept.

'You know that my daughter . . . that Millie has cystic fibrosis and, well, there are degrees of severity and, of course, the treatment is getting better and better all the time. But Millie's at the more difficult end of the spectrum and I've had to rethink my priorities.' He wiped some breath-mist from the windscreen. 'Ever since she's been born, other people have been taking care of her. Child-minders, my mother and sister. Which was fine until I realized that I was putting the job before Millie, that if I don't spend more time with her now, well . . . I've already missed a whole year of her life. I don't want to miss any more of it.'

'So you're leaving us?' Helen said, tempted though she was to delve further but seeing no point in it. 'You're doing the right thing.'

'I think so. I'll miss you lot though.'

The disappointment she felt surprised her. The ache of loneliness too.

'You especially,' he added.

'Yeah, right,' she said.

She searched her pockets for her personal mobile by way

of distracting his smothering gaze. She found it had been on her lap all the while and tried to think of something she could pretend to do with it.

'I was thinking,' he began. 'You know, now that we won't be, like, working together, maybe we could meet up and . . .'

A flash of inspiration rescued Helen. Google the Glasgow Celtic squads from the early 2000s for some Slovakian connection.

'Sure,' she said, keeping her attention on the phone screen, knowing Ben's continued to rest on her. 'Just something I wanted to check out here.'

No Slovakian in the 2003/04 squad. He watched her. Nor in the 2002/03 squad. Still he watched. A quick scan through the 2001/02 squad and Helen's head jerked back in shock.

'Bloody hell,' she said, and Ben looked down quizzically at her screen.

The shock didn't arise from finding a Slovakian player in the squad. It came with the name.

'Number twenty-five, Ľubomír Moravcˇík.' She scrolled up a head shot. The football clichés kicked in. 'Class midfielder and some shot on him.'

'I'm not into soccer, I'm afraid. Where exactly is this going?'

A text message rang in on her work phone and she dug around in her pockets for it while she spoke.

'You know what his nickname was?' she said, her spirits soaring high as a goal-scorer's. 'Lubo. Don't you see? The school report mentioned that letter reversal thing. A reversed letter b is d, right?'

'Ludo. The name on the back of the torn photo of Whitney.'

'The Larkins are all Celtic fans,' Helen ploughed on, 'and

Anton Bisjak the Slovakian was too, so they called him Lubo, after L'ubomír Moravc̆ík. Bisjak is the one torn from the photo, Ben. He has to be. We assumed Ludo was the bloody dog's name. The Larkins hid behind that assumption. And when did Bisjak disappear from view? June, July 2002. A few weeks, a month at most, after that shot was taken.'

She found her work phone in her jacket, checked the new message.

'Do you get the feeling that this thing is about to blow wide open?' Ben said.

'Holy shit,' Helen gasped. 'Those texts that Mrs Larkin got from Whitney's phone?'

'We have a location on them?'

Her mouth had gone dry, her tongue thickened. She turned to Ben.

'Tandy's Lane,' she said. 'They were sent from Tandy's Lane.'

She was perfect. She drank. She smoked. Cursed a little, laughed a lot. Knew her football and her films. Knew her books. Knew most corners of the world first-hand. She'd run a marathon. Jumped from a plane. And she made her own ice cream. She was the Empress of Ice Cream, he told her, and she got the joke because she knew her poetry too. Ev was everything Leo had wanted her to be. Except for the music that accompanied her, looping irritatingly in the background.

'You don't like it?' Eveleen divined. 'But everybody loves Bill Evans.'

'No, no. It's just that I have this, you know, this sort of amusia thing.'

'Really? I've read about that but I've never met . . . Tell me about it.'

He'd done it again. Nice one, Leo. Transformed himself from an interesting prospect into an interesting specimen.

'Not much to tell. Burst eardrum when I was a kid. And I was already tone-deaf so . . .'

'I really don't know how I'd live without music.'

Eveleen had taken his hand. He hoped she wasn't going to pat it. Good doggie.

'There are lots of things we have to live without,' Leo said.

'Such as?'

He placed his other hand on hers. They were playing some kids' game. Not the kind of game he'd hoped to be playing tonight. She covered his second hand.

'We don't have to live without it tonight, Leo,' she said.

# 39

Headlights blazing through the beech hedge startled the two detectives into wakefulness. They sank lower in their seats. Out in the lane, the car came to a halt at the far side of the hedge. Lights doused, the car's engine purred. Helen braved a brief glimpse above the dashboard. From further back in the lane, a lamp post threw some dingy light on the newly arrived car. A suggestion of the Volkswagen Beetle's curved top lines. A silvery blue hue. Helen ducked back down.

'It's Frida Goode's car,' she whispered. 'I'm sure of it. Heaven Blue.'

'Heaven?'

'One of the 2010 blues.' She knew what her levity was about. It was about fear. She wasn't sure what her fear was about. 'Never miss a new brochure, you know, in case I win the Lotto.'

A minute passed. Two. Still no one emerged from the Volkswagen. A conversation perhaps? Or a kiss? One way or the other, no movement was visible. Helen and Ben each rested a hand on their door handles. They unzipped their jackets, briefly felt for their guns. Big, wavering light filled the lane and the beech hedge again but from further off.

She got her door open, thinking the sound of the approaching car would disguise the click. And it did. Only it wasn't the sound of a car.

'Motorbike,' she said, her heart pumping when Ben opened his door an inch.

In the space of a heartbeat she saw the single headlamp and heard a volley of gunshots. Helen was out of the unmarked car before Ben. Crouching low, gun cocked at the apex of her outstretched arms, she moved along the trail through the grass. Ben followed. Another shot rang out and the two detectives hit the ground as, behind them, the bullet hit a car windscreen like a star sucked loudly into a black hole. The windscreen of the car they'd been sitting in. Helen's call was a scream.

'Police! Drop the gun!'

The motorbike's answer was a celebratory screech of tyres and a whine of acceleration diminishing rapidly as it sped towards the Coast Road. They heard the agonized moans of a woman, a man's voice breaking over her name again and again. *Frida! Frida!* Baz MacDonald's voice.

Helen plunged through the gap in the beech hedging, heart racing, locked arms hurting. The Beetle's windscreen had taken two hits, its shatterproof glass frosted over. On the passenger's side, the window had been pierced three times and was similarly opaque. The woman's voice was no longer to be heard.

Helen took the driver's side, Ben the passenger side, guns at the ready. They pulled the doors open in the same moment. Trapped by his seat belt, Baz leaned across, his bloodied hands moving uselessly about the upper body of Frida Goode.

'Cover him, Ben,' Helen said.

She pulled the door wide and took a spurt of blood on her

zip-up jacket. Then another. A severed artery – but where? When she pushed Baz back, he grabbed his left shoulder and cried out. Unconscious, Frida was pale as death. Blood shot again and again from her right wrist. The ulnar artery, Helen remembered from her first-aid classes.

'Your tie!' she shouted at Baz, but pain and shock had deafened and blinded him for now. 'Ben, give me his tie. Just pull it off him!'

Ben's every touch caused the ex-Provo further teeth-clenching discomfort. He roared like a beast at the pain as though defying it. The silk necktie came loose at last and Helen grabbed it.

'Pencil, biro, any bloody thing,' she called, and Ben delivered two plastic biros from his jacket. Helen improvised a tourniquet on Frida's arm. She twisted it tight. The biros snapped into pieces and she got a spray of blood on her lips for good measure. 'Try the boot, Ben. The car-jack, the turnscrew, whatever you call it, something! And ring for—'

Her colleague already had his mobile to his ear.

Helen raised the bloodied hem of Frida's gold lamé dress. And took another spurt of blood in the face. A second severed artery. Jesus Christ! The femoral artery. Severed for as little as two minutes, Helen knew, and you were likely to be a goner. And how many minutes had already passed?

'Ben, your shirt – rip a sleeve off! We've a femoral pumping here!'

The phone slipped from Ben's grasp as he pulled off his jacket. On the passenger's side, Baz released himself from his seat belt and moved his right foot out of the car. And on to Ben's phone. It was accidental because the man's eyes were jammed tight in pained distress but Ben was ready to take it out on him anyway.

'The boot, Ben, now! She's in serious trouble here.'

While Ben whipped up the hatchback and scrambled desperately through the contents of the boot, Helen pushed the ex-Provo through the door.

'Out! I need to lie her flat here. Go!'

Baz tumbled out on to his knees on the wet-soaked concrete. From his prayerful crouch he stared in at his lover and at Helen.

'Oh Christ,' Ben cried from the rear of the car, and in the next beat Baz asked: 'Is the wee girl OK?'

'The girl?'

'The blue trench coat on the floor at the back,' Ben told Helen. 'It just moved.'

He raced to the passenger side door and swept the wounded man aside.

'Stay on your knees, MacDonald!' he shouted.

He reached into the back of the car and grabbed the trench coat. Beneath it was a tartan blanket.

'The belt of the coat, Ben, give it to me,' Helen said. 'Who is it? Is it Whitney?'

The bearded detective reached across to her, proffered the belt and a thick wrench. Perfect. If it wasn't already too late.

As Helen got to work, Ben pulled the blanket from the crouched body behind the front seats.

'Who is it, Ben? Is she hit?'

'No, I don't think so.'

'But who . . . Shit, see to the tourniquet on Frida's arm, will you, Ben? I can't do both of them.'

'I think it's Georgia,' Ben gasped. 'She's in shock. Eyes open. Catatonic.'

He got the blanket back over the girl and slid back off the passenger seat. Helen moved Frida back and Ben took the weight, laid her head down on the seat and concentrated on the necktie tourniquet. A livid rawness filled the air that seemed composed of frost and blood. Ben leaned in close to the woman.

'She's not breathing, Helen.'

'Heart's still pumping,' she said. 'Weaker though. Much weaker. Try mouth-to-mouth.'

Ben had already tilted Frida's head back. His lips moved on to hers, passing a double breath into her, his head nodding as he counted to five and kissed her again. And again. It wasn't working.

'Keep going, Ben,' Helen insisted and loosened the coat-belt briefly on the woman's femur, tightened it again when the blood came.

They worked steadily, not thinking how this would end, not thinking anything, casting a watchful eye over the prostrate Georgia whenever either had a chance. Ben listened at the woman's lips again, his shadowed muscles pulsing, damp. He brightened, looked up at Helen.

'She's breathing.'

But Helen was looking beyond him.

'MacDonald's gone,' she said. 'Christ Almighty.'

At neither end of the dog-legged lane could they see the ex-Provo. As one they looked towards the gap in the hedge that led back into the apartment grounds. They heard a car door slammed shut, the scream of an engine starting up. No lights came on but they heard the screech and the cry of stressed car tyres shooting away from them. They didn't know which direction Baz had taken until they saw the car flash by the far end of the lane to the left.

'It's ours,' Ben said. 'He's headed towards town. Towards Chapelizod?'

'Ring Pettycannon station. Get a cordon in place around Chapelizod.'

'He just stood on my phone, made shit of it. My work one is still in the car.'

'Christ's sake!'

Helen searched her pockets with her free hand. Nothing. Not the work phone nor the personal one.

'Mine are in the bloody car too.'

They heard the lightest of whimpering from behind the front seats. A singing tone, a child's repetition of a mother's lullaby. The girl's eyes were too wide open yet to see anything or to make sense of what she saw.

Frida Goode's lips had turned frighteningly puce. An aura of peaceful finality resided in her closed eyelids. Her right hand, bent at the shredded wrist, hung lifelessly over the edge of the driver's seat. Blood trickled downwards. Helen's eyes followed its course. She reached down to some glinting thing there. A Glock 17. Baz's gun. The gun used to shoot the Libyan? And Harry Larkin?

*Wednesday 4 May*

# 40

Leo wanted to touch the cleaved perfection of her long, naked back but resisted the temptation. It was enough that he already had. Three hours at most he'd slept but he felt more rested than he'd done for weeks, months, perhaps years. He was high as a kite on nothing but female companionship. Which was more than nothing, he knew. Which was everything, and made everything possible again. Like a half-decent life. A life without masks and drugs and regrets. A life without—

His work mobile vibrated on the bedside table. A life without the damn phone always ringing.

He eased out of the bed and took the phone out into the sitting room. He felt perfectly calm. Ready for anything. He checked the mobile. An unfamiliar number, no name. The clock on the sitting-room wall said ten minutes past six and said it lightly, optimistically.

'Sir.' It was Ben.

'Christ, you're up and about early, son,' Leo whispered and moved further away from the bedroom and into the hallway. 'You got a new work phone?'

'Eh, yeah. It's been a busy night, sir. Very busy.'

And Ben wasn't exaggerating. As he listened to the

details of the shooting in Sandymount and the discovery of Georgia Goode, Leo felt his new happiness already under siege. It survived. For now.

'MacDonald escaped in your car?'

'Yeah, but we found it in Ringsend shortly after,' Ben said. 'My work phone had been taken.'

'You left your phone in the car?'

'We had to move quickly when the shooting started.'

Leo sensed the young detective's irritation and backed off.

'OK, OK,' he said. 'How serious is MacDonald's wound, do you think?'

'Hard to say. There was a lot of blood around the shoulder but it might just be a flesh wound.'

'Did we get anything from Georgia?' Leo asked.

'We didn't have much time with her before the medics had to take over. She didn't see the shooter last night. But we did get an outline of Whitney's movements last week from her.'

'Which goes?'

'Which goes: Tuesday – Georgia tells her Hadi's gone missing. Whitney says she'll persuade her family to give her money to go to Libya. Wednesday – she shows up at the gallery. No money. But now she's got a plan to blackmail the family.'

'With what?'

'Whitney had seen someone murdered in the house when she was a kid.'

'Anton Bisjak?'

'Very probably.'

The events at St Laurence Villas back in the summer of 2002 began to take shape in Leo's mind as Ben told him of Whitney's dyslexic mistake, how Lubo became Ludo. The Glasgow Celtic connection.

'So he's the one torn from the photograph?'

'Looks like it,' Ben said. 'So, on to Wednesday and Thursday nights. Whitney stays at the gallery and—'

'The Goodes were helping her then?'

'No. Whitney actually wanted to get the money for them too so they could get out of the country, and they knocked that on the head. They're thinking this blackmail thing is just another of her fantasies and she'll get over it.'

'But she doesn't,' Leo said.

'Seems not. Come Friday, Whitney's plan is to have the Larkins leave the money in a spot up beyond Kilmacud but—'

'Where David Goode was knocked down?'

'Yeah. The plan changed Friday evening when Kevin showed up at the gallery.'

Leo's brain wobbled. He put a hand out to steady himself against the sitting-room wall, which was a little further away than he'd imagined. He almost went down. A blood pressure thing, he thought. No, a pressure thing.

'Leo?'

'Yeah. The plan changed?'

'Whitney told Georgia she was picking up the money Saturday night and left with Kevin,' Ben went on. 'But Saturday morning, David got the news that a body had been found over in Libya that was probably Hadi's. Georgia rang Whitney, who lost it and hung up. They hadn't heard from Whitney all day Saturday, so eventually David went out to Kilmacud in the small hours.'

'With his laptop?'

'He'd spent most of Saturday doing these computer lessons with elderly people apparently,' Ben said. 'That's about as far as we got with Georgia last night. She passed out and the ambulance took her. Helen's at the hospital waiting to talk to her again.'

Leo slipped out of the sitting room and into the hallway. The cold tiles burned the soles of his feet.

'So, the shooting. Have we picked up the Larkin boys?'

'Our officers found Gary about two hours after the shooting,' Ben replied. 'They went to Mrs Larkin's house first. She didn't come to the door for a while and when she did she told them Gary was at his place across the river. They had to force their way into the apartment and Gary was out cold when they reached him. He'd been drinking.'

'And Kevin?'

'We haven't found Kevin,' Ben said. 'We've had the pub searched. Jimmy's house was checked too but he was home alone.'

'Why didn't you call me?'

'It was your night off,' Ben said, and moved on. 'Mrs Goode is unconscious but her condition is stable. We may be able to talk to her later in the day.'

In his mind's eye, Leo saw Kevin Larkin. Not the big un-tidy man he'd become but the kid taking a punch in the back of a car in Tandy's Lane. The kid he hadn't defended. Gone AWOL now. A party to the blackmail attempt last week. Leo's instincts led him blindly on beyond the truth staring him in the face.

'We can't assume Kevin's the shooter here. Maybe MacDonald's got other enemies wanting to get a crack at him before he leaves,' Leo said. 'Plus, Gary had half an hour, say, to get from Sandymount to Chapelizod. Ninety minutes to wash, dump his clothes, get into bed, guzzle down half a bottle of whiskey, whatever. I take it you swabbed Gary for gun residue?'

'Yeah, but you know how unreliable those tests can be.'

'Did he tell you anything?'

'Gary's making a lot of noise but, basically, he insists that the Larkins have settled any differences they had with Baz MacDonald. Actually, we may know pretty soon whether or not MacDonald shot Harry. Helen found his gun in the car while she was working on Mrs Goode.'

'First-generation Glock 17?'

'Yeah. It's with the Technical Bureau. John expects a result in the next hour or two.'

The cold of the hallway had wrapped itself around Leo's body before he realized he was naked. He ducked into the bathroom and found himself a bath-towel.

'Have you talked to Gary about this Ludo/Lubo business?'

'Yeah,' Ben said. 'Lubo wasn't Bisjak's nickname, he's claiming. He didn't have a nickname that Gary was aware of. It might take a while but we could probably check out the rest of these Glasgow Celtic Supporters Club members and see if we can verify the Lubo nickname.'

'If Gary hasn't already got a word of warning out to their pals.'

'Or his mother?'

Leo caught sight of himself in the mirror over the hand basin. His eye-patch had moved from his left eye and sat in the middle of his forehead. His scowling early-morning face was a three-eyed mask. The Tibetan Buddhist deity, Mahakala. Fierce, ugly, protective. Of Liz Larkin, he wondered, or of himself?

'What do you mean?'

'We called to her house last night,' Ben said, and the arse fell out of Leo's temporary toga.

'And?'

'Well, it seemed to us that she's the one pulling Gary's strings. Pulling all the strings, actually. Family-wise. Business-wise. Their differences with MacDonald seem to have been resolved and we wondered if these differences were real in the first place. We thought maybe she'd got MacDonald to take out her husband but Georgia's story about the blackmail more or less puts the kibosh on that theory. One way or the other, grief over Harry isn't exactly high on her agenda.'

'Meaning?'

'Meaning when our guys called to the house last night, Derek McCarthy was . . . eh, on a sleep-over there.'

The eye-patch back in place offered no great improvement in the man-in-the-mirror's looks. Leo raised the waist of his bath-towel to cover his middle-age spread. It was the best he could do with himself. The best he could do with the drift of the conversation was to change its direction.

'Getting back to Anton Bisjak,' he said. 'Let's say he was especially liked and therefore probably trusted by Whitney. What if he took advantage of that trust? It happens, doesn't it?'

Ben's reply was neither immediate nor acquiescent.

'The abuse scenario may be less likely given what we discovered last night at Mrs Larkin's,' the young detective said. 'Physical abuse certainly. We called there because John sent us on the cleaned-up photograph. Whitney's body appeared to be covered in bruises. But it actually wasn't down to physical abuse. Until she was ten, Whitney had a medical condition that left her vulnerable to bruising easily and often. We saw the medical confirmation of this.'

Leo's earlier elation was subsiding rapidly. He needed another glimpse of Eveleen to keep it alive. He wandered back along the hallway.

'Mrs Larkin also claims she got two text messages from Whitney yesterday,' Ben continued. 'Actually showed them to us and rang Whitney's number to prove the mobile wasn't in the house. I'm inclined to take her word on this.'

'You think Whitney is alive then?'

'I think Mrs Larkin believes she is,' Ben replied. 'Though much of what the woman says is . . . well, not credible. To me, at least.'

'Such as?'

'Some unpleasant allegations she made,' Ben said, and Leo knew the Bad News Fairy was about to land on his left shoulder.

'Concerning?'

'Concerning you, sir. Personal stuff. An under-age relationship you may have had with her in the past.'

Leo came to a sudden halt on the threshold of the sitting room. He held on to his bath-towel because the air had been sucked from his stomach. The muscles in there felt like they were eating one another.

'I don't believe it has any relevance to your . . . to your handling of the case, sir, but Helen—'

'But Helen does?' Leo said; disappointed, saddened and that was all right. But then he got angry. 'And what? She wants me to walk the plank? Yeah, well tell her go walk her own fucking plank.'

'I'm sure you can explain what exactly—'

'I owe nobody an explanation, Murphy. I'm not squeaky clean but I'm not the Cookie Monster.'

'No one's implying—'

'Leave it, OK? What about Mahmoud Maguin? Has he opened up to you or to the SDU guys?'

'No, not a word,' Ben said.

'I'll talk to him,' Leo said, half afraid of the threat in his own voice. 'I'll take Gary too. Send a car for me.'

'To?'

'Under the railway bridge on Bath Avenue,' Leo said. One

of Dripsy Scullion's hang-outs. Dank and dusty. The kind of place Leo used to imagine himself ending up as a permanent resident. Might end up there yet.

'For what it's worth, sir, I don't believe—'

Leo cut the call. He went back quietly into the bedroom. The sight of her in slumbering repose heartened him but it wasn't a full-on heartening any more. He grabbed his clothes, dressed himself in the sitting room and left a note. *Ev, I'll call you later. Thanks for last night. Leo.* He thought about throwing in some Xs but remembered the child Whitney's Xs for 'Ludo' and changed his mind. He left the house and left Vavasour Square and hurrying along the raw, early morning streets, couldn't help thinking it would be the last time he'd do so.

# 41

You could make yourself all kinds of promises, Helen told herself, but promising never to darken the inside of a hospital ever again was one you couldn't possibly keep. Not in this game. She sat in the same hospital she'd sat in that first day of the case. Felt almost precisely the same. Battered and aching, itchy with unwashed sweat, her short black hair an untidy mess. And tired as hell. Thirty hours since she'd last slept, this new day merely an exhausted addendum to yesterday. Garda Dempsey's silent, gawky concern on the half-hour drive from Pettycannon station hadn't helped. Feeling like shit in private was bad enough. Looking like shit in public was worse.

Anthony Goode sat at the other side of his sleeping daughter's bed. Her dreadlocks had been untangled. The long red hair, rich and thick on the pillow, made a fairytale princess of her. Apart from the stud in her nose and the heavily bandaged left hand she'd reefed back at the gallery. Her father hadn't yet spoken to Helen though this was her third visit to the bedside, scarcely moved a muscle of his long, doubled-over frame.

'I know it's difficult for you but we need your help here.'

Helen leaned forward. 'Georgia might have died in that car, Mr Goode. Your wife too. We have to know—'

'I never learned to drive,' he said.

'Sorry?'

Gazing down at his daughter, Anthony Goode might have been reciting a slow, spiritless prayer so absorbed did he seem.

'Last evening, Georgia rang me. I could tell she was in a bad way. Her voice was so weak and she seemed so confused. She'd cut herself badly but couldn't go to a hospital because they'd catch her. They, I said? You have to bring me to a doctor who won't tell, she was saying. Tell what, I said? But all I got was more confusion.'

'What time was this?' Helen asked.

'Eight, half eight,' he replied. 'I told her I'd get a taxi and pick her up. But no, the taxi-driver would see her. It was only then that I realized Frida was in the room and had heard all of this. She took the phone from me, went to her room and, you know, made the arrangements with Georgia. Five minutes later she was gone without a word of explanation.'

Make the deepest cut first, Leo had often advised. Helen didn't have to like him to follow that advice. Better still, she could actually despise him rather than herself for this hard-hearted approach.

'Were you aware of the fact that your wife was having an affair with Baz MacDonald?'

Anthony lowered his elbows and rested them on his thighs. His long upper body folded further downwards. His face fell on to his open palms. When he spoke, he stayed below and Helen had to lean closer to hear.

'I guessed she was seeing someone but I didn't know his name. Whoever he is, he's just the latest.' He sighed, splayed the long fingers of his hands together. 'Ever since our finances went belly up, she's been . . . You see, she had a lot of insecurity in her early years. Her people were Big House and all that but in reality quite down-at-heel. This isn't the first time she's had to leave a beautiful home behind, and it changed her.'

'It didn't change her. She's always been like that. She never had enough.'

They looked up. The princess had seemed prettier as she slept. Resentment exaggerated the puffy asymmetry of her young face. Helen reached into her jacket for her ID.

'Don't be unkind, sweetheart, your mother's—'

'Why do you always have to be so fucking weak, Dad?' Georgia pleaded.

'We need to talk,' Helen said, flashing her ID.

Though she was probably unaware of it given her re-bellious nature, the tall girl had something of her father's condescending mien about her. She cast barely a glance at Helen and disregarded the ID entirely.

'I thought you might be a cop all right,' she said. 'The Americans will try to extradite me now, won't they? And you lot will gladly hand me over.'

'Why would they want to extradite you?' Helen asked. 'David was the one who—'

The sudden change in the girl's demeanour was riveting to watch. From haughty dismissiveness to tearful dissolution in three seconds flat. Anthony took his daughter's free hand in his. She didn't cast it off.

'That's the terrible thing,' Georgia cried. 'They thought he was the hacker but he wasn't. He did some hacking with Anonymous two years ago but he got out of it because he wanted to go to college in the States and he couldn't afford to risk it.'

'So who . . . ?' Helen began.

Georgia, however, had a monologue in mind. A full confession of the guilt racking those teenage features that would one day, Helen thought, combine to stunning effect. For now, she had a different kind of stunning effect to offer.

'I was the hacker,' she sobbed. 'I picked up all the tricks from David. Last year, I joined a group that was attacking websites of companies with American Defence Department contracts. Then when the Libyan uprising kicked off and Hadi started talking about going over there, I got into DDoS attacks on Gaddafi's government departments.'

'DDoS?' Anthony asked, like some Edwardian gent at the wrong end of an H. G. Wells time-shift.

'We flood the website with spoof requests and close it down,' Georgia said, and the explanation meant nothing to her father. 'David was worried. He was afraid the Americans would catch me and it wouldn't matter to them if I was helping to overthrow Gaddafi. So, he got paranoid about checking my laptop. He set up some Zone Alarm software and stuff so we could pick up any IP addresses trying to wardrive our wifi.'

'But you were sussed anyway?' Helen asked, cutting through the technical jargon.

Georgia nodded. More sobs followed. Slow ones. Irritatingly slow ones. Helen wanted desperately to move on to the subject of Whitney Larkin but knew she had to keep the girl's confessional floodgates open. She waited. Georgia re-emerged from the waters of her guilt.

'We weren't sussed online,' she explained. 'The weekend before last, the Zone Alarm flashed up a warning about an IP address trying to access our wifi. I told David and he copped this silver grey car parked near the house. There was a guy there talking on the phone for, like, two hours. Pretending to.'

'Foreign-looking guy. Black hair, glasses?' Helen asked, and the girl nodded.

'We didn't realize he was Libyan,' Georgia blurted out. 'I still can't see how the Libyans sussed us. They don't have that kind of capability. David was sure it had to be the Americans and that someone in the Anonymous group had ratted on me. I shut down straight away and didn't go back online after that. But the car came back a couple of times last week.'

'And you didn't report this to the police?' her father asked naively.

'Don't you get it, Dad?' she said, raising herself. 'The Americans have no mercy. They've been hounding a poor guy over in England, a hacker with Asperger's, for nine years. Do you imagine our cops are any different?'

Helen knew that the girl's anger wasn't altogether directed at her. David Goode's sister was punishing herself for his murder. Whatever harassment she got in the future from the Americans or from the Guards here in Ireland would always pale in comparison to the self-harassment that would stay with her as long as she lived. Anthony stroked her long, girlish hair.

'Last night, you told us about Whitney, about what went on last week,' Helen said. 'You got as far as, well, as far as David's going out to Kilmacud.'

'Did I?' The girl seemed genuinely alarmed at her absence of memory.

'Has Whitney been in touch since then? A call, a text?'

Georgia didn't answer. Helen felt her stomach sink. Whitney's voice on the message minder echoed in her mind. *Whitney Larkin isn't here . . .*

'She's your friend, Georgia. Don't you want us to find her?' Helen said.

One last silent battle with her anti-establishment scruples and the girl gave in. She didn't look at Helen as she spoke. It seemed like a kind of protest, the last available to her.

'David was taking so long,' she said. 'It was one o'clock, then two. See, we've got these iPhone-finder apps that secretly switch on the phone GPS every ten minutes so you can trace it and locate it on Google maps. Next thing I see the phone's somewhere over in Milltown and that's OK because it's in the right direction. But he wasn't picking up and I was in a panic. So I tried ringing Whitney. I left a few voicemails. And no answer. Nothing. Then Dad called me about the . . . about poor David.'

Another tear-break, and Helen sat patiently through it. Anthony tried to comfort his daughter but she was beyond comfort for what seemed like eternity squared.

'But you checked again surely?' Helen said and hoped her timing hadn't been too hasty.

'Not for hours,' Georgia replied. 'I just presumed the phone was on David when he . . . Then I heard it was missing and I located it in Castleknock. I got a location because this place was in its own grounds so it was a big area but not many apartments.'

Anthony withdrew from his daughter and straightened. He stared down at her and she seemed to wither below him.

'And you never told us this?' he said. 'You knew where his . . . his killer was and you didn't tell us?'

This time it was Georgia who did the reaching out. She held her father's reluctant arm.

'But I thought it was the Americans, the Secret Service, that were on to us. So did David,' she pleaded.

Anthony stood, high above in the dark cloud of grief

and guilt hanging over his daughter. Visibility was poor up there. The girl looked out from under her great shock of red hair at Helen. Her expression was one of resignation but Helen didn't push her. Wait, she told herself. And the wait proved worthwhile.

'I texted Whitney from the hospital on Sunday morning after David . . .' Georgia swallowed back the grief again. 'And, like I said, I knew where David's phone was and I asked if the address meant anything to her. Because, you know, if it wasn't the Americans, I thought it might be someone connected to her family. I mean, he was heading up to where Whitney was supposed to collect the money, wasn't he?'

'Did she answer you?'

'Yeah. One text: "I'm so sorry". She didn't even bother to ring. After all we did for her. We really did everything we could to help her stand up to her family. I know she exaggerated stuff but her father was a Little Hitler. And her mother? She was Eva Braun all over again, pretending everything was normal in that house. And as for her creepy little brother Gary . . . she got so paranoid about him following her around that she thought he might be tracking her mobile and got herself another phone in this dodgy phone shop over on Moore Street. And that uncle of hers, leering at her, staring like a dirty old man. But still, I shouldn't have blasted her like that on the voicemail I left.'

'Do you have the number of this second phone?' Helen asked, and Georgia gestured to the phone on her bedside table.

'It's under W2,' the girl said. 'She won't answer.'

Helen tried anyway. Nothing. Not even a message minder. Might as well be trying to ring the next world, she thought, and, putting the thought away, typed the number into her own mobile.

'So, this voicemail you left, Georgia, what did you say to her?'

'I told her it was all her fault that David died,' the girl replied, summoning up whatever righteousness she could find. There wasn't a lot of it. 'And it was. Wasn't it? I had every right to say that, didn't I?'

Helen was reminded of Ricky's efforts to take her in hand back in their college days. That was the trouble with middle-class revolutionaries. They took offence when the revolution went pear-shaped and the plebs proved ungrateful.

'One last question, Georgia. Did Whitney ever explain why she had an aversion to having her photo taken?'

'She told us that photos had been taken of her in the house when she was a kid. Nude photos, like. Not by that weird uncle, she said, but she wouldn't tell us who. Couldn't have been Kevin though. He was the only one in the family she got on with. He's a nice guy.' She sniffled again. 'David sussed out a bunch of new apps that might be useful for the deaf and Kevin was so grateful. He was all, like, emotional about it. And he wanted to do something to scare off this guy who was watching us. David told him not to get involved, that it might only complicate things for us.'

'So you'd met Kevin before?'

'A couple of times, yeah.'

'Did he confirm this story about the photos?'

'We didn't talk about that. How could we? But we believed her because she really was totally paranoid about hiding from cameras. It took us a long time to convince her but eventually she let us take some photos of her and Hadi. It really helped her. At least I thought it did but I don't know now.'

'Do you have a copy of those shots?' Helen asked.

Georgia nodded, took out her mobile phone. She sent them via Bluetooth to Helen's mobile. Three shots. Whitney and Hadi, arms around each other's waists. The goth girl's smile opened out like a dark flower from tentative to shy uncertainty to a positive glow. It was no surprise that Whitney had been head over heels with Hadi. The boy, his gelled hair shaved tight at the sides, was good-looking in a dark-eyed, long-lashed way but reserved rather than engaged. Affairs of state on his mind, Helen thought, and not affairs of the heart.

'You know the craziest thing of all?' Georgia said, less unkindly now than bemused. 'Whitney thought she was in some kind of major romance with Hadi. But it wasn't true. She was obsessed with him and he couldn't get away from her. Even after her brother and his gorilla pal beat Hadi up, she threatened to kill herself if Hadi stopped seeing her. That whole thing with Hadi was totally in her head. She didn't live in the real world. Last week, when all this stuff was going on, she even tried to convince us she was carrying Hadi's child just so's we'd go along with her plan. That's how she was.'

'And you're sure she wasn't pregnant?'

'Yeah,' Georgia said. 'She had this pregnancy tester thing and she goes into the toilet and does the whole urine thing. But it was so, like, fake. We didn't say anything but I Googled the brand name afterwards and it was off a joke site. That's how she was. Not . . . bad. Just kind of . . . harmless.'

Helen stood up, readied herself to go.

'We'll talk again,' she said.

The rebel had one last gob of bitterness left in her to spit out: 'Yeah, when you come with a warrant from your American pals.'

Helen shrugged. She went out into the corridor and readied her mobile to ring Leo. She scrolled back up to Ben's number instead, shared the new information.

'There's someone here at Pettycannon waiting to see you,' Ben told her. 'She won't speak with anyone else.'

'She?'

'Mrs Al-Baarai.'

# 42

To the basement cells in Pettycannon, daylight had never been more than a rumour. One of many rumours running through the minds of their insomniac occupants. Tortured imaginings of worst-case scenarios murdered any semblance of sleep. For all but the most hardened of criminals, the cells were incubators of guilt. Mahmoud Maguin was clearly less than a hardened criminal. He lay flat on the single pillow, a blanket drawn up to his chin, his fingers clutching it. His eyes were big pools of astonishment under the bleak strip-light. He'd woken to see a nightmarish mask hanging above his bed. Then the mask introduced itself.

'Detective Inspector Leo Woods.'

Leo sat on the end of the bed and let the young intern get unsettled. The strip-light above them buzzed like a trapped bluebottle.

'I've nothing to say. I've told your colleagues I know nothing.'

The posh-boy accent held little assertiveness but a whole lot of tentativeness. He reached for his spectacles on the bedside table but changed his mind. He'd already seen more than he wanted to see.

'Mr Maguin, I've a busy day ahead of me and no space in the diary for bullshit, OK? So, straight down to the business end. This is the deal and there's no other on—'

'Don't you understand?' Mahmoud pleaded as he raised himself on to one elbow. 'My family's in Libya. My dad works in one of Gaddafi's hospitals. If I talk, they'll die. Don't you have any idea what these people are like?'

'I used to be a UN peacekeeper, son. I've a pretty good idea what dictatorships are like.'

The young intern picked up his spectacles after all and looked at Leo more closely. A hint of professional interest lay beneath his wariness.

'Bell's palsy,' Leo explained. 'Let me tell you how I see your situation, Mahmoud.'

He held up a warning hand when the young man made to object.

'OK. What do you imagine's going to happen if you don't talk to us?'

Mahmoud shrugged. He wasn't sure but he hazarded a timid guess: 'I'll be charged as an accessory to that kid's death?'

'And for assaulting a Garda detective. So, we're talking seven to ten years here,' Leo clarified, and the young man's mouth fell open, his future shrinking before his eyes. 'But, of course, the authorities over in Libya will be convinced you actually did help our deceased Secret Service friend, right? And your family will be safe.'

'Yeah,' Mahmoud said, as uncertain as he was unhappy.

'Except I have a different plan in mind, son.' Leo moved closer for effect. 'I'm going to release you without charge. The press will get hold of the story of how you cooperated fully with us and helped us to get to the bottom of David Goode's murder and to identify the murderer,

Yusef Dorda, as a Libyan Secret Service agent.'

'You can't do that!'

'The release papers are already being processed,' Leo lied. 'I reckon you'll be out of here by, say, nine o'clock.'

'What about my family? My parents, my sister.'

'Not my problem.'

'But they'll be tortured, beaten, murdered!'

'Probably,' Leo said. 'You should try and snatch an hour of sleep for yourself there now, son. You won't be getting much of it for the rest of your life.'

'You can't . . .'

Leo did the shit-happens helpless hands thing and made for the door. He got there sooner than he'd wanted to, got the door open sooner too. Almost got it closed behind him.

'Wait!' Mahmoud called. 'The deal. You never told me what the deal was.'

Leo stayed by the door, making a casual offer of it.

'The alternative goes like this,' he said, summoning up a tone of indifference. 'We charge you, hold you on remand for your own protection, and when Gaddafi falls we drop the complicity charge and see if we can work out something on the officer assault charge.'

'But if he doesn't fall?'

'He's already dead in the water, son,' Leo said. 'NATO's bombing the shit out of Tripoli and hitting his army all over Libya. He's got no friends worth a damn to him in the international community. Plus everyone's lusting after his oil. He's got two chances of surviving. Slim and zero.'

Mahmoud Maguin sat with his back to the wall and pulled the blanket up over his shoulders.

'He told me he didn't mean to run the kid down,' he said. 'It was a stupid, careless bloody accident. I'm telling you, this Dorda guy, he was a total clown.'

'So you weren't in the van when it happened?'

'No way. I never saw this Dorda guy until he showed up at my apartment on Sunday morning. He told me he was Secret Service, that I had to help him or my folks would be arrested over in Tripoli.'

'Did he tell you how he knew David Goode was the hacker?'

'No.'

'So, he forced you to go into the hospital, yeah?'

Leo approached the bed, cast a sceptical eye on the young man. Something wasn't quite adding up here.

'Isn't that a bit of a coincidence?' he continued. 'A Libyan just happens to be working in the same hospital David Goode was brought to?'

'There are Libyans working in all the major hospitals in Dublin,' Mahmoud countered. 'They do the Irish Leaving Cert in private schools over there and a lot of students come to medical school here. Law, engineering, whatever. Dorda kept a watch on the Libyan community here and knew who worked where. I'm not even the only Libyan working in the hospital. I just happened to draw the short straw.'

'What did he want you to do at the hospital? Check on David's condition? More than that, surely?' A shocking thought struck Leo. 'Finish David off?'

The blanket fell from the intern's grasp.

'No way, nothing like that,' he said. 'See, Dorda had the kid's laptop but it had one of those fingerprint security things on it. Like, you had to swipe this pad to open it.'

'And Dorda wanted you to swipe David's finger across it.'

'Yeah, but I never got close enough to the kid. I thought Dorda was going to kill me when I got back from the hospital.'

'He stayed at yours on Sunday night?'

The intern nodded, his drained expression seeming to recall the torrid hours of captivity in his own apartment.

'He was totally overwrought. He thought he was being hunted down. So he had this bullet-proof vest on him even when he lay in bed. And the gun was always in his hand.'

'Who did he think was hunting him down?'

'He wasn't sure. He told me that earlier in the week he'd had this feeling that someone had been following him. After the accident he kept saying he should've trusted his instincts and left the country when he could've flown out on one of his fake passports.'

'So, he was trying to find another way out of Ireland?'

'Yeah. He had this list of contacts but it was obviously out of date because the first guy he rang was dead. I mean, when he rang he was told the guy was dead. The next one he tried – some guy down in Kerry – he was told not to dare ring again or he'd be shot.'

'These were IRA guys, I'm presuming. Or ex-IRA, more likely.'

'I suppose,' Mahmoud said. 'The guy he was going to meet the night he was shot, he was ex-IRA for sure. Dorda told me he was.'

'Did he tell you this guy's name?'

'No. All he said was that he had to drive to the border in County Monaghan to meet him.'

'And Wilkinstown, where he gets plugged, is on the scenic route from Dublin to Monaghan,' Leo speculated.

Baz MacDonald came to mind. The ex-Provo from across the border in Belfast. Taking out this Libyan pest at the behest of his old Republican buddies maybe? The ex-Provo who now had two possible motives for killing Yusef Dorda if you believed in wild coincidence, and Leo didn't.

'Listen, son,' he said, 'I'm sorry I had to lean on you. I know you're in a real bind here but, look at it this way, if you had to serve time as an accessory it wouldn't matter whether or not Gaddafi stays in power. He could be gone, dead, but you'd still be counting the days in Mountjoy.'

'Thanks,' Mahmoud said, though he clearly hadn't yet figured out exactly what he was thanking this ugly detective for.

Out in the hospital carpark, Garda Dempsey mustered up the courage to express his concern for Helen. What he hadn't mustered up was a dash of subtlety. Nor, as yet, sufficient volume.

'How's the head, Sarge?'

Her mind was on Mrs Al-Baarai, who awaited her at Pettycannon station. She doubted the woman was bearing good news.

'How's the head, like?'

'Excuse me?' Helen said, stopping up short.

'After the box you took. You're awful sick-looking.'

Dempsey shrank from the verbal assault that seemed inevitable. Then Helen's mobile came to his rescue. John from the Technical Bureau.

'Just a sec,' she said, and covered the phone. 'Open the bloody car, Dempsey.'

Unspoken was the promise to eviscerate him later, though the young Guard clearly got the message. Apology and defeat collided on his face and left him forlorn. Helen got back to the call. It was a small phone but a big wind howled inside it.

'John. How's it going?' Her lightness was less about good humour than anticipation. Something major coming her way, she suspected. 'Are you chasing tornadoes or what?'

'Strange happenings, Helen,' he said. He sounded shaken. 'I'm out in Tandy's Lane.'

'Where Harry Larkin was shot? Why?'

'Just some routine follow-up work,' he said. 'Thought I'd get it done on my way into work. It's my side of town, you know. But this . . . this I never expected to find. I tried to ring Leo but . . .'

'What did you find?'

'I think it might be a grave. Two graves probably.'

Helen's stomach lurched. The sky in her brain fizzed with exploding stars. Don't let it end like this, she thought.

'Helen?'

'Yeah, I'm here,' she said, getting herself back on the job, leaving her emotions to explode somewhere else, some other time. 'Where exactly are these graves, John?'

'There's this house that was never completed here in the field beside the shooting site,' he said. 'The graves are out behind it. But we checked every inch of the field on Sunday. I've actually got the photos here on my laptop and the lilies are definitely not there.'

'The lilies?' she said, recalling with a chill the lilies on her bedside table at the hospital and at Liz Larkin's house.

'Bunches of lilies arranged in the shapes of two crucifixes,' he explained, his usual neutrality of tone compromised. 'They're pinned into the soil so they won't blow away, I guess. And the earth's been disturbed.'

'Jesus Christ,' Helen said. 'You don't think one of them might be—'

'Better not to think. We'll need to dig here. I'll leave it to you to tell Leo, OK?'

'Sure.'

White-coated figures swept by behind the windows of the hospital, soft-shoed nurses spectral in their gliding by.

Her world was full of ghosts. We walk with the dead, Leo had once told her, tongue in cheek, even if it takes us to hell. Too right, Leo. Pity you turned out to be such a bastard.

'More positive news on the gun front,' John said. 'A couple of the guys worked on that Glock 17 through the night. They're about as certain as it's possible to be. Looks like you've got your weapon.'

'For which shooting?'

'Same gun shot Harry Larkin and your Libyan agent both. Same guy presumably.'

'Baz MacDonald,' Helen said.

Waiting. Waiting for God only knew what the earth spat up, Leo thought. A fellow could lose the run of himself waiting.

When he was twelve years old, Leo had skipped out of St Margaret's care home one Sunday afternoon and gone to a League of Ireland football match. Tolka Park. Lovely old-style ground. The corrugated stand, its front row seating so close to the touchline you could pat the winger on the back if he'd put over a good cross. Plenty of good crosses that day from his hero, Joe Haverty, the Shelbourne winger. Back from his goal-scoring feats with Blackburn Rovers, a little slower, a little heavier. It didn't matter. The genius was still in his feet.

After the game, Leo had run all the way from Drumcondra back to Blackrock tasting for the first time that strange concoction of divine pleasure and terrified anticipation of the punishment that inevitably followed. Someone, he couldn't remember who, had brought him to wait in the head sister's office. A high-ceilinged room not unlike the Incident Room in which he sat now. Oddly, he retained no memory of Sister Benedict's arrival or of the punishment she'd meted out. He remembered only the waiting, the fear, the growing resolve not to cry no matter what followed. A similar brew of thoughts and emotions swilled in his stomach now as he waited for the coming confrontation with Helen. And for the bad news from Tandy's Lane.

Helen's message, relayed to him by Ben, had seemed conclusive. The gun in Baz MacDonald's car appeared to solve the riddle of Harry's shooting and the Libyan's murder. The graves behind the unfinished house in Tandy's Lane, added to Kevin's vanishing act, unfortunately, conjured up an alternative explanation of these incidents. Leo hoped he was wrong, hoped he'd been infected with the same air of delusion that had hovered around this case from the start. He'd kept the speculations to himself. And waited.

A rustling sound outside his door set his nerves on edge. As soon as the handle turned, Leo felt the childish urge to take a leak. The door opened. It was, at once, a relief and a let-down. It was Superintendent Heaphy.

'You were right, Leo,' Aonghus declared, all smiles, all teeth. 'I just heard about the bullet matches and the graves out on Tandy's Lane will probably be this Slovakian chap and . : . well, sad to say, of course, but probably that poor young one, Whitney. And I wouldn't be surprised if that . . . that terrorist killed the poor deaf lad too. One way or the other, we're heading for a major string of results here. All we need now is to find that Armenian fellow, and we're out in force on that. Airports covered, ferry terminals. We're bound to catch him.'

'And you're bound for glory,' Leo said, but the super was, as always, impervious to irony.

'I wouldn't say glory,' he said cheerfully. 'I'm only doing my job. And my job is to let you do your job. Isn't that what you're always telling me?'

'It is. And I'm telling you again. Piss off and let me do my job.'

Impervious too, at least for now, to expletives, for Heaphy's enthusiasm remained undiminished.

'And that young one of yours. Troy, isn't it?'

'Helen, yeah. What's your problem with her?'

'None. The opposite in fact. She performed miracles last night, I'm told. Saved that woman's life. I'm putting her up for the Scott Medal for bravery.'

'Ben was with her, wasn't he? Does he get a medal too?'

Superintendent Heaphy straightened his uniform jacket buttons, fixed his tie, removed his braided cap, brushed his almost hairless scalp and replaced the cap. The chairman of a military tribunal about to pass judgement.

'That fellow,' he said, readying himself to leave. 'He's a major disappointment to me.'

'I'm sure he had good reason not to go to Quantico on that course.'

'He's jumping ship, Leo. Resigning from the force.'

'What? Why?' Leo asked, genuinely surprised.

'He's staying home to mind the child. That's not a man's job.'

Leo leaned forward, propping an elbow on his desk, propping his chin in the palm of his hand. He felt like the manager of a half-decent Premier League team whose best players had just decided to move elsewhere.

He checked his personal mobile again. No response from Eveleen to his messages. He looked at the old, dog-eared Harry Larkin file before him. He knew that his petty concerns over the ICU nurse and Helen's new loathing of him were just sideshows. The end of the Larkin affair was drawing close and it wasn't going to be tidy. Baz MacDonald, the villain of the piece, full stop? No, it was going to be a bloody awful mess. The inevitability, the unbroken circle of it all sickened him.

'It's a man's job, all right,' Leo said. 'If the man has a child. What the hell would we know about that anyway?'

Childlessness was the one thing Heaphy wasn't impervious to. Not even on this most optimistic of mornings for him could he forget his wife's desperately surreptitious and unsuccessful effort to become pregnant. By Leo. A miracle, she'd planned to tell her husband. But the miracle end of things never quite happened and her God had intervened, piled on the guilt, forced her confession many years later.

'Sorry, Aonghus, I—'

'Fuck off, Leo, you bollocks,' the super said, and left his detective inspector speechless in wonder at this sudden outburst of profanity from a Knight of Columbanus.

# 43

Inside Pettycannon station, the public waiting area was empty except for a woman wearing a full-length black chador. She turned to face Helen. Tears overwhelmed Mrs Al-Baarai at first and Helen brought her through to an interview room. The spartan space seemed, at once, to invite desolation and to mock its expression with harsh echoes.

'Would you like some coffee?' Helen asked.

Mrs Al-Baarai shook her bowed head, towelled her face with a large handkerchief.

'Is this about Hadi? Is he . . . ?'

'No, Alhamdulillah. No. He is safe.'

The woman was calmer now but no less troubled.

'My husband found Hadi in El Salloum,' she said, though hers wasn't a good news tone. 'Hadi is fine. No injuries, nothing like that. But he will never speak to my husband again. I don't know if he will ever speak to me.'

'But why?'

'Because . . .' Mrs Al-Baarai lowered her voice. 'That poor boy David, his family would hate us if they knew.'

'Knew what?'

'That my husband is responsible for David Goode's death.'

The next question was simple enough. How? But Helen couldn't formulate it, and when she did, the question got lost somewhere between her brain and her tongue. Mrs Al-Baarai answered anyway.

'Two weeks ago, my husband met with a group of Libyans here in Dublin,' she said. 'They talked about how they might help the National Transitional Council – you know, the alternative government to Gaddafi. My husband thought they were among friends and he talked about how Hadi was getting on in Libya but he also . . . You see, when they argued before Hadi left and my husband refused to give his blessing, Hadi told him how even his Irish friends were doing their bit, how one of his friends was helping to hack into Libyan government websites. Hadi didn't say who but my husband assumed it must be David because he knew of his work fixing computers for charity and teaching. And he mentioned David's name and—'

'And Yusef Dorda was there?'

'Yes,' Mrs Al-Baarai said. 'When Dorda was killed the word went around our community very quickly about who he really was. What he really was. And I told my husband when he rang me from El Salloum. Everyone trusted Dorda. My husband wasn't the only one who was fooled but he is devastated now. Hadi will not forgive him and he will not forgive himself. What will become of us now?'

Helen didn't have an answer but she made noises enough to assuage the woman's grief. She found someone to take Mrs Al-Baarai's statement and headed for the Incident Room.

Halfway up the first flight of stairs, a text message arrived on her personal mobile. Ricky. She read the message on the move. *Talked to Jamie & got the full story. You won't like it. Ring me.*

*

'They've started digging out at Tandy's Lane,' Ben said. 'They don't know how long it might take.'

His voice echoed in the Incident Room, which Leo had cleared when the young detective arrived. Leo nodded, checked his mobile, chucked it back on the table again. He went back to the file before him. An old file. Made him feel how long he'd been on this planet to see the yellowing pages embossed with ancient lettering from some antique typewriter that was probably sitting in an attic or dump or retro shop now. The old 'Harry L/Informant' file with its secret addendum marked 'Elizabeth R'. Someone knocked on the door, opened it. Sergeant Martha Corrigan sashayed towards Leo with a couple of A4 sheets in her hand and a quizzical smile on her beguiling face.

'The personal details from your Admin file,' she said and placed the second sheet on the desk. 'And a charge sheet for Elizabeth Reilly from 1979.'

'Thanks, Martha,' Leo said but didn't offer the explanation she might reasonably have expected.

'How did your date go?'

'Swimmingly,' Leo said, struggling to get into bantering mode.

'Ah, she had a pool, had she?'

'No, just a fish tank,' he said. 'We paddled.'

Martha exited the room with a laugh and a wave. Like she'd exited Leo's life ten years before. A sickly child took her place in the doorway of the Incident Room. Helen. She sat halfway along the table and didn't look Leo's way as she outlined Georgia Goode's and Mrs Al-Baarai's revelations. He was relieved to hear that the Libyan kid hadn't been killed after all. But that was the end of the good news. Whitney's second phone wasn't giving out any signal that the service provider could tell. Worse still was the fact that Kevin Larkin had lied to him. He'd known the Goodes after all. Known too of Whitney's blackmail plans. And the photos Helen had made copies of were three punches to Leo's gut. Whitney, alongside her fantasy paramour, grew more like the smiling Liz Reilly of old with each shot.

A mobile phone rang in someone's pocket.

Leo glared at the two young detectives. They checked their phones, shrugged. The ringing ended. Leo's heartbeat fluttered in his throat. He couldn't decide whether or not to tell them his story of a little deaf boy. The phone rang again. The three detectives triangulated the buzzing to a leather jacket hanging on the back of a chair at the far end of the table.

'Martin Buck's jacket?' Leo asked. 'Isn't he in hospital?'

'Yeah, sorry,' Ben said. 'One of the SDU guys dropped it in here. He'd picked it up at Maguin's apartment.'

The mobile stopped ringing.

'How's Buck doing anyway?' Leo wondered. 'Is he all right?'

'They've kept him in for a brain scan,' Ben said.

'They'll need a microscope.'

'That's so not funny,' Helen said, including both men in her withering look.

Ben took it well. Leo didn't. He picked up the decrepit Larkin files and the A4 sheets Martha had delivered and lobbed them on the desk before her.

'Right then,' he said. 'See if you can find something to amuse you in there. Open the file. You'll see a very large fucking red circle around the date of my first clandestine meeting with Elizabeth Reilly, now Mrs Larkin.'

'Sir,' Ben objected.

'Shut it, Ben, and let me finish,' Leo thundered. 'Got that,

Helen? Our first meeting after I took her over from Blackie. Fourth of August 1980, right? Now her charge sheet from 1979. Possession of. Her DOB is on there. Twelfth of March 1960. So, she was twenty when I first met her, right? And my details from Admin – see the DOB? Nineteenth of February 1954. Which means I was twenty-six.'

Though her eyes had glazed over, Helen saw the dates quite clearly. Still no excuse, she thought, and Leo read her mind.

'These are not excuses, these are facts,' he said. 'I have no excuses. I was a married man, a careless, callow young man. Screwed up more ways than I can remember. I abused my position of authority. It doesn't matter that I didn't force myself on her. I did worse than that. I abandoned her.'

'We don't need to hear this, Leo,' Helen said, and his name on her lips softened him, woke him up to his boorishness.

'Damn it, I've upset you now,' he said. 'But there's a reason I have to finish this story. It's to do with Liz . . . with Elizabeth Larkin. It relates to the case. It explains this abuse angle I've been harping on about.'

Helen wiped a tear from the corner of her eye. She didn't know if her brain could any longer hold up to the assaults on it. Leo's pained unmasking, Jamie's latest escapade and, worst of all, the inescapable image of a grave being opened in a field in Lucan, the clay being brushed delicately from the buried face of a young girl.

'Liz was abused as a child by her father,' Leo said. 'When she told me, I stopped seeing her. In that way. Then I stopped seeing her, full stop. I'd tried to get her to take a case against him but she said he'd shagged off over to England for himself and that . . . well, that was the end of that. I never followed it up. I did everything I could to convince her not to marry Larkin because I knew it would end in tears. Worse than tears. So, yeah, when she came back on my radar, I was carrying too much baggage. I couldn't let myself think she had a part in all this mess. But the graves—'

The mobile phone in Martin Buck's jacket rang again. Leo stood up.

'Fuck this,' he said, strode down to the end of the table and pulled out the mobile from the zipped inside pocket. It stopped ringing when he'd got it clear. Angrily he checked the screen. Ten missed calls. The last three came from someone called Marie. His latest squeeze no doubt, Leo thought. The rest were from Jimmy. Not that Jimmy, surely? There was a voicemail dated 10.15 the previous evening. He opened it. The voice was male all right, if not exactly masculine. Jimmy fucking Larkin. *Answer the phone, you bastard. Martin! Martin! Drop me in the shit on this and I'll drag you down with me. Do you hear me, you bastard? Ring me. Now!*

He put the phone on loudspeaker, played the voicemail again. The two young detectives looked blankly at him. Leo was drawing blanks himself. A mess, he thought. Just as he'd expected.

Another phone rang. Helen's. The Technical Bureau. She switched her phone to loudspeaker too and took the call. There was no tornado, just a big hollow silence with a small, last-man-on-earth voice punctuating it.

'Helen, we've found the first body,' John said. 'The grave wasn't deep and it wasn't a grave. At least not a new grave. Neither of them is.'

'I don't understand,' she said, speaking for all of them.

'Some of the upper soil had been disturbed. Just enough to mark the spot basically.'

'So, they're both old graves?' she said, relieved but guiltily so.

'Yeah. This one's eight, ten years old maybe,' the CS operative told her. 'High water table here which doesn't help preservation but we do have some remnants of the clothes. Green and white top of some kind.'

'A Glasgow Celtic jersey, you think?'

The ringing of yet another mobile drowned John's answer. Ben's phone. He left the Incident Room whispering to his caller.

'Sorry, John, missed you there,' Helen said.

'A football jersey, yeah,' he told her. 'There's the suggestion of a number or part of a number on the front like the top curve of a number two. Or it might be the first digit of, you know, twenty something?'

'Twenty-five,' Helen said, and Leo looked searchingly at her. She told both men, the visible and the invisible one, what she meant. 'That was Ľubomír Moravčík's number in the Glasgow Celtic squad. He was Slovakian. The corpse is too. Anton Bisjak. What's the MO, John? Shot?'

'No. His skull's been cracked open. Blows to the top of the head and to the left cheekbone and jaw. Also looks like the killer may have performed a neck snap on his victim. The skull had fallen on its right side and we spotted a fracture of the C2 cerebral vertebra. This might have occurred before or after the other blows because—'

'Because neck snaps work well in the movies but in reality are actually very difficult to perform,' Leo said. 'And even then death isn't always instantaneous.'

A memory came close to the surface of Leo's attention but didn't quite emerge just yet.

'Exactly,' John said. 'I'd better get back to work here, OK? We've started on the second grave.'

'Yeah, thanks, John,' Helen said. 'Talk to you—'

'John?' Leo said.

He moved closer to Helen, to the phone. She stared at him. From the doorway, the returning Ben stared too. The memory had surfaced in Leo.

'Busy here, Leo. I need to—'

'An attempted neck snap, even an unsuccessful one, would leave bruising, wouldn't it?'

'We're talking about a body that's in the ground a decade here, Leo.'

'No, I've just remembered Harry's neck was badly bruised when I saw him at the hospital,' Leo said. 'Could be someone tried the same neck snap on him, right?'

'Could be.'

'The second grave there, my guess is you'll find the same neck snap,' Leo said. More astonishment. 'And, John, keep an eye out for an eye there.'

'Sorry?'

'A glass eye, John. Blue. Let me know when you find it, OK?'

'It might take time,' John said.

'And, John? Send us over a few snaps of Bisjak's bones and the piece of jersey. Like now, if you can.'

'Sure.'

'Thanks, John.'

Helen had forgotten the phone was in her hand. Leo gestured to her to cut the call, gestured Ben into the Incident Room, gestured the closing of the door. Then he sat them down and told them a story. He hoped it wasn't true, he said, especially the last chapter.

Once upon a time there was a lonely, unloved little deaf boy. A boy who, when he looked into a field one late evening in 1983, didn't piss himself because his father was a monster. Or because the young Clown Prince Leo in the front of the car with the monster frightened him. Or because the lowering mist was like something out of a Hammer movie. Or because he imagined the ghost of his mother hovering in the abandoned house construction there. He pissed himself because he knew there was a grave in that field and because he knew who was in the grave and who'd dug it. And nineteen years later another burial took place there, and the deaf boy, a man now, knew who was in that grave too and who'd put him there. Another nine years on and the deaf man marks the graves, points the finger at his brutish father. And at his wicked witch stepmother.

'Who's in the other grave, Leo?' Helen asked.

'I believe it's Liz Larkin's father, Charley Reilly.'

'So he hadn't gone to England?'

'No,' Leo said and knew, in that moment, that he'd never believed Charley Reilly had done a runner. 'Harry Larkin killed him. I'm assuming he killed Anton Bisjak too.'

'So you think that Kevin's taken advantage of the situation to avenge his rejection by the family?' Ben said. 'Marking the graves for us to find?'

'That's the more obvious possibility, yes,' Leo said. 'But, given the fact that Kevin's gone AWOL, there's another.'

He sat back tiredly in his seat. He lifted the eye-patch, took the weight of seeing off the good eye for ten seconds, quarter of a minute, half a minute. He lowered it again. The muscle of the good eye went into spasm. The world spun. Nothing, for too long a moment, seemed real. Then it was all surreal.

'The Harry Larkin shooting and the Libyan's murder, they look . . . well, they look done and dusted,' Leo said. 'Same gun used for both and we find it in MacDonald's car. The guy's got motives for definite. And he's killed before. So, it's plausible he might even have killed Bisjak. He supposedly went looking for him in 2002. Different MO,

370

of course, but plausible. And, OK, as a parting shot before he hit the road he may have decided to land the remaining Larkins in the shit by marking the graves. But I have to say it doesn't add up for me.'

'Why not?' Helen asked.

'The possible attempt at a neck snap on Harry for one,' Leo said. 'OK, I did get another explanation for it at the hospital but . . .'

Leo leaned forward. His good eye was fed up with carrying its sibling's share of the work. By way of sarcastic protest, it shed a tear. Leo left it there. Doubt spread itself across the expressions of the two young detectives.

'Listen,' he continued, spreading the fingers of his out-stretched hands, 'all of this – Harry's shooting, the murder of the Libyan, the flowers placed on the graves, the attempt on Baz MacDonald's life – is the work of one desperate, damaged soul. I'm sure of it.' He locked his hands into a white-knuckled tightness that hurt. 'Someone's writing a history of the Larkin family here in blood and tears. Jimmy's up to something but not up to this mayhem. Gary's a more realistic bet, yes. But Kevin's the one gone AWOL. And remember what he told us, Ben? Whitney couldn't break the circle. He loved her but he saw no hope for her.'

'You think she's dead then?' Ben asked.

Leo hesitated, the logic coming together only as it reached his lips.

'Look at it this way. On Saturday morning last, Whitney learns that a body likely to be Hadi's had been found and loses the plot. Now we know she made it to Sunday morning and heard about David Goode's death. It's all too much for her so she . . . well, she had this suicide ideation thing going on, didn't she? And Kevin murders the Libyan because it's David's killing that put her over the edge.'

'If everything's connected, if it's all Kevin's work,' Ben said, 'why would he take a shot at MacDonald? They seemed close, certainly closer than any of the others.'

'I don't know.'

More than ever, it seemed to Leo that he was flying in the face of the evidence, making a case against a disturbed but fundamentally decent man and, in the process, letting a gunman with a fancy moniker off the hook. But you don't go with the flow, he reminded himself, you go with the currents beneath the flow. Even if they drown your righteous soul.

'OK,' he said. 'I want both of you to prove me wrong on all of this. I want to come out of this looking like a bloody idiot. So, first off, bring me the head of Jimmy Larkin. Maybe his liaison with Martin Buck will throw up a different angle on things.'

'Might Jimmy be in on this with Kevin?' Ben suggested. 'They're both outsiders in the family. Maybe Jimmy was guiding Kevin's hand here.'

'It's possible but I don't see it,' Leo said. 'Jimmy's devious, sure, but he doesn't have the killer instinct. And I don't believe he's capable of hurting inside as deeply as Kevin. Or Gary, for that matter. He hasn't suffered like they have.'

'We have to bring Mrs Larkin in too,' Helen said, though without acrimony. 'If you're right about the other body, she must know the story there.'

'Of course,' Leo said. 'Helen, I was over the top earlier. I'm really very—'

'Sir?' Ben rescued his boss from another foot-in-mouth situation. 'That call I just took? It was one of our guys at the hospital to say that Mrs Goode's woken up. We can talk to her for five minutes, ten at most.'

In the hush of the Incident Room, the three detectives as

one drew in deep breaths. At the end of their long exhalations, they were ready to go.

'Do you want to take that, Leo?' Helen asked.

His name on her lips again was a ray of hope in the dark place he'd come to, and from it another ray emerged. Maybe he could rescue something from this painful case. Someone.

'No,' he said. 'You stay with the Goodes, OK? And listen, that kid Georgia? We should throw her a break.'

'I don't understand,' Helen said.

'This American lot, they still think David was the hacker, right?' he explained. 'So what's the point in hanging her out to dry now? She's already got herself a life sentence, it seems to me.'

The two detectives looked at him doubtfully. Youthful qualms, he thought, God be with the day.

'I'm not trying to prove I'm Mr Nice Guy, Helen,' Leo said. 'The kid's misguided but she's no criminal. Not in my eyes. So we spare her, OK?'

She nodded her assent.

'And talk to Buck. You'll have to hit him hard, girl. No mercy, no matter what shape he's in, right?'

'No problem,' Helen said.

Eyes averted, she packed up, took off. She hadn't forgiven him, Leo thought. Join the queue, Helen. It's a hell of a long one and it goes back a long way. He wondered if Ben Murphy was lining up in there too.

'Soon as those photos come in from John, we lay them on Gary,' Leo said. 'Speaking of Garys, I hear you're doing a Gary Cooper on us.'

The unshaven detective was nonplussed. Leo had forgotten quite how young the guy actually was. Sometimes it felt like everyone in the world was younger than him.

373

'Gary Cooper in *High Noon*, throwing in the badge,' he explained. 'Riding off into the sunset with Grace Kelly.'

'I asked the super not to tell you. I wanted to tell you myself. I'm sorry.'

'Don't apologize, son,' Leo said. 'You're doing a brave thing. I'd like to think I'd have done the same in the circumstances.' He smiled. Self-deprecatingly. 'Wouldn't put money on it though.'

He went towards the Incident Room door. From back at the long table, Ben called out: 'I've worked with a lot of men in here, Leo, but you're worth the whole bloody lot of them put together.'

'Thanks, old sport,' Leo said.

# 44

$G$ary Larkin was drowning. The two detectives watched his shaven head go down on the arms he'd lowered to the table. The head bobbed like a ball buffeted on a current of tears. Held loosely in one hand, the photocopied shots of Anton Bisjak's bones and shredded Glasgow Celtic jersey fluttered as though in a river breeze.

'Not such lovely bones, eh, Gary?' Leo said. 'You watched him die, didn't you? Joined in the sport maybe.'

A sound emerged from below that wasn't entirely human. Leo took it as a negative.

'You bludgeoned him to death right there in front of your eight-year-old sister?' Ben chipped in. 'We know she saw it happen. She tried to blackmail Harry with it, right?'

Before he raised his head to face them, Gary got rid of his tears along the sleeve of his black suit jacket. He came up red-eyed with humiliation.

'No way. It's just one of her loopy stories,' the ex-child actor muttered. 'I want a solicitor. I've a right to—'

'You don't have a right to a shite, son, until you start talking to us,' Leo said.

The black suit didn't hang well on the small man, the little of him there was to fill it shrinking rapidly. Leo's personal phone vibrated in his pocket. A call. He took a surreptitious look at the screen. *Unknown Number.* Might be Ev ringing from the hospital. Hopefully. He leaned across the short table, laid a firm hand on the padded shoulder of Gary's jacket. Cushioned or not, the small man's trembling registered in Leo's palm.

'You brought your pal Anton, otherwise known as Lubo, into your house, didn't you?' Leo said. 'What was he doing? Prowling around your little sister? Maybe you brought him home so's he could do just that?'

'No,' Gary said, floundering, casting about for some out but there was no out because two detectives sat between him and the door. 'He screwed us in a cigarette deal. Caught us for thousand, tens of thousands. So we sent Baz after him.'

The old family fable, Leo thought, the story they'd been sticking to since 2002.

'And Baz made a home visit of the job? Are you kidding me, son?' Leo said. 'Baz is a professional shooter not a Neanderthal skull-breaker like Lubo's killer. No, that'd be more Harry's style, right? He'd done it before, hadn't he? We've got two graves out in Tandy's Lane, Gary. But you knew there were two bodies, didn't you?'

'No way. Two graves? Who else could . . . ?'

Gary's expression did the sudden realization thing. Arched eyebrows, fish mouth. His attention wandered out of the interrogation room chasing a horrified thought. Leo's phone vibrated again. Same unknown.

'Look at the photos, Gary,' Leo said. 'Look at them. Look at the skull. Split open it is. Look. The scrap of jersey.'

Gary obeyed. Briefly. Then he jammed his eyes tight shut to hide from the photos, plugged his ears with his fists, tried some wheedling incantations to shut down his brain. Nothing worked. The world wouldn't go away and he couldn't get himself out of it.

'It was just a stupid misunderstanding,' Gary moaned. 'Lubo didn't have to die.'

'Tell us more, Gary,' Ben said.

'You only live twice,' Gary said. Twice. But it was still a mystery to the two detectives second time around.

The senior ward nurse's office in ICU was decked out in festive mode. Greetings cards, neatly wrapped and ribboned boxes of various sizes, flowers. Including lilies, from which there seemed no escape. Eveleen Morgan had recovered from her earlier moment of curious panic. She'd asked if Leo had come to the hospital with Helen. No, Helen had said, why? Oh, nothing. But the young detective knew it was more than nothing. Now she sneaked a closer glance at the cards propped on the filing cabinet as Eveleen spoke on the office phone. *Farewell & Best Wishes. Bon Voyage. You'll Be Missed!* The brown-haired nurse ended her call.

'Where are you headed?' Helen asked, indicating the cards, and noted the nurse's odd hesitancy.

'Oh, off on my travels again,' Eveleen replied. She stood, fixed the crumpled hips on her uniform. 'Dubai. We can talk to Mrs Goode now but not for long. I know you're under pressure on this but I'm already stretching the rules here.'

'Is her husband in there with her?' Helen asked.

'He's in the A&E ward with his daughter. We told him he could come in but . . .' She shrugged.

No happy ending there then, Helen thought. Maybe Leo was right in letting Georgia off the hook. Outside the office door, Garda Dempsey waited. Unhappily. Helen hadn't spoken to him on the journey to the hospital except to issue an occasional order. He made to follow the two women.

'Wait here,' Helen told him.

He sat on the chair by the office door. It felt like the subs bench. On his lap, Martin Buck's leather jacket smelled like the tannery near his home back in County Mayo. Which reminded him of the wedding. Which plunged him further into misery.

As they walked the corridors to the ICU ward, Eveleen outlined Frida Goode's injuries. A shattered femur that would probably result in a permanent limp. A shredded nerve structure in the left forearm that might or might not repair itself. One way or another Mrs Goode was going to have limited use of her hand and arm for some time to come. A broken doll came to mind, like one Helen had seen in the last few days though she couldn't remember where.

Frida Goode lay in a glassed-off area by the six-bed ICU ward. A tiny puppet, her left leg strung up by a system of wires radiating from the metal pins piercing her flesh. Helen winced. The woman's arm had been set in a thick cast, tilted slightly upwards. The rag-ends of minuscule and deathly white fingers hung from the end of the cast. Gold polish still intact made worthless coins of her fingernails.

'Frida?' Eveleen whispered as she leaned close in, checking the bank of display screens all the while. 'Everything OK?'

The perfectly arched eyelashes raised themselves. Frida Goode looked up at the nurse, nodded.

'Any pain now, you let me know,' Eveleen said, her bedside tone different to her office tone. Kinder, more patient. She brushed a hand across the small woman's damp forehead. 'There's someone here wants to speak to you, Frida. A policewoman. You don't have to if you don't feel up to it right now.'

'You're sure Georgia's OK?' Frida asked of the nurse. 'Please don't lie to me.'

'She's fine. Really. Don't be worrying now.'

'She hates me,' the woman pouted. 'She's this great rebel but she wanted some kind of housewife mummy back at home. David understood. David was so . . .'

The perfectly arched eyelashes lowered themselves.

'None of this is my fault,' her infantile complaint went on. 'I don't understand any of it. Why did all this happen?'

Her head didn't move but she scanned the room and found Helen. Recognition wasn't immediate but it did finally come.

'Why can't you people leave me alone?' she cried, and in her effort to turn from Helen reignited the pain in her shattered bones.

Eveleen put Helen on a silent warning. A waste of bloody time coming out here, Helen thought, when she could be ripping into Gary Larkin back at Pettycannon station. Or Liz and Jimmy Larkin when the squad cars brought them in from Chapelizod.

'Maybe I should leave it?' she told Eveleen, but Frida found it in herself to speak again.

'Is Baz dead?' she asked, fearful but hopeful too.

The woman's concern for her ex-Provo lover seemed to Helen worse than pathetic, a bubble waiting to be burst. Helen obliged.

'No, Mrs Goode, but he left you and Georgia for dead in that car out in Sandymount.'

Helen got two horrified looks for her troubles. And a yellow card from the senior nurse to boot. She kept on kicking.

'I saved your life, my colleague and me. And while we kept you alive, Baz did a runner.'

Eveleen let the play continue. Maybe she was coming over to Helen's side. Frida blanched and Helen put in a gentler tackle.

'OK, maybe he thought we had the situation under control,' Helen continued. 'Probably did think so actually because my guess is he'd do anything for you. Anything you asked.'

Frida's eyes slid away, down and to the left where it seemed, like a child, she could almost believe no one could see her. Only now did Helen realise that the woman's dark beauty spot had been a fake and was no longer in place.

'Mrs Goode, did you ask Baz MacDonald to avenge your son's death?'

'No.'

'We found a gun in the car, Mrs Goode. It was the gun used to shoot the man who killed your son.'

The woman sank further back into her mound of pillows. The moving graphs on a couple of the screens above her reached new peaks but there were no beeps, no alarms.

'I didn't ask him to,' she said. 'I didn't have to.'

A weight had fallen from Gary Larkin's padded shoulders. You could tell by the way he sagged back into his seat. His delivery was flat, atonal, his pinched face unpinched. He fixed his gaze on the video lens high up in the corner of the room. This was the biggest role he was ever likely to get. *Death in Chapelizod – The Sequel*, Leo thought, directed by the latest in a long and distinguished line of eye-patched directors. Nicholas Ray, Raoul Walsh, Fritz Lang. And Leo Woods.

'It was hot. Eleven in the morning and the sun was scorching already. Me and Lubo were out the back, kicking around a football cos it's, like, chaos inside with Mam trying to get Whitney and herself ready and sewing up the sleeves of my jacket cos they were too long. Whitney's hyper. And she runs out into the garden in her underwear and over to Lubo. "Am I nice? Am I nice?" she's going and he says, "Yeah, lovely." And she goes back in and we forget about it. Or I did. But Lubo didn't. See, he didn't know about that weird condition she had and—'

'Wind it back a bit there, Gary,' Leo said. 'Who took the photo? You must have seen who took the photo.'

'No, I didn't. There was people scattered around the garden, like. Could've been anyone.'

'Was Kevin there?' Leo asked.

Gary nodded.

'He told us he had the flu that day,' Ben said, and Gary shrugged.

'You sure?' Leo asked.

A nod. Why would Kevin lie about that? Leo asked himself. Because he was the one who'd taken the photo of Whitney?

Leo's phone vibrated again. Gary stared at him irritatedly. Leo peeked at the screen. *Unknown Number*.

'And Jimmy?' Ben asked.

'Yeah.'

'OK, let's get back to Lubo,' Leo said. 'He didn't know about Whitney's medical condition. This is the bruising we're talking about here, yeah?'

'Yeah,' Gary said and picked up his monologue where he'd left off. 'So, a few nights later we were out at a karaoke night in Jinky's. Me, Mam and Da and Jimmy. And Kevin was babysitting. He didn't go out much. Lubo was with us for a while and then he disappeared. We made nothing of it. So, anyway, Kevin's put Whitney to bed and gone up to his own bedroom. He can't hear nothing, of course. So he doesn't hear Lubo come in the back door or sneak over to her bedroom. It was on the downstairs, like. Kevin was upstairs.'

Gary paused, swallowed hard, tried to work up some spittle in his dry mouth, wiped his lips like they were poisoned things that belonged to someone else, something else.

'And we left the karaoke early. Me and Da and Jimmy. We had a call to make over in Finglas. So we went back home for the car and, next, we see the bleedin' flashes in Whitney's bedroom. Like, you know, camera flashes. We charge in and Lubo's there trying to hide this camera and Whitney . . . Jesus Christ . . . Whitney's there on the bed posing with nothing on except her panties.'

Gary was back there in space-time, eyes wild, pupils wilder.

'And we start laying into him big-time. Kicking the head off him. And Kevin's down from upstairs trying to hold Da back. And he's going, "Not in front of Whitney" – signing, like. But Da plants him one and Kevin swings back and Da loses it, laces into Kevin, cracks his jaw and half-strangles him and when he's done he lays into Lubo again. With a baseball bat this time. So Kevin grabs Whitney and takes her upstairs to his bedroom.'

As the small man paused for breath, Leo paused for thought. The hospital file Eveleen had found came to mind, confirming Gary's account. The deaf man was back in the spotlight toe-to-toe with Harry – every punch he'd taken a further cause for revenge perhaps.

'Lubo's not moving much now but he can still talk. He's telling me why he was taking those photos of Whitney. He's pleading with me. See, he thought the bruises were from beatings and he was worried about her. He loved the kid, he says, he couldn't bear to think of her being treated like that and he was going to send the shots to Social Services. He's still holding on to the camera and he says—'

'What happened to the camera after?' Leo interrupted,

stumbling on something, not knowing yet what that something was.

'I don't know. It's probably in the grave, right?' Gary
calmed down, finished out the story. 'And he says, "Save
her, Gary, save her, tell someone." But Da's totally tanked
up and he won't listen when I tell him it's all a misunderstanding and he catches Lubo around the neck. "You only
live twice," he says. And I'm, like, what? A James Bond trick,
he goes. And he snaps Lubo's neck. I can still hear it, that
crack, like a tree branch.' Gary looked back up at the video
camera. 'They took him away and buried him.'

'They?'

'Da and Jimmy and Kevin.'

'But not you? Why not?'

'We had to stay and clean up the mess.'

'You and your mother?' Leo asked, though he really
didn't want to, truly didn't want to.

'Yeah,' Gary said. 'But you can't clean it out of here.' He
fisted his temples. 'I couldn't. Whitney couldn't. She needed
help to do that, a psychologist or whatever. But Da was
never going to let that happen. We did the best we could for
her but what chance did we have? It was hard enough trying
to get her to forget what happened in that bedroom. How
could we get the grave out of her head? How?'

'She knew about Anton's grave?' Leo said. 'How the hell
did she?'

'We never told her,' Gary said. 'But she knew.'

Leo envisioned a corner of a twilight field, a girl-child
staring down. The stark black and white contrasts of
chiaroscuro. Camera shifts sideways left from the girl's
expressionless face. A black-coated figure. Camera angle
tilts slowly upwards along the chest, the gap of bare neck at
the shirt top. Kevin? Fade.

'Who could have told her about Lubo's grave? Who else knew?'

'Jimmy. Kevin. Baz, because Da told that bastard everything. It had to be Baz. Da knew from the start that Baz was behind the whole blackmail thing.'

'Why would MacDonald tell her about the grave?' Leo demanded.

'Fuck's sake, man, who was the first one she went to looking for the money? BAZ.'

A capital-lettered shout. And a revelatory one. Might this be why Kevin took a pop at the ex-Provo, Leo wondered? If Baz had given her the money, the story might have turned out very differently. Was that the deaf man's logic?

'But she also went to Kevin before she asked you lot,' Leo said. 'He could've told her, right?'

'No way would Kevin do that. All right, Baz didn't kill Lubo. All that stuff about him going after Lubo was just Da's smokescreen.'

'And Baz knew this?'

'Course he knew,' Gary insisted. 'So he didn't kill Lubo but the rest of it is down to him. How many clues do you need to figure that out, Sherlock? Whitney trusted him. She used to go around pretending he was her father. But she couldn't see she was just a dumb retard to him. So he goes and puts all this shit into her head about going to Libya. He must have. And, of course, she fell for it. The stupid little . . .'

Love and disrespect, Leo thought, a more common combination than people imagined. The very fuel of unhappy families. Tolstoy had it wrong. All unhappy families were the same. They loved but were somehow incapable of respecting each other. All sorts of aberrations ensued. But Gary was still trying to keep it outside the family.

'He used her to get at us. He was never going to just walk

away. He wanted to destroy us. And you know why?' The small man's chin was up again, his blood too. 'It wasn't about money or about who got to pull the strings in our ... our empire, as you called it. It was because Da told him who he really was. The Armenian, my hole.'

With a smug grin, Gary lapped up their bewilderment. He was like a man with a hammer about to hit a nail and so certain of the accuracy of his peripheral vision that he didn't even have to waste his time looking down. No, he could look up into those three eyes and enjoy the view of their dumb-fuck confusion.

'MacDonald's mother didn't go to Paris to study,' he said. 'The RA boys sent her over to London for an abortion but she didn't have it. She hopped over to France and had Baz instead. His father was one of the British squaddies they shot in that love nest up in that Belfast apartment. A fucking Paki half breed his old man was.'

Leo and Ben shared an unconvinced glance.

'You knew all this and still made a deal with Baz?' Leo said.

'Mam made the deal.' Gary fixed Leo with a clenched, malevolent stare. 'She was always easy to manipulate, wasn't she, Inspector?'

Gary relished his little triumph until Leo's short, sharp blow to the breastbone emptied his lungs. An old trick. No bruising. Gary's forehead hit the table and popped back up. He was speechless. Literally. He couldn't find his voice. Ben had trouble finding his too.

'Show some respect for your mother,' Leo said. He took no pleasure from Gary's wounded collapse. He felt like he was picking up from where Harry Larkin had left off and making too good a fist of it. He turned from the young man, looked at Ben. 'I need a fucking smoke.'

# 45

Back in the senior ward nurse's office, Eveleen Morgan sat in front of the PC on her desk. The wireless mouse guided her eyes, sending them up, across, down as she searched for Martin Buck's name on the system. All the while, Helen texted. *Mrs Goode confirms that MacDonald shot the Libyan – claims she didn't ask him to. On my way to talk to Buck now.* She sent the message to Ben, hesitated, sent it to Leo too.

'Oh.'

The nurse's surprised exclamation startled Helen. She was looking for an answer to some unspoken question. She didn't find it. Or not all of it.

'Detective Sergeant Buck has been transferred to an emergency bed in Neurosurgery,' she explained. 'No details up yet but it looks like he may have a problem.'

'I have to talk to him,' Helen said, her insistence sounding crass even to her own ears. 'If at all possible, I mean.'

'You'll have to ask when you get to Neurosurgery,' Eveleen told her. 'I'd bring you over except it's one of those mornings, you know. Three new admissions and we're about to switch off Mr Larkin. Not a pleasant task.'

'But the family,' Helen declared. 'Shouldn't they be here? All of them?'

'That's Mrs Larkin's call,' Eveleen replied, a little annoyed now. 'She's already here with some young guy. Derek something or other?'

'Derek McCarthy.'

Eveleen nodded, stood up and came round from behind her desk.

'And Jimmy? Harry's brother?' Helen asked.

'On his way, I'm told.'

'How long will it take before Harry Larkin actually, you know . . . ?'

'Every patient is different but, given his prior conditions, a few hours at most. I'll point you towards Neurosurgery.'

Outside the office door, Garda Dempsey jumped to attention from his seat when they emerged. He absorbed the nurse's directions. Dreamily. Helen, half listening while she texted Ben again to tell him that the Larkins were gathering at Harry's bedside, missed the gist. To her surprise, Dempsey guided them unerringly. She tried to make sense of this latest development. Why would Harry's wife and brother go ahead with the unplugging knowing that Gary was sweating it out in an interview room at Pettycannon station? Had they decided to buy themselves some temporary immunity from questioning, maybe stretch it out to a few days with the wake and the funeral? At her side, the heavy-jowled young Garda looked her way once too often.

'What?' Helen demanded.

'Nothing,' Dempsey said, but it was an open-ended nothing and he peeped through the gap at the open end. Hopefully. Hopelessly. 'Did you like the flowers?'

She stopped up, sent the traffic of hospital staff veering around her.

'When you were concussed the other day I—'

'*You* sent the flowers?'

Dempsey was back in school again. In trouble again. Ready to faint or find some other mode of escape.

'You frightened the shit out of me with those flowers.' Helen lowered her voice. 'I thought it was the bloody Larkins trying to mess me about. Plus I bloody hate lilies. Why didn't you put your name on the card?'

'I wanted to surprise you,' he said. 'I wanted to be in your good books when I asked you . . .'

'What?' The bar on Helen's volume control slid swiftly upwards. 'Asked me what?'

Dempsey threw in his cards. Not an ace among them.

'My sister's wedding, I was going to ask you to come with me,' Dempsey said defeatedly. 'Next left for Neurosurgery.'

'I can see the bloody sign,' Helen told him.

She sneaked a glance at his downcast, hapless side-face.

'Don't mind me, Patch,' she said. 'I'm like a bitch today. I can't remember the last time I slept.'

'I have trouble sleeping too,' he said, rather too bleakly for comfort, and she dodged into the Neurosurgery nursing station.

From there, they were directed to Martin Buck's ward. Because neither of the police officers was a relative of the sick man, no details could be divulged to them. They had twenty minutes to talk to Buck. Or rather, Helen had.

'You won't be needing me here either, I suppose,' Dempsey said when they reached the ward.

'No,' she said, but she had an errand for him. 'We're going to have to intercept Jimmy Larkin as soon as he gets here so we'll need some officers down at the main entrance and over at ICU. Can you organize that for me?'

'No problem,' Dempsey said, straightening his shoulders to the task.

He handed her the leather jacket and strode away, his

mobile phone on the ready. Helen sucked in a big breath of disinfectant-enhanced air and plunged into the ward.

Time had caught up with Martin Buck. Below the naked white of his shaved skull, his face seemed oddly shrunken, yellowed, caved in around the mouth. His dentures, Helen realized, had been removed. The breasts on his bared chest sagged, the chest hairs matted to a slimy undergrowth. Half a dozen white patches there connected him to a variety of graphed screens. When he saw her, his eyes swam slowly down, his pride sinking.

'I'm in rag order, aren't I?' he said.

'You'll be right as rain again soon,' she said, but he shook his head.

'A tumour on the brain, can you believe it? I knew I wasn't right of late, but this . . .' The weight of grey sky outside his window pressed him further down on to his pillow. 'No one came. Not one of the wives. Not one of the kids.' From the corner of his eye, he glimpsed the jacket. 'Is my phone in it?'

'Yeah, there's a few missed calls from Marie. Is that one of your wives maybe or . . . ?'

'Estate agent. I'm behind on the bloody rent.'

'Jimmy Larkin's been ringing you too.'

Helen took the mobile from the leather jacket. Tapped in 171, readied herself to press the green phone icon for go.

'He left a voicemail,' she said and played the message.

Before he made a play for her pity, she pitied him. But not after.

'I put seven kids through college,' he said. 'Three through MAs and the eldest girl just started a PhD. Cost me a fortune they did. And what thanks did I ever get from any of them? From the mothers?' He got up the nerve to look her way. 'I didn't do any of this because I wanted to live like a lord, you know. I did it for my kids.'

A variation on the blame-the-victim theme, blame the beneficiaries. In Buck's case, both categories overlapped.

'Martin,' Helen said, 'what's Jimmy freaking out over in this voicemail? "Drop me in the shit"? What shit? Is it connected to the case?'

'No. It's . . . it's another matter.'

The sheen of sweat across his face and torso was so asexual it was counter-sexual.

'That's not enough, Martin. You're the one in the shit now and you have to explain because if you don't the roof falls in on you.'

His stare wasn't hateful and it didn't last long. He turned to the window, looked out at the lowering sky as though he might find there some trickster god to blame for his misfortune.

'There were four or five gyms in Lucan I could have gone to,' he said. 'And I walked into the wrong one. Sheer bloody chance. Liz and Gary worked out there. Derek McCarthy too. And Harry when he was still able to. I got sucked in because I was skint as usual. Not that the money was major or anything. I mean it was minor shit I was helping them out on. Warnings about after-hours raids on the pub, parking fines, penalty points. Then Jimmy got himself into trouble, the stupid prick.'

'What kind of trouble?'

Buck sighed, shook his head. Something like wisdom transformed his ageing features, but it wasn't wisdom.

'I've made plenty of mistakes but at least I'm normal,' he said without a hint of irony. 'Sexually, like. I can't keep my zip closed, OK . . . or couldn't. But I was never a pervert.'

The ward had got a lot colder and, for Helen, it was a cold with the ice of dread in it.

'And Jimmy was? Is?'

'We got two complaints from the parents of young girls in that football club where he used to coach,' Buck said, then, more fervently, added, 'We're not talking rape here now, right? This was . . . mild stuff. You know. Put your hand in my pocket and see what you can feel. That kind of thing. Disgusting but not . . . not . . .'

Helen resisted the temptation to rage against the prone detective. She needed him to get to the end of his sordid tale. Then she could rage.

'I was up shit-creek money-wise at the time and—'

'This was when exactly?'

'2004. Jimmy hadn't been told who the complainants were naturally. So he asked me to, you know, pass on the info and the complaints were . . . you know . . .'

'They were dropped. He, what, threatened them? Paid them off?'

'I don't know. I don't want to know,' Buck said, regretful now but not yet done with the excuses. 'Try putting seven girls through college on the crap salary we get. Jesus Christ, I wouldn't mind but they'll all end up getting married anyway and living off some other unfortunate bastard.'

Revulsion came in many colours and Martin Buck supplied the pigments for all of them. Helen stuck to the bigger picture.

'Did the other Larkins know about these complaints? Or Baz MacDonald?'

'No. This was between me and him. They knew he was a weirdo that way. All of them did, except for Harry. He turned a blind eye to it.'

'You're telling me this has nothing to do with the case?' Helen erupted. 'Jimmy's a bloody paedophile and Whitney was a vulnerable kid. She's in the photos with Jimmy's teams and disappears from them after 2002. Chances are he's into kiddie porn too. And we have that photo of Whitney in the garden. Didn't you ever think of adding these things up and . . .'

Stirred from his guilt-ridden torpor, the cowboy detective raised himself on to one elbow. He'd found something to fight for. The last shreds of his credibility as a police officer, as a man.

'I put a gun to his head,' he said. 'And I'm not talking metaphorically here. I told him the second bullet was for me and it was, it truly was. He pissed himself. Says no way could he ever get near Whitney even if he'd wanted to and he swore he didn't. Says Liz never let him into the house if Harry wasn't there and never left him alone with Whitney. The kid hardly spoke to him because Liz had warned her off him because of these . . . these rumours about him. I swear to you, I went through his computer, went through every last nook and fucking cranny in his house to find any evidence against him, and I found nothing.'

'He doesn't sound too scared of you on the voicemail.'

Buck lay back on the bed, a hand moving on auto-pilot to fix the hair that was no longer there and giving up when his mind met his reptile brain again on the pillow.

'He's scared all right, but he thinks I'm scared too,' he said. 'Until this morning, he was right. But not any more. I've got bigger things to worry about now. I've been straight up with you because I want to do the right thing this time. I might not have another chance to.'

So unexpectedly did he take her hand that she had no time to pull back.

'Jimmy's a blind alley, girl. I've been trying to convince Leo from day one but he wouldn't listen to me just because . . . because we fell out years ago over . . .' His grip on her tightened. 'Listen, Baz MacDonald shot Harry. Jimmy told me so. Baz had already decided to quit. He was planning to go to Armenia with Frida Goode. He and Harry had agreed a golden handshake and it was all happy-camping until last week when Whitney tried to blackmail the old bastard. He wanted MacDonald to find her and deal with whoever it was that was helping her. No way would MacDonald get involved. So Harry takes the money off the table and tells him to fuck off. That's the story. Plain and simple.'

He looked at the sky again. It hadn't got any brighter. Believing in Martin Buck's newly acquired sense of honour wasn't easy but Helen was inclined to give him the benefit of the doubt. The droplets descending along his cheeks might not, after all, be crocodile tears. Only one way to confirm her instinct, she thought. Confront Jimmy. Now. Before the switch-off. If he showed up. If he hadn't already run for the hills.

There wasn't a sky in the clouds above Pettycannon Garda Station. The courtyard carpark felt like an animal pen covered with grey plastic as Leo popped the filter of a menthol cigarette, lit up and checked his phone again. No messages. No further calls from the unknown. He'd been proved a fool once already today and was well on his way to a second comeuppance. And it wasn't yet midday.

Helen's message from the hospital had pushed Kevin Larkin further into the clear. And that was OK. The prospect of being wrong about the deaf man didn't bother him. In his line of work, you had to stick your head over the parapet now and again, see which way the wind and the bullets were blowing. It didn't matter if you took a volley of shots in the face, you could get up and play again after you counted to ten. What did bother him was Kevin's continuing absence. If he was innocent and they couldn't find him, then he might be yet another victim in this sorry saga.

Love was a different game. In love, when you were alive you were truly alive and when you were dead you were truly dead in the water. He blushed at the memory of the texts he'd sent to Eveleen, the desperate missives of a fool. And Eveleen she was again. Not Ev or *love*. A distant prospect, receding. He was just another seventies man that time had overtaken. Not yet six feet under like Gerry Cooney out in Howth. Nor struck down by a brain tumour like that hapless clown Martin Buck. That was something. Not a lot. But something.

The mobile rang in his hand, drilled along the nerves in his arm and struck, he imagined, his heart. *Unknown Number.* He took the call.

'Ev?'

The name was out before he could take it back. No response emerged from the loud, sweeping background noise that had the groan of heavy-lifting works in it and the raucous scream of seagulls. The docks?

'Are you alone there?' Baz MacDonald's sharp Belfast accent sliced through the static.

'Very much so,' Leo said. Shaken, he took a drag from the cigarette to steady himself but it merely dizzied him further. 'How did you get my number?'

'You need to teach your apprentices not to leave the keys in their car, Inspector,' Baz said. 'Is Frida all right?'

'Yeah, she made it. No fucking thanks to you. I doubt she'll be joining you on the run after you left her and her daughter for dead.'

'She was never going to. I haven't rung to discuss my love life, Inspector.'

'I don't imagine there'd be a lot to—'

'I found her,' Baz cut across him. 'I found Whitney.'

It was too early for stars but they filled the sky anyway. The scream inside Leo had to stay put but it hurt his gut. Already he could see the dead child who'd haunt his dreams for weeks and maybe months ahead. If he ever slept again.

'Alive?' he asked.

'No.'

'How did she die?'

'I don't know,' the ex-Provo said. 'She's covered with a sheet. I didn't go close enough to lift it.'

'How do you know it's her then?'

'It's her.'

'Did you do away with Kevin too?'

'Right, I'm a mass murderer and I rang in to give you the details, Inspector. I'm doing your job for you. Be grateful. What I have to tell you is—'

'The gun that shot Harry and the Libyan was found in your car, Baz,' Leo said. 'Harry told you who your real daddy was. The Libyan killed your lady-friend's son. You told her you shot the Libyan, for Christ's sake. Need I go on?'

'Frida rang me, asked me if I'd done it. And I said yeah. Because it was my last chance to get her to come away with me.'

Silence fell at the other end of the phone. Then the gulls fell on the silence, fighting over it. Leo walked towards the back entrance of the station. Get some cars down to the docks, he told himself. Get the shipping list from the port authorities. When he reached the door, it was locked.

'Baz? Are you still there?'

'OK, I don't owe you any explanations on the gun, but this much I'll tell you. I don't often carry. I rarely need to. But yesterday I did.'

'Why?'

The window sills at the back of the station were almost at eye-level and Leo struggled to reach the pane.

'I was watching my back, right?' the ex-Provo snapped. 'Look, I know what you're at here. Delaying me so you can trace the call. Forget it, Inspector, I'm out of your jurisdiction. So, OK, I go to where we keep our guns and—'

'We?'

Leo got a knuckle on the window pane and tapped lightly but to no avail. He moved along to the next window thinking, Belfast port or Derry maybe? Have to alert the police up North. If he ever got back into the bloody station.

'Me and the Larkins,' Baz said. 'So, I pick up the gun I prefer to carry. I've got some markings on it so's I can tell it from the others. That's the gun your girl found in the car. Last night after the attack I obviously needed a replacement, right? So I went back to the stash. The other guns were gone so I turned the place upside down. That's when I found her.'

'Sounds to me like a tall story, Baz,' Leo said as he reached up to the tall window and knuckled it. A face appeared there, astonished, unknowing, withdrawing. A second face appeared. Ben Murphy's. Disappeared. 'Now you're going to tell me who the real shooter is and send me on a wild goose chase while you slip away. Is that how this goes?'

'One of those boys took a pop at me, Inspector,' Baz said. 'A few inches lower and I'd have taken a bullet in the heart. If I knew which one, believe me, I'd tell you. They both had their reasons, I guess.'

'Gary's pissed off that you were his daddy's favourite all these years and Kevin thinks all this blackmail stuff might never have happened if you'd given Whitney the money on day one, right?'

'Something like that.'

The back door of the station swung open. Flushed from running, Ben stopped up short before Leo's raised hand. Switching the phone to speaker, Leo gestured Ben closer.

'Where is she, Baz? Where's Whitney?'

Baz's delay in replying began to seem like a change of mind. The gulls cried wildly of freedom but the ex-Provo's voice when it came sounded like it was in prison for life.

'I should have helped her,' he said. 'Play along with the delusions. That's what they say, isn't it, Inspector? I guess I was too busy with my own.'

They were both on the same ship of fools in the treacherous sea of love but Leo wanted to push the ex-Provo overboard.

'Spare us your fucking regrets, MacDonald. Where do we find Whitney?'

'In the derelict house beside Jinky's. There's a trap door under the lino and rubble in the hallway. She's in the cellar.'

'We'll catch up with you, Baz,' Leo shouted into the phone. 'We'll have you if you're bullshitting us.'

The line went dead. A tidal rush of anger swept through Leo. He flung the mobile phone at the grey-stone wall of the station. It broke into pieces but not so many pieces as his heart did. He cursed the heavens but the boulder of clouds refused to roll away.

'Jesus wept,' he said.

# 46

On the top floor of the Neurology building, the two lift doors refused to budge. Helen had no choice but to take the stairs. Her downward passage felt whirling dervish-like and eternal. Jimmy Larkin hadn't arrived at the hospital. Garda Dempsey was sure of it. He waited for her now out in the squad car. She was psyched. Not the best time to ring her ex but that's what you did when you were psyched. The things you were normally afraid to do. She pressed green to go. He picked up as she raced down.

'Ricky? Listen, I don't have a lot of time to talk here but tell me what you know.'

'He's trapped, Helen, snookered,' Ricky said. 'Yeah, some of it's his own fault, but not all of it. Jeez, it's such a mess I don't know where to start.'

No slackening in her pace and yet she felt that strange calm that sometimes comes when the storm is still raging around you.

'OK then, Ricky. Start with the guy he owes money to. Who is he?'

'Ned Morrissey. You wouldn't know him. He came up from Cork a few years ago. He's a moneylender.'

'A moneylender and what else?'

She shot through the gap between two white coats, the faces a blur to her. She grabbed the stair rail and took a schoolgirl swing around the next landing.

'Just a moneylender. This guy's not some kind of skangy dealer or anything. He's a middle-aged suit-and-tie kind of guy and he doesn't have a gang of heavies or anything. He hires these dodgy debt-collecting outfits when he needs to collect.'

Her head swam. Baz MacDonald? Surely not. Of course not. There's thousands of those bastards in the country. She glanced out at the hospital carpark, couldn't believe it was still so far down.

'How much does Jamie owe?'

'That's the thing, Helen. He only borrowed a few thousand a couple of years back for an album he never made. But this crazy interest the guy charges, it's . . . well, it's nearly twenty thousand euro now. And counting.'

Sucker-punched again, Helen slowed, tried to kick on.

'What did he do for this Morrissey character then?' she asked. 'He must have done something.'

'He . . . well, he . . . See, this woman he's with. Deirdre. She's Ned's sister, and . . .'

Helen stopped dead. She was on the second-floor landing but her mind hadn't yet left the third floor. Jesus Christ, she thought when it arrived, married to the mob. It couldn't get any worse. Could it? Ricky's hesitation suggested it might.

'I know this doesn't sound PC or whatever,' he continued, 'but that woman shouldn't be having a kid. She used to be a junkie. Heroin, like. Now she's in and out of hospital with . . . put it this way, mental health issues. Ned's not too happy that his sister's pregnant and he wanted her to have an abortion. But she wants the baby and she wants to be with Jamie. So, Ned offers Jamie a deal.'

'What kind of deal?'

'Jamie sees Deirdre through the pregnancy, you know, keeps her clean,' Ricky explained. 'If it works out OK and they stay together, Jamie can put the house back on the market in a year or two. See, Ned's sure Jamie will split if the place is sold right away.'

'And if it doesn't work out?'

'It'll work out, cos Jamie has no intention of leaving his child in a situation like that. He really wants to do right by the kid, Helen. He really does.'

'No,' she said.

'Sorry?'

'I'll be ringing my solicitor first chance I get.' She didn't sound like herself but you never really did when you tried to be your real self. 'This is not going to happen. We sell the house and he sorts out his problems *after* that. Not *before*. No way.'

She could tell he was appalled. She was a little appalled herself but there was no other way out of emotional black-mail, she knew, than slamming the door shut, locking it, gulping down the key however much it might hurt.

'But what can he do, Helen? And what about the baby?'

Gagging on the grief and guilt of it all, she headed down the last two flights of stairs.

'He's really very sorry, Helen,' her ex insisted. 'Genuinely.'

Helen had lived apart from Ricky long enough to acknowledge that he'd had at least some endearing quali-ties. This was one of them. Gullibility.

'Listen, Ricky,' she said. 'This is what he does. Gets him-self in the shit and finds some devious way out of it. Don't let him fool you with his caring Daddy crap.'

'But the child . . . It's just that it seems—'

'Cruel, yeah, because that's what it is,' she said. 'But not selfish. Selfish is what Jamie is. Always will be. He thinks he's built himself another little comfort zone to hide in. Not this time. No way.'

She found an exit door by the end of the stairs and got herself outside. The breeze cooled her flushed cheeks. Slamming the door shut felt like an act of unforgivable heartlessness because behind it, though she didn't look back, she imagined the receding figures of her father, of Jamie, of another little girl neglected, bruised, abandoned. She felt sick with herself.

'Have to head, Ricky,' she said. 'I'm up to my eyes here.'

'We're playing the Workman's Club on Tuesday week,' Ricky said, rising unexpectedly to the occasion. 'Would you fancy . . . ?'

'Yeah, maybe I will,' she said, her gut hurting with loneliness. 'No, I'll definitely see you there.'

'Cool,' he said. Unable to find a suitable superlative, he added, 'Cool.'

Over at the squad car, Garda Dempsey shook his head as she approached. Still no word on Jimmy Larkin. She sat in the car. Every bone in her body ached. She needed a coffee so much she could actually smell it when she closed her eyes.

'They found the second skeleton,' Dempsey told her. 'Another neck snap.'

'And the glass eye?' Helen asked, still immersed in her solitary, swirling darkness.

'Yeah.'

She sat up, looked out at the carpark, at the sky where a patch of hopeful blue peeped through. Automatic pilot kicked in. She got back to work.

'Head to Chapelizod,' she said. 'Let's see if we can find this piece of shit.'

'Sarge? This is for you.'

In one hand Dempsey held a take-away coffee. In the other, a doughnut wrapped in a paper napkin.

'Where'd you get these?' she asked.

'One of the guys was heading back from the filling station with supplies. I nabbed some for you.'

And hadn't, she saw, nabbed any for himself.

'Thanks, Patch,' she said. Fuck it, she thought wearily; a day out, a new dress, mile-high heels, why not? Maybe she was still psyched but what the hell. 'That wedding, when is it?'

She made Dempsey's day, his month, his year. And there'd be no hanky-panky, like, he assured her. His occasional delighted glance in her direction as they raced to Chapelizod felt nothing like as intrusive as the other eyes that followed her. The glass one. The pair behind the bottle-end spectacles. Laughing eyes. Watching.

They went down. Two men in blues, gloved and masked. Leo led the way, reversing along the vertiginous steps. He reached up to Ben for the torch. He knew they were breaking the rules but the Technical Bureau were at full stretch out at the graves on Tandy's Lane. They'd excavated the second grave. The glass eye they'd found there haunted Leo. He imagined it peering out of the disturbed earth, its wicked intention still residing in the blue orb. Watching him. He hoped the girl's eyes were closed.

Beneath the low ceiling he stooped as Ben descended. A fug of stale cigarette smoke, rotting flowers and human decay assailed them. The beam from Leo's torch flittered along a wall of cigarette cartons. Regals. The light fell into a gap at the far end of the make-shift wall. Heads lowered under the rough boards above, they proceeded. Leo went through the gap, his torch aimed at the floor, readied himself to raise it. His vision was suddenly swamped with a snowblind glare. In the bare clear bulb, the worm of light welcomed him to the lowest depths.

'Found the switch,' Ben said unnecessarily.

Leo urged himself forward through the thicket of his shrieking senses. On a tattered old mattress on the packed-earth floor, the girl lay. The white sheet covering her burned bright but only briefly. A bunch of lilies stuffed into a cracked vase sagged, stared down at the petals they'd shed on to the floor below. Leo lowered himself on his haunches, slowly drew back the sheet from over Whitney's head.

'Oh, Jesus Christ. Oh, God,' Ben muttered.

Fallen to one side, Whitney Larkin's face was no longer a face. It was a hideous caricature, a bloated blue thing, a monstrous anomaly placed atop a tiny, child-like body. A small blood-encrusted gash tattooed her right temple. Her eyes were closed but her tongue vulgarly protruded, a shade of purple that didn't belong above ground. Leo looked at the girl through the lenses of panic and revulsion, kept on looking until he could see again. He knew at once that Whitney had been dead for days.

He drew the sheet away. A grey and black silk scarf with a spider's-web motif covered her neck. He couldn't bring himself to raise it just yet. She was fully dressed. Black blouse. Denims. Below the bottom end of the mattress a pair of pink Doc Martens stood forlornly, redundant as a Samuel Beckett prop. He checked the blue shells of her fingernails but they'd been bitten to the quick and he detected no visible signs of struggle there.

'Leo,' Ben said, and pointed at the wine racks covering the end wall. 'The money.'

Leo replaced the sheet over the girl and went to Ben's

side. A few inches thick and wrapped in a clear plastic freezer bag, the slim wad of notes seemed paltry in the circumstances. The indented shelves contained no wine but there were bottles. A lot of bottles. Small white plastic ones marked 'Airbrush Colours'. Every colour of the rainbow and every artificial shade in between. Half a dozen air brushes lay abandoned around the shelves like metal peace pipes, their bowls clogged with hardened paint. Carefully, Leo fingered another find. An insect-eyed spray-painting mask. Beneath it lay the torn left side of a photograph.

'Whitney's First Communion day photo from the Garden of Eden,' Leo said. 'Or Evil. Take your choice. Same damn thing anyway.'

The young Slovakian in the Glasgow Celtic jersey wasn't Slavic in looks. He was darker, more tanned, an almost Asiatic slant to the eyes. His expression was made of horror and alarm.

'Hungarian descent, I'm guessing,' Leo suggested. 'I did some of my UN training with a Slovakian group. Couldn't help noticing the difference in colouring among them, so I asked.'

'Similar looks to Baz MacDonald,' Ben said.

'And to Hadi Al-Baarai.'

'So Whitney has this . . . this ideal, you could call it,' Ben speculated, dared a quick disturbed glimpse at the dead girl. 'She wanted Baz as a father and Hadi for a boyfriend.'

Leo nodded, scanned the cellar, eyes adapted to the shades of horror. Logic cleared the fusty air and his thinking sharpened.

'It simply doesn't make sense that Kevin wouldn't have known the body was here. Therefore, either he killed her or he's covering for someone else.'

'MacDonald?' Ben said.

'I doubt it. If he'd been hiding her or keeping her against her will, he wouldn't have held her in a house on Main Street, Chapelizod. Not an especially busy Main Street but way too risky in any case.'

'Isn't it possible that Gary and Kevin were in this together?' Ben suggested.

'I don't think so. One thing's for sure though. Gary isn't covering for Kevin. OK, he's putting the blame on MacDonald for Harry's shooting and Whitney's blackmail efforts. But, if he was covering for Kevin, he'd have left him out of his account of what happened to Lubo. That fight between Harry and Kevin puts the deaf man centre stage. Plus Gary wouldn't have insisted Kevin was at the First Communion and not in bed with the flu.'

'So if Kevin did this, Gary didn't know?' Ben said.

'That's how it looks,' Leo said.

They resumed their search among the narrow shelving that was like a giant Joseph Cornell box containing the enigmatic curios of a life. Except the contents here were far from enigmatic.

The evidence began to pile up against the Larkin brothers, though not definitively against either one in particular. A pink laptop and a handful of mobile phones, two of them also pink – the only colour Whitney went for outside of black. On the same shelf was a tan leather wallet. Leo eased out the top half of a credit card. *Yusef Dorda*. The fake pregnancy tester kit that Georgia Goode had described to Helen was there too, alongside Whitney's passport. A Kodak 35mm camera of older vintage stood atop an old school copybook of Whitney's, a copybook opened to a drawing of a little stick man titled 'Ludo XXX'.

Leo peered desperately about the claustrophobic space knowing the Technical Bureau would be here soon and that he and Ben would have to bail out. Behind the mattress bearing the girl's remains, an abandoned rag drew his attention. Something familiar about its texture and its colours. He crouched low on his hunkers, opened out the cloth carefully with his gloved hand. The image of a snow-capped peak unfolded. Mount Ararat. Baz MacDonald's gift to Kevin, the tag still in place, just as it had been when the deaf man had handed it to Leo yesterday to wipe away the crocodile tears.

'You recognize this?' he asked.

'Christ,' Ben said. 'Yeah.'

'She couldn't break the circle,' Leo said.

'Sorry?'

'Just after I handed this tea-towel back to Kevin yesterday he said exactly those words.'

'So Kevin broke the circle?' Ben said. 'Because she told him she was pregnant like she told the Goodes? Because this time he believed her?'

'Maybe.'

Leo's bones felt permanently and painfully locked into this crouched position. He wanted to move, get the hell out of this pit of despair, but knew he wasn't done here yet. And besides, the prospect of what lay ahead in the world above grieved him. Liz Larkin would have to be told that her daughter was dead. And he was the one who would have to tell her. He owed her that much at least. He wished it was as simple as that, him doing the honourable thing. But his motive, he knew, would be ambiguous. If Gary was the culprit here after all then his mother would know or at the very least have sensed the truth. He almost hoped he was right about Kevin.

'It's all too neat, Leo,' Ben said. 'All the evidence in place. It stinks of a set-up.'

'Too obvious for a set-up,' Leo insisted. 'We were meant to find all of this, yes. But by the killer himself. He wants us to know who did it.'

'But why so violent?' Ben wondered. 'If we're talking a mercy killing of some perverse kind, this seems just . . . too vicious. That blow to the head, and the scarf. He's probably snapped her neck too.'

'We're not looking at rational here, Ben. But even the irrational has its own logic.'

Leo drew back the sheet again and slowly untied the silk scarf from around the girl's neck. He stared hard, wondered if the light was lying until Ben spoke.

'No bruising. The neck hasn't been snapped.'

'So he's placed her head to the side, covered her neck to draw our attention to it.'

'Which means that he doesn't just want us to know who did it but why he did it.'

'Exactly. He's linked Whitney's killing to Bisjak's. Liz's father's killing too, I'm pretty damn sure. This is the metaphor linking a very dark narrative, Ben. And it may not be over yet.'

'He might be going after Jimmy? And Liz?'

'Yeah. Better check the hospital again. And pronto.'

'No problem,' Ben said and took out his phone. No signal, have to go up into the house, the expression on his face suggested. But he had some doubt to express first. 'I still don't see how the Libyan fits. I mean, his neck wasn't snapped for starters.'

'His head was half blown away. How could you snap his neck in that state?'

'I suppose. But how did our perp know where to find Dorda?'

'He had Whitney's phone,' Leo said. 'He saw the text

Georgia sent from the hospital and got the location. Sent the texts to Liz Larkin, no doubt, while he was out planting lilies in Tandy's Lane.'

'But why? Why would he want to kill Dorda?'

'Because he obviously appreciated what David did for Whitney,' Leo said. 'I mean the kid wouldn't have been up there in Kilmacud at all if he hadn't been concerned for her. And Kevin's clearly psyched up on all the shit that's happened to Whitney. He's looking for culprits everywhere. Plus you heard what Georgia told Helen. The guy wanted to do something to scare Dorda off last week.'

From above came the pad and squeak of vinyl boot covers. The Tech boys had arrived. Leo stood up too quickly and took a blow to the top of his head from the low ceiling. It hurt, but it didn't hurt enough to distract him from what came next.

'Are you OK?' Ben asked. 'Leo?'

'Yeah,' Leo said. 'Aren't you the lucky man to be escaping from all this shit?'

'You could escape too if you wanted to. You've put in the years.'

Leo looked around the cellar. Already it seemed less than nightmarish to him. It was filthy air but he could breathe it. The ceiling loomed low but he could bend to it. Past death-throes echoed from its chalk-damp walls but if he kept talking to himself, he'd stop hearing them. Eventually.

'No, I belong here,' he said, and went chasing after some invented quote, some one-liner redolent of irony. He found nothing. 'OK, Ben. You deal with the Tech boys, and head back to Pettycannon station when you're done. Get a few snaps of this poor kid and work Gary with them. Really work him. And tell Helen to swing by Maiden's Lane and wait for back-up. I doubt Jimmy's there but you never know. I'll head to the hospital and talk to Mrs Larkin.'

'I could take that if you like,' Ben said.

'Thanks, Ben,' Leo said. 'But this time around I don't get to walk away.'

# 47

Leo parked his car at the back entrance to the main hospital building. He took a few last long pulls on the filterless menthol cigarette. The smoke-filled car was like an antechamber to hell. Not all of the French philosophers were up there with Cantona, he reflected. Sartre, for example. Hell was other people, he'd written. Wrong, Jean-Paul. Hell is our individual self. The flames burn from the inside. They burned in Leo now. He got out of the car and snapped the remote lock. Oddly, the hazard lights on the car next to his, a dingy grey Ford Focus, flashed too. He looked at his car keys and then looked around the parking area.

At first, Leo didn't recognize the man approaching from the hospital building. Dark, ill-fitting suit, grey-haired and gaunt, slow on his pins. Then he saw the plastic voice box on the man's long neck. The security control room officer, Gus Ewart. He looked like a man all dressed up for a funeral. His own.

'Inspector,' Gus rasped.

'Gus,' Leo said, and for want of something better to add asked, 'Off-duty today, are you?'

'Took a half day. A staff do. We're starting out early.'

Every struggled-for word the security officer spoke sounded a health warning to Leo.

'What's the occasion?'

'Ev's leaving. She's off to Dubai.'

It was the second time in his life that Leo had been beaten up in a carpark. The first time, he'd fought off three Sinn Féin goons and did more damage than he'd shipped. Here, there was no one to fight back against. He took another shot in the stomach.

'I knew she'd go,' Gus continued, the claws of his voice scraping Leo's brain. 'She's never been the same since Mr Loughney had the stroke.'

'Mr Loughney?'

'He was a consultant here. Top notch. Married but he and Ev were an item for a couple of years.'

Leo didn't want to hear any more but his legs weren't ready to carry him away yet.

'Poor bastard,' Gus piped morbidly on. 'Lost the use of his left leg, his arm and his face was . . .'

He raised a hand to his cheek. Then he looked at Leo's face, made a strangled effort at an apology and walked away.

Leo went into the hospital to find the woman he'd once used, feeling battered and bruised. And used. Payment in kind from Fata Morgana, the wicked witch of Fate.

'Switch off your phone, please,' the senior nurse at ICU ordered.

'It's on silent,' Leo said.

'I mean *off* off,' she clarified. 'I really don't see why this can't wait. This is a very private moment you're intruding on.'

The nurse wasn't brown-haired or brown-eyed, her name wasn't Eveleen and she wasn't heading off to Dubai without so much as a goodbye. Her name was Bowles, but Leo could tell she wasn't one for playing games. Such as Screw the Doppelgänger. They'd got off to a bad start as soon as he'd flashed his archaic ID. She hadn't believed it was him and his self-deprecating joke hadn't impressed her either. We never are who we think we are, Nurse, are we?

'The press will be swarming outside the doors very soon,' Leo told her patiently. 'I don't want Mrs Larkin learning of her daughter's murder from that lot, do you?'

'I suppose not,' the nurse agreed. 'But can you make it brief? Mr Larkin might pass at any time.'

'Mightn't we all?' he said and took possession of the door handle as the nurse took extravagant offence.

He went inside, deliberately seeing nothing at first, battling the assault on his senses with idle, wild speculation. What would you call a room for the dying anyway? The rest-is-history room? The last-post room? Old Goethe would have liked it here. *More light*, his last words. Too much of it in here. And no windows, which didn't seem right even to an old heathen like himself. No escape for the released spirit, no escape for the spirits trapped inside the living here either.

'What do you want?'

The young man's voice brought the room into focus for Leo. Seated at the bedside next to Liz, the black-haired guy might have been a Spanish bullfighter except that his eyes were less than courageous. Derek McCarthy, Leo presumed.

Liz continued the Spanish theme. She had a black lace mantilla wrapped around her neck, ready to be raised over her head when the moment came. Her back held straight, her legs set primly to one side, she didn't look up at Leo. On the bed, Harry had shrunk visibly since he'd last seen him. No tubes, masks or machines. That was how it went at the

412

end, Leo thought. No attachments. How it went, for some, long before the end.

'Can you excuse us for a moment, Derek?' Leo said.

'Are you a consultant or what?'

Only when the bullfighter stood up did Leo notice the small plaster over his right eye, the bruise on his right cheekbone. He was tall and wide but his muscles were for display purposes only. Leo flashed his ID. Briefly.

'Detective Inspector Leo Woods,' he said, and the young man wilted. 'Been in a scrap, have you?'

'An accident at the gym,' Derek said, not masking very well his shiftiness. 'I was lifting weights and—'

'Leave us, Derek,' Liz said, her voice coarse-grained, all emotion roughly sanded from it. 'We're old friends, the inspector and me.'

Looking from one to the other, Derek shook his head perplexedly and left the room. Into the waiting arms of three uniformed officers.

As Leo took his place beside Liz Larkin, her unseeing gaze dwelt on some midway point between her and Harry. They'd shaved him, sorted his hair, given him back his teeth, covered his belly with a pyjama top whose collar covered the bruising on his neck but not on his chin. Someone had placed a rosary in his joined hands. Just in case he was up to one last strangling before he popped his clogs, Leo thought.

'Elizabeth,' he said, 'I'm sorry, but I've more bad news for you.' Nicely put, Leo, subtle.

She didn't move. Not an eyelash. She stayed in that far-off zone, expressionless, every line of her sun-dried face bearing a filigree of shadow.

'We found Whitney,' he said. 'I'm sorry.'

Her eyes closed. Nothing moved in her but her breath

and that was shallow, barely perceptible. Leo waited for the collapse, the questions, the accusations. Nothing came but tears. No wailing or gnashing of teeth either. People reacted differently in these situations, Leo knew. The silence of inner paralysis was more common than the movies suggested. But he knew Liz too, or thought he did. The Liz he knew would have fought off this truth, refused it, or at the very least pointed the finger at some culprit, demanded revenge. When she spoke, Leo's suspicion deepened.

'Was it . . . Did she suffer?'

She raised her hands to her neck, fixing the lace mantilla, holding it in place. The truth was Leo didn't know for sure whether the girl had suffered or not. He might have lied, said she hadn't. But it was the other, more cruel lie he had to go with. He had to break Liz. Again.

'Looks like it,' he said. 'I'm sorry.'

A low-decibel groan emerged. She clutched more tightly at her mantilla. Leo waited again for the outburst. And waited. The dry air sneaked in under the patch to his bad eye. He fished out a tissue from among the cigarette filters, spilling a few. They fell at her feet. Stiffly as an offended monarch, she turned her upper body towards him.

'Pick them up,' she demanded. 'Pick the fucking things up. Look at the mess you made, you bastard, you ugly, ugly bastard.'

'We just dug up your father's body and Anton Bisjak's,' Leo told her. 'Someone left lilies on the graves so's we could find them.'

She stood quickly and slapped his face. The bad side.

'We know Harry killed them,' he went on. 'Same neck snap both times. Is that why you stayed with Harry all these years? Because he punished your father for what he did to you? And you stayed with him even after he killed Bisjak right there in front of Whitney and Gary? But that was an honest mistake, you thought, right? He thought he was defending Whitney but—'

She slapped his face again. The bad side again. A strange unearthly cackle split the air and they looked at Harry. His head had fallen to the side, foul waters leaked from his slack mouth. Harry Larkin was dead. But he was watching them. Liz wavered, reached out to Leo. He steadied her, brought her to her chair. As he lowered her, the mantilla came loose and she clutched at it, bunched it up around her neck too urgently. Leo's heart skipped. He imagined a purple neck-lace of bruising beneath it. She looked askance at him. His mind somersaulted. Someone had tried to snap her neck? Not Kevin because she'd have shopped him, especially now that her daughter had been murdered. So it was Gary? And Derek with his cut eye saved her?

'What are you hiding, Liz?'

As the squad car pulled into Maiden's Lane, Helen felt sick. Ben's description of the discovery in the cellar had been harrowing enough. Knowing that only the other day she'd stepped across that rubble-strewn opening piled a layer of superstition on to her sense of failure. She'd walked on the girl's grave. Bad luck must follow. More bad luck. Beside her, Patch sniffed back the furtive tears he'd been manfully withholding since the news came in.

'I can't believe it ended like this,' he said.

'It's not over yet, Patch.'

They tried the bell, peered in the front window of the terraced house for a couple of minutes before a fair-haired young woman emerged from next door. Behind her stood two little miniatures of the woman still in their nighties, long fair hair and sky-blue eyes big and awestruck by Garda

Dempsey's uniform. His reassuring smile didn't reassure. They ducked back into the house.

'Mr Larkin is not at home, I think,' the young woman said, her accent East European, her disposition not altogether friendly, her grip tight on the half-open door. 'His brother is dying. I think he went to the hospital.'

'Do you have any idea what time he left this morning?' Helen asked.

'The taxi came at eight? Maybe before.'

'The taxi?'

A wariness entered the young woman's expression. She shielded her eyes from the sun and from the glare of Helen's persistence.

'Did you actually see him get in a taxi?'

The woman shook her head. She seemed to be reconsidering her reticence as she looked from Helen to Garda Dempsey, whose newly serious expression made him look more harmless than ever.

'I think you ask Mr Boyle,' she said.

'Mr Boyle?'

'The taxi man. I show you card with his number. Please, a minute.'

The woman closed the door and went inside. Helen heard the little girls' worried whispers, the soothing tones of their mother's answers. When the woman returned to the front door, she'd lit herself a cigarette and done some more reconsidering. She proffered the calling card. *Boyle's Cabs: Faster than a boiling kettle!*

'I have Mr Larkin's keys,' she said, and tentatively raised the bunch. Helen took it. 'I am cleaner for him. Two days a week.'

'Were you in there this morning?'

'No. Tomorrow.' The young woman took a nervous pull

from her cigarette. 'Mr Larkin will not be happy if he—'

'He won't know. I'll drop these keys back when we're done, OK?'

The woman nodded and closed her door abruptly. Helen tried the number on the punning cabman's card. He was slow to pick up. Waiting for his bloody kettle to boil, Helen thought irritatedly. Just as she was about to give up, a cheerful-sounding man came on the line.

'You wanted a taxi?'

'Mr Boyle?' she said. 'Detective Sergeant Helen Troy here. Did you call to Jimmy Larkin's house in Maiden's Lane this morning?'

The man hesitated. Then he prevaricated. Or tried to.

'How do I know you're actually a—'

'Listen, Mr Boyle,' she told him, 'this is urgent. This is a murder investigation. Did you bring Mr Larkin some-where?'

'No, I swung round by the house but no one answered,' the cabman said. 'I reckoned Jimmy must've been called to the hospital earlier so I didn't hang around.'

'He'd booked a taxi for the hospital?'

'Yeah, rang last evening,' the man said. Some shuffling and a brief consultation at the other end of the line. 'At nine-fifteen. He was heading in to see Harry this morning at eight. Poor old Harry's dead, is he?'

Helen cut the call and turned to Dempsey.

'Let's take a look inside,' she said.

The protest died on Dempsey's lips when Helen tossed an unspoken warning his way. It had *wedding* written on it. She turned the key and was, too abruptly, inside. She paused, listened. All she could hear was Garda Dempsey's quick, faltering breath behind her. The stern-faced woman in the enlarged photo on the end wall seemed to be asking her what she was doing there. The open door to the right of the hallway invited Helen forward. She stepped into the doorway. And stepped back, a hand to her mouth.

'What?' Dempsey asked. He peered by Helen and gasped. 'Oh God.'

The curtains in the sitting room were closed but there was light enough from the hallway. Too much. In the far corner of the room, Jimmy Larkin sat naked, tied to a chair, his mouth heavily taped, his bloodied head too blue and weirdly askew to sustain life. Another neck snap, Helen thought. Placed before the old PC on the table beside him was a digital camera. She took a pair of Crime Scene gloves from her pocket, pulled them on. She approached the body, trying to look beyond it, not see it. Dempsey didn't follow her in.

The digital camera was a Canon Powershot G3. The camera used for the First Communion day shot of Whitney had been an old 35mm model. So what was the significance of this one? Helen wondered. The PC hummed. She touched the mouse gingerly. Her question was answered. Graphically. Before her were the photos taken by Anton Bisjak. In them the child Whitney sat naked but for her panties on a tousled bed, her flesh festooned with bruises. Innocence and incomprehension troubled her expression. Helen couldn't bear to look. She turned away.

Out beyond the door, Garda Dempsey was halfway up the stairs, frozen in mid-stride. He stared upwards like a pilgrim paralysed by a visitation from God or one of His saints. Or a devil. Helen lowered the zip of her jacket, reached in for her gun. Dempsey raised his arms slowly, started backwards down the steps. Locking her two arms in position behind the gun, Helen stepped across towards the door. Halfway there, she stopped, caught a glimpse of a gun bearing down on Dempsey. A Glock 17, she felt certain. A bloodied shirt sleeve followed, inching down. Baz MacDonald, she thought, recalling last night's attack, the West Belfast Armenian's shoulder wound. Maybe he wasn't outside their jurisdiction after all. She tried to move from the spot where she was rooted but couldn't.

'Take off the mantilla, please,' Leo said.

'Leave me alone,' Liz Larkin cried. 'Go find that bastard MacDonald. He murdered my poor child. It has to be him. Or . . . Kevin? If it's not Baz, it must be Kevin. Why aren't you out there looking for—'

'We'll find your daughter's killer. Harry's too. The mantilla. Please.'

She stood up, stepped in close to him, obscenely close. Grief had gone manic in her, ripped her sense of reason apart. Or was it something more primal even than grief? A mother's protective instinct.

'Take it off yourself, Leo,' she said, at once wild but quiet. 'You were always good at that, weren't you?'

'Jesus, Liz, don't make this any harder than it already—'

The unintended double-entendre stuck in his craw. He felt the same seedy uncleanliness he'd been feeling since this case began. On the bed, dirty Harry sneered in eternal repose. The air in the death room had become unbreathable. Tears trickled from beneath Liz's shuttered eyelids. He raised his hands to her shoulders, lifted the mantilla. No bruising. Or not of the neck-snap variety.

'Love bites?' he said in astonishment. Derek McCarthy, he thought, in further astonishment.

'Love?' she said. 'What do we know about love, Leo?'

*

Garda Dempsey had reversed from Helen's door-frame view of the stairway and the gun, descending haltingly, began to gesture. Down, get down. Then its bearer entered the picture.

Kevin Larkin.

The big man saw Helen, saw her gun pointed at him from out of the half light of the sitting room, pointed his in her direction. She couldn't tell if he could see her eyes, the fear in them, but she saw his. Fear in them too, and pain so deep that Helen felt her bones ache.

'Put the gun down, Kevin,' a voice said that sounded very much like Helen's and was, she realized a moment later, her own voice – futile in the silent world of Kevin Larkin.

She braved a forward step. With a high-decibel and incoherent reproach, he backed himself against the wall, the gun in his hand becoming more insistent. He stared at her. A take-this-cup-from-my-lips kind of stare. Helen didn't lower her gun. Kevin lowered his. Then he turned it inwards on himself. Up along his chest, above his neck, his chin, to his mouth.

'Don't do it,' Dempsey's voice came from the hallway with the words Helen had been searching for.

Kevin's stare had turned inwards too. His life, it seemed to Helen, was passing before his eyes. He didn't think much of it. His future too. He didn't think much of that either. The gun was all there was now. Him and the gun. His opened mouth and the gun. He closed his eyes.

'Ah, Jesus!' Dempsey cried. 'Ah, no!'

At first, Helen thought the silhouette that lengthened into the hallway must be her uniformed colleague's.

'Stay where you are, Patch,' Helen called, and Kevin opened his eyes, looked down into the hallway, startled, entranced.

The shadow came to a halt. It wasn't Dempsey's. Long hair. An ankle-length and billowy, diaphanous dress. A nightdress. One of the little girls from next door, Helen thought. And couldn't think what else to think, what else to do. Kevin could. He lowered the gun, sat on the stairs, put the gun down. Helen edged forward, sneaked a look into the hallway where Dempsey knelt at the foot of the stairs, his hands behind his head. The child stood on the footpath outside the front door, less frightened than curious while Kevin gazed at her with infinite sadness.

Helen smiled at the girl and crossed the hallway to the stairs. She took the big man's gun, stuffed it in the back of her jeans. The girl appeared to be waiting stubbornly for an explanation. Inspiration failed Helen. Kevin came to her rescue. He made a circle with a thumb and forefinger and put it to his eye, wheeled the other hand like he was cranking an old silent film camera. A Charades gesture.

'We're making a film, love,' Helen said, and the child was whisked from sight by a hysterically scolding mother.

Liz Larkin clung to Leo, wept uncontrollably. Her voice muffled on his chest, he couldn't hear the word she kept repeating but he felt it there at his heart, its vibration two-syllabled, short and long, short and long. Whit-ney. Whit-ney. Whit-ney. Her face, though she didn't know it, was pressed against a photo in Leo's inside pocket. A photo of Whitney, the arm of a rebel Libyan boy over her shoulder, a smile lifting the dark mantle of her gothic gloom. He couldn't decide whether or not to show it to her. Maybe later, he decided. When the real storm broke on her. When she discovered what was, at last, perfectly clear to Leo. The stepson they'd cast from the family nest had come back to blow it apart.

'We should call a nurse,' he said, but Liz wasn't listening.

'I knew she was dead but I couldn't let myself believe it,' she cried softly. 'I thought she'd battle through. Like I did. But how could she? What hope did she have in this rotten family, with this rotten mother?'

'You're not rotten, Liz. You've had it tough all the way,' Leo said, but Liz still wasn't listening.

'Another few years and Whitney's heart might have hardened like mine did. She might have put all that fantasy stuff behind her. I did. I used to dream about you and me living out there in Ballsbridge and nobody would know who I was or what hole I'd crawled out of.'

'I'm sorry, Liz.'

'Don't be,' she said. 'I got over it. I got real. Whitney never did. But, you know . . . I shouldn't say this, but I'm glad she didn't have to grow up to be a woman like me.'

He knew how the world would judge her, had already judged her. The matriarch of a perverted, amoral clan. A black widow. The *mum* in that other Larkin's much-quoted poem. But some mums, and Liz was one of them, get fucked up long before they become mums at all.

'You're a bloody saint, girl, to have survived what you survived.'

She drew back from him a little but still held him.

'I'm no saint,' she said, glanced at her dead husband. 'I made a murderer of that man. Yeah, he was a bully and a cheat and whatever else, but he was never a murderer until . . .'

Leo placed his hands on her shoulders, held her firmly, sternness in his tone as he spoke.

'No. You knew nothing about that killing. You didn't ask Harry to do it. He didn't tell you he'd done it. And you knew nothing of the Anton Bisjak killing. Nothing.'

'But—'

'You've already served your time, Liz. Full stop.'

She sank towards him again, heavier than before, a dead weight, nothing left in her of any lightness or hope.

'I tried so hard to make a family of us, Leo,' she said. 'I did my best for my children. Now they're all gone. There's nothing more this world can do to me.'

'You've still got Gary.'

After he'd served his stretch as an accessory in the murder of Anton Bisjak and for his assault on Helen, Leo thought. He offered Liz an underestimation.

'He won't get any more than two or three years.'

'He despises me more than he despised Harry,' Liz said. 'I suspected him, Leo. Last night I asked him straight up, and if it wasn't for Derek . . . Harry was just a bully but I'm a whore. That's what my son told me last night. After all the sacrifices I made for him, all the shit I put up with from Harry so's Gary could get his chance in the acting game . . . Jesus, Leo, when do I stop getting punished? I was getting punished before I knew what a sin was and it never stopped, never will. Never.'

She was right, of course, but Leo told her differently, raised her chin, cajoled her, *listen to me, listen to me.* He gave her false encouragement, false hope, false estimations of the human capacity for survival. He gave her everything but the truth because, sometimes, the only comfort lay in delusion. Sometimes, life had to be a movie and not some sepia-toned art-house film that kicked the shit out of your soul for ninety minutes and dumped you out on to Bleak Street.

# 48

Detective Inspector Leo Woods took his usual late-show seat. The side of the bed, facing the cul-de-sac. No one was about, which was a mixed blessing. The street was safe but had nothing to offer by way of entertainment. Over at the tracks opposite Serpentine Crescent, the commuter trains had stopped running for the night. These were the longest hours, and Leo had already tried and failed to fill the first of them. He'd watched five minutes of the DVD that was still in the player since Sunday morning. Then he'd lugged the wicker laundry box from the end of the bed to the mask room, taken one look at the masks it contained and thought better of rehanging them. He'd smoked a joint to see if he could bend time into a less linear shape. No joy. He lit another because he had another.

Silence reigned, though not benignly. Silence and quiet were two different things, Kevin Larkin had told him earlier. Too right, Kevin. As with Harry, it was Leo the deaf man had wanted to talk to. A long hour that had been too. Not a dark corner in the fluorescent-lit interview room. Not much darkness in Kevin either, just that curious phenomenon Leo had witnessed so many times in the secular confessionals of Garda stations all over the country. The return to sanity.

He'd sensed the strangeness Kevin felt, that man-who-fell-to-earth sensation. The weightlessness of a man who came from a place where no one else lived. He'd gazed at his hands a lot, touched things – the table, the cuffs of his shirt, his hair – felt their substantiality.

As always, precious little consolation was to be had from the telling of a man's sins. But there was some. The deaf man hadn't murdered his sister. Probably hadn't. No one would ever know for sure. Except for Kevin. The immediate cause of death was clear, the pathologist's initial report confirming that Whitney had fallen from a height of six to eight feet and suffered a brain haemorrhage from the blow to the temple. A Luminol test at the foot of the attic steps in the deaf man's sitting room had revealed the bloodstains that Kevin had tried to remove. Leo believed Kevin's version of events because his own more melodramatic, *breaking the circle* scenario had so upset and offended the deaf man. The truth was that Whitney had died accidentally before the investigation had even started which for the searchers was a bitter consolation.

The Friday night drop-off of the money which Whitney herself had arranged was a trap. Gary and Derek McCarthy would be lying in wait for her or for whatever emissary she might send. Kevin had sussed the plan earlier in the day when Gary told him things would be sorted that night and she'd come to her senses once they'd caught her. Though she'd never replied, Kevin had continued to text her in the previous days. When he texted to tell her that she was being set up, she responded. This time, Kevin made the arrangements. Then fate intervened.

On that Saturday morning when she'd got the word that Hadi's body had likely been found, Whitney fell apart. Kevin calmed her, Xanaxed her. It worked for a while. Until

Whitney sneaked down those steep attic stairs to his bathroom. From the kitchen, he saw her dart back towards the stairs, a bunch of his tab-pads in her hand. She'd made it almost to the top of the stairs before he grabbed her arm. And the sleeping tablets fell from her grasp. And she tried to chase back down after them. And fell. And fell. Leo knew that the vertigo of Whitney's fall would forever dizzy the deaf man's brain. The accident, as accidents often do, kick-started the automaton of revenge.

Out on Tandy's Lane, Harry Larkin's reaction to Kevin's approach went quickly from sneers to tears. He refused to believe Whitney's death was an accident, blamed Kevin, blamed Bisjak for destroying Whitney's innocence and her love for him, took none of the blame himself for the damage he'd done to all of them through the years. None of which mattered anyway. The deaf man had already decided to kill his father. He'd taken a Glock 17 from the stash in the chimney of the derelict house beside Jinky's. The stash they shared with Baz MacDonald. He'd tried the neck snap on Harry but the old man summoned the strength to free himself, jump back in the car, almost reach the keys in the ignition. And Kevin unloaded the Glock 17 into him.

Georgia's text to Whitney's second phone had alerted him to Dorda's whereabouts. Late Sunday evening, Kevin went to the Oak Lodge apartment complex in Castleknock and hid in the grounds to wait for the Libyan to appear. The brief description Whitney had got from the Goode kids last week had proved sufficient. That and the silver grey car from which he saw the guy take some things in the early hours of Monday morning, get into a white van and drive away. Kevin followed on a motorbike he kept in a lane on the other side of the river back in Chapelizod. Dorda's progress had slowed a little more at each junction on the long uninhabited stretch of road around Wilkinstown. There weren't enough signposts. Never were, Leo thought, not in this life. When Dorda pulled into a siding, Kevin used the same Glock 17 he'd used to kill Harry. Later on Monday, he cleaned the gun and left it back in the stash. This was the gun, Leo realized, that Baz MacDonald had grabbed on Tuesday afternoon.

Baz had become a target because he'd been suspicious of Kevin ever since Whitney dropped out of sight the previous week. He didn't say as much but Kevin could tell. Besides, the ex-Provo had always treated Whitney with disdain despite, or maybe because of, her deluded idolizing of him. And, yes, it hurt that she'd asked Baz for the money first, but none of this might have happened if he'd given it to her.

So, he'd deliberately used Baz's preferred gun on Harry and Dorda? Leo had asked. Yes. And he was sorry he hadn't killed the guy but sorrier still that he'd fired so recklessly and injured Frida Goode so badly as well as endangering Georgia's life. As for Jimmy, he'd always suspected his uncle had taken Lubo's camera that night in June 2002. With nothing left to lose, Kevin had decided to torture the truth from Jimmy. And finished him with the contempt he deserved.

And was Liz next on his list? Leo had asked. A nod. And Gary? A shake of the head. And yourself, Kevin? A slow, emphatic nod.

Leo lay back on the bed and stretched an arm across to where he'd foolishly hoped Eveleen Morgan might some day lie. The faint scent of her perfume remained on his shirt. It didn't matter any more that he'd unwittingly played the ghost of her lost lover. The truth revealed itself to him in all its rational clarity. Lucidity in the face of experience, as that other great French footballing philosopher had put it. Eveleen too had played a phantom's role. Every woman he'd ever slept with since Iseult had done the same. Still, it had felt damn good being with Eveleen and he was glad he'd seized the moment when it had come. He closed his good eye into the eye-patch dark and the night had passed when the ringing in of a text message on his mobile welcomed him to the brightest of mornings. Dripsy Scullion. *The brother left me 500 euro – Paddy Power's here I come!*

Laughing aloud, Leo saw Dripsy in his mind's eye breaking from a limp into a sprint as the betting shop door beckoned. He sent a reply: *Carpe Diem.*

On his bedside table was the new ID he'd tossed there last night. He laughed too at the memory of his grumpy reply when the young woman taking the shot had asked him to smile. *I am fucking smiling.* She'd blushed then and apologized much as this sunny May sky seemed to be doing for the unseasonable weather of the past week, for the clouds it had blanketed over the lives of innocents, for the weak sun that had refused them lasting warmth. He wished to Christ he could have raised Whitney Larkin into the light of this new day, rescued her from captivity and brought her back to her mother's house. But he was no John Wayne and the greatest eye-patched director of them all, John Ford, wasn't calling the shots. Chance was calling them. Blind Chance, wearing not one eye-patch but two.

Another text rang in. Dripsy again. *Can't find Carpe Diem on the race sheets – where's he running?*

The smile insisted on setting up residence on the good side of Leo's face so he left it there. Get up, he told himself. Get dressed and seize the day. It might not be there to seize tomorrow.

*Sleeping Dogs* is Mark O'Sullivan's tenth novel. His work has won several awards in Ireland and France and been translated into six languages. He has also published short stories and poetry in various magazines and journals. His first crime novel featuring Detective Inspector Leo Woods, *Crocodile Tears*, was published to critical acclaim. Mark is married with two daughters and lives in Thurles, County Tipperary.

# CROCODILE TEARS
## Mark O'Sullivan

'Leo Woods is a memorable character . . . Studded with
dark humour, elegant in style and clever in its execution,
*Crocodile Tears* is a remarkably assured first outing'
Declan Burke, *The Irish Times*

Detective Inspector Leo Woods' life is a mess. Work
keeps him sane. More or less. On an ice-cold winter
morning in an affluent Dublin suburb, he stares down
at the bloodied corpse of a property developer.
Dermot Brennan's features, distorted in terror,
are a reflection of Leo's own disfigured face. Life
does that kind of thing to Leo. Makes faces at him.

With the help of ambitious but impetuous Detective
Sergeant Helen Troy, Leo uncovers a frosted web of
lies, where nobody is quite who they seem. As ice
and snow grip Dublin, Woods and Troy find
themselves battling forces as malevolent as the
weather: jealousy, greed and betrayal. Can they
identify the murderer before things get even uglier?

'Well written, gritty, with dark humour and some striking
metaphors . . . reminded me of Mankell's Wallander'
*Irish Independent*

'Splendidly idiosyncratic and with a leading man who
makes Inspector Morse look positively cheerful,
this is fine crime writing'
*Daily Mail*